MIDNIGHT WARRIOR
"A magical, memorable story tinged with enchantment and brimming over with passion and perils."
—*Romantic Times*

THE BELOVED SCOUNDREL
"All the makings of a classic romance—an intriguing hero, a strong and endearing heroine and a fascinating plot." —*USA Today*

THE MAGNIFICENT ROGUE
"Iris Johansen demonstrates her unique and incredible talent with [this] romantic drama."
—*Affaire de Coeur*

THE TIGER PRINCE
"If you are looking for a unique, unforgettable reading adventure, this book is for you!" —*Rendezvous*

THE GOLDEN BARBARIAN
"Sizzling tension . . . an exciting tale . . . the stuff which leaves an indelible mark on the heart."
—*Romantic Times*

STORM WINDS
"Johansen serves up a diverting romance and plot twists worthy of a mystery novel."
—*Publishers Weekly*

LION'S BRIDE
"Lion's Bride is all any reader could ask for . . . and more."
—*Rendezvous*

ALSO BY IRIS JOHANSEN

LION'S BRIDE
MIDNIGHT WARRIOR
THE BELOVED SCOUNDREL
THE MAGNIFICENT ROGUE
THE TIGER PRINCE
THE GOLDEN BARBARIAN
THE WIND DANCER
STORM WINDS
REAP THE WIND
LAST BRIDGE HOME
THE UGLY DUCKLING
LONG AFTER MIDNIGHT
AND THEN YOU DIE . . .

And coming soon in hardcover
from Bantam Books

THE FACE OF DECEPTION

DARK RIDER

Iris Johansen

BANTAM BOOKS

New York Toronto London Sydney Auckland

DARK RIDER

A Bantam Book / May 1995

ISBN 0-553-29947-6

Published simultaneously in the United States and Canada

*Bantam Books are published by Bantam Books, a division of Bantam
Doubleday Dell Publishing Group, Inc. Its trademark, consisting of the words
"Bantam Books" and the portrayal of a rooster, is Registered in U.S. Patent
and Trademark Office and in other countries. Marca Registrada. Bantam
Books, 1540 Broadway, New York, New York 10036.*

PRINTED IN THE UNITED STATES OF AMERICA

RAD   15 14 13 12 11 10 9

DARK
RIDER

Prologue

September 15, 1795
Marseilles, France

"Y ou demon from Hades, come back here!"
Cassie jumped over a small cask and darted around a sailor.

"You know what will happen if I have to come after you!"

Oh yes, she knew. She would be forced to listen to one of her nurse's long lectures and then be locked in the ship cabin for hours and hours. But she had seen the crew load horses, two beautiful horses, and she would not lose this opportunity because of Clara's threats. Some things were worth any punishment her nurse could inflict.

She glanced over her shoulder. Clara was stalking after her, her face twisted with anger.

Darting around a corner, Cassie dived behind a pile of trunks. She held her breath as she heard the swish of Clara's stiff skirts.

She waited two minutes more before peeking

around the trunk. Clara was not in sight. Her breath released in an explosion of relief. She started running back the way she had come.

"And what have we here?" Papa was standing at the rail with another man. "Come here, wild one."

She skidded to a stop in front of him and sighed resignedly. It could have been worse. She could not count on her father to stop Clara from punishing her, but he might lessen the sentence. Papa was not like other grown-ups; he didn't shout or frown or shake his head. There was even a chance she might persuade him to go with her to see the horses.

"What a sweet child." The man to whom her father had been talking was looking down at her. "How old is she?"

Her father smiled proudly. "Cassandra is eight. Cassie, this is my friend, Raoul."

Raoul knelt before her. "I'm delighted to meet you, Cassandra."

He was smiling, but his gray eyes were as cold and unblinking as the garden snake she had put in Clara's bed last week.

"You're a lucky man, Charles. She's as lovely as your beautiful wife."

Why was he lying? Clara had told Cassandra over and over that she was as ugly as a toad. She had said that beauty was founded in obedience and a bad girl like Cassandra would never be anything but homely. She had come to realize that Clara didn't always tell the truth, but there was a chance Clara was right about Cassie's lack of beauty. Mama was always gentle, always obedient to Clara, and no one could deny she was pretty. Cassandra set her jaw and said clearly, "That's not true."

The brilliant white smile on Raoul's lips never

faltered. "Modest as well as comely." He patted her cheek and rose to his feet. "We must be sure to find a suitable match for her when you return."

"Match?" Her father looked dismayed. "You think I'll have to be gone that long?"

"We both know that's a possibility. Naturally, I'll let you know the moment it's safe for you to return." He clapped her father on the shoulder. "Don't look so morose, my friend. Tahiti is supposed to be a beautiful land. I was just talking to Jacques-Louis David about it last week, and he was saying what a thrill it would be to paint in such a place. You may be inspired to create a great masterpiece."

"Yes . . ." He lifted Cassie in his arms and gazed blindly down at the dock. "But it's so far away."

"Distance is safety," Raoul said softly. "You're the one who came to me in a panic. You even moved from Paris to Marseilles to escape him. Have you changed your mind now? There's a possibility you may be safe here for a time. Do you wish to stay and chance letting him find you?"

"No!" Her father's face paled. "But it's not fair. I didn't mean to—"

"It's done." Raoul cut into his sentence. "Now we must protect ourselves from the consequences. Why do you think I intend to change my name and cut all my former ties? Now, do you need more funds for the journey?"

"No, you've been more than generous." He tried to smile. "But you'll remember to let me know as quickly as possible? My wife has a delicate constitution and is not pleased to be going to such a savage land."

"She will thrive in Tahiti. The climate is much more pleasant than that of either London or Marseilles." Raoul smiled again. "Now I must go. Good journey, Charles."

"Good-bye," he said faintly.

"And good journey to you, little mademoiselle." Raoul turned his smile on Cassie. "Take care of your father."

Exactly like the garden snake. Her arms tightened fiercely around Papa's neck. "I will."

They watched him move down the gangplank and walk across the dock.

Papa tugged at her hands. "A little air, *ma chou*." He chuckled. "You cannot protect me if you choke me to death."

Her gaze never left Raoul's retreating back. "I don't like him."

"Raoul? You don't understand. He's my good friend and wants only what's best. You heard him say he wanted you to take care of me."

She was not convinced, but grown-ups never paid attention when she argued with them. She laid her head on his shoulder and whispered, "I'll always take care of you, Papa."

"My big girl. I know you will." He bit his lower lip as his gaze went back to Raoul, and he added absently, "But it's not Raoul who is the danger, it's the Duke."

Cassie knew about dukes. Clara had told her with great enthusiasm of all the aristocrats who had lost their heads on the guillotine. Clara was English, like Mama, and had no use for French aristocracy. But, then, Clara had little use for anyone. "Like the dukes who died in the Place de la Concorde?"

"No, he's a British duke." He suddenly turned away from the rail and set her down. "Now I must return you to Clara and your mother. The ship is about to depart."

"I want to stay with you."

"Do you? I'd like to stay with you, too, but Clara will be most upset with both of us." His eyes suddenly lit with boyish mischief. "Where will we hide?"

She was already prepared. "Down with the cargo." The cargo hatch had been her destination when Papa had caught sight of her. "We can stay with the horses."

He laughed. "I should have known you'd find horses even on a ship."

"Beautiful horses. Clara won't look there; you know she hates them. I'll get your easel from the trunk, and you can paint them."

"Excellent idea." He took her hand and set off down the deck. "You see, you're already meeting all my needs."

As she always would, she resolved, her hand tightening on her father's. Mama had told her once that Papa was not like other men. He was an artist who needed all their love and care so that he would be free to paint beautiful pictures and give his gift to the world. He must not be bothered with the concerns that plagued lesser men. That rule surely meant he must never be as frightened as he had been a few moments ago. She knew how terrible fear made you feel. When she was smaller, she had let Clara frighten her.

Yes, she would protect him from Clara and the snake he had called Raoul, and this British duke. She would protect him from everyone who might ever hurt him.

One

April 4, 1806
Kealakekua Bay, Hawaii

"Come with us, Kanoa," Lihua called out as she waded into the surf. "Why stay here on the shore when you could be where there is fine food and finer gifts? The English are beautiful and make love like Gods."

English. Cassie gazed out at the gleaming lanterns lighting the sleek lines of the ship in the darkness. The *Josephine* was smaller than the other ships that had come to the bay, but that did not mean it did not bring danger. She had been uneasy since she had come to the village that afternoon and Lihua had told her of the ship that had sailed into the bay two days ago. She had attempted to convince her friends that these foreigners might be a threat, but the village women had laughed at her. Still, she had to try once more.

"You know I can't go. I've already been here too long." She clenched her hands as she watched a dozen women run into the water. "And you should not go, either. Have you learned nothing? You should not sleep with the English. They bring disease and they care nothing for you."

Lihua grinned. "You worry too much. It's not certain that Captain Cook's sailors gave our people the French sickness, and these English care enough to bring me pleasure for the night. It is all a woman can ask."

It was all Lihua ever asked, Cassie thought with exasperation, all any of them ever asked. Pleasure for the present, pay tomorrow. Ordinarily she had no quarrel with the philosophy, but not when she could see danger looming.

"Come with us," Lihua coaxed. "Besides the sailors there are two who lead, a chief and his uncle, who captains the ship. I will let you have the chief, who knows many ways to please a woman. He is very beautiful and has the grace and the lusty appetite of that stallion you love so much."

"Chief? There is a noble chief on board that ship?"

"The sailors say it is the same as our chiefs. They call him Your Grace."

A duke. She felt a faint stirring of memory of that long-ago day in Marseilles. Foolishness—there could be no connection. "What is his name?"

"Jared."

"No, his last name."

Lihua shrugged. "Who knows? Why should I ask such things? It's not his name that makes me cry out with pleasure. It is his big—"

"Lihua, come along," Kalua, Lihua's sister, called from the surf. "You cannot convince her. And why give her the chief? We will share him as we did last night. She would not know what to do with him." She added with teasing scorn, "She is a virgin. She lies with no one."

"It is not her fault," Lihua said defensively. "She did not choose not to give and take pleasure." She turned to Cassie. "I know Lani decided for you because she fears the ugly one will punish you, but surely just one time would not hurt. You can swim out to the boat and taste the English chief and then swim back. A woman *should* have a stallion for her first lover."

"He will be too big for her," Kalua protested. "If I'd had such a one for my first man, I would never have taken another."

"You were only thirteen. She rides that huge horse, her woman's veil cannot still be there. The fit would be tight but not—"

"What is he doing here?" Cassie interrupted, her gaze on the ship. She was accustomed to their frank discussions of a sexual nature and no longer paid attention to them.

"I've just told you." Lihua giggled. "But I refuse to tell you more; his skill is beyond description. You must find out for yourself."

"These English don't sail into a harbor just to bring pleasure to women. Ask him why he is here."

"Ask him yourself." Kalua turned and struck out for the ship. "I have other things to occupy me."

"I must go." Lihua waded farther into the sea. "Kalua may decide not to share the Chief."

"Do you know nothing about him?" Cassie called after her. "How old is he?"

"Young."

"How young?"

"Younger than the uncle."

"How old is that?"

"I pay no attention to a man's age, if his vigor is strong. You know it's of no importance to me."

It might be of importance to Cassie. Her father had never mentioned the Duke again after they had fled from Marseilles, but he must have been at least her father's age to inspire such terror.

"What is there to know?" Lihua asked. "He is English, he comes here from Tahiti and knows our language. He probably wants something from King Kamehameha, as all the other English did." She reached deep water and struck out after the other women. "And he is a true stallion. . . ."

"Find out his name," Cassie called, but she doubted if Lihua heard. It probably didn't matter. The memory of that day was so faint, she couldn't remember if Papa had mentioned a name. Besides, the prospect of there still being a danger to Papa was slight. British ships had come and gone over the years with no ill consequence. Not many men would travel halfway across the world to destroy an enemy.

She could hear the laughing chatter of the women as they called back and forth to one another in the darkness. She should not linger there. Coming to the village was forbidden, and if she did not get back to the cottage soon, Clara would discover where she had been. What did it matter? Clara would probably find out anyway, and she wanted these final delicious moments of freedom.

She drew a deep breath of the soft salt-laden air and dug her bare toes into the wet sand. She thought she heard Lihua's laughter. Her friends were swimming happily through the cool, silken water. Soon they would be welcomed on board the ship and coupling with joy and vigor. Sweet heaven, her nipples were actually hardening as she envisioned the act, she realized ruefully. Of late her body was constantly betraying her. Lani said it was natural, that her body was ready for a man and the ripening was as beautiful as the blooming of a flower. Yet, if that was true, why wouldn't Lani let her lie with—

"Are you truly a virgin?"

She stiffened and then whirled to face the man strolling out of the thatch of palms. He spoke in the Polynesian language she had used with her friends, but there could be no doubt that he was not one of them. He was as tall, but leaner, and moved with a slow, casual grace, not with the springy exuberance of the islanders. He was dressed in elegant tight breeches, and his coat fit sleekly over his broad shoulders. His snowy cravat was tied in a complicated fall, and his dark hair bound back in a queue.

He is very beautiful and has the grace and lusty appetite of that stallion you love so much.

Lihua was right. He *was* beautiful. Exotic grace and strength exuded from every limb. High cheekbones and that well-formed, sensual mouth gave his face a fascinating quality that made it hard to tear her gaze away. A stray breeze ruffled his dark hair, and a lock fell across his wide forehead.

Pagan.

The word came out of nowhere and she instantly dismissed it. Clara used the term to describe the islanders, and she would deem it totally unfitting for civilized young noblemen. Yet there was something free and reckless flickering in the stranger's expression that she had never seen in any of the islanders.

Yes, he must be the English, and he was coming from the direction of Kamahameha's village, she realized. Lihua was right, he probably wanted only supplies or trade rights, as the other English did. She did not have to worry about him.

"Well, are you?" he asked lazily as he continued to walk toward her.

He might not be a threat, but she answered in Polynesian with instinctive wariness. "You should not eavesdrop on others' conversations. It's not honorable."

"I could hardly keep from hearing. You were shouting." His gaze wandered from her face to her bare breasts and down to her hips swathed in the cotton sarong. "And I found the subject matter so very intriguing. It was exceptionally . . . arousing. It's not every day a man is compared to a stallion."

His arrogance and confidence were annoying. "Lihua is easily pleased."

He looked startled, but then a slow smile lit his face. "And you are not, if you're still a virgin. What a challenge to a man. What is your name?"

"What is yours?"

"Jared."

The Duke, not the uncle. The last of her concern vanished as she realized that this man could not be more than thirty. What threat could have been posed by the boy he was then? "You have another name."

His brows lifted. "You're not being fair. You've not told me your name yet." He bowed. "But if we must be formal, I'm Jared Barton Danemount."

"And you're a duke?"

"I have that honor . . . or dishonor. Depending upon my current state of dissipation. Does that impress you?"

"No, it's only another word for 'chief,' and we have many chiefs here."

He laughed. "I'm crushed. Now that we've established my relative unimportance, may I ask your name?"

"Kanoa." It was not a lie. It was the name Lani had given her and meant more to her than her birth name.

"The free one," the Englishman translated. "But you're not free. Not if this ugly one keeps you from pleasure."

"That's none of your concern."

"On the contrary, I hope to make it very much my concern. I've had very good news tonight, and I feel like celebrating. Will you celebrate with me, Kanoa?"

His smile shimmered in the darkness, coaxing, alluring. Nonsense. He was only a man; it was stupid to be so fascinated by this stranger. "Why should I? Your good news is nothing to me."

"Because it's a fine night and I'm a man and you're a woman. Isn't that enough? I hate to see a woman deprived of—"

He broke off as he came to within a few yards of her. Then with disgust he said, "Christ, you're nothing but a child."

"I'm *not* a child." It was a common and most annoying mistake. She was very small-boned and tiny compared to the Junoesque islanders and was always being thought younger than her nineteen years.

"Oh, no, you must be all of fourteen or fifteen," he said sarcastically.

"No, I'm older than—"

"Of course you are."

He didn't believe her. It was foolish to argue with a man she would probably never see again. "It doesn't matter."

"The hell it doesn't," he said roughly. "I heard what Kalua said about having her first man when she was thirteen. Don't listen to her. Pay heed to this old one. You have no business swimming out to foreign ships and coupling with sailors."

"But it's entirely proper for you to fornicate with my friends."

"That's different."

She snorted inelegantly.

He blinked, and then his lips twitched as he tried to suppress a smile. "You disagree?"

"Men always make themselves the exception to every rule. It's not fair."

"You're right, of course. We're very unfair to females."

She felt a flicker of surprise. She was not accustomed to such easy acquiescense on this subject. Even Papa became defensive when she tried to discuss the issue of man's injustice to women. "Then why don't you stop?"

"Because taking advantage of women makes the world a very comfortable and pleasant place for us males. I'd wager we'll never be anything but unfair until we're forced to it."

"And you will be. It cannot last forever. Mary Wollstonecraft has even written a book that—"

"Mary Wollstonecraft? What do you know of her?"

"Lani was taught by the English missionaries. The Reverend Densworth's wife gave her a copy of Miss Wollstonecraft's book, and she gave it to me."

He groaned. "Good God, and I thought I was leaving the teachings of those Bluestockings behind when I left London."

She frowned in puzzlement. "Bluestockings?"

"Learned ladies like Miss Wollstonecraft. I never thought they'd invade a paradise like this."

"Truth and justice cannot be hidden," she said earnestly.

"I see," he replied solemnly. "Is that what your Miss Wollstonecraft says?"

She felt a hurtful pang. "You're making mock of me."

He frowned. "Dammit, I didn't mean—"

"Don't lie. You did mean it."

"All right, I was mocking you. It's all I know. I'm not accustomed to talking to youngsters like you."

"Well, you don't have to talk to me any longer." She started to turn away. "I won't stay to listen to—"

"Wait."

"Why should I? So that you can mock me again?"

"No." He grimaced. "I'm feeling unusual twinges of conscience. I believe I need absolution." He smiled coaxingly. "Stay and give it to me, Kanoa."

His eyes no longer appeared cold, and his entire being seemed to exude a glowing persuasiveness that was nearly mesmerizing. She had a sudden desire to take a step closer, move nearer to that warmth.

"Why . . . should I?" she asked again.

"Because you have a kind heart."

"You don't know that I do. You don't know anything about me."

"I know that you were concerned about your friends. Surely that denotes a kind heart."

"It's easy to give kindness to friends. You're a stranger."

His smile faded and he looked out at the sea. "Yes, I am."

Loneliness. She had the sudden feeling that he was speaking of a constant state, and felt an odd sense of kinship. She knew about loneliness.

Foolishness. He was a nobleman, and Lihua had

certainly not found anything in him to pity. Yet Cassie found herself saying haltingly, "If you're asking forgiveness, then I give it freely."

He turned to look at her. "Do you? How extraordinarily generous." When he saw her frown with uncertainty, he shook his head. "No, I'm not being sarcastic. I believe you mean it, and the women to whom I'm accustomed give nothing freely." He smiled crookedly. "But, then, you're not yet a woman. You have time to learn the way of it."

The flare of annoyance burned away any pity she had felt for him. "It's no wonder you must pay for your pleasure when you make stupid judgments and your tongue stings like an adder."

He chuckled with genuine humor. "My tongue can do other things than sting. I must show you—" He broke off and sighed. "I keep forgetting that you're not fair sport. I think we'd best discuss something of mutual interest." He glanced over his shoulder at the palm thicket from which he had emerged. "Is that your horse tied to the tree?"

"Yes."

"A fine stallion. I might be interested in buying him, but first I'll have to watch him move. I've seldom seen a more splendid animal."

"He's not for sale." She added flatly, "And you've *never* seen a more splendid animal. Kapu is without equal."

He threw back his head and laughed. "I beg to disagree, but I approve your loyalty. How did you come by him? I've never heard of islanders raising horses."

"You've not been here long. How could you know anything about us?"

"I've annoyed you again."

He did annoy her. His easy assurance made her feel uncertain, and his physical presence was most disturbing. She sensed the heat of his body only a few feet away and caught the aroma of musk and leather that surrounded him. So different from the men of the village, who carried the scent of salt and fish and the oil of coconut; different also from her father, who usually smelled of brandy and a lemony cologne. Everything about Jared Danemount was different; she had the impression of tremendous strength in spite of his lithe leanness. His light eyes were either blue or gray and very cool. No, that was wrong, they were hot. No . . . she didn't know what they were, but looking into them was making her uncomfortable. She said in a rush, "You think you have a horse finer than Kapu?"

"I know I have a horse finer than your stallion."

She felt another flare of annoyance at his confidence. "Only a fool would make such a claim after one glance at a horse."

"I took more than a glance. I've never been able to resist good horseflesh, and I had a chance to examine him very closely while you and your friends were playing on the beach." He smiled. "It was only when the conversation became so interesting that I was distracted."

She stiffened. "How close to him?"

"Enough to note the usual things—hooves, teeth . . ."

"You lie," she said curtly. "Kapu would never let anyone that close. I would have heard him."

"But you didn't."

"And you would not be here now. The last time anyone tried to check Kapu's teeth, he lost a finger."

"Perhaps he likes me. Horses have been known to find me trustworthy."

"You lie," she repeated. It could not be true. Kapu belonged only to her.

His smile disappeared. "I don't lie. I may be guilty of many sins, but that's not one of them."

"Prove it. Go bring him to me."

"I don't take orders from children."

"I thought as much," she said, relieved. "You're afraid of Kapu, like everyone else."

"You're beginning to irritate me." His tone had taken on a steely edge. "I do not lie, and I'm not afraid of your horse."

She glared at him. "Prove it."

Studying her intently, he asked, "Why is it so important to you?"

"I don't like liars."

"No, I don't think that's the reason." He shrugged. "But you shouldn't issue challenges unless you expect them to be accepted." He turned and moved toward the thicket. A moment later he disappeared into the shadows of the palm trees.

He wouldn't be able to do it, she told herself desperately. In the entire world Kapu was the one thing that was fully her own. He would never betray her by yielding to a stranger.

She heard the Englishman's soft murmurings, his voice gentle, tender, almost loving, as different from the silken sharpness with which he had spoken to her as dawn from sunset. Then he emerged from the thicket and came toward her . . . leading Kapu.

Astonishment and then pain tore through Cassie. Kapu was moving as meekly and contentedly as if she held his reins.

Jared continued murmuring until he stopped before her and extended the reins. "Your horse, I believe."

She could not believe it. She *would* not believe it. She swallowed to ease the tightness from her throat. How stupid to want to weep because someone else had managed to gain Kapu's confidence enough to perform such a simple act. Even Lani was able to lead Kapu on occasion. He was still Cassie's horse. "An easy task."

"You didn't seem to think it easy when you sent me to fetch him."

Dear God, Kapu was pushing affectionately at Jared's back with his nose.

"Ride him."

He shook his head. "I fear I'm not dressed for riding."

"Ride him!" she said hoarsely, blinking back the stinging tears.

He stared down at her and said slowly, "I don't think you want me to do that."

"You can't do it. I know you can't."

"But you want me to try."

She didn't want him to try, but she had to be sure. She had to know Kapu was not completely swayed from his allegiance to her. "Ride him."

He hesitated. Then he stepped to the side, removed his coat, and dropped it onto the sand. He jerked off his cravat and tossed it on top of his coat. "As you like." He stood before the horse, motionless.

"What are you waiting for?"

"Be quiet," he said impatiently. "It's not right. I need—" He broke off as he saw her expression. "Damnation!"

He leaped onto the back of the horse!

For an instant Kapu was perfectly still.

Cassie's heart sank, and her hands closed into fists at her sides.

Kapu exploded! The stallion reared upright, came down hard, and went into a frenzy of bucking. By some miracle the Englishman stayed on his back.

She heard him curse as his legs gripped Kapu's heaving sides. His dark hair came loose from the queue and flew wildly about his face and shoulders. His lips set in a grim line, and his eyes narrowed with fierce intensity. He was everything savage and primitive; no particle remained of the elegant man who had strolled out of the thicket such a short time before.

Kapu gave up the violent gyrations and bolted toward the palm trees!

Cassie's heart stopped. "Watch out. The tree!"

The Englishman had already divined the horse's intention and swung his leg across Kapu's back as the stallion careened by the trunk, missing it by inches. Then, before Danemount could recover his seat, Kapu began bucking again.

Danemount was tossed over Kapu's head and landed a few yards away in the sand. Kapu neighed triumphantly and stopped in his tracks.

Cassie had a terrible idea she knew what was coming. "Don't," she whispered. "Oh, no . . ." She ran toward the palms.

Kapu turned and thundered toward the fallen man.

"No, Kapu!" Cassie stopped before Jared, thrusting herself between him and the horse. "No!"

"Get the hell out of the way!" Danemount said as he rolled over and tried to get to his feet. "He'll trample—"

Kapu skidded to a stop in front of her and reared again.

"Shh," she crooned. "Easy, Kapu. He's not the

same. He won't hurt you. I won't let anyone hurt you."

Kapu reared again.

Yet she could see signs she was getting through to him. He backed away from her but did not move again when she followed him and laid her hand on his neck. "It's all right. Everything is fine."

It took her a few minutes more of quieting him before she could turn to see if Danemount had come to any harm. "Are you hurt?"

"Only my pride." He raised himself on one elbow and flinched. "And perhaps a few parts of my body."

"You'll recover. The fall couldn't have done much damage. The sand is soft as a cushion. Get up."

When he didn't move, she felt a flicker of concern and walked quickly toward him. Her emotions had been in such a turmoil, she had not thought that he might truly be hurt. "Well, perhaps you'd better lie still for a moment. I'll see if you have any broken bones."

He lay back down on the sand. "I admit I like that suggestion better than the others you've made recently. Does it amuse you to lure strangers into riding that devil of a horse?"

"Kapu is no devil." She knelt beside him and began moving her hands over his limbs. His thighs were all lean, iron-hard muscle, she noted absently, a horseman's thighs. "He's just very particular." She glanced at Kapu, and an intense wave of happiness flowed through her. He was still her own. "He doesn't like anyone on his back but me."

The Englishman's gaze was fixed on her face. "So I found out."

She could afford to be generous now. "You did very well." Having found no breaks in his legs and

hips, she began running her hands over his arms and shoulders. Sleek, smooth, corded muscle . . . like Kapu's. She must be hurting him; he was tensing beneath her touch. "Is there pain?"

"More of an ache," he muttered.

"A sprain?" She gently probed his shoulder. "Here?"

"No, definitely not there."

"Where?"

"Never mind. You can't help."

"Of course I can. I'm very good with sprains. I take care of all of Kapu's hurts."

"I don't have a sprain and I'm not a horse, dammit."

She felt a twinge of pain and tried to cover it with tartness. "No, Kapu is more polite when I try to help him."

"The help can be more troublesome than the cure. I don't—" He broke off when he saw the determination in her gaze. "Christ, do whatever you want."

She sat back on her heels. "It's not as if I want to do anything for you. I feel it my duty since I—" She stopped before she made the admission.

"Since you made me ride the stallion," he finished.

She didn't try to deny it. "It was a mistake. I didn't think." She pulled a face. "Lani says it's one of my worst faults and could prove very dangerous."

"And who is this Lani? Your sister?"

"My friend."

"Then your friend is very perceptive." His gaze searched her expression. "Why did you do it? You knew he'd try to throw me."

"I wasn't sure he would," she whispered. "He liked you. He was mine but he liked you."

"And that's forbidden? How selfish of you."

"I love him," she said simply. "He's all I have. I was afraid."

"I know."

He was smiling faintly, and she realized he had somehow sensed the emotions that had driven her. Had she been that transparent? Probably. She had never been good at hiding her feelings. She quickly averted her gaze and moved her hands from his ribs to his abdomen. "When I first saw you lead him out of the thicket, I thought you must be a Kahuna."

"Kahuna?" He shook his head. "No, I'm not one of your island priests, and I certainly have no magic."

"He's never behaved like that with anyone else. It took seven months for him even to let me in the same stall with him."

"Then you must have done all the hard work. I had only to follow in your footsteps."

He was not the sort to follow in anyone's footsteps. She felt a surge of warmth at the unexpected kindness from a man who said he knew only mockery. "Is it only Kapu?"

"I have a certain gift. I told you, horses have a fondness for me. Perhaps they realize I possess the same animal instincts and feel a kinship." He smiled crookedly. "Which brings me to the suggestion that you'd be wise to remove your hands from my body."

"Why? I'm not finished."

"But I've definitely started." He looked into her eyes and said roughly, "You may be a virgin, but you're no ignorant miss. You know what arouses a man. I'm beginning to forget how young you are and imagine how tight you'd feel. Get your hands off me."

She suddenly realized the muscles of his stomach were clenched and locked beneath her palms. Heat burned in her cheeks as she jerked her hands away. "You're very rude. I was only trying to help."

"If I didn't believe that, you'd be under me, not over me." He sat up and said wearily, "Run along back to your village and stay there."

Stung, she jumped to her feet. "I certainly don't want to remain with you. I've spent too much time here already." She moved toward the stallion. "And Kapu was right to dump you onto the sand. I should have let him pound you into it."

"But you didn't." He rose to his feet. "As I said, you have a soft heart. It's a very dangerous fault in a woman who wishes to maintain her independence." He met her gaze. "Not to mention her untouched state."

She found her anger ebbing as she stared at him. Why was she still standing there? She should leave him as he had ordered her to do. She certainly didn't want to stay with him.

A warm breeze lifted his dark hair from his forehead and molded the material of his shirt against his body, the same wind that was caressing her naked breasts and causing the hair at her temples to brush across her cheeks. She became acutely aware of the salty scent of the sea, the rhythmic sound of the waves rushing against the shore, the grainy roughness of the sand beneath her bare feet. The air seemed suddenly thick and hard to breathe.

"Go on!" he said sharply.

Her hands shook as she mounted Kapu. She was about to turn away when she noticed how pale his stern face appeared in the moonlight. She hesitated before asking, "You're sure you're unhurt?"

He drew a deep breath and said with great precision, "I'm not hurt, Kanoa." An unexpected smile banished the grimness from his face; then he inclined his head in a bow. "I won't say it's been a complete pleasure, but it's certainly been interesting making your acquaintance." He stepped forward and slapped Kapu's rump. "Run along."

The startled stallion lunged forward.

"And, dammit, if you won't cover yourself, stay away from the shore until we're gone," he called after her. "Some of my seamen won't care how old you are."

She was several yards down the beach before she glanced over her shoulder. He was standing where she had left him, gazing after her.

He smiled faintly and lifted his hand in farewell.

She didn't return the gesture. Staring ahead once more, she urged Kapu to go faster. The episode that had taken place had been most unsettling, and she wanted to put time and distance between herself and the Englishman. He had no role in her life, and yet for a moment he had seemed to have the power to dominate it.

Most disturbing . . .

"Well, I see you've found something to interest you."

Jared turned from watching the girl flying down the beach on the back of the black stallion to see Bradford strolling toward him. "I take it you grew bored with waiting."

"I finished the bottle of brandy," Bradford said mournfully. "Most distressing. I should have noticed that it was only half-full."

"Three-quarters full," Jared corrected. "I wonder you can still walk."

"No, you don't. You know that I seldom get that foxed."

It was true. His uncle had an amazing capacity. He was always a little drunk, but Jared had seen him under the table only a handful of times. "You should have come with me to see King Kamehameha instead of staying on board. They served a heady brew that you would have appreciated."

He grimaced. "Too primitive. I prefer good French brandy."

"I enjoyed it."

Bradford nodded. "But that's because you also have a primitive side to your nature. I noticed it while we were in Tahiti." His gaze went to Kanoa, who was now almost out of sight. "Fine horse. Beautiful gait."

Jared should have known Bradford would notice the horse first.

"I can't tell much from this distance," Bradford went on, "but the woman appears equally fine." He slanted a sly glance at Jared. "I thought you were getting along quite nicely. What did you say to her to make her run away?"

"She isn't a woman, she's a child," Jared said curtly.

"They grow up fast here in the islands."

"But I have no desire to be the catalyst."

Bradford's brows raised. "Good God, you sound positively virtuous."

"She's just a child," he repeated. But one with a strange mixture of qualities—wary and eager, impulsive and caring, bold and yet uncertain.

"Then what was she doing stroking you?"

Christ, he had hoped Bradford had not witnessed that. He would enjoy the explanation far too much. "She wasn't—" He stopped and then admitted, "Her horse threw me."

Bradford stared at him in astonishment. "Indeed?"

"Yes."

He started to laugh. "Amazing. You haven't been thrown since you were a boy. Have you finally found an animal who doesn't appreciate you?"

"Possibly." He shrugged. "I didn't prepare him enough."

"Why not?"

"What difference does it make? I was careless."

"You're never careless. Not with horses." He gazed at him speculatively. "Why?"

"How do I know?" Bradford was right—the impulsive action was not at all like him. It had been evident the stallion was high-strung and dangerously unstable, he should have talked to Kapu longer, soothed him, let him grow used to his touch before mounting him. He deserved that toss and was lucky not to have been trampled. If the girl had not been there, he would have paid heavily for that impulse.

Bradford's gaze went back to the girl and horse. "Pretty?"

Pretty? He didn't suppose so. Except for the thick mane of shining dark hair that flowed nearly to her waist, Kanoa's features were too bold and striking for her to be called pretty. Her jaw was too firm, her lips full and a little pouty, her brows winglike over huge dark eyes that dominated a triangular face. Those eyes had challenged him, and yet he had sensed something fragile and vulnerable about her when she had looked up at him with desperation. He repeated, "She's a child."

Yet not completely a child. Though small, her naked breasts had been perfectly shaped, the nipples dark and pointed. . . .

Bradford chuckled. "That's not what I asked. She must have been a veritable Venus to have you so besotted you can't answer a simple question. Did you find her at Kamehameha's court? Maybe I should have gone with you."

"I didn't go to Kamehameha to find a woman."

"But you found one anyway." Bradford sighed blissfully. "I must admit I've enjoyed our sojourn in this paradise. Beautiful women who give pleasure and no guilt. Can a man ask for more?"

"It seems he can. French brandy."

"Ah, yes, but every paradise has a serpent. This one is fairly innocuous." His gaze returned to Kanoa. "But you shouldn't have been so selfish. Why didn't you invite her to the ship so that we both could enjoy her?"

The flare of hot resentment Jared felt was as startling as it was totally unreasonable. He and Bradford often shared women, and these island beauties had proved eager for the diversion the two men offered them. "For God's sake, why don't you listen? The only thing that child wants between her legs is her damned horse." He turned on his heel and strode down the beach toward the cove. "Forget her. We have more important things to do."

"Not so fast," Bradford complained. "I may not be drunk, but I'm not so steady that I can run."

Smiling affectionately, Jared slowed his pace. "I was thinking only of your dire need for brandy. The sooner we get back to the ship, the sooner you can tap a fresh bottle."

"Well, perhaps I can run . . . a little." He fell into step with Jared. "Did Kamehameha tell you what you wanted to know?"

"Yes." He felt a return of the excitement that had surged through him when the King had so casually given him the information he had been striving to learn since that hellish night in Danjuet. He had traveled to Paris and Marseilles, then had spent almost a year in Tahiti following Deville's trail before arriving on the islands. It had seemed almost unbelievable that the long search had ended. "He's here."

"Deville?" Bradford pursed his lips in a low whistle. "Are you sure?"

"Charles Deville, a Frenchman who lived in Tahiti for a short time and then came here. It must be he. Everything matches too closely with what we've uncovered for it to be anyone else."

"Did he fit the description?"

"Exactly."

"The wife and daughter?"

Jared nodded. "His English wife died a year after he came here, and he took a Polynesian woman as mistress. There's a daughter, Cassandra, but she never comes to Kamehameha's court."

"Does DeVille?"

Jared nodded. "It seems Kamehameha has made something of a pet of him. Deville's done several paintings of the King and his wives. He's permitted to roam all over the island, painting and living off the land."

"Will the king let you take him?"

"He'll have no choice." He smiled with tigerlike ferocity. "If I find him, he's mine."

"I've no doubt he will be. I only hope that Kamehameha isn't too fond of him. I'd hate to have his warriors use one of those exceedingly ugly war clubs on you."

"I don't look forward to that prospect either. I'll have to take him unaware." He thought about it. "The king made a few hints about his desire for British guns. He might be persuaded to turn a blind eye to my taking Deville if he thinks there's a possibility he'll get what he wants."

"Still, it would be easier to kill Deville than try to take him hostage."

"But then I'd have no chance at getting Raoul Cambre. I want both of them dead."

Bradford shook his head. "I hope you get what you want, Jared. It's been a long time and the trail is very cold."

"That's why I have to leave Deville alive until I can squeeze information out of him. Deville was only the weapon—Cambre was the guiding hand."

"Does Deville have a house here on the island?"

"Yes, a cottage in the foothills, but I understand he's seldom there. It appears he has a passion for painting volcanoes. I think it's best to go to Lihua's village tomorrow morning and hire a guide who knows the mountains. We'll try the cottage first, but I want to be prepared."

"I suppose I should be the one avenging John's death. He was my brother, and everyone would say there is some sort of duty owing." Bradford smiled lopsidedly. "I've always had trouble with duty. It has a damnable habit of getting in the way of pleasure."

"I've never blamed you."

"No." Bradford paused. "I've always had trouble with hatred too. I've never hated anyone. I've often thought it was left out of my character. It's hard to kill someone when you feel no hatred for him." He shot Jared a wry glance. "However, *you* don't suffer from a lack of hate."

"No, I have an abundance of it. Enough for both of us."

"Yes." They had come to the longboat drawn up

on the sand, and Bradford began to push it into the surf. "Which is why I left the matter in your hands."

And everything else, too, Jared thought without resentment. When Bradford had been saddled with a thirteen-year-old orphaned nephew to raise, he had resolved the issue by simply treating Jared as if he were a grown man instead of a boy. Jared had attended his first orgy shortly after arriving at his uncle's London lodgings and in the following years was never chastised for drunkenness or licentiousness. The one and only beating he'd received was when Bradford had thought he'd ridden one of his horses too hard. He suspected Bradford loved his horses far better than any human being.

But it was a passion they shared and one that had probably been Jared's salvation.

He didn't have Bradford's head for liquor and soon found he couldn't ride in a race while reeling in the saddle from drunkenness; therefore, it was only sensible to embrace moderation. He'd also learned that if you cuckolded too many husbands, you were in danger of becoming ousted from court, where all the interesting racing took place; therefore, liaisons were formed with carefully chosen demimondaines.

Until tonight.

He had been right not to pursue the lust he had felt at the moment the girl's hands had been on him. He had thought himself a jaded womanizer, but she had somehow managed to touch something soft in him. For an instant her loneliness and vulnerability had reminded him of the boy he had been, the boy who had come back from France and used every bit of recklessness and ferocity at his command to hide the pain and desolation. Now that he had found Deville, he could permit no hint of softness to hinder him.

Besides, virgins could be trouble even in this society, where an untouched state was looked upon only with friendly scorn and amazement. He should be content with the women who swam out to the *Josephine* and offered themselves. Tonight he would rid himself of this lust with Lihua or her sister and forget all about Kanoa.

And tomorrow he would seek out Deville.

Lani met Cassie in the stand of trees at the foot of the hill leading to the cottage. "Come quick," she said as she thrust Cassie's riding habit at her. "The old woman is pacing like a tiger."

Cassie jumped from Kapu's back, ripped off the sarong, and hurriedly dressed.

"What kept you so long?" Lani asked.

Cassie avoided Lani's glance. "Nothing."

Lani's shrewd gaze narrowed on Cassie's face. "I think your 'nothing' may be 'something,' but we have no time to talk now. The old woman has no idea you went to my village. I told her that you hiked up to the volcano to be with your father. She may spit venom but won't punish you, if you keep silent."

"I'll keep silent." Cassie pulled on her boots, trying to subdue her exasperation. Such a waste of effort to dress and undress for the benefit of one poisonous woman.

"You always say that you'll keep silent," Lani said, "but you seldom do."

"I lose my temper."

"And taste the old woman's sting." Lani frowned in concern. "Be careful tonight. With your father away I may not be able to save you."

Sometimes Lani could not save Cassie from punishment even when her father was at the cottage, but she always tried. Cassie felt a warm surge of affection as she looked at Lani in her starched blue gown and high-bound hair. Life was probably more difficult for Lani than for herself. After running free on the island until her sixteenth year, Lani had come to her father's bed and a household ruled by Clara Kidman. Cassie remembered well those first days of rage and conflict. Poor Lani—she had to fight not only Clara, but Cassie as well, who was as rebellious as an imp of Satan. In time a guarded peace was established, but Lani had been forced to make compromises. Charles Deville would seldom support either Lani or Cassie against Clara. After Cassie's mother's death Clara had become the housekeeper and had dominated everyone in the family. Deville's solution was wonderfully simple and comfortable: he was just not there. It was rare indeed when he was at the cottage for more than one week every month.

"Hurry," Lani urged. "Her anger will only grow as time passes."

Cassie pulled on her other boot, gathered her hair in a bun on top of her head, and rose to her feet. "Go back to the house. I have to take Kapu to the stable."

Lani shook her head. "Tie him to the tree. You were supposed to be on foot. I'll come back for him while you're talking to Clara and put him in his stall."

Cassie tethered Kapu and started up the path toward the cottage. "Wait!" Lani hurried after her, plucked the ginger flowers from her hair, and dropped them to the ground.

Cassie looked down at the flowers. She felt a pang of sadness as she remembered the feeling of freedom and happiness she had experienced when she had tucked those blooms into her hair earlier in the day. It should not be that way, she knew. Beauty should not be ground into the earth or hidden like something foul and forbidden. "This isn't right."

"No, but it's necessary."

"It shouldn't be necessary." She whirled on Lani. "Why do you stay? You'd be much happier back in your village. There's nothing for you here."

"There is you." A radiant smile lit Lani's face. "That is much. And there is your father."

"Who is seldom here, and when he is, he uses you and then leaves you to face your problems alone."

"That does not matter."

"It *does* matter. You should leave him."

Lani's brows lifted. "If he's so terrible, why do you not leave him? Why do you not take your fine horse and go live in the valley on the other side of the mountain, as you're always telling me you're going to do? What of the herd of wonderful horses you're going to breed?"

She lifted her chin. "I will do it."

"When?"

"I need a mare to equal Kapu."

"And are you going to find her in this cottage on the hill?"

"Of course not."

"Then why don't you leave this terrible man you call Father and go make a life of your own?"

"He's *not* terrible. He's just—it's not the same. You're not bound to him as I am." She burst out, "He *needs* me."

"And you love him," Lani said gently. "It's easy to love Charles. He is gentle and kind, and it's not his fault that he was not given the will to withstand adversity. It's very hard to walk away from a man who needs you, isn't it?"

"Is that why you stay?" Her brooding gaze went to

the cottage on the hill where Clara waited. "Because he has need of you?"

"It's a strong bond. I'm a woman who must be needed." She touched Cassie's shoulder with a loving hand. "Fulfilling that need enriches me. I feel blessed that I was allowed to come here."

Cassie blinked back tears. "You have no sense." She went into Lani's arms and gave her a hug. "We're the ones who are blessed. We don't deserve you."

"That is probably true," Lani said serenely, then laughed. "Particularly if you cause me more trouble with the old one this night."

"I'll be good." Cassie stepped back and moved quickly up the trail. "I'll be no trouble at all. I promise you."

"You're always good."

Cassie snorted. Nothing could be less the truth. Even when she tried to school herself for Lani's sake, she nearly always failed. "Is that why I ran away today and left you as my father always does?"

"I know you could not stand it any longer. I could see it seething within you yesterday when she was pecking at you with her sharp tongue. You don't have a gentle spirit and sometimes passion overcomes you."

Passion overcomes you. . . .

Lani had not meant the phrase in a carnal sense, but Cassie had a sudden vision of the Englishman on the beach. He had both angered and stirred her. Was this part of the turbulent nature Lani spoke of? The memory of that queer breathless moment before she had left him caused heat to rush through her. It was most unsettling; she would not think about it. "I won't run away again. It's not fair to you."

"You'll do what you need to do. I knew you'd return once your anger had lessened."

"Someday I won't come back. Someday I'll make it happen. I'll take you and Kapu to the other side of the island, and we'll never set foot here again."

"Someday." Lani smiled. "But not while he still needs us. Yes?"

Cassie nodded resignedly. "Yes."

"Now, don't be so gloomy. Did you have a good day? How is Lihua?"

"Good." She paused. "There's an English ship in the bay. She and the others have been swimming out to couple with the sailors."

Lani frowned. "That is not good. She may get the disease."

"I told her. She wouldn't listen."

"No, not when the blood runs hot." Lani added, "I remember when I was only fourteen, a ship from Russia docked in the bay. My mother told me that there was some talk of the foreigners bringing disease, but I paid no attention. I swam out with the others and chose a sailor of my own. He was very strong and brought me much pleasure." She chuckled. "Such foolishness. I was lucky that he did not have the disease."

"Yes." Cassie looked away from her and asked haltingly, "Can you truly have pleasure with a stranger?"

"Of course. As long as there is no cruelty and the man has skill."

"Then why do you say I shouldn't couple with any of the men from your village? They're not even strangers and would be kind to me. Would that be bad?"

"Bad?" Lani grimaced. "Now you're talking like

the old one. Have I not taught you better? Love is never bad. It would just be unwise for you."

"Why?"

"You might have a child, and the old one would be very cruel to you, to both of you. You would have to choose between your father and the child." She shook her head. "You have a very loving heart, and to deny either one would hurt you. It is better to wait until the situation alters. Do you understand?"

"Yes."

Lani gazed at her curiously. "Why have you never questioned me about this before? Have you found a man you wish to pleasure?"

"No!" Cassie tried to shrug casually. "I just wondered. Sometimes it's difficult for me when I go to the village. I don't feel like a foreigner, but I'm not one of them either. I don't belong anywhere."

"Then you must find your own place."

"I will." She smiled at Lani and repeated, "Someday."

Lani nodded. "It may not be—" Her gaze on the veranda, she broke off and her pace faltered. "There's the old woman. I must leave you here, or she will suspect I told her falsehoods." She moved toward the shrubbery at the side of the trail. "I'll go back and get Kapu, but I may not be able to come to you before morning. I told the old woman I was going to bed. Have you eaten supper?"

"Yes," Cassie lied. Lani had already risked too much for her today. If she admitted that she had not had anything but a piece of fruit since that morning, Lani would move heaven and earth to make sure she was fed. "Go."

Lani gave her another fleeting smile and was gone.

Cassie braced herself and moved quickly toward the woman waiting on the veranda.

Clara Kidman stood straight and forbidding, silhouetted by the candlelight streaming from the room behind her. "Good evening, Cassandra. I trust you had a pleasant day," she said coldly. "How is your father?"

"Well." Cassie walked hastily toward the bamboo door. "He should be home within a few days. He gives you his regards."

"And did you tell him of your rudeness to me?"

Cassie didn't answer.

"Or your undisciplined behavior?" Clara questioned grimly. "I think not. You probably gave him sweet smiles and told him lies about me. It will do you no good. When he comes back, I'll tell him the truth, and he will let me punish you as I see fit."

"Perhaps." She felt the familiar anger tightening her chest. She had made a promise to Lani. She must escape to her room before Clara found a way to get under her guard.

"He knows that such unbridled behavior is not to be permitted. You're turning into as much a pagan as that whore he uses for his lust."

Cassie stopped but did not look at her. "She's not a whore."

"A whore," Clara repeated. "Whore and Jezebel and lost to all goodness."

"She *is* good. She's kind and generous and—"

"Are you defying me again?"

Cassie wanted to strike out at Clara, but that was what she expected. She knew that Cassie could withstand verbal abuse directed against herself, but an attack on Lani invariably brought a response. She would not lose her temper. She had promised Lani.

"I'm not defying you," she said, trying to keep her tone even. "But my father would not like you talking in that fashion about Lani. He truly cares about her."

"Blasphemy. A man who was wed to a woman as pure and saintly as your mother would never feel anything but lust for a harlot who bares her breasts to all the world."

"She doesn't do that anymore."

"Only because I convinced your father how sinful it was to expose you to such behavior. I told him that if he permitted such conduct from her, she would soon be having you running around half-naked."

Cassie felt an instant of satisfaction over her state of undress that day. Lani had taught her that the human body was the most beautiful of creations and she must never be ashamed to bare it. She had an almost irresistible temptation to tell Clara she had not won that particular battle. Her resolve was clearly weakening, and she had to get out of the room before she exploded. "I'm very tired. Good night, Clara."

"If you ponder your sins, I doubt if the night will be good for you."

Don't answer her, Cassie told herself. Keep your promise.

"Cassandra."

She glanced back over her shoulder at Clara. The old one, the ugly one, the Polynesians called her, but at first glance Clara was neither. She had only a few strands of gray in her dark hair that was pulled back in a bun, and her face was clear and unlined. Her features were regular, and she might even be considered handsome if it weren't for her tight expression and the bitter aura that surrounded her.

"This disobedience must stop," Clara said. "I won't permit you to go the way of that native whore.

It's time you returned to the civilized world. A few years of schooling in a convent would prove of vast benefit in curbing your behavior."

It was an old threat, but Cassie still felt a ripple of disquiet. "This is my home. My father won't send me away."

"You think not? He gets a little less stubborn each time I speak of the matter." She smiled again. "Good night, Cassandra." She turned and went back out to the veranda.

She was satisfied now that she had caused Cassie uneasiness. What made any person so vindictive as to wrest pleasure from others' pain? When Lani had first come, she had tried to make Cassie understand that people were not born evil, that experiences made them what they were. But now even Lani found it hard to be kind. Clara seemed to thrive on the power she had wrested from her position here, and each year she grew more greedy.

Cassie shivered and looked away from the woman who now stood quite still at the wooden balustrade, looking up at the moon. She went to her room down the hall and closed the door. Safe. Clara had removed the locks after her mother had died, but she seldom intruded here. Cassie crossed to the window and threw open the shutters. Had she given Lani enough time to get Kapu to the stable?

With relief she saw Lani moving toward the house from the direction of the stable. She would avoid the veranda, slip through the back door, and be in her room before Clara could discover her. All secure.

But Cassie did not feel safe. She felt unsettled and unsure. She had the odd premonition that everything had changed tonight. Yet nothing had really hap-

pened. She had merely met an Englishman who had
aroused in her strange and disturbing emotions.

Well, she must forget him. His world was far away
and incomprehensible to her. Her world was going to
be in the beautiful valley across the island. She and
Lani and Papa would raise fine horses, and they would
be as free as Lihua and the other villagers.

Lihua was probably in the Englishman's bed now,
writhing, crying out . . .

Cassie's knuckles turned white as she gripped the
shutter. The sudden surge of anger took her off
guard. Jealousy? Impossible. She had never experienced jealousy before and would certainly not envy
her friend any pleasure. She had lived too long among
the islanders not to have accepted their belief that all
possessions should be shared.

But she had known jealousy when she had seen the
Englishman leading Kapu toward her—jealousy and
possessiveness and desperation that the treasure of
Kapu's affection would be taken away. Perhaps she
had not absorbed as much of the generosity of Lani
and the islanders as she had hoped.

She closed the shutters and turned away from the
window. She would go to bed and forget everything
that had transpired tonight. No doubt when she was
less weary, this strange restlessness would vanish.

Two

The messenger from Kamehameha came to the cottage shortly before dawn.

Cassie woke to hear a pounding at the front door and then Lani's swift, light footsteps down the hall.

Papa!

She jumped out of bed and ran from her room. She was being foolish. The summons did not have to mean any danger to her father. It was only that unsettling experience on the shore that had fueled this fear.

Lani already had the door open, and light from the torch borne by the huge bare-chested islander fell on her frowning face.

"What is it?" Cassie asked. "Is it a message from Papa? Is something the matter?"

"No," Lani answered, then spoke in a low tone to the islander. He smiled and bowed and then was gone, running on swift bare feet down the hill.

Lani turned to Cassie. "The message isn't from Charles. It's from King Kamehameha. He wishes to let your father know he may have a visitor. An English chief was at his court tonight making many inquiries regarding your father. Since the Englishman is a great chief and the king wished no problem with the English, he judged it wise to tell the man what he wished to know."

"What?"

"He told him of this cottage and Charles's habit of painting near the volcano." She paused. "The Englishman's manner was polite and unthreatening, but the king said to tell Charles that a typhoon often starts with the gentlest breeze."

Chill rained through Cassie. "What was the Englishman's name?"

"Jared Danemount, Duke of Morland." Lani's eyes narrowed as she heard Cassie's sharp intake of breath. "It is the one? The enemy?"

"Papa told you about him?"

Lani nodded. "You know Charles must share all his troubles. But he said only that he feared the coming of an Englishman. Could he be the one?"

Cassie wished she could remember more of her father's words that day in Marseilles. "I don't know— I'm not sure." She had been almost certain the Englishman could not be the man her father had fled France to avoid. "Did you send the messenger to the hills to warn him?"

"Am I a fool? Of course I did." She nibbled at her lower lip. "If he is the man, is there truly danger?"

"I can't be sure." She tried desperately to recall every trait of the man on the beach that might prove deadly. Power, strength, recklessness. What if they were turned against her father? "Yes, I think so."

"Then we must not rely on the messenger. I told him of a few places Charles likes to go to paint, but he may not be able to find them." She grimaced. "And he may not try too hard. My people tread warily on Pelée's ground."

"I'll go," Cassie told her as she headed back to her bedroom. "If the Englishman comes here first, try to send him away."

"What is this?" Clara Kidman appeared in the doorway of her room, the light from the candle in her hand lighting her grim expression. "Who was at the door?"

"It was a messenger from the King," Cassie tossed over her shoulder. "I have to go find my father."

"You'll do no such thing," Clara said. "Respectable people don't go running to do the bidding of heathens. You can wait until he returns to—"

"I'm going." Cassie slammed the door behind her.

She hurriedly threw on the riding habit and boots she had discarded only a few hours before. The clothing would offer protection from the brush and rocky trails. She would have to go on foot; the country was too wild for horses.

A few minutes later she flew out of the room but stopped warily when she saw Lani and Clara still in the hall.

"It's all right, Cassie," Lani said quickly. "I've explained to Clara that Charles would want you to go."

"And I'm not sure I believe it. I'll expect you back before dark," Clara said coldly. "With a note from your father that your journey was both necessary and important."

Cassie didn't even know if she could locate him before dark. Her father drifted around the hills like a piece of ash from the volcano; there was no telling where he was today. "I'll do my best to find him as quickly as possible."

"Before dark," Clara repeated.

Anger flared through Cassie. What was she supposed to do? Whisk him out of thin air? All the tension and worry suddenly exploded. "I said I'll do—"

"Come along, I'll walk you down the hill." Lani took Cassie's arm and pulled her away from Clara. "I don't think you'll need a torch. It will be dawn soon. Are you warmly dressed?"

"Yes." Lani, as usual, was stepping between them, trying to divert Clara's venom and Cassie's rage. Cassie knew Lani was right; she shouldn't waste her time battling Clara when Papa might be in danger. She pulled away from Lani as soon as they were out on the veranda. "I'm sorry, I'm over it now. I'm just worried about Papa."

"I'm worried, too," Lani said gently. "And there's nothing to be sorry about. I understand."

Lani always understood. "Go back inside," Cassie said gruffly. "You're wearing only your dressing gown, and it's cool out here."

Lani nodded. "Go with God, my friend."

Charles would be no match for this man, Lani thought as she gazed at the face of the Englishman. It had taken only a glance after she had opened the door to his knock to realize that Jared Danemount possessed the cool, deadly confidence she had seen in the finest warriors in her village. She and Cassie had been wise to take extra precautions. "I regret you have come this far for no reason, Your Grace. Charles is not here."

"And where is he?"

"He took a boat to the island of Maui. There is much to paint there."

"Indeed?" His expression didn't change, but she was aware of a slight edge to the silken politeness of his tone. "I heard he was content to paint here." His gaze wandered to the trail leading up to Mauna Loa. "Or near the volcano."

"He's an artist and they are never content." She started to close the door. "Now, if you'll excuse me, I have duties to perform. Good day, Your Grace."

"Wait!" He put his foot in the door. "I need to find—"

"Who is this?" Clara demanded as she came toward Lani. "Disturbance after disturbance. Is it another of those heathens?"

She could not have come at a worse time. Lani had hoped to have the Englishman gone before Clara appeared. "No, it's an Englishman, but he's going now."

"Not quite yet." Danemount threw open the door. "I have a few more questions." His gaze went to Clara. "I'm Jared Danemount, Duke of Morland. And you are . . . ?"

"I'm Clara Kidman. I'm housekeeper here, and you have no—" She broke off and frowned. "A duke? A British duke? Truly?"

He nodded. "I wish to know the whereabouts of a Monsieur Charles Deville. I understand he has left the island?"

"Of course he's not left the island," Clara said. "He's gone to that volcano again."

Danemount's cool glance moved to Lani. He murmured, "Really? I must have misunderstood."

"But he may be returning soon. A courier from the king came earlier today, and his daughter took the message to him."

Lani gritted her teeth in sheer exasperation when she saw the flicker of wariness cross Danemount's face.

"You could wait for him here," Clara said grudgingly to Lani's surprise. It was seldom Clara offered hospitality to anyone.

"No, I don't think I will. My business is of some urgency." He bowed mockingly to Lani. "Good day, ladies."

She had to make one last attempt at diverting him. "The mountains can be dangerous for a man alone. You could become lost."

"I'm not alone. My uncle and a guide are waiting on the trail below." His lips twisted in a cynical smile. "But my thanks for your concern."

She watched him go down the veranda steps and then move quickly along the palm-bordered path until he was lost to view.

"This was not a good thing you did," she muttered.

"It's only what I'd expect of you," Clara said. "You tell that heathen who came bursting in here in the middle of the night where Monsieur Deville is to be found, but you lie to a civilized British gentleman."

"That gentleman may prove—" She broke off as she realized Clara would not listen. Patience, she told herself. She had known the burdens she would face when she had come to this house, and she was determined to bear them with grace. "It was not a good thing," she repeated as she crossed the veranda.

"Where are you going?"

"To work in my garden." She needed the soothing balm of delving into the earth, and it was the one pastime to which Clara could not object, since it provided fresh vegetables for the table. "Unless you need me in the house?"

"I've told you that you're not needed here."

Many times and in the cruelest of fashions. But she

was needed by Charles and Cassie, and she could withstand the old woman's cuts.

As she knelt before her vegetable patch, she gazed uneasily up at the mountain. It was nearing noon and Cassie had been gone for hours. Had she found Charles yet?

Cassie did not find her father until nearly twilight. He had painted the place he called Pelée's Breath so often, she had not thought he would return to do another picture. Yet there he was, standing at his easel, on the highest plateau overlooking those barren foothills where clouds of steam drifted like phantom snakes from the jet-black earth.

"Papa!" Cassie waved before carefully traversing the rocky incline leading to the plateau. It was always slippery both on this incline and on the foothills themselves. The black lava was constantly coated with the moisture from the steam that rose from between the cracks in the earth. Since the first time her father had brought her here as a small child, she had been frightened of the strangeness of the place. The seething silence broken only by wind and the hiss of escaping steam had seemed more threatening than the red-orange molten fire in the heart of the volcano. She had always thought it odd that her father, who was nervous of even touching Kapu's mane, was comfortable in this eerie place. As she reached the top of the plateau she said, "I need to talk to you."

"Good afternoon, Cassie," her father replied abstractedly. "I'll be with you shortly. I just have to complete this shading on the lava rock. Do you see how it glows with the steam? It's really quite—"

"Did the messenger reach you?"

"Messenger?" His gaze never left the canvas. "Did you send one? I don't believe that—"

"King Kamehameha sent a message. Someone wants to find you. An Englishman."

Her father's brush stopped in midmotion. "An Englishman?"

"The king said he doubted the man was a threat, but that you should know he had told him of the cottage and that you often painted near the volcano."

He stared straight ahead. "His name?"

"Danemount."

Her father's eyes closed. "Dear God," he whispered.

She need no longer wonder if Danemount was the threat. Her father was terrified. She had not seen him really afraid since that day they had left Marseilles. She took a step forward. "Why is he looking for you?"

His eyes opened. "To kill me," he said dully. "He wants to kill me."

"But why?"

"The hand of *le bon dieu*," he muttered. "I always knew it would come. God's will."

"It's not God's will," she said fiercely. "What are you talking about? God would not condone this man murdering you."

"God's will," he repeated. Then he shook his head as if to clear it. "I don't want to die, Cassie. I've done bad things, but I'm not a bad man. I don't deserve to die."

"Of course you don't. And you could not have done anything very wrong. We'll go down and face the Englishman and tell him—"

"No!" He whirled so quickly that he knocked the easel over. "How can I face him? What would I say to him? It wasn't my fault. Raoul told me that nothing would happen, and I believed him. At least I think I believed him. Raoul was always so certain about everything, and I was never certain about anything. Yes, it's Raoul's fault."

Raoul. He had called the man who had come to the ship that day Raoul. Cassie frowned in bewilderment. "Then we'll tell the Englishman that whatever happened, the blame is not yours."

"He wouldn't believe me. Not without proof. He wouldn't listen to me. Why do you think I ran away? It was the uncle who was making inquiries, but I knew the cub would come after me. I remember his eyes . . . burning, glaring at me." He picked up the half-finished painting and started down the incline, stumbling in his hurry. "I have to get away. I have to hide. I knew he'd come. . . ."

Cassie ran after him. "But where are you going?"

He stopped in midstride and looked around him dazedly. "I don't know. There has to be someplace. . . ."

"If you think there's danger, go to King Kamehameha. He'll protect you. This Englishman is nothing to him."

"Perhaps," he muttered. "I don't know. I can't seem to think."

And if he continued to blunder around in this state, Danemount would be here before she could get her father to safety.

She took his arm and shook it. "*I* know. Listen to me. Go to the king and tell him this Englishman is a danger to you. He'll send his warriors to rid you of him."

"I couldn't do that. I won't have his blood on my hands, too."

Too? A chill rushing through her, she asked, "Would you rather it be your blood spilled? I'll kill him myself before I see that happen."

For an instant the fear left his expression, and a faint smile lit his face. "My fierce Cassie." He reached out and gently touched her cheek. "You're the best part of me, you know. But I can't remember ever being as true and loyal and brave. I've not been a good father, but I've always loved you."

His words sounded terrifyingly final. "Don't be foolish. You've been a very good father."

He shook his head. "It was always too much trouble. I should have—" He broke off and went rigid. "What is that?"

She had heard it, too. The sharp sound of boots on the rocky path. It could not be the king's messenger; the islanders did not wear footwear. They both turned to look down the path.

No one appeared to be in sight, but in the half darkness Cassie wasn't sure she would be able to discern anyone. The steam was now a thick mist that glowed malignant yellow-purple in the dusk. Her hand tightened on her father's arm. "Listen to me," she spoke quickly, forcefully. "Climb back up the plateau and go down the other side. Then cut across the mountain and circle back when you reach the shore. I'll go down and try to lead him away from you. In the darkness he'll think I'm you."

"No!"

"I'll be safe. Would this Danemount kill an innocent woman?"

"I know little about— I don't think— No."

"Then go to Kamehameha. I'll come to you there tomorrow and we'll make plans."

The sound of booted footsteps on stone came again, closer.

"Hurry!" She grabbed the canvas from him and deliberately threw it down to the left of the path.

"What are you doing? My painting . . ."

"You can paint other pictures. We need to leave a trail." She pushed him toward the plateau. "Go!" She jumped over the painting and began to half run, half slide down the steam-coated lava rocks.

His hoarse exclamation echoed loudly in the eerie silence. Glancing back over her shoulder a few minutes later, she saw to her relief that he had almost reached the plateau again. She had feared he would follow her. The next moment he was lost to view.

The footsteps were even closer now, coming from just beyond the mist at the foot of the hill. If the Englishman had heard Papa's exclamation, all the better. Between the vapor and the twilight she would be only a shadow to any pursuer and could easily be mistaken for her father. She had only to give him a quarter of an hour's head start, and they would never catch him before he reached the king.

She left the path and carefully began winding her way through the cracks spouting vapor. She heard a cry from behind her. Her heart leaped as panic soared through her. She had been seen!

Stupid response. She had wanted to be seen. She glanced behind her but could discern only three dark, phantomlike silhouettes on the trail. Good. She must look the same to them. Her pace quickened.

"Deville!" The Englishman's voice carried across the barren rocks like the horn of Gabriel. "Stop, goddammit!"

She didn't look around as she moved along the side of mountain.

Darkness, falling fast.

Steam writhing and hissing from the cracks around her.

The rocky path steeper and more slippery.

The crunch of footsteps behind her.

Hurry. Keep moving.

She could barely see in the dimness. Was that another fissure ahead?

A sudden burst of steam exploded from the ground in front of her!

She cried out and instinctively jerked back. Dear God, too slippery . . .

She was losing her footing.

Falling!

She reached out and tried to catch her balance as she rolled down the rocky incline, trying desperately to dig her nails into the hard rock.

Blackness.

"He's down!" Exhilaration surging through Jared, he moved quickly over the black rocks toward the slumped figure at the bottom of the hill. After all the years of tracking and hunting he had the bastard. "By God, we've got him!"

"Be careful," Bradford called as he followed at a slower pace. "Or you'll end up down there on those rocks beside him."

"Lakoa, light that torch," Jared ordered the native guide. He drew his knife as he approached the fallen man. Deville was still, but that didn't mean he was not dangerous. Desperate men were always a threat.

"Jared, wait," Bradford told him. "I think—"

Jared had already stopped a few yards from Deville. Only it wasn't Deville. It was a girl, her dark hair loose and covering her face, her black serge riding habit torn.

"Is it the daughter?" Bradford asked as he and Lakoa reached Jared.

"Who the hell else could it be?" Sharp disappointment mixed with concern as Jared fell to his knees beside the still figure. Instead of Deville, he might have succeeded in murdering a girl. "Dammit, I called out his name. She must have known it was he we were after."

"I suppose Deville is long gone," Bradford murmured. "She kept us following her for over twenty minutes."

The girl moaned and restlessly moved her head.

At least she was alive, Jared realized with relief. He pushed aside the hair covering her face.

He went still.

"What's wrong?" Bradford asked.

"It's not Deville's daughter."

"Oh, yes." Lakoa stepped forward. "It is her. I know her. She is the friend of my sister Lihua. It is Kanoa, the daughter of the one who paints." His brown eyes filled with concern. "Lihua has great affection for her. This is not good."

"No, this is not good," Jared muttered. Nothing about this situation was in the least good. Not Kanoa's injury, nor her deceit, nor Deville's escape.

"We must get her to Lani," Lakoa said. "She will know what to do."

Lani must be the Polynesian woman at the cottage, Deville's mistress, Jared decided. Lakoa was right; the cottage was not close, but it was nearer than the village. He checked the wound on Kanoa's temple. It had stopped bleeding, and the cut did not appear deep. The fall itself had rendered her unconscious.

He cradled her in his arms and rose to his feet. "Let's go."

Bradford frowned. "Are you sure? It's miles back to the cottage. We could camp here and send Lakoa for help."

"It will be quicker to take her ourselves." He moved down the hill. "You lead the way, Lakoa. It's getting black as pitch on this damn mountain."

Papa was carrying her, holding her close and safe, keeping away the darkness.

No, it couldn't be Papa. He hadn't carried her in his arms since she was a little girl. Since the time Clara had told him that such coddling would spoil her. It must be someone else. . . .

She struggled to open her lids. She gave it up; it was too hard.

"I'll take her for a while. You must be tired, lad."

"I'm damnably tired. I'd like to drop her off the side of the mountain."

"Then why didn't you leave her? I told you an hour ago carrying her all this way was too much strain. We should have done what I first suggested."

No answer but a low curse.

Both voices had been deep, masculine, but neither had been Papa's.

Danger. There was something she should remember. . . .

She managed to raise her lids this time. Why, that was Lakoa bearing the torch on the trail ahead. She had known him since she had been a child, played with him in the village. "Lakoa," she whispered.

"Don't talk." The words were clipped, reverberating beneath her ear.

She looked up and met the gaze of the man who

was carrying her. Blue eyes, clear and cool as the lake in her valley across the island. She remembered those eyes but couldn't recall why they brought this feeling of uneasiness.

"Is she awake?"

She caught a glimpse of another face. Heavy features; curly, gray-flecked dark hair; eyes the color of strong tea.

The arms tightened around her. "Barely."

His scent drifted to her—musk, leather. The scent was also familiar. . . . Why couldn't she connect it to the man? He had been close to her once like this and had spoken words, disturbing words. . . .

"Who are . . . ," she whispered.

He looked down at her, his eyes gleaming like the blade of a knife.

Gleaming with anger . . . and something else.

She closed her eyes to shut him out. She could not deal with the uneasiness looking at him brought. The blackness was rushing back, and she had to concentrate on the fight to keep it at bay.

Only a few seconds later the battle was lost, and darkness claimed her once more.

At Jared's first knock the door of the cottage was thrown open.

"What have you done to her?" the Polynesian woman demanded, staring at Cassie in dismay. "Why did you hurt her? She did nothing to—"

"I didn't hurt her." Jared pushed past her and strode into the sitting room. "She hurt herself. The blasted girl fell down the mountain and hit her head."

"And you had nothing to do with it?" Lani asked with sarcasm.

"She was skipping along the rocks in the dark trying to make us think she was Deville." He laid Cassie down on the sofa. "I assume this is his daughter?"

Lani knelt beside Cassie. "Of course it is."

The confirmation came as no surprise, but he had hoped Lakoa had been mistaken.

"Did she wake at all on the way here?" Lani asked.

"Once. She appeared to be confused. I've sent Lakoa and my uncle to King Kamehameha to bring a physician here."

"I've seen many head wounds before. If she woke, then the danger is probably not great. Sleep is the medicine she needs." Lani looked at him. "Charles?"

"We didn't catch him." He gazed directly into her eyes. "But we will."

"So that you can break his head, too?"

"I didn't break—" He drew a deep breath and tried to control his temper. "I don't go around breaking girls' heads—even if they deserve it."

"To try to save a father's life is such a heinous crime."

His hands clenched into fists. "It's not criminal, but it's damn foolish. She could have died on that mountain."

She tilted her head and gazed at him curiously. "You are concerned about her."

"I'm *not* concerned. Anyone who is stupid enough to risk everything for a man who— Why are you just kneeling there? Do something! At least wash the blood from her face."

"I will do so." She paused. "If you wish to be helpful, you could keep Clara out of my way. She's bound to hear me, and she thinks no one does things properly but herself."

Clara? He vaguely remembered the woman. "The housekeeper? Very well."

"And you could carry Cassie into her room. She will be more comfortable there."

Jared lifted Cassie again and followed Lani down the short hall. After he had placed Cassie on the narrow bed, he stepped back. God, she was pale.

"Now leave the room," Lani ordered. "She will be disturbed if she wakes to a stranger."

Jared hesitated. He didn't want to go, blast it.

"You have no place here." Lani's soft voice held a note of steel. "You're the enemy, and I won't have her made afraid when she's ill."

Of course, he was the enemy. Did the woman think he would forget it? "I have a place here until I find Charles Deville." He turned on his heel. "I'll let you have your way, but I've not noticed Kanoa is burdened by an overabundance of fear."

As he closed the door behind him, Clara Kidman appeared in the hall.

"What's happening?" she asked sharply. "What are you doing here?"

He opened his lips to answer with the same rudeness, then changed his mind. The woman was as sour as an unripe grape, but in the house of the enemy you gathered any ally you could. He injected all the powers of persuasion at his command into his smile. "Ah, I was just coming to tell you all about it, Miss Kidman. It appears we have a desperate situation and need someone of your obvious intelligence and efficiency to help us solve it."

The scent of lavender soap, vanilla, and ginger flowers drifted to Cassie even before she opened her eyes.

Lani.

Lani's beautiful, serene face above her, Lani wiping her forehead with a cool cloth. Everything was all

right; safety, love . . . Not quite all right, she realized the next moment as a throbbing pain shot
through her temple.

"My head hurts." The words came out in a croak.

Lani smiled. "It's not surprising when you tried
your best to break it open. Does your throat ache?"

She swallowed. "A little."

"I've been able to get only a little water down you
in the last few hours." She took a cup from the bedside table. "Drink."

It wasn't water but sweetened coconut milk, Cassie
recognized. She must be ill. From childhood Lani had
always given her the same drink when she'd been sick.
She had made up a story for Clara that though the
drink was bitter tasting, it had special healing proper-
ties. Cassie remembered the secret laughter they had
shared as she had feigned reluctance even to taste the
milk.

Her lips curved in a smile before she made a face.
"What foul stuff."

Lani's eyes twinkled. "But it's so good for you."

She took another sip. "Am I sick?"

"You don't remember? You fell and hit your head
at Pelée's Breath. But don't worry, the doctor was
here just a few hours ago and said no true harm had
been done." She wrinkled her nose. "I didn't need
him to tell me that."

Pelée's Breath. What had she been doing at Pelée's—

She sat upright in bed. "Papa!"

"Lie back down," Lani said. "All is well. At least I
think it is. The Englishman has not found Charles
yet. Do you know where he is?"

"Yes." Ignoring Lani's order, she threw the cover
aside and swung her legs to the floor. Then she had to

clutch at the mattress as dizziness overwhelmed her. When it cleared, she cautiously lay back down before asking, "How long have I been here?"

"Danemount brought you back late last night. It's a little after noon now. He found you lying in a faint at the bottom of Pelée's Breath. You'd hit your head on a rock."

Cassie suddenly remembered that moment of waking on the trail. "He was angry. . . ."

"Extremely," Lani said. "He came here first, and when he couldn't find Charles, he set out for the volcano." Her lips tightened. "I tried to keep him here, but Clara told him that you had hurried off early that day to give your father a message from the king."

"Splendid."

Lani shrugged. "She appears to be mildly enthralled with His Grace. I suppose we shouldn't be surprised. He's an English duke, and even a British peasant is better than the king of any other country."

"Haven't you told her he's Papa's enemy?"

"When has she ever believed me? I'm a heathen."

It had been a foolish question. Cassie doubted if Clara would have listened to her either.

"But is he really your father's enemy?" Lani asked. "What did Charles tell you?"

"He said Danemount wants to kill him."

Lani's face paled. "Why?"

Cassie shook her head. "He kept saying, 'God's will.' "

"Danemount is no angel sent from heaven. Quite the contrary, I'd judge. But he can be charming when it suits him, and he's made an effort to make himself pleasant to Clara." She was silent a moment. "He's a very clever man, isn't he?"

Cassie could not miss the significance of the question. Lani suspected things were not as they appeared on the surface, and Cassie knew she should tell her of that meeting on the shore. Yet she was reluctant to do so. She wanted only to block it out, forget it. "How should I know?"

Lani raised her brows. "When he brought you back, he called you Kanoa. Of course, Lakoa could have called you by name, but his manner was definitely familiar. What knowledge do you have of Danemount?"

She looked away and said haltingly, "I . . . met him on the beach. We talked for a few moments." She burst out, "He was a stranger. I knew nothing about him."

"But now you know he's your father's enemy."

"Of course I do," she said fiercely. "Do you think I would—"

"Shh." Lani put her fingers on Cassie's lips. "You didn't tell me of your meeting, and I had to be sure. He's a man who's practiced in molding women to his will. Even Clara has weakened before him. She believes everything he tells her."

"I can't imagine that happening."

"You'll see." Lani sat down on the bed. "Now we must talk about your father before they know you're awake."

Cassie's gaze flew to the door. "The Englishman's still here?"

She nodded. "He's been here since he brought you back. He told me to call him when you woke." She grimaced. "There are also two of his sailors from the ship wandering about the grounds 'for our protection.'"

"They think Papa will come back."

"Will he?"

Cassie shook her head. "I told him to go to Kamehameha, and I'd come to him. Can we count on the king to rid us of Danemount?"

Lani frowned. "Kamehameha has a fondness for Charles, but he won't help him against the Englishman. He wants British guns to fight his wars."

"But he'll hide Papa until the Englishman leaves the island?"

"Unless it proves uncomfortable for him. But how do you know Danemount will leave? I've rarely seen a more determined man."

"He'll grow tired of looking for Papa," she said with a confidence she didn't feel. The man she had met on the shore was not the kind who gave up easily.

"And what if Charles becomes worried about you and comes here?"

That possibility had also been Cassie's concern. "Can you send him a message?"

Lani shook her head. "I doubt if it would reach him without leading Danemount to Charles. The Englishman is watching us closely."

"Then I'll have to go to him."

"You can't even get to your feet."

"Then you must watch for him until I can. I should be fine by tomorrow."

"I will go to him."

Cassie shook her head. "He's expecting me. I have to talk to him and decide what we're going to do." She whispered, "He's so afraid, Lani."

Lani glanced at the door. "He has a right to be afraid with that man as a foe." She got to her feet. "I'll get you water for bathing and a little broth. I'll keep Danemount from coming to you until later this evening. Try to rest."

Rest?

Cassie lay back against the pillows. She was not likely to rest, but she had to try. She would need all her strength for the battle ahead. From what Lani had said, Danemount had been busily weaving a cocoon to imprison them here at the cottage. A cocoon that could prove a deadly trap if her father tried to reach her.

Cassie felt much better after the bath and meal, but not well enough to try to get out of bed until later that afternoon. It was the sound of loud male voices just outside her window that finally stirred her to the attempt.

She slowly sat up and swung her feet to the floor. No dizziness. Good.

She slipped on a dark-blue dressing gown over her nightgown and stood up. A slight feeling of nausea, but nothing she couldn't deal with. She carefully made her way to the window and threw open the shutters.

Two roughly dressed men were strolling about Lani's garden. She decided they must be the sailors from the *Josephine* Lani had mentioned.

"I see you appear to be doing much better than I was told."

She whirled away from the window to see Jared Danemount standing in the doorway. He looked slightly raffish, and the lack of elegance made him appear even more threatening. He was without a coat, his shirt was open at the throat, and a day's growth shadowed his lean cheeks.

But his eyes were just as cool as she remembered them. She instinctively drew the dressing gown closer about her. "Good evening, Your Grace."

"Were you contemplating leaving through that

window?" He came into the room and shut the door. "I wouldn't advise it."

"This is my home. Why should I leave it as if I were a thief in the night?" Her knees were beginning to feel weak, so she crossed the room and sat down on the edge of the bed. "I was just looking out at the intruders blundering around the grounds. They're ruining Lani's vegetable garden."

"I'll give her adequate compensation."

"Can you compensate her for her distress and disappointment, for all the hours she spent planning and nurturing?"

"Enough gold can soothe most disappointments."

She shook her head. "Perhaps in your world. Not here."

"Then she will have to be disappointed." He came toward her. "And I didn't come here to discuss vegetable gardens."

She gazed at him defiantly. "It's all I'll discuss with you."

"Where is your father?"

She stared at him in silence.

"I'd advise you to tell me. It will be easier for you."

"I don't want it to be easier for me. You have no business here. Go back to England."

"On the contrary, I have very important business here."

"Murder?"

He was silent a moment. "Retribution."

"I know my father. He could never have done anything that would deserve death."

His expression hardened. "Yes, what a kind and sacrificing father he must be. He fled like the coward he is and left you to lead me away from him. You could have died on that mountain."

"It wasn't his fault I was clumsy. He didn't want to leave me. I made him go."

"And you weren't as important to him as his neck."

"My father *does* love me. I told you, I made him go."

"He loves you so much, he goes off into the hills and lets you run wild and half-naked where any man can assault and rape you," he said violently.

"There's no shame in nakedness, and no islander would take me by force." She stared at him scornfully. "They're not like you English."

"I didn't take you by force. I didn't take you at all. I thought you a child. Another lie. According to what I was told, you were eight when you left Marseilles. That would make you near your twentieth year now."

"I didn't lie."

"You didn't make any real attempt to dissuade me."

"Why should I care what a stranger believes?"

"You were lucky that this particular stranger believed you to be an innocent child instead of the half-naked voluptuary you obviously are."

"What do you mean?"

"You know exactly what I mean."

She inhaled sharply as heat burned her cheeks. "What would you have done? Ravished me? Kill the father, rape the daughter? What a splendid man you are."

"I don't rape women." His mouth tightened. "And how was I to know you were that bastard's spawn? Respectable women don't wander around beaches at night and masquerade as natives."

"I wasn't masquerading. I was with my friends, who are just as respectable as any of your English-women. You're the intruder. You're like all the other foreigners. You come here and lie with the women, give them a few beads, and then sail away."

"These women you say I victimized were not only eager but aggressive, and I didn't come here to take advantage of them." He paused. "You know why I came here."

"I won't let you do it," she said fiercely. "My father isn't without friends here. Even the king is fond of him."

"But he's fonder of the prospect of guns to make war on the chief of the neighboring island."

Cassie had hoped he would not make that discovery. Lani was right, he was very clever. "And will you give him those guns?"

"Let us say I would do almost anything to have your father."

Dead. He meant he wanted Papa dead, she realized, feeling sick. "Why? You don't know him. He's a kind man who wants only to paint and live his life in peace."

Danemount's eyes were suddenly merciless. "He's a butcher and deserves to be butchered in turn." He turned and moved toward the door. "Go back to bed and rid yourself of any idea of going to him. My men have orders to stop anyone from leaving."

"Then it's true? We're to be prisoners here?"

"That's not the precise term I'd use." He opened the door. "Bait for the trap. We'll see how much love your father has for you."

She shivered as she watched the door close behind him.

Bait for the trap. It mustn't happen. She had to find a way to get out of the cottage and down to Kamehameha's village.

. . .

Bradford looked up as Jared strode out on the veranda. "How is she?"

"Stubborn," Jared said curtly as he dropped down in the chair opposite his uncle. "Other than that I'd say she's recovering rapidly."

"She's fond of her father?"

"Yes." Jared poured a whiskey. "God knows why. He apparently ignores her most of the time and has clearly brought her up as a savage."

"The life of a savage can be very pleasant." Bradford leaned back in the chair and lifted his glass. "And it's not uncommon for a woman to love an undeserving lout and give him her loyalty. Though not many of them would go to the lengths she did. She must be brave." He shuddered. "I wouldn't have wanted to go sliding along that mountainside in the dark."

Jared took a long drink. "It wasn't altogether dark."

"Close enough for me." Bradford tilted his head. "You're still angry with her. Why? You would have done the same in her place."

"I wouldn't have been in her place. My father was not a butcher."

"He was no angel either," Bradford said quietly. "John was a brave man but he had his faults. Even though you were only a lad of thirteen, you must have realized that he was arrogant as the devil and even more of a womanizer than I was."

"That didn't mean he deserved to be murdered." He took another drink. "He was in Danjuet to save lives, and Deville betrayed him." His hand tightened on the glass. "You weren't there. You didn't see them slice him to ribbons. I think even you would have learned to hate, Bradford."

"Perhaps." Bradford's eyes were sympathetic. "I

wish it had been I who had seen it instead of you, lad.
But you shouldn't be angry at the daughter for the
father's sin."

"Shouldn't I?" He looked down into the amber
liquid in his glass. "Stay out of this, Bradford. I won't
have you interfering. She's the key I need to get to
Deville."

"And what happens if she won't cooperate?"

"Then I do whatever I have to do."

Bradford frowned. "I don't like this. There's too
much anger in you."

He finished the brandy and poured another. "I've
waited a long time."

"Not to hurt the innocent as well as the guilty."

"Only if the innocent help the guilty."

"You seem more angry with her than with him."

Because he would not have it any other way, dammit. Jared's anger at Deville was cold and sharp,
honed through the years, but he had to work to keep
his anger at the girl fresh and hot. In the past twenty-
four hours she had aroused him to anger, pity, fear,
and an admiration he would not admit even to Bradford. Anger was safe. If he yielded to a softer emotion,
then he would lose his key.

But lust need not be soft. It could be hot and frantic and iron hard.

The thought came so swiftly that he knew it had
been waiting just beneath the surface. She was not the
child he had thought was forbidden to him. He could
reach out and take . . .

Christ, what was he thinking? Who could be more
forbidden than Deville's daughter? He was her enemy, and he wouldn't pretend to be anything else.
Frustration surged back in a storm of rejection.

"That's your third brandy," Bradford observed

with interest. "Are you returning to your days of depravity?"

He hadn't realized he'd poured another brandy. He was tempted to drink the whole damn bottle. No, he was too close to his goal and would need a clear head in the next few hours. He pushed the glass aside. "No."

"Too bad." Bradford sighed. "It's a sad and mournful cross for a man to be forced to be depraved alone."

"You bear it well." He stood up. "Come along."

"Where are we going?"

"To the stable."

Bradford immediately brightened, as Jared had known he would. "Is there something worth looking at?"

"You thought there was last night. I believe you said he had a lovely gait."

Bradford's brow wrinkled in bewilderment. "I did? When did—" His eyes widened. "On the shore? The woman?"

Jared didn't answer as he went down the steps and set out for the stable. "Are you coming?"

Giving a low whistle, Bradford followed him. "I'm beginning to understand." He chuckled. "You were telling the truth when you said he'd raised her as a savage. I thought you were referring to her manners."

"I don't want to talk about her anymore. We're going to see the horse."

"Ah, yes, the horse," Bradford said. "But you must admit your meeting was an interesting coincidence. Most unusual. Almost as if it were fated."

Jared made an obscene remark.

"Don't be impolite. There are a great many people in this world who believe in fate."

"You're not one of them."

"No, but I wish I did. I wish I believed in something," Bradford said wistfully. "It would be pleasant, don't you think?"

"I think you've had too much brandy."

"You're probably right. I always become melancholy after the fifth glass. Are you ever melancholy, Jared?"

"No."

"Of course you're not. You never let yourself feel anything so mawkish. You allow yourself lust and an appreciation of beauty, a hunger for knowledge . . . even an affection for my humble self." He opened the stable door. "But nothing that would strike deep, no sentimental nonsense for you."

"Isn't that what you taught me?"

"No, I taught you only to be cautious. You built the other walls yourself. Sometime when I'm sober, I must have a talk with you about the danger of— What have we here?"

"Someone who belongs." Lani turned away from the stallion's stall and set the bucket of oats down on the ground. "As you do not. Isn't it enough that you injured Kanoa? Do you also intend to steal her horse?"

"I didn't injure her," Jared said, trying to keep his temper. "And we came only to look at the animal in the daylight. Were you thinking of riding out and going to your lover?"

"No, I was feeding him." She moved toward the door. "No one rides Kapu but Kanoa."

"What a pity," Bradford murmured as he eagerly moved toward the stall. "Jared, he's magnificent. Look at those lines . . . the shoulders." He reached a hand out to touch the white star between the stallion's eyes. "And he moves with—"

"Don't touch him!" Lani hurried forward and slapped his hand down.

"I wasn't going to hurt him."

"I know," Lani said grimly. "But I have no desire to bandage your hand after he savages you. Kapu doesn't like strangers."

"He apparently likes you." Bradford looked at her with interest before bowing low. "I don't believe we've been introduced. I'm Bradford Tyndale Danemount."

"I know who you are. You're the uncle."

He sighed. "Such is my boring fate. The brother, the uncle, never Bradford Danemount the extraordinary, the bold knight, the wise sage, the—"

"Stay away from Kapu," Lani interrupted. "You have had too much to drink, and Kapu likes drunks."

"If that's the case, then we should get along splendidly."

Lani's smile gleamed white with wickedness. "But Kapu likes to see them dead. He trampled his former master until one could not tell he had ever had a face."

"Who was his master?" Jared asked as he stepped closer to the stallion.

"An Englishman who stopped here on his way to Australia. When he was drunk, he beat Kapu unmercifully. One day he grew careless and Kapu was equally unmerciful. The king tried to claim Kapu for his own, but he was too vicious. They were going to put him to death until Charles went to Kamehameha and begged him to sell the horse to him."

"Nothing I've learned about Deville indicates he has a fondness for horses," Jared said.

"But he has a fondness for Cassie, and she was in

love with the stallion." She added caustically, "And this is the terrible man you wish to kill." She watched Jared move to stand before the stallion. "You're too close. I told you—" She broke off and stared in astonishment when Jared reached up and stroked the stallion's muzzle. Kapu nickered softly and pushed against his hand. "Magic."

"No." Jared gazed into the stallion's eyes. "We just understand each other."

"Jared is very good with horses," Bradford said.

"Kahuna," Lani muttered.

It was what Cassie had said on the shore, Jared remembered. She had looked at him with that expression of desperation and fear, and he had felt as if he had been cruel to a helpless child. The abrasive memory roughened his voice. "Nonsense."

Bradford chuckled. "He's definitely no priest. Though I've often thought he delves in sorcery when dealing with horses . . . and the gaming tables."

Jared shot him an amused glance. "Intelligence."

"Luck," Bradford replied.

Lani looked from one to the other and then shrugged. "Neither will do you any good here. This is a bad thing you seek to do to Charles, and God will not be with you." She moved toward the door. "Test how far your good fortune lasts, Your Grace. Let the drunken one stroke Kapu."

Bradford watched her leave the stable. "Unusual woman. I feel quite intoxicated." He laughed. "But then I felt intoxicated before I met her, so it's difficult to judge." He turned back to the stallion. "Magnificent."

"Yes."

"You want him."

"Oh, yes." Now that he had a closer look in full daylight, he wasn't sure even his Morgana could compare to the stallion. Another frustration to add to the mix.

"A difficult situation."

"Without the slightest doubt." He gave the stallion a final pat and backed away. "And probably going to grow more difficult as time goes on. I want you to go to the king and make discreet inquiries regarding Deville. Make sure the king knows we're staying here at Deville's cottage."

"If Deville is under his protection, then I may get a blow instead of an answer. He'll know by now that your intentions aren't friendly."

"I don't think there's any danger. He won't want to jeopardize the possibility of persuading me to furnish him weapons. Would you rather I go?"

"No, I'll do it. Braving the savages will make a fine story when we return to England. You're staying here to watch the girl?"

Jared nodded. "If Deville went to the trouble of pleading for that horse for his daughter, he must have some feeling for her. If he thinks she may be in danger, then he might come here."

"You're beginning to speak of him as if he possesses a few human qualities."

"I always knew he was human. There's usually a balance of good and evil in every man. When I was a boy, I found Deville quite amusing." A sudden memory of Charles Deville sprawled in the chair in that hidden little room at Danjuet came back to him, Deville's pencil moving rapidly on a sketch pad, his bearded face alive with humor as he joked with Jared. "That doesn't mean I don't realize what he is."

"But it makes it harder to execute a man who isn't a complete villain."

He smiled thinly. "Try me." He turned away and moved toward the door. "If you find out anything, let me know. Otherwise I'll expect you back here tomorrow evening."

Three

"Danemount was down at the stable looking at Kapu," Lani said as she brushed Cassie's hair. "He has quite an amazing way with horses."

Cassie stiffened. "He didn't try to ride him?"

"No, I said he was looking." She paused in midmotion to meet Cassie's gaze in the mirror. "You should not care for Kapu this much. He's only an animal. You cannot expect total loyalty from him."

"He *is* loyal. He knows he belongs to me."

"But he won't—" She broke off and shrugged. "Why should I argue? I'm wasting my breath."

Cassie reached up and took her hand. "Because you don't want me hurt. I won't be, Lani."

"Yes, you will. It is inevitable." Lani smiled. "But thank God you have the strength to heal yourself. It's a great gift." She squeezed Cassie's hand. "Now, how do you feel? Can you eat some supper?"

"Yes." Her brow wrinkled thoughtfully. "Is Clara having supper prepared for the Englishmen?"

Lani nodded. "Of course. A meal fit more for a king than a duke."

"Then I'll come to the table."

"You wish to eat with them? Why?"

She quickly looked away from Lani. "It will do us no good to have me cowering in my room all night. I may learn something that may help us. You can't defeat the enemy without knowing their strength. Where are the Englishmen now?"

"Having brandy on the veranda." She made a face. "The uncle drinks like a fish. Pity."

"Why is it a pity? Surely such a weakness is good for us."

"But I think he is not weak. He is just . . . I hate waste. But you're right, any flaw will help. You won't find much weakness in the other one to use." She turned away and moved toward the door. "I'll tell Clara that we'll be joining them for supper. I'm sure she'll be delighted."

"No, wait." Cassie jumped to her feet. "I'll tell her. You go on and change."

"Why? I can do it before I go to my room. You have to dress yourself, and it will take you longer since you're still weak."

"Go on and dress," Cassie said again.

Lani turned to look at her speculatively. "This is the first time I've ever seen you so eager to confront Clara. What are you about?"

Cassie could not involve her friend by telling her the truth, but neither could she lie to Lani. So she merely repeated, "I'll do it."

Lani hesitated, then turned and left the room.

Dear God, but could she do it? She must stop this waffling; she had no choice. She had to reach her father before he arrived and was trapped. It seemed impossible that merely a few days ago her only problem had been Clara's overwhelming oppression. Now she was being forced to commit an act that filled her with revulsion.

Don't think about it. Just do what has to be done.

She drew a deep breath and moved quickly toward the armoire across the room.

"What an enchanting surprise," Jared murmured as he and Bradford pushed back their chairs and rose to their feet. "To what providence do we owe the grace of your presence?"

"I was hungry." Cassie strode brusquely onto the veranda. "You keep forgetting this is my home. Why shouldn't I come to supper?"

"You're also joining us for supper? Extraordinary."

This was neither the girl on the beach nor the defiant waif he had confronted in the bedroom, Jared thought with dissatisfaction. She still looked a mere child, but now everything about her was tight and confined. She wore a high-necked gray silk gown that fell straight to the floor, hiding any hint of a possible curve. Her dark-brown hair, scraped back from her face and captured in a bun on top of her head, looked too heavy a burden for that slim neck. Jared had a sudden desire to take out the pins and let her hair flow free, as it had that night on the beach.

"Not at all unusual, Jared. She's quite right," Bradford said as he moved swiftly to escort Cassie to a chair. "But as he said, a lovely surprise. We thought that your injury would keep you to your room. Please sit down."

She shook her head. "I came only to tell you that I refuse to hide in my room like a culprit."

"Sit down anyway. You must conserve your strength." Bradford smiled. "May I get you a glass of wine?"

"No." She sat down and perched on the edge of the chair, her back rigid. "And I don't need to conserve my strength. I'm much better now."

"I can see you are," Bradford said warmly. "You have a lovely color in your cheeks."

Jared watched the color deepen. Bradford was right: her cheeks were flushed and her dark eyes shone brilliantly, almost feverishly. She clearly wasn't as well as she claimed. Why the devil hadn't she stayed in her room and rested?

"You're the uncle?" she asked.

Bradford nodded. "Forgive me. I feel as if I already know you after that trip down the mountain. I'm Bradford Tyndale Danemount."

She studied him. "I remember you . . . I think."

"I consider that very promising." He slanted a glance at Jared. "You see, even out of their senses, women find me unforgettable."

"They would have to be out of their senses," Jared said.

Bradford flinched. "What a cruel blow." He turned to Cassie. "You can see how afflicted I am. I raise the lad from boyhood, and he gives me nothing but insult. Are we also to be honored by the presence of the beautiful lady I met at the stables? Lani . . ." He looked at her inquiringly.

"Her name is Lani Kalnarai. And, of course, she'll be here. What a stupid thing to ask. She belongs here, too."

"So she told us."

"Do you doubt it?" she asked, bristling. "Do you think because she's not married to my father that he honors her any less? Lani is stronger and kinder and more clever than any woman you've ever met. She may have been raised an islander, but that doesn't mean she's ignorant of your ways. She's always reading and learning and is probably better educated than either of you."

"I didn't mean—"

"It's not the custom in England to house a mistress in the same domicile as a man's daughter," Jared interrupted. He met her gaze. "And it's also not the custom in France."

"That means nothing. We're no longer in France."

"Your father is a Frenchman. If he holds the woman in as much honor as you obviously do, then he would have wed her."

She glared at him. "Does that mean you don't want to see Lani at the table? Well, I will not—"

"I didn't say that," Jared said. "This is your home and we are your guests." He sat back down and reached for his glass of brandy. "I was merely defending my uncle, as you were defending your friend. He meant no insult, but you're clearly used to jumping to your Lani's defense. I wonder why . . ." He glanced speculatively at the doorway. "Your housekeeper?"

She stiffened. "Has Clara been telling you lies about her?"

"I'm not on such intimate terms with the lady. Does Miss Kidman usually tell lies?"

At first he didn't think she would answer, but then she said curtly, "She hates Lani."

"She doesn't appear to be on good terms with most of the world."

"Lani says that Clara finds you most agreeable," she said bitterly. "It didn't surprise me."

"Since we're two such detestable creatures?"

"Yes."

"Then why have you chosen to dine with me? Unpleasant company is certainly not good for the digestion."

The words seemed to disturb her. He could see the leap of her pulse in the delicate hollow of her throat. "This is my home."

"Why?" he repeated.

She met his gaze. "I gain nothing by avoiding you."

"Ah, then this is an exploratory foray?"

"Call it whatever you like."

"Or perhaps you wished to persuade me to abandon my plans for your father."

Her eyes widened. "Don't be ridiculous. How would I do that?"

Her surprise was genuine and free of coyness. She knew nothing about the sensual games women of his world played. He felt a flicker of annoyance, and he realized he had wanted her to display that familiar coquetry. It would have given him reason to indulge in the same game. No, not reason, he amended in disgust. An excuse. "It was only a thought."

"A very stupid one," she said bluntly.

Bradford chuckled. "Yes, where is your perception, Jared?"

Jared ignored the gibe. "Why did you say your name was Kanoa?"

"It is my name. Lani gave it to me when she came here. She said that since we were to be sisters, she wanted me to have a Hawaiian name."

"That's not what I mean. You knew I thought you Hawaiian."

"Why should I correct your mistakes if you jump to foolish conclusions?" She lifted her chin. "Besides, I am Hawaiian even if I'm not an islander. I belong here and I should have an island name."

"Do you? I've noticed your friend Lani seldom uses it."

Color flushed her cheeks. "There are certain difficulties here. Clara can be— I don't have to make explanations to you."

"I take it you have no desire to return to France?" Bradford interceded quickly.

"What is there for me?" she said simply. "Here I have everything."

"Including a very fine piece of horseflesh," Bradford said. "You wouldn't care to sell him?"

"Never." She added, "And certainly not to you."

"I didn't think you would, but I had to try. Magnificent animal." He lifted his glass. "And it would have been a great coup to own the horse that dumped Jared into a sand dune."

A tiny smile tugged at her lips. "I admit I value him all the more for his good judgment."

"You should. Jared hasn't been thrown since he was—"

"What are you going to do with the stallion?" Jared interrupted. "Keep him as a pet to ride around your beautiful island?"

She stiffened at the faint sarcasm beneath the silkiness of his tone. "If I choose. Why not?"

"Because it's a damnable waste. A horse that fine should be put to stud and sire horses equally splendid."

"I do intend to breed him. I'm going to have a horse farm on the other side of the island."

"You have a mare?"

"Not yet. I haven't found one suitable."

"And I doubt if you will on this island."

She glared at him. "I found Kapu."

"One chance in a thousand."

"Fate," Bradford murmured. "It appears that destiny has a special fondness for this place."

"Not enough to provide a fit consort for the stallion," Jared said. "And do you have enough money to buy her if you do find her?"

"I *will* find a way to get her."

"You won't find a mare by playing in the sand and dreaming about it," he said tauntingly.

"What makes you think that's all I do?" Her hands clenched the arm of her chair. "You know nothing about me."

"Jared." Bradford's tone carried both puzzlement and warning.

Christ, Jared thought. The girl was gazing at him with defiance, but her eyes were glittering with moisture. He had clearly stumbled on a dream she was desperate to fulfill, and he was as puzzled as Bradford at his desire to rob her of it. He had found a weakness and had instinctively attacked. "My apologies. You're correct, I know nothing about you."

"I've been looking for a mare," she insisted. "I meet every ship and talk to the captains. I've traveled all over this island. I was going to Maui next month to see if—"

"I said I was sorry," he said roughly. "It's not my concern."

"No, it's not." She stood up and moved quickly toward the door. "I'll be back. I must see what's keeping Lani."

Bradford shook his head as she left the room.

"Don't say it," Jared said.

"I don't have to, do I? I just wondered if you were planning on sticking pins into her during supper. If so, I really prefer not to be around."

Jared didn't answer.

"Of course, there's the possibility she won't join us for supper. I don't know many women who would come back for that sort of punishment."

"She'll be there."

"You seem very certain."

He was certain. All through that barbed exchange he had been aware of the core of strength beneath her fragile, childlike exterior. She had not yielded; she had only retreated because he had struck her in a vulnerable spot. "She'll join us for supper."

"And you will be a cordial and well-mannered gentleman," Bradford said with firmness.

Jared looked at him in surprise. "Good God, gallantry?"

"On occasion."

"Not one I've witnessed."

"I make sure I'm seldom in a position where it's required. It's a most uncomfortable state for a rogue such as me." Bradford yawned and leaned back in his chair. "But I'm forced to defend mistreated horses and helpless children. So if you have a fondness for me, don't make me expend the effort. Behave yourself, Jared."

"By all means," he said mockingly. "I wouldn't want to disturb you."

"Splendid. Now, pour me another brandy."

Cassie stopped just inside the veranda door to gather her composure. She should not have let his criticism disturb her so much. She did not care what he thought of her.

You won't get her by playing in the sand and dreaming about it.

Those were the words that had struck home. Had she been dreaming like a child instead of acting to make her vision of a horse farm come true? She had made several attempts to find the mare, but had she tried hard enough? Had she used Papa as an excuse to avoid venturing forth? There had seemed no hurry, and she had let time drift by. . . .

"Are you ill? Perhaps you should go back to your room."

Cassie looked up to see Lani coming down the hall, a concerned frown on her face.

She smiled with an effort. "I'm fine. I was just coming to look for you."

"I was in the kitchen trying to keep Uma from hitting Clara with a pot and going back to her village." She grimaced. "It wasn't easy. Clara is being more difficult than usual about the meal preparations for the English. She was raving about heathen servants and people who got in her way while she was doing her duty. I gathered the last volley was aimed at you."

"I didn't stay in the kitchen very long."

"Long enough to annoy her." Lani looked beyond her to the veranda. "If you're not ill, then you're upset. What did they say to you?"

She should have known she could not deceive Lani. "Nothing important." To distract her, she said quickly, "Is supper ready?"

Lani nodded. "Clara sent me to inform our honored guests."

Cassie's stomach clenched with apprehension and dread. "Then let's do it."

"Wait." Lani's gaze was on her face. "You're sure you're well enough?"

"Of course." She turned and moved toward the veranda. "It's only dinner. It will be over before we know it."

• • • •

It was a strained meal that seemed to go on forever. Neither Cassie nor Lani were eager to speak. Jared was fastidiously polite and cool as the North Star. Bradford was affable but gave up after a few attempts at conversation and devoted himself to the food.

Clara Kidman marched into the dining room after Uma had removed the main course. "I hope everything met with your approval, Your Grace."

Cassie looked at her in amazement. It was the first time she had seen Clara in Danemount's presence and was bewildered by the servility in her manner.

"It was absolutely delicious." Jared smiled. "I've not had such a fine meal since I left London. But it's only what I expected. I could tell the moment I met you that you had the reins of the household firmly in your hands."

A faint tinge of color flushed Clara's cheeks. "I know it's not what you're accustomed to, but it's the best I could do with only these heathen islanders to help me."

"Uma is not a heathen," Lani said quietly. "She studied with me at Mrs. Densworth's school."

Clara met Lani's gaze. "It takes more than a few lessons to make a silk purse out of a sow's ear."

"You have a fine cook," Jared interjected quickly. "But I'm sure it was your expert supervision that carried the day."

"The meal was adequate," Clara said grudgingly. "But I couldn't trust the dessert to anyone but myself. I'll have it brought in at once."

"Thank you, but I seldom eat dessert."

Clara frowned in disappointment. "It's my own special lemon syllabub."

Cassie lifted her brows in mock surprise. "Perhaps

he would rather trust his digestion to the heathens, Clara."

Jared's lips tightened as he met Cassie's challenging stare. "Nonsense." He turned to Clara with another brilliant smile. "I'd be delighted to try your syllabub."

Clara gave Cassie a triumphant glance and hurried from the dining room.

"Charming woman," Bradford said, looking at the doorway through which Clara had disappeared. "Am I supposed to compliment the witch on this delicacy?"

"With fervent enthusiasm," Jared said. "She may still prove useful."

Bradford shifted his stare to Lani. "I think not. You do it, Jared. It would stick in my throat."

"Because the old woman insulted me?" Lani asked coolly. "There's no wound. I'm accustomed to her venom."

"And Deville permits it?"

"She doesn't do it when he's here."

"But does he know?" Bradford probed softly. "That's the question."

Lani shrugged. "Why should I bother him with something he cannot change?"

"She's a servant," Jared suddenly bit out with leashed violence. "He could change it if he wished. Why do you defend him?" He whirled on Cassie. "Why do either of you defend him, dammit?"

"Here it is!" Clara sailed into the room with Uma trailing behind her bearing a tray. "I'll wager you won't find anything tastier even at Brighton. It has a fine, tart bite."

Jared pulled his eyes away from Cassie as Uma set the plate before him. "I'm sure you're right," he muttered. "Tartness appears to be the rule of thumb on this island."

"You could hardly expect anything else," Cassie said.

"I expect nothing." He dipped his spoon into the syllabub and tasted it, then smiled at Clara. "Excellent."

She beamed. "I told you. My mother taught me the recipe. She was a cook for the Earl of Belkarn."

Cassie experienced another ripple of surprise. Clara had never spoken of her background before. "I didn't know that."

Clara's smile faded and her expression became guarded. "Did you think I would have been accepted into your mother's household without proper recommendation? I grew up in service."

"Wonderful," Jared said. He glanced meaningfully at Bradford. "Try it. It's superb."

Bradford hesitated, then shrugged and began to eat the dessert.

Clara looked at him expectantly.

"Very good," he said without expression. He eyed Cassie's untouched dessert. "You're not eating."

"She and Lani have no liking for my cooking," Clara said. "And no manners to make the pretense."

"We're more accustomed to island fare now," Cassie said. "You seldom honor us with your efforts."

"No doubt you've noticed her deplorable lack of civilized schooling. I've done the best I can but to no avail. I've told her father he must send her to a convent in England."

"An interesting solution," Jared said impassively. "But not one I'd judge entirely suitable."

"My father refused to send me away from him."

Cassie defiantly met his gaze across the table. "He cares as much for me as I do for him."

He smiled coolly. "We shall see."

He meant that if her father truly cared for her, he would walk into the trap, she realized with a shiver. It would not happen. She would not let it happen.

"More syllabub?" Clara asked, hovering over Jared.

Cassie held her breath.

He shook his head as he finished the last bite. "Too dangerous. I'm afraid I'll become too spoiled to enjoy even the most elaborate repast when I return to England."

Cassie's breath expelled in a rush, and she jumped to her feet. "I'm going to my room. I'm suddenly feeling tired. Lani, will you come and help me?"

"Of course." Lani stood up and followed Cassie to the door.

Both men rose to their feet.

"Good night," Bradford said. "Pleasant dreams."

Jared bowed slightly.

Cassie said over her shoulder, "Clara, perhaps you could serve the gentlemen their after-dinner brandy on the veranda? They seem to find it pleasant out there."

"I don't need your suggestions. I was going to do just that."

"Of course you were," Cassie murmured, and fled the room.

Lani caught up with her as she reached the door of her room. "What's happening?" she asked. "And don't tell me nothing when you're shaking like this. You wouldn't have put us through an evening this uncomfortable without reason."

"Come!" Cassie pulled her into the room and

slammed the door. She collapsed against it and took a deep breath. "I need your help."

"That's why I'm here." She wrinkled her nose. "And clearly not to help you into bed. You're going to your father tonight?"

"Can you distract the two seamen watching the house?"

Lani nodded. "But you still won't be able to reach the road without being seen from the veranda."

"Yes, I will," she whispered. "I hope. If I gave them enough."

Lani stiffened. "Enough?"

"Laudanum. The laudanum that we had left after I had the fever last summer. Remember? It was in the medicine chest in the back of my armoire."

Lani's eyes widened. "Mother of God."

"I slipped it into the lemon syllabub when I was in the kitchen talking to Clara. I know you never eat syllabub, and I hoped the strong taste of lemon would disguise it."

"Why didn't you tell me?"

"I didn't know how much laudanum to use. I thought I remembered how much the doctor had given me, but I couldn't be sure. I tried to be careful, but I was afraid I'd—" She broke off, unwilling to put the dread into words.

"Kill them?"

She shivered. "I had to take the chance."

"But you didn't want me to take it with you." Lani shook her head. "You shouldn't have done it. We could have found another way."

"There's no *time*. What if Papa comes tonight?"

She shrugged. "Well, there's nothing else to be done now. I'll distract the sailors, and you get to your father."

Cassie grabbed her shawl from the bed. "Lani . . ."

Lani smiled understandingly. "I know. Don't worry. I'll watch over the English and make sure the sleep is not too deep."

Relief surged through Cassie. "I know they're Papa's enemies, but I don't want them to die. I don't want anyone to die."

"Then get to your father and tell him he must hide until the English leave."

"I will." Cassie gave Lani a quick hug. "I'll be back before they wake. I won't leave you alone to take the brunt of their anger."

"I've survived Clara for years; these English are nothing." She opened the door, looked both ways before pushing Cassie down the hall in the direction of the veranda. "Give Charles my love and tell him . . . Never mind. The decision must be his alone this time."

"What decision?"

"We cannot do everything for him this time, Kanoa," she said gently as she moved swiftly toward the back door. "There comes a time when a man must come to terms with himself."

Cassie stared after her in puzzlement. They had always protected her father in every way, and now Lani was saying there were limits. Well, there might be limits for Lani, but not for her.

Cassie braced herself and then walked slowly toward the veranda, dreading what waited for her. If she had given them too little, then all her plans were for naught. If she had given them too much . . . No, she did not even want to consider that possibility.

She stood in the doorway of the veranda. Both men

were slumped in their chairs. Asleep? Dear God, they were so terribly still. Dead?

She moved slowly toward Jared until she stood before him. No, he was breathing, she saw with profound gratitude.

Then his eyes opened and he stared up into her face. Shock held her riveted. His eyes were ice-blue, cold as a sword striking at her.

"Luc . . . rezia," he muttered. "What a . . . fool . . ."

His lids closed again.

She backed away from him, afraid he would wake again and fix her with that accusing stare. It was unreasonable to feel that she had betrayed him. He was the enemy, and she had done the only thing possible.

She ran down the veranda steps and fled along the path toward the road.

Four

"**C**assandra!"

She skidded to a halt, her heart leaping with terror when she saw the man coming up the path toward her. "No!"

Her father stopped in his tracks. "Are you all right, Cassandra? Lakoa said you'd had a fall."

"It was nothing. Just a bump on the head." She glanced over her shoulder at the cottage. "You shouldn't be here."

"You were hurt," he said simply. "Where else should I be?"

"The English are here."

"I know."

She ran forward and dragged him into the underbrush beside the path. "You have to leave. Go back to the village."

"I can't do that," he said quietly. "I can't hide any more. Eleven years is long enough to be a coward."

"You aren't a coward. It's not cowardly to try to keep a madman from killing you."

"He's not mad. He merely wants justice done." He

looked back at the cottage. "How much does he hate me, Cassandra?"

She shivered as she remembered that last icy glance from Danemount. "You have to leave here."

He grimaced. "That much?"

She took his arm and pulled him through the bushes toward the road. "I think we should leave this island. I've been wanting to go over to Maui for a long while to see if I could find a mare for Kapu, and you must be tired of painting that volcano. You could go first and find a place for us."

"You mean a hiding place."

"Only for a little while. When Danemount leaves, we'll come back here."

"You believe he'll give up? What makes you think he won't follow us?"

She knew as well as her father did that the Englishman would follow. "Then there are other islands."

"Not for me." He stopped when they reached the road and turned to face her. "Have you spent much time with the boy?"

She frowned. "Boy?"

"Danemount." He shrugged. "It was a slip of the tongue. I still remember him as a lad. It's difficult for me to realize he's a man now. But even as a boy he was *très formidable*. Is he the same?"

She could think of no more accurate description for Jared Danemount. "Yes."

"But just? Would you call him just?"

"Not if he wants to kill you."

"But in matters not connected with me?"

"Yes, I suppose so," she said impatiently. "Why are you asking these questions?"

"Because I have to be certain that you and Lani

will be safe when I return to France. A just man wouldn't wreak vengeance on the innocent."

She went still. "France?"

"There's an American ship docked on the other side of the island that's due to sail for Boston at midnight tonight. The king has arranged passage and supplied me with funds to take me on to Paris once we reach Boston. He's also promised to make sure that your needs are taken care of until I return." He added ruefully, "He appears to be glad to be rid of me. My departure will evidently solve certain diplomatic problems for him."

She barely heard anything but the first part of what he had said. "Why are you going to France?"

"Raoul Cambre is there. I have to find him. I have to know—"

"What?"

"If I've been as much a fool as I suspect. I've been doing a good deal of thinking while I've been waiting in the village. I thought Raoul was my friend, but Danemount shouldn't have been able to find me. I covered my tracks in Marseilles very carefully."

"You believe Cambre betrayed you?"

"I don't know. I have to find out. Only Raoul knew I was going to Tahiti." He frowned. "No, that's not true. He might have told Jacques-Louis David."

"Who is that?"

"An artist . . ." His tone was abstracted. "Yes, he could have told David. They were close friends."

"What difference does it make now? It's all in the past."

"Not to me." He looked back at the cottage. "Not to him."

"Then you should forget about Cambre and worry only about hiding from Danemount."

"I'm weary of hiding." He turned to face her. "And I'm weary of making you hide. You should be back in Paris going to balls, surrounded by young men courting you."

"I'm not hiding. I love it here. I wouldn't know what to do at a ball."

"Exactly." He touched her cheek. "*Pauvre petite*, I fear I've done you a great disservice. Clara is right, this is no life for you."

Why was he talking about balls when there was so much else at stake? "Go to Maui," she said desperately. "There's no need for you to find this Cambre."

"There's every need. It may save my life. If Cambre did use me for his own ends, I'll have no compunction about surrendering him to Danemount." He added beneath his breath, "Though God knows if one life will be enough for him after what happened at Danjuet."

"What are you talking about? Danjuet?"

He shook his head. "There is no time. I must go. The Captain will sail without me."

"Wait!" She grabbed his arm. "What can you do even if you do find Cambre?"

"I told you, bring him to Danemount."

"Are you mad? He's not going to come meekly to be murdered by the Englishman." She shivered as she remembered Cambre's cold reptilian eyes. "He'll try to hurt you."

"Maybe. Or perhaps he's weary of hiding too." He leaned down and kissed her on the forehead. "Keep well, Cassandra. Watch over Lani."

"If you're going, I'm going with you."

"To protect me from Raoul?" He shook his head. "Not this time."

"But you'll *need* me."

"It's too dangerous. Raoul was always clever. I didn't realize how clever. I've no doubt he'll have gained back all his influence under Napoleon's regime."

"All the more reason for me to go." She turned back toward the cottage. "Wait for me here. I'll just go tell Lani that—"

"No, Cassandra." His tone was frighteningly final.

"If you leave me here, I'll just follow you to the ship," she called after him.

"Then I'll tell the Captain you're not to be permitted on board." He started down the road. The smile he gave her over his shoulder lit his face with sweetness. "Don't be so concerned, *ma chou*. Nothing will happen to me. I'll be back almost before you realize I'm gone."

"Papa!"

He did not look back again.

Her hands clenched into fists at her sides, she watched him walk away from her. Why would he not listen? She had never seen him this resolute. She had always been able to sway him on matters of importance, and yet in this question, which might mean life and death, he stood firm. Should she follow him to the ship? No, it would be a waste of time.

But she could not just let him go alone to face that snake. Her father was a dreamer, and dreamers could be easily fooled. The hunter could well become the hunted.

When he was out of sight, she moved heavily up the path toward the cottage. She could not let him go into danger alone, but she could not see her way clear to stop it. She would have to think about it. In the meantime she must make sure Danemount did not interfere with her father's departure. Cambre was a distant threat; the Englishman was the immediate danger.

Lani was sitting on the veranda and rose to her feet when she saw Cassie. "What's wrong? Why are you here?"

"I met Papa on the path." She glanced worriedly at the Englishmen. Lani had tucked quilts over them and placed pillows beneath their heads. They did not look ill, only peacefully asleep. "Are they all right? The laudanum wasn't—"

"It was not too much," Lani assured her. "Their sleep is very light. I was even worried they would wake before you got back and follow you to the village."

"Really?" She frowned. "We can't let them leave before morning. Papa is sailing for France at midnight tonight."

Lani did not look surprised. "Then you're right— we must make sure he gets away and out of their reach."

Cassie suddenly realized Lani might be hurt that her father had been so near and made no attempt to bid her farewell. "He was in a great hurry. He'll be back as soon as he can. He needs to find a man who can—"

"Hush." Lani smiled. "You don't need to defend Charles to me. I know he would not desert me. He's a good man and he cares for my happiness."

Cassie felt a rush of relief. Of course he would not abandon Lani. She had not realized until this moment how Danemount's words regarding her father's relationship with Lani had disturbed her. She would never have been as tolerant as Lani in the same circumstances. "He made arrangements for us to be cared for by Kamehameha."

"Which is not going to be necessary," Lani guessed shrewdly. "Is it?"

She shook her head. "But he won't let me go with him, and France is far away. It's going to be difficult."

"We will find another way." Lani moved toward the door. "I'll go tell the old one the English have fallen asleep out here and not to disturb them. It's fortunate she wishes not to displease them; she may actually obey me. I'll be back soon and we'll take turns watching them."

"No, I'll do it. You stay inside and make sure Clara doesn't come out to the veranda."

Danemount suddenly stirred.

Cassie stiffened in alarm, but he didn't open his eyes. Thank the Lord. She was not prepared to confront him yet. "Lani, would it be possible for you to go to the stable and bring some rope?"

Lani nodded. "Good idea. I'll see if I can get past the guards in the garden."

After Lani left, Cassie slowly sat down in a cushioned chair and gazed at Danemount's face. Even in sleep he looked guarded and dangerous. What would he be like when he woke?

She would have to worry about that later. She had other concerns right now. She leaned her head against the back of the chair and tried to relax. She had a little time before the Englishman woke, and she would spend it trying to find a solution to the problem facing them.

Danemount stirred three times in the hours that followed. Cassie tensed on every occasion but then relaxed when he returned to sleep. It was near three in the morning before he finally opened his eyes.

She held her breath as she saw his drowsiness vanish. "My God, you poisoned me."

"I did not," she said quickly. "I only drugged you."

"Only?"

"It was necessary."

"I'm sure Lucrezia Borgia said the same after she used her poison ring."

Lucrezia. That was whom he had meant when he had called her by that name. "Lani said that there's some doubt Lucrezia Borgia ever used poison, and I certainly did not. I only used a few drops of laudanum in the syllabub to put you to sleep."

"Laudanum? That can be a dangerous potion. How did you know how much was safe to give us?"

She squared her shoulders, prepared for battle. "I didn't know. I took a chance."

"I suppose I should count myself fortunate to wake at all," he said with lethal softness. He glanced at the still-slumbering Bradford. "Is he alive?"

"Of course he is. He should wake soon."

"He had better." His gaze moved back to her. "Or you'll join him in his sleep."

Dear God, he was angry. His voice was low, almost silky, his face without expression, but she could sense an icy rage beneath that composure. "Threats will do you no good. I'm not afraid of you."

"You should be. If you knew my— What the devil!" He had started to sit up and discovered the cords around his wrists. He went rigid. "You've bound me!"

His rage was no longer controlled, and she tried to ignore the fear that spiraled through her. "Yes, both wrists and ankles." She added with bravado, "Trussed like a pig for the roasting."

He stopped struggling. "Or for the assassin's knife? When do you expect your father, Madam Borgia?"

"I'm not—" She broke off and drew a deep breath. "And my father would never kill a helpless man."

"No more than his daughter would chance killing a man with a potion she knows nothing about."

"Would you have stood by and let someone set a trap for a person you loved without trying to stop him?"

"I would have tried to find—" He wearily shook his head. "No, I suppose I would have done the same."

His honesty took her off guard, and a little of her anger ebbed. "I tried to be careful with the laudanum," she said haltingly.

"How comforting." His lips twisted. "You didn't answer. When do you expect your father?"

"I don't. I've already seen him." She paused. "And by now he's no longer on the island."

"You expect me to believe that?"

"No, you'll probably go to Kamehameha and question the islanders and waste a good deal of time. It will do you little good. Kamehameha wanted my father safe and arranged to send him away."

He studied her. "By God, I believe you're telling the truth. Now, why would you tell me he's no longer here? It would give him a head start if I searched this island first before going to the other islands."

"Because I don't want him to have too much of a head start."

Surprise flickered in his expression. "Would you care to elaborate?"

"I wanted him to go to Maui, but he wouldn't do it. He sailed for Boston at midnight. From there he'll make his way to France."

"Indeed," he murmured. "Now, why did he do that?"

"Raoul Cambre."

His expression hardened. "Ah, yes, like to like. He went running to beg help from his fellow conspirator."

"He's not like that man," she said fiercely. "And he didn't go for help. He went to see if he was wrong in his judgment of Cambre. He wanted to know if—" She broke off as she saw his skeptical expression. She would never be able to convince him of anything he didn't want to believe. "What difference does it make why he went? You don't care."

"But I do care where he's hiding. Where in France?"

"I don't know."

"But you have an idea."

"Perhaps." She had pitifully few scraps of information garnered from that long-ago encounter with Cambre, and only one name—Jacques-Louis David. She was not even sure the artist was still alive. "Perhaps not."

"Now the pertinent question. Why tell me anything at all?"

"Because I couldn't afford to have you waste time here when we could be on our way to France."

He didn't speak for a moment. "*We?*"

She took a deep breath and then said in a rush, "I'm going with you."

His expression remained impassive. "I don't believe you were invited. Why should I be interested in taking you with me?"

She had known he would ask that question and was prepared. "For the same reason you were keeping me prisoner here. I'd be a hostage to draw my father into your net."

"My, how accommodating you've become. You're now willing to be bait for the trap?"

"No, I'll escape at the earliest opportunity. I'm merely telling you what advantage you'd see in taking me. I didn't say that it would be a true advantage."

He looked taken aback, and then the faintest smile quirked his lips. "I see. You wish to use me and then flee."

She nodded. "Few ships stop here, and it might be months before I'd be able to follow my father to France."

"And why would you want to follow him?"

"I don't want my father destroyed. I don't trust Cambre."

"Nor me."

"Of course not."

"So you intend to save him from both of us." He shook his head. "You won't succeed."

"I *will*."

"Shall I let you try?" He tilted his head as if to consider it. "Untie me and we'll discuss it."

She shook her head.

"Why not?" he asked softly. "If your father has really left the island, then you have nothing to fear."

"Not until dawn. I want to make sure he's well away before I let you go."

The answer clearly did not please him. "I dislike intensely being bound like this," he said through his teeth. "I have no fondness for feeling helpless."

She could see he didn't. A man of his control would hate being robbed of it, but it was the strength of his response that she found most unusual. He appeared to resent the ropes more than the drugging. "At dawn."

"No, by God. *Now.* I won't—" He broke off as he saw her stubborn expression. "I could cry out and bring the guards from the garden."

"And I could put your pillow over your face and smother any sound." She added desperately, "I wouldn't want to do it, but you would force me."

"I seem to be the complete villain. I force you to poison me and then to smother me."

"Not you, only any sound, and I did not poison— But you are a villain."

"I certainly can be." He leaned back on the pillow. "You have no idea of the scope of my villainy. But I believe you may have the opportunity to learn."

Her heart gave a leap. "You'll take me with you?"

"Oh, yes." His blue eyes glinted recklessly in the moonlight. "*If* Deville is on his way to France, then I definitely need a hostage."

"I've told you the truth."

"Or you could be leading me away from him the way you did on the mountain."

She sighed resignedly. "You're going to waste time questioning the islanders."

"Forgive my suspicious nature, but I'd be a bit foolish to trust a woman who has deceived me, drugged me, and threatened to smother me."

She frowned. "I suppose you're right."

He gazed at her in astonishment, then started to laugh. "Suppose?" He looked down at his bound wrists, and his smile faded. "I'm going to remember this, you know. I'm a man who believes in revenge."

She moistened her lips. "I'd be a fool not to realize that fact by now."

"I'm going to sit here and look at these ropes . . ." He raised his eyes to her face. "And I'm going to think of all the ways a man can make a woman helpless. I know a great many, Cassie. Shall I mention a few?"

She felt heat burn her cheeks. "No."

"You prefer to be surprised?"

She didn't answer.

"It's very unwise of you to go with me. I have no intention of treating you with honor. Do you understand?"

"I have no choice. I have to go with you."

"Do you understand?" he persisted.

"I'm not stupid. You mean you intend to rut with me."

"At the earliest opportunity."

"Because you wish to punish me."

"Partly." His gaze roamed from her face to her breasts. "And partly because I've wondered how tight you'd feel around me since the moment I saw you on the beach."

She felt the muscles of her stomach clench, and for a moment she was robbed of speech.

He looked down at the cords around his wrists. "It would go easier for you when we come together, if you'd take these off. They make me angry and I'll remember, Cassie." His gaze lifted and he said softly, "I'll remember how helpless I feel and the frustration and the rage. Believe me, you don't want that."

"It's not going to happen. I won't let you—" She met his gaze and shook her head. "And I won't take off the ropes. Not until dawn."

"As you like." He closed his eyes. "But I believe you'll regret it."

Silence. No sound but the night birds in the trees. It seemed impossible, but she thought he had actually fallen back asleep. How could he relax when she was so tense she felt as if she would break apart with every breath?

"He's not worth it, you know."

She jumped, her gaze flying to his face.

His lids had lifted to reveal those cold eyes. How foolish to believe he might have been asleep. He had only been trying to subdue his frustration and gathering strength for another foray. He added roughly, "He's a coward and a murderer. Forget him. Stay here in this tropical Eden and raise your goddamn horses."

"He's not a murderer. He couldn't do anything like that."

"Not by his own hand. I told you he was a coward. Judas. How many pieces of silver did he receive, Cassie?"

"I don't know what you mean."

"I mean Danjuet. What else could I mean? Why did he—" He broke off as he saw her expression. "My God, you don't know. He didn't tell you."

"I'm sure there was nothing to tell."

"Christ, he didn't tell you." He laughed incredulously. "He let you risk your life on that mountain, and he didn't bother to tell you why."

"He would have told me," she defended. "There wasn't time."

"Fourteen years."

"He wanted to put everything in France behind him." She added quickly, "But not because he did anything wrong."

"You don't believe that."

God's will.

She tried to block out her father's words. She could not believe him capable of any real sin. "It's not possible. He's kind and gentle."

"Judas."

"No!"

"I saw him." His tone was relentless. "I know it."

"You're mistaken."

"How can you judge when you don't know anything about Danjuet. Shall I tell you?"

"I wouldn't believe you. It would be lies."

"I don't lie." He smiled crookedly. "And unlike your dear father, I think it only fair you know the man for whom you're staking so much."

Is he a just man? her father had asked her.

She had answered in the affirmative, but she did not want to admit Danemount's fairness now if it was coupled with this merciless hardness.

"Are you afraid to hear the truth?" he taunted.

"What you *say* is truth."

"Then judge for yourself." His gaze held hers as his words spiked out with hammered precision. "Danjuet was the home of my father's cousin, Paul Brasnier, Compte de Talaisar and his wife, Gabrielle. During the madness when aristocrats were being butchered at every turn, he couldn't believe it would happen to him. He wanted to stay in the land of his birth and thought the madness would run its course before it touched him. His wife had borne him a child two years before, and she insisted the babe was too frail to travel. My father decided to go to France to convince them to flee to England before it was too late. We arrived at Danjuet the night the neighboring estate was burned to the ground and the owner taken in chains to Paris for execution." He smiled sardonically. "It was enough to sober even cousin Paul. He agreed to allow my father to arrange transport for his family and himself. Before leaving England my father had taken the precaution of obtaining the name and address of a young artist who had been helpful in aiding the escape of another family a year earlier. Charles Deville.

"He sent for him. In the meantime we hid in a small secret room in the dungeon of the château. Deville came; he agreed to give us his help and set the escape plans in motion. My father had arranged to have a ship anchored in a cove off the coast, but we had to get there. It took two weeks before Deville completed the forged documents, and another two days to bribe the border guards. Then we were ready to go." He paused. "I remember Deville looked very somber when I looked back at him from the window of the carriage. I thought it was only concern. Your father was so very charming. None of us even suspected him of villainy."

"He's *not* a villain."

"No? You wouldn't have been able to convince my cousin and his wife as they knelt before the guillotine. The carriage was stopped not twenty miles from the château by agents of the Committee of Public Safety. The soldiers knew exactly who would be in the carriage. The Compte and his wife were taken prisoner and set out under guard for Paris. The soldiers would have killed their child on the spot, but my father intervened. They had other instructions for our disposition that did not include immediate slaughter, so he was allowed to take the child himself."

"Surely they wouldn't have murdered a child."

"You think not? During those days it was not unusual to use aristocrats as canon fodder."

She shuddered with horror. She had been too young to really comprehend the tragedy going on around her. She had heard only stories recounted with grim relish by Clara, and they had seemed no more real than a bad dream. Now those tales were being brought vividly to life. "My father couldn't have had anything to do with their capture."

"Judas," he said flatly. "When my father and I were brought back to the château, Deville was in the courtyard talking to a man who was obviously in charge of the soldiers."

"Then he might have been a prisoner, too."

"He turned white when he saw me staring at him. He backed away, mounted his horse, and rode out of the courtyard. Free." He added bitterly, "And probably considerably richer than when he had arrived two weeks before."

"There has to be some explanation," she whispered.

"I'm giving it to you. You just refuse to accept it."

She shook her head. "It can't be. There has to be another answer. Who was the man he was talking to?"

"Raoul Cambre."

"And he was a soldier?"

"No, I found out later he was loosely attached to the Committee of Public Safety, which was charged with the persecution of the enemies of the state. Very loosely. He astutely kept out of the light of public attention, gathering riches from the estates of the aristocrats he sent to the guillotine, riding the crest of the wave until it turned. After Robespierre was beheaded and the terror ended, he simply disappeared." He met her gaze. "Like your father."

"I keep telling you, he's not at all like my father." She was shaking, she realized. She crossed her arms to keep him from noticing. "If you want to kill someone, kill Cambre. He was clearly to blame."

"Were the Romans more to blame than Judas?"

She drew a long breath before saying unevenly, "I'm sorry your cousins were killed, but I—"

"Not only my cousins. My father was butchered."

"But you said the soldiers had orders not to hurt him," she said, shocked.

"My father was a very reckless man and had the temerity to speak to Cambre with less respect than he thought he deserved. Raoul Cambre gave the order that he be taken into the forest and cut to pieces. I watched them do it."

"Please." She closed her eyes to shut out the image. "I don't want to hear any more."

"I have no intention of giving you any bloody details. I think you've heard enough."

Too much. Danemount's clear, cold words had rung with truth and shaken her more than a passionate utterance would ever have done.

"Do you still think I'm lying?" he asked.

She forced herself to open her eyes and face him again. "I think you believe you're telling the truth."

"Christ." He stared at her in exasperation. "Don't you ever give up?"

"Sometimes the truth isn't clear," she said desperately. "You have no evidence."

"I *saw* Charles Deville."

"And I trust him," she whispered. "And even if I didn't trust him, he's my father. I couldn't let you kill him. It had to be a mistake. Everyone makes mistakes. We have to forgive them."

"Not a mistake of this magnitude." His lips tightened. "I don't forgive mistakes until they're paid for."

"Not even your own father's mistakes?"

He looked at her in surprise. "My father?"

"You said you were only a boy. What right did he

have to take you from safety to a country in which he knew you'd be in danger?"

"I wanted to go."

"It was still a mistake. You could have been killed and it would have been his fault. He was a fool."

"We're not talking about my father."

"I'm not talking at all." She leaned back and tried to gather the tattered remnants of her composure about her. "It does no good. We cannot agree."

He was silent a moment and then said roughly. "You're right. I knew you wouldn't be dissuaded when I started. Why in Hades should I keep trying to save you, when you won't save yourself? I assure you it's not my nature. I always accept whatever fate offers me, and I'm already anticipating this particular delicacy." He smiled cynically. "By all means, come with me. It's been a long, frustrating search, and it's only right that I take a reward for my labors."

Lani came out onto the veranda just after dawn, and Cassie breathed a sigh of relief. It was good to have an ally nearby. Danemount had not spoken again, but she could sense his anger and tension as he lay those few feet away.

"Good morning," Danemount greeted Lani coldly. "May I take it that you're also actively involved in all this?"

"As actively as Cassie would permit. She didn't tell me about the laudanum." Lani walked over to Bradford, tilted his head back, and peered into his face. "I expected him to be awake by now. It must be all that brandy. . . ."

"I am awake," Bradford murmured. "I'm just afraid to open my eyes. My head feels like a broken coconut." He cautiously opened one bloodshot eye. "Ah, but the sight of you is worth any pain. You truly have the face of an angel."

"Your judgment has no value. You've clearly had no dealings with heaven or any of its beings."

Bradford flinched. "Cruel . . ." He frowned in puzzlement. "I seem to be restrained." He tugged at the bonds. "Your doing?"

"I believe we can lay the blame at Mademoiselle Deville's door," Jared said. "Along with the laudanum."

"Laudanum. No wonder I have such a throbbing head."

"I'm sure it's little worse than you usually suffer in the morning." Lani turned to Cassie. "It's time to release them. Clara will be rising soon."

Cassie nodded eagerly. Thank goodness this nightmare was over. "It should be safe now."

"You're wrong," Danemount said softly. "You've never been less safe."

Avoiding his gaze, she reached below her chair and drew out the carving knife she had put there in readiness. She cut Bradford's bonds.

"Thank you," he said politely. "Though I doubt if such extreme measures were necessary in my case. I'm not a warlike man."

"Too much effort?" Lani asked.

He beamed at her. "Exactly. How pleasant to be understood."

Cassie braced herself before moving toward Danemount. He silently held out his wrists.

She hesitated for an instant. He seemed no longer tense, almost relaxed, his lean body graceful, loose-limbed, but full of danger. She felt as if she were about to release a bound panther.

He lifted his brows. "Well?"

It had to be done. She slashed through the ropes, then tossed off his blanket and cut the cords binding his ankles. She hurriedly took a step back.

"Don't be afraid." He smiled mockingly as he rose to his feet. "I'm a patient man. I can wait. Come on, Bradford. Let's go back to the ship."

"Now?" he asked as he struggled off the couch. "I seem to be a little confused. Have I missed something?"

"I'll explain on our way back to the beach." Jared paused at the top of the steps and looked back at Cassie. "It should take me at least a full day to ascertain if you've told me the truth. The guards will stay here until I do." He grimaced. "Not that they've been overly successful in this enterprise so far. They might as well not have been here."

"You shouldn't waste your time," she said impatiently. "We could leave right away."

"*If* I decide you're not trying to deceive me again, we'll leave tonight. I'll send a message to the guards to pack up your belongings and bring you to the beach at sunset."

Cassie heard Lani's quick intake of breath but did not look away from Danemount. "You needn't bother. I'll be there."

"It's no bother." He smiled sardonically. "I appreciate your eagerness, but there's a protocol regarding the treatment of hostages. I fear guards are de rigueur."

He went down the steps followed by Bradford. She and Lani watched them until they disappeared from view.

"What is this?" Lani asked Cassie.

"I have to go with them. There's no one else to take me," Cassie said. "It's not what I want, but at least I'll be on the same side of the world as Papa. I'll have to find a way to escape from them once I reach France."

"There is always a way. We will find it."

Cassie didn't look at her; she didn't want Lani to know how relieved she was at that calm assumption of togetherness. She was suddenly feeling very uncertain and alone. "You don't have to go with me," she said haltingly. "I won't ask it."

"Good. Then instead of chattering we can concentrate on packing our bags and dealing with Clara's tantrums at our leaving. Charles left me with a little over a hundred pounds for emergencies. It's not much but it will help." Lani moved toward the door. "I'd judge we have another quarter hour before Clara wakes. Let us make the most of it."

Five

"I t's not a wise move," Bradford told Jared as the longboat drew close to the *Josephine*. "You should leave the girl here."

"I need a hostage." Jared smiled mockingly. "As the lady pointed out to me."

"She's not a lady; she's little more than a child."

"She won't remain that way long," Jared said. "Life has a way of forcing us all to grow."

"Life or Jared Danemount?"

Jared didn't answer.

"You intend to bed her."

"Do I?"

"Was it the ropes? She didn't know, Jared."

"It wasn't only the ropes."

"I was afraid it was more." He sighed. "I could see it coming."

"How perceptive of you."

"It's not wise," Bradford repeated. "You'll regret it."

"Why should I?"

"Because you're a just man, and you'll find it difficult to make the daughter pay for the sins of the father."

"I'll steel myself. And may I remind you that she's committed a number of sins against us on her own."

"Enough to provide you with an excuse to force her to your bed?"

"I didn't say I'd force her," he said, stung. "I don't force women to couple with me."

"Not as yet." Bradford tilted his head as if in thought. "There may be other ways, of course. She will be completely in your power. Perhaps if you refuse to feed her, you could starve her into submission."

"I will not starve her," Jared said between his teeth.

"Or you could stake her out on the deck for the seamen to ravish. I'm sure your bed would appear very appealing in contrast to that experience."

"You know I'm not— Good God, I've never seen you this protective over a woman."

"She's very brave. I like courage. It's the one quality that is instinctive, undefiled by what we're taught. It comes from the heart and not the mind." He smiled. "But don't worry about me. When I get drunk enough, I'll forget all about gallantry and helpless innocents. I'm sure it's only a temporary aberration anyway." He looked back at the shore. "Maybe it's this place. Golden and clean and without a sense of sin . . ."

"And a king trying his best to find weapons to kill his nearest neighbors. Napoleon builds armies and so does Kamehameha."

"How do you intend to avoid the issue of guns after you dangled the carrot in front of the King?"

"Sail away before he knows our intention. Which

is why any questioning we do must be done with the utmost care."

"You don't think she's telling the truth?"

"Actually, I do. I think she'd do anything to save Deville," Jared said. "But she wouldn't want to do it from thousands of miles away. She would want to make sure of his safety from close quarters."

"You appear to be very knowledgeable about a lady you've known only for a few days."

He did know her. He knew that bravery of which Bradford was so fond. He knew her impulsiveness, her stubbornness that was laced with bravado, and most of all, he knew that damnable loyalty. "Well enough. A good deal has happened in those few days."

"And you think she's desperate enough to risk anything to help her father."

"Don't you?"

Bradford shrugged. "I prefer not to think at all. It's much more comfortable in these circumstances. Make your own decisions . . . and your own choices."

"That's my intention."

"But do remember to supply me with a bottle of brandy on the night you decide to ravish her. Screams are as disturbing to me as thinking."

"I'll remember," Jared said through his teeth. God in heaven, would Bradford never stop pricking him?

Bradford beamed. "Excellent."

"You're going to leave me here alone in this savage land?" Clara asked from behind Cassie.

Cassie carefully folded her gray gown and placed it in the large portmanteau. Clara had been glowering and muttering since she had been told of their departure, and Cassie had been expecting the attack all day. She supposed she should be grateful Clara had held her tongue until it was almost time to leave. "The king will protect you. If you wish to return to England, petition him to find a ship that will take you."

"I suppose it's what I should expect from you. Where is your gratitude for the hours I've spent serving you and your father?"

"My father isn't here. If you wish gratitude, wait until he returns."

"And you?"

Cassie gave her a level glance. "You've never given me understanding or kindness. Sometimes I've felt as if you hate me. Should I feel gratitude for hatred?"

"You need me. Take me with you."

"I've never needed you. I have to help my father. You would get in the way." She closed the case and fastened the buckle. "It's not going to be an easy time."

"It's that heathen strumpet," Clara spat. "You would take me except for her. Ever since she came here, she's been twisting you into an image of her sinful self."

She must not lose her temper. Only a few more minutes and she would be gone. "I sincerely hope you're right. I could have no better example than Lani. I'll be fortunate if I'm half as good a woman."

"She's a whore."

"Be quiet!" Cassie's control broke, and she whirled on Clara with blazing eyes. "I don't have to permit this any longer. You won't malign Lani to me."

"No?" Clara's smile was malevolent. "Then I'll go to that whore of Babylon and tell her what I think of her. You think she's such a good example? Wait until you get out into a world not populated by savages. They will scorn and laugh at you and see her for the harlot she is. I wish I could see it." She headed for the door. "Yes, I think I'll go to your precious Lani and let her feel the edge of my tongue. She will— What are you doing?" She clawed at Cassie's arm encircling her neck from behind. "Let me go!"

Tightening her grip, Cassie dragged Clara toward the open armoire. It was no easy task. Clara was surprisingly strong, and she was struggling fiercely.

"What do you think you're doing?" Clara's elbow whipped backward and struck Cassie in the stomach. She temporarily lost her breath but held on. Just a few more steps . . .

She gathered all her strength and flung Clara into the armoire.

"Cassandra!"

Cassie slammed the door and turned the key.

"Let me out of here!"

"No more, Clara. It's not going to be easy for Lani to leave her island and her people. I won't have you making it worse for her." Cassie brushed back a lock of hair and moved toward the bed. The seaman had loaded the other cases into the wagon; she would have to manage this one herself unless she wished Clara discovered before she left. It should prove no burden. She felt as strong and confident as Hercules. In one gesture she had broken the shackles of a lifetime of oppression and abuse.

"I could die in here," Clara cried out. "What if no one finds me?"

"What a pleasant thought," Cassie murmured. She was tempted to let Clara struggle with that frightening idea for a while but relented. "I'll tell Uma to let you out after we leave." Oh, what the devil. Why not make her just a little uncomfortable? "But you're not always kind to Uma, are you? Just last night you insulted her, and you know how we savages can be. She may decide to leave you there for a while."

She smiled happily at Clara's screech of outrage. The solid oak doors of the armoire were thick, and Clara's scream couldn't be heard for more than a few feet. If Cassie could get out of the room before Lani came looking for her, Clara might be imprisoned for hours. Unfortunately, Lani wouldn't care if Clara deserved the punishment or not; she would probably release her.

Cassie was dragging the portmanteau down the hall when Lani appeared. "That's too heavy for you to handle alone. Why didn't you call me?"

"It's not too bad. I thought I could do it myself."

"Is this the last one?"

Cassie nodded. "Where is Uma?"

She gestured. "Standing beside the wagon waiting to say good-bye. It's almost time to go. Have you said your farewells to Clara?"

"Yes."

"She's been seething like a volcano since we told her we were going. Was she difficult?"

Cassie smiled. "No, actually she was quite . . . subdued."

"She's riding the horse," Bradford murmured, his gaze on the little party coming toward them on the beach, Cassie mounted on Kapu and behind her a wagon driven by one of the sailors. "I didn't expect her to bring the stallion."

Neither had Jared. The scarlet rays of the setting sun glowed satin on Kapu's ebony back and lit Cassie's upswept hair. She was dressed in a black riding habit and looked as annoyingly prim as she had appeared last night.

He took a step forward as she reined in before him. "You intend to take the horse?"

"Of course. Who would feed him with Lani and me gone? He won't let anyone else near him."

"Lani?" For the first time he saw the Hawaiian woman in the back of the wagon.

"You didn't expect me?" Lani jumped down, and without waiting for an answer, she turned to the sailor on the wagon seat. "Unload those trunks, and be very careful not to spill that basket of grass. Cassie wants no sand in it."

The sailor scowled and muttered something beneath his breath.

"Now," Lani said so softly the steel in her tone was barely discernible. "Be quick, if you please."

To Jared's surprise the burly sailor obeyed.

"Why are you bringing grass?" Bradford asked with interest.

"Kapu's journey here from England was not a pleasant experience," Cassie said as she dismounted. "I'm hoping he'll settle better if his food tastes and smells familiar."

"Excellent idea."

Lani studied Bradford. "Are you sober enough to help with the trunks? We must hurry. Cassie wants to get the horse on board before darkness falls."

"I'm always sober enough to help a lovely lady." He plucked the smallest valise from the bed of the wagon. "As long as the task isn't too strenuous."

"I'm sure you won't overstrain yourself with that piece. I could have lifted that valise when I was a child fresh from the cradle." She frowned. "Cassie tells me you act as captain of this ship."

He bowed slightly. "I have that honor."

"Then I'll learn how to do it myself. I've no confidence in you, and I've no desire to be run aground or sunk because you decide to blind your senses with strong liquor."

"You needn't worry. I'm always sober when there's a challenge in the offing."

"I don't trust you. You'll show me the navigation maps when we board." She turned to Jared. "Two hostages are better than one. You have no quarrel with my coming?"

"Why should I? A man's mistress could be a greater draw than a daughter. I just didn't anticipate your eagerness to sacrifice yourself. Come ahead. Welcome." He paused. "As long as you don't get in my way."

"I won't get in your way." She moved toward the longboat. "If you walk the path of peace."

Which nullified the first words very neatly, Jared thought dryly. He turned to face Cassie and watched her stiffen, then brace herself.

"I'm taking Kapu," she said defiantly. "I know he'll be a great deal of trouble, but I'll not have it any other way."

"You seem to have a strange idea about the privileges of hostages. They don't make demands."

"I'm taking him," she said flatly. "You can argue all you please. He goes—"

"I'm not arguing." He took a step nearer and touched Kapu's muzzle. "I thoroughly approve. It will give me the opportunity to persuade you to sell him to me. I have only one question."

"Yes?" she said warily.

"How the devil are we going to get him on board? There's no dock here, and the ship's anchored a good half mile out in the bay."

"Oh, the same way he was taken off the ship when

he was brought here. I still have his halter." She moved to the back of the wagon and pulled from its bed a web of leather-bound canvas straps and iron rings. "We fasten this around Kapu's middle and you attach it to a pulley on the deck of the ship and we pull him out of the water."

"How simple," he said caustically.

"Not simple but it works."

"Providing you can get the horse to swim that far out and then keep him from killing himself or us when we try to attach the ropes to the straps."

"It's the only way." She unfastened Kapu's saddle and pulled it off. "I can do it. Kapu and I swim out farther than that when we play together."

Jared frowned, still absently patting Kapu's muzzle. "But if he panics, you won't have the strength to hold him."

"Yes, I will. I'm very strong."

Jared shook his head. "You go on board with Bradford. I'll do it."

"No!" She stepped forward, putting herself between Jared and the stallion. "He's my horse. I'll do it."

"For God's sake, I'm not trying to take him away from you. You're mad if you think I'd enjoy going for a swim with a fear-crazed animal. I'm merely saying it's only reasonable that the strongest rider do the task."

"He's my horse." She turned her back on him and grabbed Kapu's reins. "Take his saddle and go back to your ship and set up the pulley. I'll stay here with Kapu until I see you wave. If it's dark, light a lantern and swing it three times."

His lips tightened. "You're not staying here."

"Are you afraid it's not safe? I'm not going to run

away. You're taking Lani to your ship. Do you think I'd leave her?"

"No, I'm not afraid you'll run away. Dammit, it's too dangerous. You can't—"

"You're wasting time." She slung the halter over Kapu's back and began fastening the leather straps. The stallion neighed and shifted uneasily. "Kapu's already getting nervous."

"Not nearly as nervous as he'll be when we try to fasten those ropes to him," he said grimly. "You'll be lucky if he doesn't crush you against the ship. I have a chance of keeping him away but you— What are you doing?"

"Taking off my clothes." She finished unbuttoning the jacket and shrugged out of it, revealing only a thin cotton chemise. "This riding habit is too heavy. It will drag me down once I'm in the water." Her skirt dropped to the sand and she stepped out of it. Her hands went to her petticoat.

"Wait!" He cast a glance at the longboat, where the four sailors were watching with delighted grins and Bradford with an expression of startled bemusement. Only Lani's expression was impassive. "You can't strip naked here."

"I most certainly can." The petticoat fell to the sand, and she held on to Kapu while she took off her boots and stockings. She stared at him with impatience. "Why are you so upset? You've seen me wearing less."

But somehow that nudity on the beach had not been as provocative or stirring as the sight of her standing here in those flimsy undergarments. He was acutely aware of the curve of her small breasts beneath the thin cotton chemise, the contrast of smooth golden skin against the soft white garment. The curve of her bare calves beneath the drawers. He was ready-ing, and, goddammit, he knew his arousal was being echoed by those gaping seamen in the boat. He wanted to step forward and bundle her back into the riding habit, veil her from their eyes, from any man's eyes. He gestured furiously toward the longboat. "But they haven't seen you, blast it."

"Not me, perhaps, but Lihua and the others."

"You're not Lihua."

"I'm no better or worse. I feel no more shame of my body than she does in hers. It's you and those others who take and then try to heap shame on us."

"I haven't taken anything from you yet," he said curtly. "I just want you to put that habit back on."

"I won't do it." She shrugged. "But I don't have to take off anything else. The chemise and drawers are light, and I may need whatever protection they offer."

"What protection? That cloth is thin as cobwebs. Put on the habit."

She glared at him. "Would you rather I drowned?"

"I'd rather you kept your clothes on and let me ride the blasted horse."

"That's not a choice. I told you that I was going to do it."

"Because you're too stubborn to admit how dan-gerous it is for—" He broke off as he realized she wasn't listening to him. She had made up her mind and was closing him out. He muttered an impreca-tion, snatched up the discarded habit and saddle, and turned on his heel. "Go on. Ride the damn horse. Dive into the sea as naked as Venus. Let him crush you. Why should I care?" He strode down the beach toward the longboat.

"I take it you lost the battle," Bradford asked as

Jared climbed into the boat and tossed his burden to a seaman. "She wouldn't listen?"

"She'll be lucky if he doesn't kill her," he said savagely.

"Kapu loves her," Lani said. "He won't hurt her."

"Even when he's mad with fear?"

"She's given him patience and love and care for two long years," Lani said quietly. "He will know she means him well."

Shaking his head in disbelief, Jared glanced back at the woman on the shore. She was standing beside the horse, talking quietly to him while she stroked his mane. She looked small and frail and infinitely breakable beside the big stallion. He tried to hold on to his anger, but he could feel it ebbing out of him, replaced by cold fear. "Christ."

The sun had gone down, but it was still twilight when Cassie saw Jared wave from the *Josephine*. That was good, she told herself. Kapu would be less nervous if he wasn't swimming in darkness.

Maybe.

She took a deep breath and pulled herself onto the stallion's back. He shied nervously, and she instantly bent over and whispered in his ear. "Easy. It's going to be fine. I wouldn't let anything happen to you. We're just going for a swim." She nudged him gently forward into the surf. "You like the water, remember?"

He might like water but Kapu didn't like ships. He had too many memories of neglect and starvation and a master who wandered drunkenly down into the cargo hold to beat him. When she had first seen Kapu after he had been brought ashore, the fresh whip marks on his body had filled her with anger. It would be a miracle if he submitted meekly to having the ropes put on him.

But it had to be done. She couldn't leave him here. "It won't be like the last time," she murmured as he reached deeper water and began to swim. "No one cared about you then. We're together now. I'll take care of you."

His ears were back, listening, but she could feel his muscles tense beneath her thighs. He sensed this was not like their other swims.

A quarter way to the ship.

He didn't know their destination. If she could keep him turned slightly away from the ship until the last minute . . .

She lifted her head and saw Danemount leaning over the rail, watching, his expression grim. But he always looked grim and intense.

No, that wasn't true. That night on the beach he had been sensual and free, and his smile had lit his face with pagan recklessness.

He had been happy because he had found her father.

Halfway to the ship.

She whispered to Kapu, "Just stay with me. We can get through this."

He neighed softly as if he understood.

Surely that was a good sign. It was possible he might have forgotten his experience on the ship. It had been two years, and she had made sure he had known only kindness since then.

Almost there.

She kept Kapu's head turned away as she angled toward the ship.

"That's right," Danemount said quietly. "Edge him just a little closer. The rope can't reach him yet."

What did he think she was doing? she thought in exasperation.

"Two feet closer. Just a yard or so more and the rope—"

Kapu jerked his head sideways, toward the ship.

Dear God!

She could feel his muscles bunch beneath her thighs as he saw the ship less than four yards away.

"It's all right," she said frantically. "It won't hurt you. I won't let it—"

He went wild! He screamed with rage and dived under the water, his legs thrashing wildly.

Cassie's mouth and nose filled with salt water as she fought her way off Kapu's back. She grabbed wildly for the reins.

Missed.

Reached again.

Leather! Her grasp closed on the reins as Kapu surfaced, pulling her with him.

"Drop the reins!" Lani's voice.

But she couldn't drop them. It was her only way of controlling Kapu. They would both drown if—

Blinding pain streaked through her shoulder. She had struck the side of the ship.

"Let go, dammit!" Not Lani, this time. Danemount, she realized. He was in the water, only a few feet away. "I have the ropes to fasten him. Let go of the reins before he kills you."

He had the pulley ropes. "Give me one of them," she gasped.

"Get away from him. I'll do it."

"He'll drown before you fasten both of them. You take one side and I'll take the other. We have to get him out of the water."

His eyes blazed at her. "Get *him* out of the water? Swim to the ladder and let them pull you up."

"We don't have time to argue. He may decide to strike away from the ship. Give me one of the ropes."

"Damn you!" He threw one of the pulley ropes to her. "Stay away from his legs."

She dived below the water, trying to avoid Kapu's flailing hooves. She could dimly discern the white canvas webbing of the halter. Where were the steel rings?

Her lungs were bursting as she fought to hold her breath. She could see Danemount on the other side of Kapu, his hair billowing about his face like seaweed. She felt a sudden surge of confidence. Together they could do it; together they could do anything.

The salt stung her eyes as she searched desperately for the ring that—there it was!

Kapu's hoof narrowly missed her head as she dived beneath his belly and passed the rope through the ring.

Hurry. She had to hurry. Her breath was almost gone.

Once through the ring and then back. Knot. The knot had to be very secure to hold his weight.

Done!

She fought to the surface.

No Danemount. Panic iced through her.

No, there he was, surfacing about ten feet away.

"Did you—" She broke into a fit of coughing.

He nodded as he drew in great gulps of air. "You?"

She nodded.

He waved his arm to the men on the deck. "Take him up."

She moved closer to Kapu. He was going to be so

frightened. "It's all right. I'm here. It will be over in a moment."

"Stay away from him," Danemount said.

"I can't. He needs me."

"He'll need you more when he's pulled on board the ship." He added grimly, "He may explode once he's out of the water. We may all need you at that point."

He was right. It was more important that Kapu sense a friendly presence when he reached the deck of the ship. She struck out for the rope ladder.

Danemount reached the ship before her and was already climbing the ladder.

She heard Kapu's terrified squeal behind her as he was lifted from the water by the pulley. She forced herself not to look back as she climbed the ladder. Soon the stallion's ordeal would be over. They would be together on the ship, and she could comfort him and make him feel safe again. Dear God, she was weary. Now that the task was done, all the strength seemed to be seeping out of her.

Danemount reached the deck, turned, and lifted her the final two rungs. He was no longer the sleek, fastidious nobleman, she thought dully. His shirt and trousers were plastered to his lean body, and his long hair hung in wet strands about his face.

"All right?" he asked tersely. When she nodded, he didn't give her another look but instead went to the rail to watch Kapu's ascent.

"How's your shoulder?" Lani was there beside her, wrapping her in a blanket.

"My shoulder?" That's right, she had rammed it against the hull. Only now was she aware of a painful throbbing. "It's not bad."

"It doesn't seem to be bleeding anymore."

"Bleeding?" she repeated, startled.

"There was blood on the water when you surfaced. That's when Danemount dived overboard. He swims very well . . . for an Englishman." She added grudgingly, "And he has courage. Not many men would have been willing to risk being maimed by Kapu to fasten those ropes to the halter."

Cassie scarcely heard her. Kapu was being lowered to the deck. He wasn't struggling; he appeared frozen with terror. She dropped the blanket and hurried to the rail.

"Stay back," Danemount snapped. "Look at his eyes."

She could see what he meant. Kapu's eyes were glittering with panic. She stopped before the stallion, who was still suspended a few inches above the deck. "Put him down."

"Not yet."

"I said put him down. He's afraid. He hates this."

"He'll savage you."

"He won't hurt me. Not now." She reached out and touched Kapu's muzzle with a loving hand. "Is there a stall prepared for him?"

"Yes." He jerked his head toward an open doorway several yards down the deck. "There's a ramp leading down to the cargo hold."

"Then put him down and leave us alone. I'll lead him to the hold when he's ready."

For a moment Danemount didn't move. Then he motioned for the stallion to be lowered the final few inches. "Stand back and leave the halter on him until he's calmer."

She didn't answer as she stepped forward and buried her face in Kapu's mane. The horse was trembling but stayed still beneath her touch. She began to talk to him.

She was only vaguely aware of the others moving away.

"The worst part is over," she crooned. "It will never be this bad again. Soon I'll rub you down and feed you your grass. But not yet. We'll just stay here and get used to the feel of the ship and being together. You don't have to move until much later. . . ."

Bradford glanced over his shoulder at the woman and the horse as he walked with Jared along the deck. "I think you should know that you're never going to get that stallion away from her. She's besotted with the animal."

"Do you think I don't realize that? She almost died for him today."

"I just thought I'd mention it. I didn't want you to have any false hopes. By the way, the two of you worked quite well together to save him. Does it foster a feeling of comradeship in your breast?"

"Not a whit."

"I think it will. It's almost impossible to ignore such a bond."

"The only things I can't ignore at present are your erroneous pronouncements and these sopping-wet clothes." He glanced about him. "And where is our other guest? In her cabin?"

Bradford nodded toward the forecastle, where Lani was standing quietly looking down on Cassie and Kapu. "Watching over her charge. She's very protective. A fine quality. You should appreciate it since you apparently have it in abundance. What a splendid gesture. My heart was quite touched when you dived into the sea." He snapped his fingers. "But of course—it wasn't due to your concern for the girl herself. It was the horse and the possibility of losing a hostage."

Ignoring the mockery, Jared looked back over his shoulder. It was fully dark now and he could see Cassie only as a gleam of white and Kapu as a stiff, unmoving bulk. There was no telling how long it would take to bring the horse to a state calm enough to be moved, and Cassie would not hurry him even if it took all night.

"Shall we set sail?" Bradford asked.

The movement of the ship would only make Cassie's task of quieting the stallion harder. "Not for a while. There's no hurry. I'll tell you when."

"For God's sake, get out of that stall. Do you want him to trample you?"

Cassie raised her head from the straw to see Jared standing in the doorway of the cargo hold. The candle in his hand cast shadows on the planes of his face. Shadows . . . He was always half in shadow, she thought. The outer shell sleek and glittering, and beneath . . . darkness and mystery. She raised herself on one elbow. "He won't trample me. He's much calmer now."

"And what will he do once we set sail?" He moved forward to stand at the door of the stall. "Will he still be calm when the ship is no longer rocking like a cradle but skittering and pitching?"

"That's why I'm here." She sat up and brushed her hair back from her face. It was stiff and wiry from the salt water, and too dry. So was her skin. Everything about her felt parched and taut, and she thought longingly of the coconut oil they had packed in Lani's trunk. "I've been waiting for you to up anchor. Why haven't you done it?"

"My apologies. I foolishly thought that you might need a little time to get the horse adjusted." He hung the lantern on the post beside the stall. "I told Bradford to up anchor and set sail in a quarter hour. I hope that will be satisfactory?"

"Yes." She was too weary to bristle at his sarcasm. Besides, he had done her a great service by helping to save Kapu. "I only wondered."

He raised his brows in surprise. "No stinging retort? Are you quite well? Perhaps it was your head and not your shoulder that was damaged."

"I'm not always argumentative. You're the one who—" She stopped and then said, "You see. It's you who sting. I'm trying not to be unpleasant."

"Why on earth?"

"Kapu." She lowered her eyes and said haltingly, "Not that I couldn't have managed by myself, but you made things a good deal easier."

"Thank you."

Sarcasm again, and she felt shamed. His action had been both brave and generous and deserved a generous response. She lifted her gaze and met his directly. "All right. There's a possibility I might not have been able to get the ropes onto Kapu. You helped me and you have my thanks."

He was a silent a moment and then said, "No thanks are necessary. I acted on impulse. I saw a fine horse in danger and did what had to be done." He smiled crookedly. "So you needn't dilute your hatred with gratitude."

"I don't hate you." The words had tumbled out, but she suddenly realized they were true. Her emotions toward Danemount were confused, but hatred was not among them. "Not yet. But if you hurt my father, I'll hate you. I'll hate you and I'll hurt you."

"Only an eye for an eye? I'm surprised you're being so magnanimous."

"You believe you're doing what's right. Lani taught me that I had to try to see both sides of an argument. She even made excuses for Clara."

His expression hardened. "I don't need excuses made for me."

"Because you've always lived a perfect and righteous life?" she flared. "It must be splendid to be able to cast the first stone."

"I wasn't the one who cast the first stone. It was your father."

"You can't be sure. You have no proof." She drew a deep, ragged breath. "I will talk no more about this with you. It does no good."

"On the contrary, it completely purged you of that annoying flash of gratitude. You must be much more comfortable now. You can be as—" He broke off when the ship suddenly dipped and swayed. Kapu neighed and half reared! "On your feet and out of that stall! We're putting about."

Cassie scrambled to her feet but inched closer to Kapu instead of leaving the stall. "Shh, it's all right. It's going to be fine." She put her arms around his neck. "You'll get used to it."

"Keep talking to him." Jared stepped into the stall with them. "But stay away from those hooves." He began to stroke Kapu's head and talk in the same low, soothing tone as Cassie.

The stallion was quieting, Cassie realized in relief. He was responding to Jared in the same magical fashion as he had that night on the beach. Strangely, unlike that night, she felt no resentment—only gratitude. Together they were calming Kapu, making him safer. She was aware of that same bond with Jared that she had felt in the water when they were trying to get the pulley ropes fastened.

It was over a quarter of an hour before Kapu was calm enough for Jared to step away from the stallion. "I don't suppose you'll feel safe enough tonight to leave him and go to your cabin?"

She shook her head. "I'll stay here. The straw is soft. When I first got him, I slept in the stable for more than a month."

"May I point out that you hadn't fallen down a mountain or been dashed against a ship?" He shrugged when she didn't answer. "I didn't think so." He sat down on the straw in the far corner of the stall.

"What are you doing?"

"I'll stay awhile." He grimaced. "Not a month. I'm not that much of a Spartan. Only a few hours to make sure the progress we've made isn't ruined by any rough weather. Sit down." When she didn't move, he added impatiently, "For God's sake, sit down before you fall. I'm not in the least tempted to ravish you at the moment."

"I know that." She settled herself in the corner farthest from him. "You'd have to be extremely lacking in taste to desire a woman who looks like a bit of stringy seaweed."

"Maybe I like seaweed." He leaned back against the wall. "I've been known to have more perverted appetites."

"Really?" she asked curiously. "What?" Then, as she saw him smile, she added quickly, "Lihua says most foreigners are perverted and that they should realize the direct way is best."

"Indeed?" His brows lifted. "I don't recall Lihua

ever complaining of my perversions. She must have realized how brutal I'd be if she angered me."

"You know she thought you—" She stopped when his smile widened.

"A God?"

"Lihua has little judgment."

He clutched his chest with a mock groan. "What a sharp thrust." His smile faded. "Though I tend to agree. She should certainly have used better judgment in discussing such subjects with you."

"Because you think what you do is sinful? It's all right to perform such acts but not to subject them to the light of day?"

"Oh, I enjoy subjecting them to the light of day. Morning is a particularly felicitous time to—"

"You know what I mean," she cut into his sentence. "You think Lihua and the other islanders are sinful, but you take advantage of that sinfulness."

"You've made that accusation before." He asked quietly, "You're calling me a hypocrite?"

"What else is there to call you?"

"I don't know. Perhaps you're right," he said wearily. "I admire the islanders, and I envy their honesty and openness, but everyone is raised to think his own way best. It could be that some part of me does condemn them for being different from me. But that part is not my mind or my will."

When she had made the accusation, she had been seeking to put up barriers between them and had not wanted him to answer with such simple honesty. First gratitude, and then the bond of shared danger, and now she was beginning to understand him. Dangerous. She searched desperately for a way to distance herself. She said tartly, "Well, it's certainly not your lower parts that condemn their difference."

The gravity vanished from his face as he threw back his head and laughed. "No, by God, that part of me is totally mindless. I accept everything with no prejudice whatever." He met her gaze. "As you will learn to do."

She felt a tightness in her chest and that curious sensation of breathlessness. She said unevenly, "But you'll not be the one to teach me. You don't really want me. You only want to punish my father."

"The *hell* I don't want you. Deville has nothing to do with this."

She was shaken by the violence in his voice. "Of course he does. Otherwise it makes no sense."

"Carnal pleasures seldom do. Passion can strike out of nowhere. You should know that since you must have seen it every day on your island."

She had seen it, but it had always happened to Lihua and the others, not to her. She shook her head in disbelief. "It's not true. I'm not beautiful like Lihua or Lani. I'm not the kind of woman for whom a man conceives such a passion."

"Shall I convince you?" He leaned forward, his eyes blazing recklessly in the dimness. "I lied, you know. You're right, you look like a scrap of flotsam. You're dirty and tired. You have straw clinging to your hair and body and salt coating you from head to toe. You should have no appeal at all for me. Do you know what I'd like to do to you right now?"

She moistened her lips. "No."

"I want to take off that chemise and lick the salt from your breasts." His eyes fastened on the damp cotton veiling the swell of her breasts. "I want to taste you. I want to pull at your nipples with my teeth. I want to make a feast of you." His gaze never left her body. "And I think you want me to do that, too."

Blood was pounding through her veins. She felt on fire, her skin tingling. "No," she whispered.

"Look down at yourself."

She didn't have to look down, she could feel her breasts swelling beneath his eyes, her nipples hardening and pushing against the soft cotton barrier. "It doesn't mean anything. It's just . . . I'm startled."

"You're ready," he corrected softly. "Beautifully ready."

"I couldn't be." She swallowed to ease the tightness of her throat. "Not with you."

"Because you regard me as your enemy? It doesn't make any difference. Not in this."

"Of course it makes a difference," she said fiercely. "I'm not an animal. I have control of my body. I wouldn't let myself—" She broke off and then said, "Go away. I don't want you here."

"Unfortunate." He leaned back against the wall. "But I'm not leaving until I'm sure the stallion is settled. After all, nothing has changed. I told you I have no intention of ravishing you tonight. You've had a bad time, and I find myself deplorably brimming with the milk of human kindness. Most unusual."

He was wrong. Something had changed. Her body had betrayed her, was still betraying her. She felt weak and vulnerable and needed time to rebuild her defenses. "I don't need you. Go away."

He didn't move.

She closed her eyes, but she could still feel him staring at her.

"But I'm not so filled with sympathy that I won't give you something to think about." His voice was soft and sensuous. "One of the times I'm going to take you will be in a stable. You'll be naked and feel the faint abrasiveness of the straw against your breasts and belly as I move inside you. Have you ever seen a stallion mount a mare?"

She didn't answer.

"Of course you have. You're planning on having a horse farm of your own. Did the mating excite you? The drive, the hard thrust, the joining . . ."

She felt a tingling between her legs as she remembered the sight of that mating. *Don't think of it.* She was not an animal, a mare for the mounting.

The hay smelled clean, and she was aware of it prickling her skin through the thin cotton. She was acutely aware of him only a few yards away: man . . . stallion.

"Did the mare scream when he entered her?"

"Yes," she said hoarsely.

"But she wanted it, didn't she? She backed toward him?"

"Of course she did. She was in season."

"Like you. You're in season, aren't you?"

"No . . ." Her lids flicked open to see his eyes fixed on her with glittering force. The air seemed heavy and hard to breathe. "I told you that I'm not an animal."

"We're all animals in that final moment. I guarantee you won't care whether I'm an enemy or friend when I'm inside you."

His tone was so confident, it frightened her as much as the image his words brought to mind. Jared inside her, riding her as he had ridden Kapu, those hard, muscular thighs holding her still while he . . . "Go away," she whispered.

He shook his head.

"Then don't talk to me. I don't want to hear this."

"I think I've said enough."

He had said too much, and she must not think about any of it or its effect on her.

You're in season, aren't you?

She had denied it, but perhaps that was the reason her response had been so powerful and beyond her control. Before she had even seen him, she had been aware of the growing sensuality of her body. Yes, that was it, she grasped at the explanation eagerly. He wasn't the cause. He could have been any man. It was just her time for mating. He was more sensual than any man she had ever encountered, and surely it was natural that she had responded. But response did not mean surrender. "Stay or go." She carefully kept her tone indifferent. "I don't care. I shall only ignore you."

He smiled. "Will you?"

She looked away from him and fastened her gaze on Kapu. Damn him. So confident, so comely. Even when she didn't look at him, she could *feel* him there. She could remember the line of his thigh outlined in the closely fitting trousers, the careless grace, his mouth . . .

I want to lick the salt from your breasts.

No, not again. She would *not* feel like this. He was not the cause. She desperately reiterated the thought over and over like a chant to ward off demons. It was only her time for mating.

It was not him.

Six

"I s she still down there?"

Jared turned, squinting against the brilliance of the morning sun to see Bradford strolling down the deck toward him. His uncle was shaved, exquisitely garbed in beige buckskin trousers and coat by Worth, and amazingly bright-eyed. "What are you doing up so early? I haven't seen you out of your bed before noon this entire journey."

"You exaggerate. I usually let you drag me from slumber on the more interesting occasions."

"But seldom voluntarily."

"True. But, then, we're all spurred to greater effort when something appears on the horizon that intrigues us."

Jared stiffened. "And may I ask what intrigues you?"

Bradford chuckled. "My, how ferocious you sound. What treasure are you protecting from my lustful avarice? The girl or the horse?"

Jared cursed the reaction, which had been purely

instinctive. He forced a smile. "The horse, of course. I know where your passion lies."

"Do you? How sad that I'm so transparent," Bradford said. "You didn't answer me. Is the girl still down in the cargo hold communing with our equine friend?"

"Presumably." He glanced away, and his pace quickened as they approached the door to the hold. "Providing the stallion hasn't trampled her."

"Oh, I don't think he'll do that. Even when he was almost mindless with terror, he let her come close." His brow wrinkled in thought. "She gives me hope."

"Hope?"

"I've always envied your way with horses. It's like magic." He made a face. "But magic is not within the grasp of ordinary mortals. What comes so easily to you is impossible for me."

Jared stared at him in astonishment. Bradford had never mentioned any of this and certainly not expressed resentment. "Nonsense. You're the finest horseman I've ever met."

"But I'm not a Kahuna." He smiled. "And perhaps I don't have to be. That young girl in the hold isn't a Kahuna, either, but she has a power of her own."

"What power?"

"I hesitate to say the word." He paused. "Love." He shuddered. "Good God, what an outmoded and maudlin emotion. Yet it gives her a power that's both embarrassing and quite foreign to both of us. We don't understand it and she probably doesn't either. But she's not ashamed to feel it. When I watched her with the stallion, it opened a new door."

"And what's behind the door?" Jared asked mockingly.

"I don't know. As I said, I think it's hope. Though

hope is also an outmoded emotion, and I may not be able to recognize it." He stopped as they reached the cargo hold. "But I thought it worthwhile to make the effort to explore."

"Are you going down with me?"

He shook his head. "I'll wait here. The hold has a variety of unpleasant smells."

Jared opened the door. "So much for exploration."

"I never said I was Christopher Columbus." Bradford paused. "Do you know, she reminds me a little of Josette."

Jared went still. "She's nothing like Josette."

"Oh, not in looks, but there's the same recklessness, the same obstinacy. I think, under different circumstances, she might have the same beguiling way about her."

"She and Josette have little in common."

"Because you don't want to admit any comparisons?" Bradford asked softly. "Would it make you uncomfortable?"

"Not in the least." Jared smiled sardonically. "Though I'm sure you intended it to do just that."

"Maybe. It could be I wanted to throw open a few doors of my own. However, the comparisons may come into play willy-nilly if Josette and she come together." He grimaced. "Heaven help us all."

"They won't come together," Jared said. "Josette has nothing to do with this."

"She might disagree with you." He turned away and leaned on the rail. "We shall have to see, won't we?"

"No, because Josette won't enter the picture." Jared closed the door and moved quickly down the steps into the darkness, glad to escape Bradford's strange mood. No, not only his mood—Jared's real-

ization that he had unintentionally hurt Bradford and
never known. Well, what the devil could he have
done, even if he had known? He was sure Bradford
wouldn't have wanted him to neglect his talent with
horses. At times Bradford seemed to rejoice in it.
Seemed? Of course he had rejoiced. Jared was questioning everything, and all because Cassie Deville had
moved into their lives and sent out waves of disturbance.

He could see Kapu's dark shape moving restlessly
in the stall. "Steady," he said quietly as he lit the
lantern beside the steps. "There's nothing to fear."
He moved slowly toward the stall. "You know me."
Where the devil was the girl?

She was asleep, curled in a corner of the stall, so
exhausted that even his voice had not stirred her.
Christ, she looked helpless. Her hair was spread about
her in a wild tangle, her cheek had a smudge that
could be either dirt or a bruise, and her slim form
beneath the cloak that covered her appeared breakable. When she was awake, he was aware only of the
wariness and the challenge, but now she appeared totally without defenses, as young and guileless as
Josette. . . .

No, dammit, she was nothing like Josette. Bradford
had deliberately put that thought in his mind. Cassie
had drugged him, deceived him, and even now she
was seeking to use him for her own ends. He would
not feel this blasted softness for her. He would use
her as she was using him. It was not—

She sighed and stirred, shifting closer to Kapu. In
another minute the idiot girl would be under the stallion's hooves. Goddammit!

·   ·   ·

"For God's sake, it's morning. Go to your cabin and go to bed!"

Cassie drowsily opened her eyes to see Jared frowning at her. He had come back. She wished he hadn't. She was tired of being on guard. Too much effort . . .

"Did you hear me?"

How could she help it when he was shouting? "I have to stay with Kapu."

"I'll stay with the damn horse." He entered the stall and jerked her to her feet, then steadied her when she swayed. "Get out of here."

The haze of sleep was clearing. "Kapu needs me."

"He doesn't—" He broke off as he saw her expression. "I'll call you if I can't keep him calm. I'm too selfish to spend this voyage pacifying a wild horse. I have other plans for my time." He released her shoulders and pushed her toward the stairs. "Eat, take a bath, and go to sleep. You may not get another bath in fresh water until we reach Tahiti. I don't want to see you here until sundown."

"I'm not leav—" A bath. How she yearned to rid herself of this salt. He had instinctively said the words most likely to persuade her. She cast a hesitant look at Kapu. He seemed calm, and Jared had promised to call her. . . . "Only a few hours."

"Sundown." Jared settled himself on the hay. "Or I'll have you locked in your cabin."

She had no intention of obeying him, but she was too tired to argue right then. She moved toward the door. "Be sure to call me if Kapu—"

"I said I would." He rolled over and turned his back on her. "Get out."

No hint of silken sensuality about him now. He was gruff and rude and angry. Good. She could cope much better with his rage than any other part of his complex nature. "I'll do as I please. I'm going because *I* wish it." She hurried up the steps and slammed the door behind her. When she reached the deck, the light blinded her. She reached out and grabbed the door, waiting for her eyes to adjust.

"May I help you?"

She turned to see Bradford standing a few feet away.

He bowed and said, "You look a trifle dishabille. Perhaps you'd care to go to your cabin and refresh yourself."

"Where's Lani?"

"In her cabin, I presume. Jared has given you quarters next to her. May I escort you there?"

"I don't need—" But she did need his help. She had no idea where Lani's cabin was, and she had no desire to prowl all over the ship searching for it. "Yes."

He gestured politely. "This way."

She fell into step with him. Since Bradford appeared willing to oblige, she might as well continue to make use of him. "I need a bath," she said haltingly. "Will you see to it?"

"It will be my pleasure." He smiled. "I love to have women indebted to me. You can never tell in what form a favor will be returned."

"Never mind," she said curtly. "I'll arrange it myself."

His smile faded. "I was joking. You don't have to be afraid of me. I'm not your enemy."

"You lie. You're his uncle. His father's brother. Are you saying your loyalty is not to him?"

"Oh, yes, I'm loyal to Jared. Completely. But that doesn't mean you're my enemy. It's much too fatiguing to carry all that antagonism around. I'd much rather be friends."

"Friends?" She looked at him in amazement. "We can't be friends."

"Why not? It's a long voyage, and you'll be much more comfortable if you have a friend."

"I already have a friend. I have Lani."

"Then take pity on me," he coaxed. "I have no one but Jared, and I've no doubt he'll be moody and restless as a caged tiger on this trip. Since you're to blame, you should at least bear me company on occasion."

"I'm not to blame. I'm not the one who came to the island and tried to—"

"Granted," he interrupted. "But you're the one who is causing Jared all this disturbance of spirit. So you must accept part of the responsibility."

"Disturbance?"

"I was trying to put it discreetly. But I suppose there's no proper word for what Jared is feeling now." He paused. "Lust."

She could feel heat sting her cheeks. "No, that's not in the least proper."

"I make it a practice never to interfere, but I thought I'd warn you. I admire courage, and you deserve to be given one weapon in the fray."

"Fray?"

"Engagement, battle." He shrugged. "Whatever it is between you and Jared."

"There's nothing between me and your nephew."

"There will be." He sadly shook his head. "You shouldn't have tied him. I think he was trying to fight it before you did that. He goes wild when he's bound. He remembers—" He stopped.

"What?"

"Nothing."

"What does he remember?"

He chuckled. "What a persistent chit you are. That's a very sensitive subject, and I have no intention of betraying Jared in that fashion." He stopped before a door. "This is your cabin. I'll have a tub brought and water heated. Will you and your Lani join me for dinner at two?"

"No."

"How sad." He bowed. "When the hour approaches, I'll send someone to see if you've changed your mind."

"I won't change my mind."

His expression sobered. "You'd do much better to bend a little. You and Jared are very much alike. Stubborn, driven, unable to compromise. But he has more weapons than you, and you'll be hurt if you confront him directly." When she didn't answer, he said with a sigh, "I don't think I'm reaching you."

"You are not."

Cassie and Bradford turned to see Lani standing in the doorway of the next cabin. "So why don't you be on your way?" she continued. "There must be a bottle awaiting you somewhere."

"Always. How kind of you to remind me." He bowed again. "Talk to your Lani, mademoiselle. She appears to be a woman of some experience and infinite insight." He bowed again and moved leisurely down the deck.

Lani dismissed him without another glance. "You look terrible." Her gaze raked Cassie from head to toe. "How is your shoulder?"

"Fine." She opened the door of the cabin. "I don't have much time. I have to get back to Kapu. He's calm now, but I'm not sure how long—"

"Who is with him?"

"Danemount."

"Then you have time. He appeared to have a way with the stallion." She smiled. "Besides, it should give you great satisfaction to use an enemy as stable boy." She followed Cassie into the cabin and undid the button at the throat of her cloak. "You've set yourself a hard task; there may not be many such triumphs. Enjoy them while you can."

She was tired of all these dire warnings. "Why are you talking like this? You sound like Lord Bradford."

"Did you expect me to lie and tell you that Danemount will let you use him to get to your father without exacting a price? We both know that's not true."

"He has me as hostage."

Lani lifted her brows. "You believe that's why he permitted you to come? You're either a fool or you think I am. He wishes to bed you." She added shrewdly, "And I'd wager he's already approached you on the subject."

She did not deny it. "I won't do it." She moved to her chest and threw open the lid. She didn't look at Lani as she pulled out clean undergarments and gown. "And he's mad to think I will."

Lani went still. "And does he think that?"

Cassie nodded. "I told you he was a madman. Mad and arrogant and without—"

"He's not mad." Lani was gazing at her thoughtfully. "I'd judge he's a man of great experience and perception. Which means he must have reason to think you might be persuaded. What do you feel for him?"

"What do I feel? He wants to kill my father."

"But you find him desirable?"

"Of course I don't."

"Because it would be a betrayal to Charles?" Lani suggested. "You feel lust and it makes you ashamed?"

"I don't feel—" She stopped, biting her lower lip. She had never lied to Lani. She would not start now. "I don't want to feel like this," she whispered. "It's not him. You said it was my time for mating. What I feel has nothing to do with him."

"Then stop feeling shame."

She said haltingly, "He says passion is mindless, but it should not be so. Not for me. I should be able to restrain it."

"You're too hard on yourself," Lani scoffed. "How many times have I told you that to couple with a man is nothing unless it has meaning? It's over in a few moments and is totally without importance after the final ripple has faded. But it's a natural act, and to desire it is also natural. We cannot choose what moment it will strike us. Next you will be preaching of sin, like Clara."

"You don't think . . . it's not . . ." Cassie trailed off and then said, "Papa."

"You're not betraying him by feeling lust. Danemount is a splendid peacock of a man, and the forbidden is always the most attractive to a woman." Lani took her by the shoulders and looked into her eyes. "No matter what you feel, will you not do everything necessary to try to save your father?"

She stared at her in astonishment. "Of course."

"Then stop being stupid."

Lani was, as always, tearing through all the bewildering doubts to get to the truth. Cassie laughed shakily and gave her a quick hug. "I will. It's only sometimes . . . I get confused."

Lani nodded grimly. "It's not surprising when Clara and your father have always tried to impose their foreign ways on you."

"Not Papa," she said quickly. "How can you say that?"

"Because it's true. Charles will always be foreign to me and our island." She added simply, "It does not matter. I love him still. I am content."

If he holds the woman in as much honor as you obviously do, then he would have wed her.

Lani's words were close to the charge that Danemount had made. But Lani had always said that wedding vows were of no importance to her. For the first time Cassie was beginning to question that claim. "He does love you, Lani."

"But he does not understand and accept me." For an instant Lani's expression was wistful, and then she smiled with an effort. "He gave me a friend who does, though . . . when she doesn't forget my teachings and become stupid."

"I'll try not to be stupid again." She shakily smiled back at Lani. "I don't know what's wrong with me."

"You're growing up. Everything is simple and clear when you're a child. Then for a while everything becomes muddied. Thank God the clarity comes back in time." Her smile faded. "But you've been robbed of time. You must think clearly and act boldly if we're to save Charles." She glanced over her shoulder at the knock on the door. "Your tub. We'll talk later." She opened the door to let the sailor with the tub enter. "I'll go get the coconut oil and rub you down after your bath. You're shriveled as a fish washed up on the beach."

· · ·

"Roll over," Lani said as she sat back on her heels beside the bunk. "I want to rub some oil into your back and that bruised shoulder."

"You shouldn't wait on me," Cassie protested even as she rolled over onto her stomach. It felt so good to be clean again, and Lani's gentle touch was strong, loving, and made her feel treasured. "I can do it."

"It's easier for me, and being busy helps me to think." Lani's hands moved slowly, delicately, rubbing the fragrant oil into her flesh. "Your muscles are knotted. Relax."

She was relaxing, surrounded in a haze of soothing affection and warm coconut oil.

She was close to dozing off when Lani spoke absently, "I may have to couple with the Englishman."

Cassie went rigid with shock. "What? Lord Bradford?"

"No, the Duke. The uncle is not dangerous to us." Lani's fingers massaged the line of Cassie's spine. "I've not decided, but it may be the wisest course."

"You're not making sense," Cassie said dazedly. She must have misunderstood. Lani's tone was as casual as if she had just told Cassie she was going to plant tomatoes in the spring. "Why would you want to do that?"

"I didn't say I wanted to couple with him. I said it might be the wisest course." Her index and forefinger moved in circles up and down Cassie's back. "We'll gain nothing by fighting with the English on this journey. It would be better to spend our time seeking out weaknesses and trying to alter Danemount's purpose."

"Impossible."

"Nothing is impossible. The woman in a man's bed can often change his mind." Lani gently spread the oil over Cassie's bruised shoulder. "This bruise isn't as bad as I feared when I saw you crash against the ship. You're lucky you didn't crack the bone."

Cassie scarcely heard her through the thoughts whirling through her head. "You mustn't do this. You won't change his mind. He'd take your body and still go after Papa."

"So what will I have lost? My body will still be my own, and I'll forget the Englishman and walk away. And you may be wrong. Foreigners have strange thoughts about coupling. It affects their minds as well as their bodies. Danemount is ruthless but not completely without softness. He treats Lord Bradford with kindness." She made a face. "And that must prove a great trial to anyone's patience. Yes, there are many advantages. If I couple with him, my chance of finding out what's going on when we reach France is much greater than if I'm locked away from him behind closed doors. We may need that information. Also, even if I can't persuade him not to kill Charles, he may find the killing more difficult if he has been intimate with his enemy's mistress. This is not a bad thing."

"It's a very bad thing," Cassie said harshly. "You know Papa wouldn't like it."

"True." Lani sighed. "Charles also has strange ideas of pride in possession. That's why I've never yielded to another man since I came to him. If I decide to do it, it will be kinder not to tell him."

"You won't do it." Cassie turned over and sat up. "I know you won't do it."

Lani smiled serenely. "I shall if I deem it wise."

"You're doing it for me."

Chuckling, Lani stood up and reached for a blanket in which to wrap Cassie. "To save you from the attentions of this wicked scoundrel? Don't be absurd. You're strong enough to save yourself, and neither of us is important right now. I do this for Charles." She leaned forward and kissed Cassie on the forehead. "Now sleep for a few hours. I'll go to Lord Bradford and tell him we'll be delighted to join him for dinner. Perhaps we'll learn something that will prove valuable."

"About how to pleasure his nephew?" Cassie asked bitingly. "You're far more beautiful than Lihua. You should have no trouble."

"Perhaps a little trouble." Lani rose to her feet. "At present he has a passion for you, and it's necessary to shift his interest. But a man seldom refuses an invitation to couple with a woman."

Certainly not a woman as beautiful as Lani, Cassie thought with an inexplicable pang.

"Sleep well." Lani moved gracefully toward the door. "I'll call you when it's time to dress for dinner."

"Lani!"

Lani glanced inquiringly over her shoulder.

"Don't do this. If Papa finds out, he'll be so angry he'll—" She stopped.

"Cast me out?" Lani nodded. "Sometimes risks must be taken. So far you've taken all the risks. Now I must share them. You won't tell Charles, and I don't think Danemount is a man who would take his revenge in that fashion."

"You don't know anything about him," she said desperately.

"It appears I may be going to learn a great deal regarding his—" Lani stopped, her gaze raking Cassie's expression. "Don't be so upset. All will be well." With a last smile she was gone.

Don't be upset? She was trembling, Cassie realized

as she drew the blanket closer about her. Trembling with fear and shock . . . and rage. Yes, rage. Lani was wrong. This wasn't the way to help Papa. They might not have many weapons, but she did not have to sacrifice herself and—

But for Lani it would be no sacrifice. Sex and love were separate to her, and coupling with Jared would mean nothing. She might even enjoy it.

The rage soared to new heights as she imagined Lani in Danemount's bunk, his hands on her breasts, his hips moving—

No!

She drew a deep breath and tried to block out the vision and the realization it had brought. She did not want to admit her rage was founded on anything but frustration. Yet she had to admit it, or she would be guilty of avoiding the truth.

You've been robbed of time. You must think clearly and act boldly.

Very well—the rage had been partially caused by jealousy. Her body felt cheated because it was being denied. The emotion had been driven by primitive instinct that had nothing to do with reason. But Lani had said this instinct was not shameful as long as the acts of the body were separate from the mind and soul. She must cling to that truth.

She closed her eyes and forced her tense muscles to loosen. She must forget the picture of Lani and Jared lying together, their bodies intertwined. . . .

"Ah, ladies, you've decided to take pity on me." Bradford rose to his feet and seated Lani, then Cassie at the damask-draped table. "I hoped you would."

"Since you've ordered two extra places set, I'd say you expected we would," Lani said dryly as she shook out her napkin. "And pity has nothing to do with this."

"No? I'd judge you to be prone to pity." Bradford nodded to the servant standing by the door to begin serving. "Why else would you choose to grace the bed of a man old enough to be your father?"

"According to Clara, grace did not enter into our union. She claims I seduced him with my barbaric wiles." She smiled. "And my people believe age makes no difference; it only serves to refine and make the act more beautiful."

"Lani loves my father," Cassie said. "And your remark was very rude."

"Yes, it was," Bradford admitted as he reached for the bottle of brandy at his elbow. "Extraordinary. I'm usually the most polite of fellows."

Lani glanced at the bottle. "How would you remember?"

"Are you suggesting my brain is pickled? Not yet. I'm keen as a sword blade until nightfall." He smiled with surprising sweetness. "For instance, I'm fully aware that it's not my charming company that brings you here, but I forgive you."

"Forgive us?"

"You intend to inveigle information from me, do you not?"

Lani hesitated and then said bluntly, "Yes."

"It will be my pleasure to be inveigled . . . within certain boundaries." He took a long drink of his brandy. "As I told your friend, it offends me to have Jared fight an opponent who has so few weapons. In most circumstances it would offend Jared also. He's a just man."

"I don't believe that," Cassie said flatly.

"You should." He took another drink. "You'll find

he's scrupulously honest. I've seen him forfeit a race he desperately wanted to win because of the possibility of chicanery. He's very respected in racing circles. You'll see when we get to England."

"England?" Cassie stiffened. "I have no intention of going to England."

"That's unfortunate, since that's where this ship is going," Bradford said. "Jared decided that it will be some time before Deville manages to make his way from America to France, and it would be wiser to stay at Morland and put his contacts in France on watch. When your father surfaces, we'll leave for France."

"And we're supposed to stay at this Morland and wait?" Cassie asked.

"That's the plan. I regret it doesn't meet with your approval."

"It certainly does not." She was caught off guard by Jared's decision. It would have been much easier for her to escape from the Duke on French soil. She had planned to flee the moment they arrived. How was she to get across the Channel and make her way to Paris?

"But we'll make the adjustment," Lani said. She reached over and encouragingly squeezed Cassie's hand. "Won't we?"

Cassie nodded. "Of course." She turned to Bradford. "How close is this Morland to the sea?"

He burst out laughing. "Do you intend to swim? I wouldn't advise it. Our northern waters are much colder than your warm sea."

"How close?"

"Quite close." He was still chuckling. "Morland is located on a cliff that overlooks the channel."

One advantage. And she might discover more once they reached England. She mustn't be discouraged by this first setback. "How long do you think we'll have to wait?"

He shrugged. "A month. Two. Who knows?"

Months. It seemed a long time, but she might be able to turn the delay to her advantage. Danemount would surely be receiving messages from his contacts in France. If she could intercept any of those messages, she might learn much more than she could on her own.

"Will His Grace be joining us for supper?" Lani asked.

Cassie tensed as her gaze flew to Lani. The disturbing news Bradford had imparted had momentarily caused her to forget Lani's equally disturbing intentions.

"Providing the stallion is calm enough to be left alone," Bradford said. "Are we again to be favored with your company?"

Lani's lips parted in her brilliant smile. "Oh, yes."

Bradford turned to Cassie. "And you?"

Of course, she wasn't going to sit at Jared's table and watch him be captivated by Lani. She intended to stay with Kapu, where she had a place and purpose.

"Yes, I'll be here." The words tumbled from her lips, surprising her as much as they did Bradford. Yet she knew she would not take them back. She could not stay in the cargo hold and not know what Lani was doing with Danemount. "If Kapu can do without me."

"Let's hope he won't deprive us of your stimulating presence."

She glanced at Lani and found her friend staring at her with speculation. She could hardly blame her; Cassie didn't seem to know herself what she was going to do from minute to minute.

Lani turned back to Bradford. "Tell us of this Morland. I wish to know more than the temperature of the water."

That evening Lani wore her yellow silk gown that turned her into a brilliant bird of paradise. At supper she glowed, she smiled, she told amusing stories of island myths and daily doings. Cassie had never seen Lani like that. Freed of Clara's oppressive presence, she bloomed like a golden orchid. She kept both men entertained and intrigued, effortlessly drawing them into her spell. Bradford responded eagerly to her sallies, and even Jared relaxed and displayed a wry humor.

Cassie watched him in fascination as he leaned forward, dark, cynical, yet totally at ease, his gaze on Lani's face. This must be the way he was in his own world, she thought, sitting at dinner tables at Brighton or London.

At the end of the meal Jared turned to Cassie while Lani was talking to Bradford. "You're very quiet. You've been sitting there watching and scarcely saying a word. Should I be worried you're planning on poisoning me again?"

"No." *Quiet* was a fitting word for her, she thought in disgust—quiet and mouselike and nondescript in Lani's shadow. She said stiltedly, "I don't feel like talking."

His eyes narrowed. "And you don't feel like being here. Why are you?"

"I have to eat somewhere."

"So you choose my table?"

"Lord Bradford invited us."

He looked at her skeptically before glancing back

at Lani. "Your friend is very splendid tonight and obviously trying to be . . . obliging."

"Yes."

"A lovely gown."

"Papa bought it for her."

"How kind of Papa." He added with sudden harshness, "He should have taken the trouble to purchase something of equal quality for you. That gown you're wearing is quite detestable. Don't you have anything else?"

"Yes, but they're all much the same." She was wearing the same gray silk gown she had worn that night at the cottage. How odd that his cruel condemnation on such a trivial subject could hurt her. "Clara chose them. Papa knew that it didn't matter to me."

"It should have mattered to him." He took a drink of his wine. "You look like a nun wrapped in a shroud. It's an abomination."

"Then don't look at me," she said.

"I *have* to look at you." A little of his wine spilled on the damask cloth as he set the wineglass down with some force. "And why in Hades aren't you fighting me? Are you ill?"

"No." But perhaps she was ill. She felt stifled, and beset by a queer nagging pain every time she looked at Lani. At any rate, she could bear no more tonight. The legs of her chair screeched as she abruptly pushed it back. "It was a mistake to come. I shouldn't be here. I have to go see if Kapu is all right."

"No, you don't. I have one of the men watching him." He shook his head as he saw her eyes widen with alarm. "From a distance. He was only to watch and come get me if he thought the horse was becoming restless."

She breathed a sigh of relief. Events were clouded enough without her having to worry about Kapu trampling someone. "You need not bother. I'll change and go to him now."

"I said you don't need to go," he uttered between his teeth.

Ignoring him, she nodded to Bradford and murmured a quick good night to Lani, then almost ran from the room.

Danemount caught up with her before she reached the door of her cabin. His hand fell on her shoulder, and he whirled her to face him. "Why?" he demanded grimly.

His hand felt heavy, warm and disturbing. She shrugged it off and stepped back. "I told you why I'm going to Kapu," she said, her gaze fastened on his cravat. "Because he needs me."

"You know that's not what I mean. Why is your friend Lani shining like a crystal chandelier, giving us sweet smiles and sweeter words?"

"What difference does it make? You seemed to enjoy it."

"Of course I enjoyed it. She's a charming woman . . . and an honest one. Which is why I don't understand all this."

"Don't worry, she won't poison you. She disapproved of my putting the laudanum in Clara's syllabub." She tried to turn away, but his hands tightened on her shoulders. "Let me go."

"In a moment. Look at me."

"I don't want to look at you. I've seen enough of all of you tonight."

"You'd rather stare at your horse, no doubt."

"Yes."

"Christ." He drew a deep breath and said with measured precision, "Very well, we won't talk about Lani. Tell me your reason for coming to supper tonight."

"It was a mistake."

"And what reasoning engendered the mistake?"

"I wasn't thinking clearly. I wanted to see—" What? Lani as alluring as Venus. Danemount attracted in spite of himself. If that was her intention, she had certainly got what she wanted. Why had it made her so confused and miserable? "I don't know."

"I think you do know."

"Then you're a fool." She tore away from him. "And I don't want to talk about it. Leave me alone."

He gazed at her a moment before saying slowly, "By God, I wish I could."

He turned and walked away from her.

And back to Lani—beautiful, wonderful Lani, who would give him much more than sweet smiles tonight if he asked it of her.

She ran the short distance to her cabin. Lani was doing what she thought best. Lani was the wisest person she knew. If she thought this way would help Papa, then who was Cassie to argue with her?

So why did she feel this torment? It made no sense that—

A growl, low and menacing . . .

Her head swiftly lifted, her gaze flying to the horizon. Thunder? The moon was shining brightly overhead, but in the distance she could see a churning mass of clouds.

"No, please, don't come closer," she whispered. Storms meant pitching decks and loud thunder. Kapu would go crazy in a storm. There was even more danger for him in the confines of the stall than in the water. If he became excited, he might break a leg or ram his head—

To devil with bothering to change her gown.

She turned and ran toward the cargo hold.

Seven

Thunder. Closer. No longer a growl but a roar.
Jared rolled over on his side to face the window next to his bunk, watching as a jagged bolt of lightning tore through the sky.

Dammit, he had hoped the storm would pass. He had no desire to go back down in that cargo hold and face Cassie Deville. He had wanted to distance himself, give himself time to rid his mind of the restraints Bradford had skillfully placed on him. If he went to her now, it would be again as a comrade sharing peril. He didn't want the blasted woman as a comrade—he wanted her in his bed.

Another lightning bolt lit the heavens.

He didn't have to go to her. She had assured him she could handle Kapu by herself.

The ship began to list as the wind quickened.

He could send one of the seamen to watch and make sure there was no real danger.

A crash of thunder shook the ship!

"Damnation!"

· · ·

"No, boy, don't fight it. It will be gone soon." Cassie's arms tightened frantically around Kapu's neck. Dear heaven, how she had prayed the storm would be gone. Every crash of thunder was causing a ripple of panic to go through her.

Kapu tried to back away, his nostrils flaring as the ship dipped sharply. She followed, talking to him. Let him not rear or batter against the wall. "Easy. Just be calm. You know it will break my heart if you hurt yourself."

"Stand back from him."

Cassie looked over her shoulder to see Jared standing at the top of the steps in the open doorway. He was barefoot, his shirt buttoned only halfway, his hair wild and wind torn and his expression forbidding.

None of that made her fearful. She wasn't alone anymore. Jared had helped her save Kapu before—maybe he could again. "I can't stand back. He's afraid. He's calmer if I touch him."

Jared muttered a curse before battling the wind to jerk the door closed. A moment later he was in the stall, on the other side of Kapu. It was like the night they had brought Kapu on board. Surely, the result would be the same, she thought desperately; Kapu would quiet, and the danger would be over.

A crash of thunder!

Kapu reared straight up, taking her with him!

Jared tore her arms from the neck of the stallion and pushed her to one side. He jerked something from the waistband of his trousers and tossed it to her. "Cover his eyes."

Black cloth. She recognized the cravat he'd worn at supper. "Blindfold him?"

"He'll be able to hear and feel the pitch of the ship, but he won't be able to see his world topsy-turvy.

Anything might help." He stepped closer beside the stallion. "Hurry!"

She moved in front of Kapu and inched closer. No thunder, she prayed; this pitching was bad enough. *Just give me a few minutes more. . . .*

Kapu was backing away from her.

"Please . . ."

Was she pleading with God or Kapu? Jared was talking, too, stroking the stallion, trying to distract him.

It was no good, she realized in despair. It would never work this way.

She took a deep breath and jumped on his back!

"Christ!" she heard Jared cry out. "I didn't say to—"

"Be quiet." Her legs and arms held Kapu as she talked to him softly. Then she leaned forward and draped the cloth over Kapu's eyes. "Quick. Tie it."

Jared didn't argue. He had the cloth knotted in seconds.

Cassie held her breath, waiting.

Kapu half reared as he became aware of his blindness. He landed hard and tried to turn in a circle!

But Jared was there talking, stroking. Cassie held tight, hugging him close, glued to his back. *Please, no thunder. Let him get used to the darkness.*

The ship pitched and slid on the swells, but there was no thunder.

One minute. Two minutes. Every second was a gift.

Kapu was quieting, becoming accustomed to the darkness.

"Get off him." Jared's voice was still soft and soothing, but she was aware of the sharp wire of tension threading it. "Dammit, you don't mount a horse in the middle of a thunderstorm."

"I do." Her tone was as soft as his. "He likes to feel me on him. It helps. Now, stop telling me what I should do and keep talking to him."

"He doesn't know whether I'm talking to him or you."

"Of course he does."

Thunder.

Kapu reared straight up! Cassie's thighs tightened around him, her heart pounding. "We're here. Don't be afraid. We won't let anything happen to you."

He came down stiff-legged, the impact jarring. She closed her eyes, waiting for him to rear again or try to bolt.

He did neither. He stood there, trembling in every limb.

More thunder.

Miraculously, he stood still as they talked soothingly.

The first terror was over. She could feel the tears flowing down her cheeks. He was safe. Thank God.

The ship rode out the storm two hours later.

"Will you get down now?" Jared asked, pronouncing each word distinctly as the last thunder rolled into the distance.

"I don't know if I can," she said wearily. Every muscle was stiff and sore with the tension of the last hours.

Jared went around Kapu and lifted her off the stallion.

She held on to the horse's mane while she steadied herself. "Thank you," she whispered.

"You're a madwoman." His eyes were blazing down at her. "I'll be surprised if you live to be twenty. You should never have gotten on him."

"But then we wouldn't have been able to blindfold

him." She patted Kapu before burying her face in his mane. "You're a great deal of trouble, boy."

"Not nearly as much as his mistress."

She ignored the pang the jab brought. "How did you know a blindfold would help?"

"When I was a boy, I had a horse who was terrified of storms," he said as he pushed her away from the horse. "He's worked up a sweat. Sit while I rub him down."

"I can do it."

He glanced at her ruin of a gray gown. "I wouldn't think of having you become more bedraggled. We've already discussed how enchanting I find that garment."

She didn't argue. She wasn't sure she had the strength to move. She dropped down on the hay and leaned back against the wall of the stall.

He took up a cloth and began to wipe Kapu's coat. "No reply?"

She roused herself to respond, "Why should I? I don't care what you think of my gowns, Your Grace, and Lani says it should bring me great satisfaction to use an enemy as a stable boy."

"Lani is a wise woman. But don't you think you should address me by my given name, considering the humble status you've given me?"

"Perhaps." She watched him move around the horse, his movements swift, precise, yet gentle. He was all lean, compact muscle and athletic grace. He might be performing a stable boy's duty, but there was no servility about him; barefoot, dark hair wild, he looked more the arrogant warrior caring for his battle steed. His shirt was totally open now, and she could see the triangle of dark hair that thatched his gleaming chest. She had touched that chest, felt the washboard muscles of his belly that had tightened beneath her hands and—

"Why are you staring at me?"

Her gaze flew up to his face and saw that his eyes were narrowed on her.

She glanced hurriedly downward, trying desperately to think of something to say. "Your feet are bare."

"I was in a hurry to get to you," he said slowly. "I regret if it offends you."

"No, it was good of you to—I didn't mean—" She was stuttering like an idiot, she realized with annoyance. "Why would it offend me? I often go barefoot."

"And your feet aren't the only portions of your body you bare," he said with a distinct edge to his voice. "Though no one would guess it by looking at you in that shroud."

She kept her gaze fixed on his feet. "You won't have to look at me in it after tonight. It's beyond repair."

"Good."

Silence fell between them. The only sounds were the soft swish of the cloth on Kapu's back and the distant whisper of thunder.

"That should do it." He tossed the cloth aside and gave Kapu a final pat. The stallion whickered and pressed his face against Jared's bare chest. He laughed and pushed the horse away before he turned to face her. "Anything else?"

"What?"

His eyes were glittering recklessly, and she stiffened as he moved toward her.

"Are there any other services you require?" He dropped to his knees in front of her. "Lani said you should make use of me. Don't you always do as Lani says?"

"Most of the time." She moistened her lips. "She's usually right."

"Is she? Then use the enemy," he urged softly. He took her hand, his thumb stroking the inside of her wrist. "As I intend to do."

She felt as if every stroke were sending little tingling ripples up her arm. Her throat tightened and she could scarcely breathe. He was so close she could smell the clean scent of him, feel the heat his body emitted.

"Let me go," she whispered.

"I'm not holding you." He smiled. "Not really. Not the way I want to hold you. Just this tiny touch on your wrist." His thumb leisurely moved up to her forearm. "And here . . ."

It was not true. He *was* holding her. She felt as if she were chained in place. The tingling was spreading to her shoulders and her breasts, and a strange languid heat was flowing through her.

He lifted her wrist until she could feel his breath on her skin with every low word. "You've seen what a good stable boy I am. Kapu enjoyed my wiping him down. Would you like me to do it to you?"

Her eyes widened in shock.

"First, I'd rid you of that nun's gown." He blew softly on the veins of her wrist. "Then I'd lay you on it so that the hay wouldn't mark your skin. You have such soft skin. . . ."

She was shaking as if she had the fever. "No . . ."

"Would you rather feel the roughness?" His tongue gently touched her wrist. "Whatever you want. I'll give you whatever you want. Just give me what I want in return."

"You can't give me anything. It's not—" She broke off as a long shudder went through her. He was licking delicately, sensuously, at her wrist as if she were some rare, exotic tidbit.

I'd like to lick the salt from your breasts.

The memory of his words pounded through her mind as she felt his warm tongue on her skin. What was the matter with her? Why couldn't she move? It was as if he were weaving some magic spell about her. Kahuna. Beautiful, seductive Kahuna . . .

"Rough or gentle. You tell me." Dark plum color flushed his cheeks and his voice was thick. "Let me open your thighs and put my hands on you, in you. I'll make you feel things you've never known before. You'll like my touch as much as Kapu did. I promise you, Cassie. Just let me—"

"No." She meant the word to be firm, but it came out a weak, mere breath of sound. She was not weak, she told herself frantically. She could break this spell. She jerked her arm away and scooted back from him. "How could you think I would do that?" she asked unevenly. "I don't want any of this."

He reached out as if he would touch her again, and then his hand dropped. "Do you think I do?" His voice was suddenly harsh. "But it's here. It's real." He paused and tried to temper his tone. "So compromises must be made. I've grown used to compromises over the years. We can't always have what we want. You must have discovered that, living with your father and sweet Clara Kidman."

And he had lived a life of privilege and self-indulgence. What wealth had not provided he would have won by that seductive charm. "I don't think you've ever made a compromise," she told him.

"Then you'd be wrong." He smiled cynically. "I

made one two minutes ago when I didn't throw you down in the straw and have my wicked way with you."

She inhaled sharply.

"Don't look like that. I don't want to force you. But, dammit, I'm not accustomed to celibacy, and I'm not going to be able to keep myself from—" He rose to his feet, his entire body charged with leashed frustration. "So you'd better learn to make a few compromises yourself. You were very close to letting me have you tonight. If you won't admit it to me, at least be honest with yourself."

"I won't—" Her voice was agonized. "I can't."

"Come to terms with it. Before this voyage is over, you're going to be in my bed. And you're going to want to be there. I don't care how you justify it to yourself. It's going to happen." He stopped and drew a long breath. "Think about it." He strode toward the steps. "God knows I will!"

The door slammed behind him.

She crossed her arms over her chest to help still their trembling. He was wrong. She had not been near surrendering to that powerful sensual force. True, she had been dazzled, held captive for a moment, but only because she was weary and strained and—

If you won't admit it to me, at least be honest with yourself.

You've been robbed of time. You must think clearly.

Use me. I intend to use you.

It's going to happen.

Lani's words. Jared's words. Both were whirling, mingling in her mind like the winds of the storm.

She leaned her head back against the wall and closed her eyes. What had happened tonight had torn aside the protective veil she had drawn around her, and she felt naked . . . and hurting.

Think about it.

Good God, how could she do anything else?

Lani was walking on deck when Cassie left the cargo hold the next morning. She made a face as she caught sight of Cassie. "You look terrible. Didn't you sleep at all?"

"A little. It was a terrible storm."

Lani nodded. "I slept little myself. I've no faith in that drunken sot as a captain." She added grudgingly, "Though he appeared to display a surprising control of the vessel last night." She dismissed the subject of Bradford as her gaze raked Cassie. "Well, that gown is certainly a disaster." She suddenly chuckled. "Which is one good occurrence in a bad night." When Cassie didn't agree at once, her smile faded. "What's wrong? Was Kapu hurt?"

Cassie smiled with an effort. "He's fine."

"I was about to go to you when the thunder started, but I saw our kindly host on his way to the hold, and I knew he'd be more help than I."

"He was a great help."

Lani frowned. "Then why do you look as if you're—" She stopped as Cassie looked away from her. "Talk to me, Cassie."

"There's nothing to say." She quickened her pace. "I only need to bathe and then go to my bed."

And come to terms with the frightening decision she had made after those long hours of searching her mind and emotions. She didn't want to be with any-one right now, not even Lani. She felt as finely bal-anced as a tightrope walker who would topple at a whisper. "I'll see you after I wake, Lani."

She was aware of Lani's puzzled gaze on her back as she hurried away.

"You look superb tonight." Jared bowed over Lani's hand before glancing around the dining hall with assumed casualness. "And will your friend be joining us for supper?"

"I think not." Lani gave him a dazzling smile. "As you know, she had a bad night with Kapu and is very weary. She prefers to eat in her cabin."

"I've not seen her all day," Bradford commented as he seated Lani. "Is she well?"

"Oh, Cassie is never sick."

"Except when she falls down mountains or tries to drown herself riding half-mad stallions," Jared said dryly.

"She never did any of those things before you came to our island," Lani said with great gentleness. She turned to Bradford. "I do hope you've chosen the wine tonight. You have such a depth of experience to draw on."

It seemed Lani was not all sweetness tonight, Jared thought as he watched her during supper. She was still glowing, still entertaining, but there had been a subtle shift of mood as demonstrated by those first velvet sheathed barbs.

Yet the smile she gave him at the end of the meal was as warm as sunlight. "Will you walk with me to my cabin? I would have words with you."

"We'll both go with you," Bradford said, pushing back his chair.

"No." She didn't look at him as she rose to her feet. "Stay and enjoy your brandy. It clearly means so much to you."

Bradford flinched. "Dismissed." He reached for the bottle. "Well, why not?"

Jared followed her from the cabin.

She looked up at the sky and drew a deep breath. "It's lovely, isn't it? It reminds me of the nights when I was a young girl, racing down the beach with my friends."

"Yes, lovely," he said absently. The night sky was clear, with no hint of last night's storm, and the motion of the sea as calm as the rocking of a baby's cradle. The stallion should be no problem tonight. Was Cassie down in the hold with Kapu now? Probably. She hadn't been there when he had gone to check on the horse earlier in the evening, but she couldn't stay away from the damned stallion.

Lani suddenly turned to him and asked bluntly, "What did you do to her last night?"

He went still. "I beg your pardon?"

"When Cassie came back to her cabin this morning, she was"—Lani hesitated—"different. Quiet. I don't know." She shook her head in frustration. "She wouldn't talk to me. She was not herself." She met his gaze. "I didn't like it. Cassie is my little sister. She thinks she's a woman, but she's still half child. I won't have her hurt."

He looked at her in astonishment. "Am I to assume you're asking my intentions?"

"No, I know your intentions. They are the same as all men. I'm merely telling you that on no account will I permit you to force her."

He stiffened. "I'm not in the habit of forcing women."

"I didn't think you were, but Cassie was very . . ." She trailed off and then said, "This is too perplexing.

I had intentions of— I don't like being uncertain about things."

"You're not alone. I've not the slightest idea what you're talking about."

"You would have had a very clear idea by now if Cassie were not—" She broke off again, and her pace quickened the last few yards to her cabin. "Perhaps tomorrow . . ." The door of the cabin slammed behind her.

Jared stared at the door for an instant before he whirled on his heel and strode back toward his cabin. What in Hades was that all about? Lani was not a woman to be unsure about anything, but her conduct tonight had been hesitant in the extreme. Well, he had no patience with delving into another woman's vagaries when he had Cassie's tormenting him.

His pace slowed before he reached his cabin, his gaze on the door leading to the cargo hold. Should he go down and see her? Last night, he knew, she had been closer than she dreamed to surrender.

She was not herself.

I will not have her hurt.

Dammit, he had no intention of hurting her. He just wanted to— He would make sure she enjoyed it as much as he did. She *wanted* it. He was experienced enough to know when a woman was ready for him. It would not have been force.

Christ, why was he arguing with himself? He had spent a hellish night, tossing and turning, heavy and aching, after he had left her. Why not just go down and take what he wanted?

He took a half step forward and then stopped. It could be she wasn't even with Kapu. Lani had said she was weary. Perhaps it had not been the excuse he had thought it. The trials she had undergone during the past few days would have been wearing on anyone.

Softness again, he realized impatiently. The chit had him hesitating and caviling like a boy with his first mistress.

He turned back to his cabin. It would do no harm to let another day pass before he resumed the hunt. That wasn't quite true, he corrected himself ruefully as he threw open the door. He would no doubt spend another tormented night and would soon be cursing his decision and the foolish impulse that—

"Good evening." Cassie rose from the chair and faced him, a touch of bravado in her stance. "I thought you'd never come."

His eyes widened as he stood frozen in the doorway. "Good God."

She was barefoot, bare-breasted, and her hips were draped in the sarong she had worn the night he had met her. His gaze slowly moved over her, from flowing hair to pink-tipped breasts, and then lifted to her face. Her cheeks were burning with color, but her eyes met his with defiance.

"I've been waiting a long time," she said.

The sheer lust that tore through him was so violent, it shocked him. It was immediately followed by fierce triumph. By God, she was *his*.

He stepped into the cabin and closed the door. "But it's said all good things come to one who waits. I'll try to see if I can't reward you for your patience."

She had not felt naked until he walked into the cabin. Her breasts swelled as his glance touched them, and her knees felt weak as she stood before him. But she was not weak; she must show him only strength, or she would be lost. She took a deep breath to ease the

tightness in her chest. "I'm not patient. I *hated* waiting for you."

"Well, I'm here now." He paused, his gaze wandering down to the sarong. "Kanoa, I presume? I know I said I detested that gown, but I'm surprised you went to such lengths to please me."

"I didn't wear this to please you, I did it to please me. I feel more comfortable in it." She lifted her chin. "What you want means nothing to me."

"Then why are you here?"

She moistened her lips. "Why do you think? I'm not the first island woman to come to your cabin."

"You're certainly the most interesting." He leaned back against the door and crossed his arms over his chest. "But I'd prefer you put it into words."

She couldn't say them. She had not thought it would be this difficult. She started across the cabin toward him. "To devil with words. You know why I'm here."

"You've decided to let me have you?" he asked softly.

"No." She stopped before him and stared directly into his eyes. "I've decided to use you."

His smile faded, and she thought she saw a flicker of anger in his expression. "I see. I suppose I should have expected that response. May I ask in exactly what manner?"

Her gaze went to the bunk. "It seems very clear."

"Nothing has ever been clear between us."

She drew a deep breath, then said in a rush, "I've reached the time when my body needs a man. You will do as well as anyone."

"Thank you," he said caustically. "How flattering."

She couldn't help it if he was displeased. It was his own fault; he had asked for an explanation. "I've thought about what you said. For some reason I find you . . ." She hesitated, searching for words. "You draw me. I cannot understand it."

"Oh, I can. I'm a very charming fellow."

"You're my father's enemy," she said flatly. "And my body should be more selective. But since it is not, then I must find a way to please both my body and my father's needs."

"Then, by all means, let me—" He smiled sardonically. "The temptation to lie to you is almost irresistible. I believe I must be more virtuous than Bradford thinks, or I wouldn't bother. If you think by playing Delilah I'll soften toward your father, you'll be disappointed. I'll be more than happy to please your body, but it won't change my intentions."

"Don't be ridiculous. First, you call me Lucrezia and then Delilah. I didn't poison you, and I wouldn't know how to go about playing Delilah. But Lani thinks—" She stopped.

"What does Lani think?"

She shrugged. "She thinks you're not as hard as you'd like to be. She says you might have second thoughts about killing Papa if—"

"If you couple with me?" he prompted.

"I told her it wouldn't do any good, but she thinks that you're—" She broke off again and gestured impatiently. "It doesn't matter what she thinks. I know you have no softness, but if I'm close to you, I'll still find a way to use you."

"A challenge," he said softly.

"I don't mean to challenge you. You wanted an explanation. I gave it."

"With your usual honesty and bluntness. I do believe I must teach you a bit of diplomacy for the sake of my self-love."

"I don't care about your self-love. I don't care anything about you."

He lifted a brow. "Yet you wish to give yourself to me."

"You keep saying that. I'll never *give* myself. That's not why I'm here."

"Isn't it the same thing?"

"Not to me," she said. "And I don't think it's the same to you, either. You'd like to think I'd meekly surrender to you."

He slowly shook his head. "You're wrong. I'd be very disappointed if you surrendered, and I can't imagine your doing anything meekly." His gaze moved down to her breasts and his smile was purely sensual. "It's my earnest hope you'll display no meekness whatever."

A tide of heat enveloped her, and she had to take a moment to steady her voice. "Then you'll not be disappointed. I'm coming to you because it suits me to do it. After we couple, I'll get up and walk away. It will mean nothing to me."

Rage momentarily crossed his face before he said lightly, "What a peculiar attitude for a woman."

"Only peculiar to a man. You all wish us to be meek and faithful and let you be the ones to get up and walk away. Your world is very unfair, and I won't live by your rules."

"All of this is more of your Lani's teachings, no doubt. Do you know, I believe I value your virginity more than you do. I actually felt quite guilt ridden before I overcame it."

She shrugged. "Because you're a foreigner and have strange ideas." This pose of boldness was growing more difficult by the moment. Why wouldn't he stop talking and begin their coupling? Anything would be better than this tension. "Why are you just standing there? I don't want to talk anymore."

"But I do. I find it fascinating to explore your reasoning in this matter."

"Why? You told me to use you as you intended to use me, and you said I'd come to your way of thinking."

"But not this quickly." His gaze went to the sarong. "And not in this charmingly barbaric fashion. Now, I wonder why you chose to present yourself in this guise."

"It's no guise. As I've said, I feel most comfortable dressed this way."

"It's the way Kanoa would feel the most comfortable," he corrected. "Not Cassandra Deville. Kanoa would dress like this. Kanoa would not hesitate to come to my bed. I'd wager you came to me like this because at the moment it's easier pretending to be Lani's little sister."

"I'm not pretending." She had acted purely on instinct when she had donned the sarong. She had not even thought about it. "I don't need excuses to do what I choose."

"Kanoa doesn't need excuses, but what of Clara Kidman's charge?"

She was beginning to think he might be right and was becoming uneasy that he knew her so well. "What does any of this matter? Don't you want me?"

His mockery vanished. "God, yes, I want you," he said thickly.

She inhaled sharply. "Then stop arguing. What difference does it make? I told you why I came here."

"To use me." He repeated the words with a grimace. "For some odd reason the term bothers me."

"You don't make sense. It's the term you used to me."

"I know." He unfolded his arms but still did not touch her. "But it's difficult to think coolly at a time like this." Suddenly he laughed harshly. "Christ, I can't believe I'm still standing here instead of inside you on that bed."

He reached out and touched her upper lip with his index finger.

She stiffened at the gentle touch as if he had struck her with a torch. Her lips felt as if they were swelling, softening, ripening at the caress. She involuntarily jerked her head back.

"No." He took a step closer and his finger outlined her upper lip. "No, Kanoa, let me . . . This is why you came here."

She stared up at him in helpless fascination as wave after wave of heat washed over her. "I don't think that this is all I came for."

He chuckled. "You're damn right it isn't. But I have to start somewhere. I've never had a virgin before, and this seems fairly innocuous."

Not to her. Everything he did or said, everything about him shimmered with sensuality—the scent of him, the planes of his face, the tension of his body. She was drowning in it, and her gaze clung to his as if to a safe mooring. No safety there, only glittering promise.

His fingers brushed the upper swell of her breast.

She shivered, and the muscles of her stomach contracted in response.

"You'll take me and then get up and walk away?" he murmured.

"Yes."

His fingers were at the knot of her sarong. "It will mean nothing to you?"

She had to force the answer through dry lips. "Nothing."

The sarong fell to the floor. She was naked.

He unbuttoned his shirt and threw it aside. "The hell it won't." He buried his hands in her hair and tilted back her head. His eyes were blazing. "I won't be nothing to anyone, goddammit." He pulled her into the cradle of his hips. Arousal. Stark, bold, merciless against her nakedness. "Is this nothing?" His palms cupped her buttocks, lifting her, rubbing her against him.

Shock tingled through her. The hair of his chest was brushing against her nipples, and they were growing more sensitive and hard with every passing second.

"Is it?" he asked again.

She could barely remember the question. "It's very pleasant . . . I think."

"And this?" His head bent, his tongue touched her nipple.

She cried out, her spine arched.

He lifted his head and he smiled. "Pleasant? I think you'll find that too tame a word." Then his lips closed on her breast, sucking strongly.

Fire. Hunger. Emptiness. It seemed impossible they could exist together, but they did. She reached out, her fingers burying themselves in his hair, holding him to her. Dear heaven, even the feel of his hair between her fingers was causing a tingling heat. She wanted to scream, moan . . .

He switched to her other breast, sucking, licking. His hands began to open and close on her buttocks. Pressure. Heat. Her heart was beating so hard it filled the cabin—no, it filled the world. Darkness and flame . . . and hunger.

He finally lifted his head and looked down at her dazed face. "I can't take this anymore," he said hoarsely. "I have to be inside you." He took her hand and pulled her toward the bunk. "Come."

She followed him docilely. In that moment she would have followed him anywhere.

Then he was over her, parting her thighs and moving between them. His hand was on the curls surrounding her womanhood, patting, stroking. "So soft." He tugged gently as he positioned himself. The muscles of her stomach clenched as a bolt of heat went through her. He nodded. "You like that? I'll give you more after I—" He stopped, not moving. "Christ." He looked down at her. "I don't know anything about this."

She looked at him in bewilderment through the haze of lust he had so skillfully built around her. What on earth was he talking about? It was clear to her he knew everything about this. "You appear to be very . . . well versed."

"Not with virgins, dammit. I don't know— It's supposed to hurt. I should take more time."

More time? When every nerve in her body was on fire? "No!"

"But I don't want to—" He broke off when she took matters into her own hands and lunged upward. His eyes closed as her tightness closed around him. "Damnation."

He plunged hard and deep!

Pain. Fullness. Joining.

Her teeth sank into her lower lip as sensation after sensation stormed through her. She felt so stretched, she was sure she could take no more. Yet, as the pain subsided, she was beginning to feel again that throbbing emptiness that had to be satisfied.

He was frozen within her, every muscle of his body knotted and strained. "Shall I move?" he asked in a low voice.

She would die if he didn't. "Yes."

"Thank God!" Some of the tension left him, but he was still braced as if on the rack. He moved stiffly, the first few thrusts slow, easy. "I'll try to—" he whispered. "It's no good. I'm sorry. I can't do—"

He exploded, thrusting short, long, fast, frantic.

She clutched his shoulders, desperately holding on to him as that emptiness grew and the hunger sharpened. She tried to help him, thrusting upward, instinctively clenching around him to keep him inside her when he left her.

"No, don't do that," he gasped. "I can't—"

She had to do it. She had to have all of him. Her head thrashed wildly from side to side on the pillow. She could feel the wetness on her cheeks, and she realized tears were streaming from her eyes. Lani had said this unbearable hunger was supposed to end. Why didn't it? Why was it growing and changing, making a slave of her body until she could only move mindlessly to the rhythm Jared set?

"Please, make it—" She didn't know what she wanted to ask of him. Make the torment stop. Make it go on forever. Belonging. Every stroke was drawing them closer. Jared. Possession. Darkness. Hunger. Faster, harder, Jared's breath was a harsh sob above her.

Or was she the one who was sobbing? It didn't matter, they were one.

"Now!" he said through his teeth, plunging to the heart of her.

She screamed as the dark hunger exploded, splintered into a brilliance like nothing she'd ever known. Jared collapsed on top of her. "Dear God."

It seemed they lay joined together a long time, but Jared's breath was still harsh and uneven when he leaned forward and his lips brushed her closed lids. "I think it's safe to assume you found me 'pleasant.' You're definitely more Kanoa than prim Cassandra."

His voice was a velvet reverberation in the darkness, Cassie thought dreamily, as lazily seductive as a summer breeze. This was beautiful, but she wanted it to start again. Soon he would touch her, stroke her, and the flames would start.

She opened her eyes. He was only a heartbeat away, looking down at her, his eyes so blue and clear she felt as if she were looking into forever. She wanted it to be forever. She wanted to float on and on in this special place until there were no more tomorrows. "Ku'aihelani," she murmured.

"I beg your pardon?" He kissed the tip of her nose. "I don't believe I know that word."

"It's not a word, it's a place. It's where—" She broke off as she came fully awake. This was not forever. This was no Ku'aihelani. What was she thinking? "Never mind."

"But I do mind. I'm a very curious man." He tugged at the lobe of her ear with his teeth, pressing just hard enough to send a tiny tingling through her. "I want to know about this Ku'aihelani. I want to know everything about you."

So that he could possess her mind as he had her body. Panic shot through her as the memory of that joining surged back. Dear God, what had possessed her? She knew the answer. *He* had possessed her, and dominated her and made her forget everything except what he had wanted her to feel.

She pushed him away with all her strength, catching him unawares. She jumped out of bed, looking around wildly for her sarong.

"Where the devil are you going?" Jared raised himself on one elbow. "Come back to bed."

"Why?" She picked up the sarong from the floor and jerkily wrapped it around her hips. "It's over. I'm going back to my cabin."

"It's not over. We've barely started."

She whirled on him. "It's *over*. I chose to come here. I choose to leave. You have nothing to do with it."

His lips tightened. "I beg to disagree. I had considerable to do with it ten minutes ago. I'm reluctant to be cast aside so arbitrarily."

"I told you that I'd walk away. I told you coupling with you would mean nothing to me." She brushed her hair back from her face with a shaking hand. "Nothing at all."

His gaze narrowed on her face. "Then why are you running away?"

"I'm not running away."

"I think you are." He held out his hand in invitation—naked, powerful, infinitely sexual. "Prove it," he said softly. "Stay. I've only begun to show you the way of it. Pleasure has many faces."

And his was the most alluring she had ever known. She took a half step forward before she realized what she was doing. She moistened her lips. "I'll come again . . . when it pleases me."

"Now." There was steel beneath the velvet.

She glared at him. "Only when it pleases me. I set the pace."

"The devil you will." He swung his legs to the floor. "You forget where you are. I can do what I will with you." He moved across the cabin. "Get back into that—" He broke off as he saw her face. "By God, I believe you're afraid."

"I'm not afraid."

"Did I hurt you?" He touched her cheek with infinite gentleness. "I know I was rough, but I didn't think I—"

"You didn't hurt me." His touch was causing her to tremble again. She wanted to lean forward against him, she wanted to reach out and—

She took a step back. "Why should I fear you?"

"I don't know." He studied her for a moment before adding roughly, "But, then, I never know what you're thinking. I keep forgetting what a child you are. Christ, maybe this is how all virgins respond after—" He turned away from her. "Get the hell out of here."

She stood unmoving, surprised by the sudden reversal.

"Leave," he said harshly. "Before I change my mind. You may have had enough of me, but I'm not so easily satisfied."

Neither was she, she realized in despair. She turned toward the door.

"Wait!" He snatched up his shirt from the floor and crossed back toward her. "Put this on."

She shook her head. She needed to be completely removed from him. She wanted nothing of his to remind her of that feeling of possession.

"Damn heathen shamelessness," he muttered. He forced her arms into the shirt. "There are seamen on duty out there."

"I know. I saw them when I came to you."

"And they saw you, no doubt." He started to button the shirt. "I don't want you to come to me like this again. At least wear a cloak."

"It's too warm for a cloak." The shirt smelled of him, and the soft linen was like a caress against her breasts, his caress. "And I don't want this. Take it off."

"If I do, I won't let you out of here until morning," he said grimly. "By God, I'm not letting any other man see you naked. You're so fond of being the one to choose. I warn you, make the right choice now."

She opened her lips to argue and then changed her mind. She wanted only to get away from him. "It's not worth discussing." She opened the door. "Good night."

"I doubt it," he muttered. "I'll see you tomorrow night."

She tensed, not looking at him. "I'm not sure— I may not decide to come to you tomorrow night."

"Then I'll come to you."

"No! *I* choose."

"It doesn't work that way. I'm willing to let you go tonight, but I'm no tame pup waiting for you to pick me up and play with me." He shook his head. "Poor Cassie, things aren't working out the way you expected, are they? Well, they aren't working out the way I thought, either. I hoped I'd be able to take you and then forget you. But it seems it's going to take more than one night." His tone laden with determination, he repeated, "I'll see you tomorrow night. I'll give you until midnight to come to me."

"I won't be here." The door slammed behind her.

Free. But she didn't feel free. His scent was on the shirt, on her skin, and she felt as if his hands were still on her body. She moved quickly down the deck toward her cabin. Once she was alone, she would scrub her skin until no hint of his touch remained.

But the memory would remain, the memory of the way he looked, the way he felt within her. . . . Sweet Mary, she was beginning to tremble again. Lani had never told her that she would feel like this afterward. If coupling meant nothing, why did she feel as if a tight chain bound her to Danemount even when she was no longer with him? She had the odd feeling that if either of them moved too far away from the other, the chain would tear them apart.

Imagination. She had lost her virginity this night, and perhaps she had paid more heed to Clara's words than she had realized. Clara had said a woman must come chaste to her husband's bed and cling only to him, or she would burn in hell. Well, Cassie had burned tonight. She had burned and trembled and cried out as he took and took and took. . . .

Don't think about it. Tomorrow she would be fine. Tomorrow she would realize that nothing had happened to her that had not happened to generations of women before her. She would laugh at this panic. She opened the door of her cabin. Tomorrow she would be herself and know—

"Are you well?" Lani asked quietly. She was sitting on the bunk across the room. "He did not hurt you?"

Cassie stopped in the doorway. "No," she whispered. "How did you know?"

"I came to see you when I returned from supper. You were not here." She smiled and shook her head. "It took no great intellect to guess where you had gone."

"But you didn't come after me."

"You know I never interfere with your decisions. It

would be an intrusion. But I wish you'd told me." She held out her arms. "Come."

Cassie flew across the room and dropped to her knees in front of Lani. Lani's arms enfolded her—warmth, safety, love. She buried her face in Lani's shoulder. "I had to do it," she whispered.

Lani stroked her hair. "Why?"

"You were right. It made sense for one of us to be close to him, if it could help Papa. We have to know when he receives word from France. But why should you have to do it when it might hurt you if Papa found out?"

"I was willing to take the risk."

"But you shouldn't have to do it when I—" She nestled closer; her words were muffled. "I wanted him."

"Shh, I know you did. Why are you so full of guilt? I told you that it was no betrayal if the passion was of the body alone."

"But I didn't think it would be like this."

Lani stroked her hair. "And how was it?"

She couldn't describe it, even to Lani. "It wasn't as you said. I . . . didn't want to walk away. It frightened me."

"But you did walk away?"

"Yes."

"Then it was no betrayal." Lani sighed. "But I wish you had not done it. I was hoping your first man would be pure joy. Was he kind to you?"

Kind. Had there been kindness in that storm of passion? She wanted to deny it, but there had been gentleness in his surprising hesitation before he had taken her. "He didn't hurt me." She lifted her head. "He wants me to come to him again."

"And are you going to do it?"

"It would be foolish of me not to, wouldn't it? This night would be for nothing." She paused. "But I don't . . . Why am I afraid, Lani?"

"You'll have to answer that yourself." She smiled. "I will tell you what I think, if you like. You suspect that you're not as strong as you'd thought. It's not true. You're stronger. You will see. You'll do whatever is necessary."

"Will I?" She felt a sudden surge of confidence. "Of course I will." She sat back on her heels. "I was afraid only because the coupling was . . . different from what I'd expected."

Lani leaned forward and kissed her on the forehead. "If you wish to refuse him, do it. We will make other plans." She rose to her feet. "I'll leave you to sleep. Rest well. I'll see you in the morning."

"Yes." She watched the door close behind Lani. She had been foolish to be frightened. She had the strength to keep mind and body apart when with Jared. She rose to her feet, quickly unbuttoned the shirt, and stripped it off. She could take what she wanted of him and discard him just as she had his shirt. She untied the sarong and tossed it on top of the shirt, then padded naked across the floor to the washstand. It would be easier the next time. She would be more prepared.

She would learn to walk away without a second glance.

Eight

S he was not in the least apprehensive, Cassie told herself as she walked into the dining cabin the next evening and saw Jared talking to Bradford. She'd had time to think over the events of last night and had come to the conclusion that her panic had been totally unreasonable. Lani had said there was no guilt, and Lani—

Jared turned to look at her, and she instinctively braced herself. His expression impassive, he said something to Bradford, then moved leisurely toward her. "I do believe that garment is even worse than the gray gown." Jared grimaced as his glance raked the high-necked, long-sleeved puce gown. He lifted Cassie's hand to his lips. "Didn't that dragon believe in revealing even one inch of skin?"

"You don't like it?"

"I abhor it."

She smiled serenely. "Good." She pulled her hand away. "But, then, you don't really know what you like, do you? Last night you were upset with me for displaying too much skin."

"That was different." His gaze narrowed on her face. "You appear to be in good spirits."

"Did you expect me to hide in my cabin? It's true I was a little discomposed afterward, but it didn't last long. After I talked it over with Lani, I felt much better."

He frowned. "You talked me over with your friend?"

"Of course. We agreed that nothing of any importance had occurred." She glanced around the dining hall. Bradford was now standing at the window across the cabin, but she did not see Lani. "Where is she?"

"I have no idea," he said through his teeth. "And I don't give a—" He broke off and suddenly threw back his head and laughed. "Christ, I just may heave you overboard before we get to England. My self-love is being stung at every turn."

She wished he had not shown that glimpse of rueful humor. It was easier to keep the barriers in place with a man who refused to laugh at himself. "I was only telling the truth."

"Truth is seldom kind. May I point out that it's definitely not the thing to denigrate the man who strove to make your deflowering as 'pleasant' as possible?"

He knew that word was too tame to describe his stormy possession. She had been trying all day to forget the details of their joining. "I didn't think there were social rules for behavior after a deflowering." She changed the subject. "Are you going to escort me to the table or stand here talking nonsense?"

"By all means," he murmured. "You clearly need sustenance to keep that tongue blade sharp." He took her arm. "I've changed my mind. I believe I approve of your wearing that gown."

She glanced at him in surprise. "You do?"

"I know it's a disappointment, but I expect to enjoy looking at you across the table tonight. Do you know why?"

She shook her head.

He looked straight before him, his voice soft. "Because I'm going to think of what's underneath that gown. I'm going to pretend you're as naked beneath it as you were last night. I'm going to consider that gown as rather ugly wrapping around a delightful present. I've always enjoyed removing the wrapping from my gifts. You cheated me of that last night."

She could feel heat sting her cheeks. So much for her confidence. Her heart was pounding wildly, and she suddenly felt unsure and shaken.

"I'm going to look at you across the table, and you'll know that I'm remembering what I did to you last night." His voice deepened. "Someday I'll persuade you to wear nothing beneath that gown. We'll dine alone, and you'll let me slip the gown to your waist so that I can see those lovely breasts. Later, while we're having coffee, you'll come and sit on my lap. I'll lift your skirt and look at you and press my palms on—"

"Stop it," she hissed. Even the roots of her hair felt on fire. They were only words, she told herself. Yet the picture he painted was there before her. She could feel his lean hardness beneath her thighs, feel his intent gaze.

"Have I upset you? I only thought you should know what's in store for you." He added silkily as they reached the table, "Though I realize you regard my attentions as totally 'unimportant.'"

She should have known he would find a way of getting back at her. No one could sting Jared without being stung in return. "You've not upset me. Imagine what you like. It won't bother me at all."

"Oh, I think I may have inserted some small— Ah, here's the lovely Lani."

With relief she turned to see Lani glide into the cabin. Bradford was already halfway across the room, his expression lit with eagerness as he hurried toward her. He looked remarkably boyish, she thought absently. Jared was the one who appeared older, more experienced, steeped in cynicism.

"Bradford is quite enthralled with your friend," he said idly. "One can't blame the poor man. She's done her best to dazzle him."

She said without thinking, "No, she didn't. It was supposed to be you."

"What?"

She hadn't meant to blurt out the truth. Oh, well, it didn't matter now. "Lani was going to be the one to couple with you."

He went still. "Indeed?"

"But Papa wouldn't have liked it."

He said silkily, "So you decided to sacrifice yourself instead. I can't tell you how enchanted I am to know that fact. Tell me, did you draw lots to see which one of you would come to my bed?"

Such a little thing to irritate him. "No. I told you, Papa wouldn't have liked her to do it."

"I'm getting very tired of hearing about Deville's opinions." He strode to the head of the table. "Bradford! We're waiting."

"Coming," Bradford said over his shoulder. "Don't be impatient. I'm merely telling this lady how lovely I find her."

"I'm the one who is impatient." Lani ignored him

and swept toward the table. "I have no time for compliments. I'm hungry."

"I admire a woman of appetite," Jared said with a sideways glance at Cassie. "It's a quality to which I can relate. By the way, I was just telling Cassie how interesting I find her gown."

Cassie stiffened. He surely would not shame her by discussing the intimacies he had suggested to her. Or perhaps he would. It was clear he was very angry with her.

"Are you mad?" Lani asked as Bradford seated her. "It's very ugly."

"How cruel. I find anger has infinite potential." Jared motioned to the seaman at the door to begin serving. He dropped the subject. "Wine?"

As Cassie breathed a sigh of relief, Jared turned to her and gave a tigerish smile. He might have spared her shame, but she knew he wouldn't let her escape unscathed.

Yet during the entire dinner it appeared he would do just that. For the first time since she had met him, Jared acted the charming, courteous host, teasing Lani, speaking with dry humor to Bradford. Only with Cassie was he coolly polite.

It was exactly how she wanted him to behave, she assured herself. As long as he was cool to her, that dangerous intimacy would be kept at bay.

When the meal was almost over, Jared turned to Lani and asked casually, "By the way, do you know where Ku'aihelani is located?"

Cassie's gaze flew to his face. It seemed the truce was at an end, but she had not expected it to be broken in this manner.

Lani frowned in puzzlement. "Ku'aihelani?"

"You've never heard of it?"

"Of course I've heard of it. The question just surprised me." Her eyes were suddenly twinkling. "It's not often one is asked directions to paradise."

"Paradise?" He didn't look at Cassie as he picked up his glass of wine. "Is that what it is? I merely picked up the word somewhere."

From her own idiotic lips, Cassie thought with annoyance. She wished she had torn out her tongue before she'd let that word slip out.

"Ku'aihelani is the place of legend," Lani said. "And I couldn't tell you where it is, because, according to ancient mythology, it's a floating island. It's always drifting, never in one place long enough to be corrupted or destroyed. Paradise."

"How interesting," Jared murmured. He turned to Cassie and asked politely, "Don't you find it so?"

She wanted to slap him. She said curtly, "Not particularly." She pushed back her chair and rose to her feet. "I must check on Kapu. Good night."

"Oh, yes, Kapu." Jared stood and bowed slightly. "We mustn't forget about your wonderful stallion. But do be careful of that gown. I wouldn't want it destroyed like the gray one."

You'll let me slip it to your waist.

Her annoyance vanished, submerged in the flood of heat surging through her. She turned her back so he wouldn't see her face as she hurried toward the door.

"Wait!" Jared was beside her, opening the door. "I'll escort you to the hold."

"I need no escort. Go back to Lani and Bradford."

He lowered his voice. "I'll be expecting you later."

She looked straight ahead. "Will you?"

"There's no reason why not, is there? Since it means so little to you? To refuse me would put too much weight on the matter." He added mockingly, "You wouldn't want me to think you were running away after the first foray."

She didn't answer.

"And I'm a man who needs constant attention. If you don't come, I might have to seek solace with Lani, and that would displease Papa."

Her gaze flew to his face. "You would do that?"

"You'll never know unless you fail to provide me with your . . . company."

"Damn you."

His face hardened. "You should not have supplied me with a weapon if you didn't expect me to use it." He turned back to the table and gave Lani and Bradford a brilliant smile. "Be there."

When Cassie opened the door of his cabin, Jared was lolling naked on the bunk. The golden glow of the candlelight gilded his lean, tough body and heightened his aura of lazy sensuality. But all hint of laziness vanished when he saw her.

"Dammit, I told you to cover yourself," he said roughly. "Do you get pleasure out of flaunting yourself to every man who sees you?"

"I owe you no obedience." She closed the door. "I don't flaunt myself, and I'm sure your sailors are used to naked women by now." She stood looking at him. "If you don't like me as I am, then send me away."

"Not bloody likely," he muttered. "Take off that nothing bit of material and come here."

Her hands were trembling as she unknotted the cloth. "I didn't like your asking Lani questions tonight. It was an intrusion." The sarong dropped to the floor. "Don't do it again."

"I'll do as I please." He shifted on the bunk as she

came toward him. "You have so few weaknesses, you can't blame me for probing the ones I find." He pulled her down beside him and bent over her. "Just as you will do." His lips hovered over her breast, each word a burst of air that teased the sensitive nipple. He said thickly, "You have exquisite breasts, full . . . firm. After you left last night, I could still taste them, feel my tongue on you. I was so heavy and aching, I was cursing you. I wanted you back."

"So you forced me to come."

"Does this feel like force?"

He knew it didn't. He was exerting the same overwhelming seduction he had the night before, and she was responding in the same mindless manner. She felt as if she were melting, every muscle of her body helplessly yielding.

His hand was between her thighs, delicately exploring. "This part of you doesn't think I'm forcing you," he murmured. "You're ready for me."

Yes, she was, she realized in despair. She had been ready for him since the moment she had walked into the cabin.

"And God knows I'm ready for you." He suddenly rolled over onto his back and lifted her to straddle him.

She looked down at him, startled. "What are you doing?"

"You appeared so sad. I want you to be happy," he said mockingly. "You see, now you're the one in control, and I'm only the poor captive beneath you."

"I don't want—"

He thrust deep inside her.

She gasped at the sensation of the clublike fullness within. In this position she felt as if he had plunged to the quick. Her head fell backward, and she closed her eyes at the sheer sensual pleasure. She didn't feel in control. She felt captive as never before.

His hands reached up to squeeze her breasts. "Ride," he whispered. "Pretend I'm that precious stallion. You know you want to do it."

She didn't think she could move. She felt chained, anchored.

His hands moved down to her hips and held her sealed to him. "Ride me!" he gritted through set teeth.

His hips thrust forcefully upward.

She gasped as ripples of pleasure went through her. She reached out blindly and grasped his shoulders, instinctively tightening her thighs around his. "That's it." He lifted her and then pulled her down, slowly, teasingly, letting her feel every inch. "You know the way of it. Ready yourself and then—"

She was moving, rocking, riding, frantically taking him. She had thought their coming together last night savage, but this lust was all consuming.

"More," he growled. "Give me more." He jerked her down, his mouth enveloping her breast, sucking voraciously as his hips bucked frantically.

The combination of sensations was too much. She bit her lip to keep back the scream. It was no use. She screamed as release tore through her a moment later.

"Yes!" His arms tightened around her with such force, she could scarcely breathe. She was dimly aware of his release seconds later.

His arms loosened, and he lifted her off him and onto the bed beside him. "Force?" he whispered.

She had no breath to answer as she lay there looking up at him.

He smiled. "Ku'aihelani?"

"No! I didn't mean . . . I was half-asleep." She drew an unsteady breath. "I must go."

He threw his arm across her stomach. "No, you don't."

"I *want* to go."

He raised himself on his elbow to look down at her. "Then I'll have to change your mind, won't I? I have a fancy to wake you tomorrow morning in the most pleasant of ways."

His eyes were half-closed and shimmering; one tousled curl lay in disarray on his forehead—pagan, wicked, totally sensuous. She could feel that dark tide stir within her just looking at him. "You've won tonight. You're done with me. Why won't you let me leave?"

The lazy smile left his lips. "I don't feel as if I've won. I feel—" He broke off and removed his arm from her middle. He said roughly, "Go on. But you'll stay tomorrow night."

She shook her head as she slipped from the bunk.

"Why not?" he asked sharply. "What difference does it make? By now every man on this ship knows you're coupling with me. You've certainly not been trying to hide it with your parading around with no clothes."

"I don't care what they think." She had a sudden thought. "Does your uncle know?"

"Not from my lips, but I'd wager he does. Bradford has a way of knowing everything going on around him even through a haze of brandy." He paused. "Why? Do you mind?"

"No . . . I just . . . he was kind to me."

"And he'll continue to be kind to you. He would never think of intruding on us, and I'm the one who will get the edge of his tongue." He shrugged. "So there's no reason for you not to stay the night."

"There is reason." She put on her sarong. "I don't want you to . . ." She would not explain her dread of the intimacy that would be engendered by hours spent in his arms. Passion was dangerous enough. "I won't stay the night with you. I'll come to your bed, but then I'll go."

His gaze narrowed on her face. "Persephone?"

She frowned in puzzlement.

"Persephone was the woman with whom Hades, the God of the Underworld, was so besotted he permitted her to spend half the year on earth in sunlight as long as she came back to his dark world for the rest of the year." He glanced around the shadowy, candle-lit cabin. "There are certain similarities."

"Nonsense. You're certainly not besotted, and I will not ask your permission for anything."

"True." He slowly nodded his head. "Very well, we'll indulge in this most delightful of pastimes and then we'll part. There are certainly advantages to remaining strangers. No boring discussions, no necessity for protestations of affection we don't feel." He lay back down and put his arm beneath his head. "Why should I complain as long as you come to me and give me what I want?"

"You should not."

"Exactly." He closed his eyes. "One hour after supper tomorrow night I want you walking through that door. And don't wear that sarong again."

"I'll wear what I please."

"If you come to me with naked breasts, the next night I'll come to your cabin instead. Your beloved Lani's in the cabin next door. Do you want her to hear you scream with pleasure?"

Dear God, she didn't want that to happen. Lani might understand that it was her body and not her mind that was in thrall to Jared, but Cassie would know shame for showing her weakness. "No."

"Then don't make me angry. I won't have you running naked about the ship."

She slammed the door behind her.

Her hands clenched into fists at her sides as she stalked down the deck. The arrogance of his last words had been the final straw. She had lost too much tonight. When he had taken her, she had felt completely dominated, totally possessed. She couldn't let him have total victory.

The next night she paused outside Jared's door to gather her courage. How foolish to be shaking like this. She had made the decision and she would not back down. She mustn't think, just do it.

Cassie drew a deep breath and threw open the door. She strode into the cabin and slammed the door behind her.

"One hour after supper, Your Grace. Just as you commanded. I hurried to be sure I wouldn't anger you."

He stared at her in astonishment. "My God."

"Why are you glaring at me? I've done everything you told me to do." She touched the sarong she had wrapped around her upper body and shoulders. "And I'm no longer bare-breasted, you see? Doesn't that please you?"

She was naked from waist to feet. His gaze moved from bare hips to the tight curls that surrounded her womanhood. "Damn you."

Triumph. She felt a fierce surge of satisfaction. "I passed two of your seamen on the way to you, but I

assure you they didn't get one glimpse of my breasts."
He was rising from the bed and she braced herself.
"Though they did stare somewhat and—" She broke
off when he grabbed her shoulders. She lifted her
chin and injected a mocking note into her voice. "I
told you that you didn't know what you wanted.
Surely this isn't reasonable. Why are you so angry?"

"You know very well why I'm angry," he said
through his teeth as his hands tightened with bruising
force on her shoulders. "I could *strangle* you."

She glared at him. "You can't have everything your
way. I won't have it."

He shook her. "So you parade like a whore inviting
every man to use you. You're lucky you weren't raped
before you reached here."

"What difference if I'm raped by them on deck or
you here in the cabin?"

"Believe me, you'd know the difference. I've never
raped you." He shook her again. "Have I?"

"You're hurting me. Isn't that the prelude to
rape?"

"I want to hurt you." Nevertheless, his hands loosened slightly. "I'd like to—"

"Strangle me," she finished for him. "I know. You
needn't repeat yourself. It grows boring."

She saw at once she had gone too far. "I would hate
to bore you," he said silkily. "Let me see . . . now
what can I do to entertain you?" His hands left her
shoulders and moved down to cup her hips. "You obviously want attention paid to this portion of your
body. The invitation is so blatant."

"You know I meant no invitation."

"Part your legs."

"No."

His fingers moved probingly, skillfully. She tensed as a ripple of heat went through her.

"You know you like my hands on you."

"That doesn't mean I'll let you"—she gasped as his fingers stroked that most intimate part of her—"fondle me."

"Fondle?" He searched and found; his thumb and forefinger plucked at the nub. "Do you mean this?"

She shuddered as the muscles of her stomach clenched with need. She didn't answer.

Her silence seemed to make him even angrier. "Damn you." He stripped the sarong from her upper body, picked her up, and carried her toward the bed.

"I don't want you to do this," she said desperately.

"Then why did you come? You knew what would happen." He sat her down on the bed and knelt on the floor in front of her. He pushed her legs apart and looked at her. The blood surged to where his gaze was fastened, pulsing, hot, tingling. She felt naked, exposed, owned.

He said thickly, "I suppose I shouldn't blame you for wanting to display this treasure. You're very beautiful here."

She tried to close her legs, but he held them open with merciless grip.

"But I *do* blame you." His eyes were suddenly blazing up at her. Three fingers entered her, deep, thrusting.

She gasped as the intrusion sent a bolt of heat through her.

He withdrew and plunged and plunged again in pace with his words. "I—don't—want—you—ever—to—do—it—again."

Dark pleasure was cascading through her. She must not give in to it. This was not the sensuality he had shown her last night—this was violent and merciless. "I'll do—what I wish. You can't force me to—do otherwise."

"The hell I can't." He pushed her back onto the bed and loomed over her. "I'll see that you're not tempted to—" He stopped and closed his eyes. "God." His features contorted, then he got off her and stood up. "Did I . . . bruise you?" he asked curtly.

His withdrawal had come so suddenly, she couldn't quite comprehend it. She just stared at him.

"Well, did I?"

"No." She felt as exhausted as if she had been through a hurricane, but there was no pain.

He lay back down beside her and drew her into his arms. "Don't do this to me again." His words were muffled in her hair. "It's not safe. That's the closest I've ever been to raping a woman."

His embrace was tender, and that was as bewildering to her as the violence. She had never really known tenderness from him. She wanted to stay there, to yield to it just for a moment. "You don't understand, I can't let you—" She broke off and then said wearily, "I cannot promise."

He lifted his head and looked into her eyes. He didn't say anything for a moment. Then he rolled away from her and onto his back. "I see."

She had the uneasy feeling he spoke the truth, that he had seen her desperation to retain some control in these encounters.

He said, "Very well, but I'd advise you to find tamer ways to challenge me."

She had no other way. He held all the weapons. "I'll wear what I like."

"The devil you will. Don't you ever give—" He

shook his head. "All right, wear whatever suits you. Come to me naked. Come to me in a ball gown. I don't care."

She was surprised at the surrender. "You don't?"

"Well, I'd prefer the ball gown." He smiled crookedly. "You'll remember I like to unwrap my packages."

His words brought back that scalding discomposure she had felt at supper. Ridiculous that mere words could shake her when she had just experienced the most sensual of intimacies with him. "I don't have a ball gown."

"No? We must take care of that once we reach England." His hand reached out and lazily rubbed her belly. "Red, I think. I like red, and it would be beautiful with your dark hair."

"I've never worn red. Clara thought it was a heathen color." She stiffened beneath his touch but then relaxed as she realized the caress was without sensuality. It was soothing, almost affectionate, and as sexless as the way he stroked Kapu. "Don't be foolish. What would I do with a ball gown? I'm not going to England to go to balls."

"That's right." He snapped his fingers. "How could I forget? But I do go to balls on occasion. I suppose if you're to remain close to me, you'll have to masquerade as a footman." His gaze wandered to her breasts. "No, the encumbrances to that plan are too . . . sizable. Oh, well, I'm sure you'll think of something."

He was joking, she realized incredulously. After the tumult and intensity, it took her off guard. "That's not amusing."

"I'm devastated you don't appreciate my wit. It is a

bit crude for the taste of most women of my acquaintance, but you're not like them."

She felt an odd pang. No, she would never be like the women of Jared's world. She would never have the gentleness or meekness. She would never have the grace or sweet ways.

"What's wrong?" His smile had faded as his gaze searched her face.

"Nothing." She didn't look at him. "I wouldn't want to be like your fine ladies, but I'm not crude. I would bring no shame to myself in your grand ballrooms."

"Christ, I didn't say you were— Look at me."

"I don't want to look at you."

He reached out and grasped her chin and turned her face toward him. "Now I truly have hurt you."

She shook her head.

"Listen to me. You're not crude. You have courage and an honesty that I've never seen in any other woman." He added gruffly, "You're also impulsive, hot-tempered, and the most obstinate chit I've ever encountered. I might want to strangle you, but I'd never be ashamed of you."

He meant it. He was staring directly into her eyes and she couldn't look away. She was drifting, drowning, floating away from every mooring she had ever known. Dangerous. Dear God, how dangerous. She tore her gaze away from him. "I have to go," she whispered.

Something changed in his expression. His hand dropped away from her chin. "Yes."

She hadn't wanted him to agree with her, she realized at once. She had wanted him to keep her, make her stay. More dangerous than she had imagined. She slipped from the bed.

"How is Kapu?" he asked.

"Nervous. Some days are better than others." She found her sarong and wrapped it around her hips. "I'll be glad to get him ashore."

"Are you still sleeping in the cargo hold?"

"When the sea's at all rough." A memory suddenly came back to her. "You once said you have a horse better than Kapu."

"My mare runs like the wind. She's won any number of purses for me."

"A mare?" She shook her head. "No mare could match Kapu."

"You told me that I shouldn't judge a horse by glancing at him, and yet you're guilty of that trespass. You haven't even seen Morgana."

"That's different."

One corner of his lips lifted. "Because it threatens your beloved stallion. Shall I tell you how I got Morgana? She came almost as far from England as your Kapu."

Curiosity suddenly sparked. "Did she? Where? I thought—" What was she doing? Conversation led to intimacy, and that was forbidden to her. "I don't care where you got her."

He smiled. "Ah, how easy it is to fall into the pit of curiosity. I sympathize completely. I want to ask you a hundred questions, but that's forbidden, isn't it?"

"Yes." She ignored the taunt and opened the door. She didn't look at him as she asked, "Are you going to insist on coming to my cabin tomorrow night?"

He went still. "I told you what would happen if you came to me in that sarong."

"I don't want—" She would not plead with him. "Oh, do what you wish."

"That's my intention." He paused and then

shrugged. "But as it happens, I prefer you to come here."

She felt a rush of relief. "I'll still wear what—"

"You've made your choice of wardrobe eminently clear," he interrupted. "Good night."

"Good night." She left the cabin.

He had been terribly angry. Why had he spared her? Kindness? She didn't want him to show her kindness or understanding. Either one rendered vulnerable the barriers she had lifted against him. Yet tonight he had shown her both. She had not dreamed defiance and conflict could lead to revelation and bonding.

It would be all right. The barriers still held firm.

She must just make sure not to draw any closer to him.

Ku'aihelani.

Floating, blissfully drifting, sunlight . . .

She must not say it out loud. He must not know.

She moved closer and whispered, "There were no sailors on deck tonight."

He kissed her temple. "Yes, there were. Just not on this side of the ship. I told them I'd throw them overboard if I caught them within view of this cabin."

That he had made sure he had his way even while giving her victory was characteristic of him. "Unreasonable," she answered him softly. "They've already seen—"

His lips covered hers. "Shut up," he said roughly when he lifted his head. He parted her thighs and moved between them. "They won't see you again. No one will."

"If I choose, they will. You cannot—"

He entered her again with one deep thrust. "They

won't." His hips lifted and fell as he started that wild, pagan rhythm. "Dammit, is this the only way I can keep you from arguing?"

Argue? She couldn't even remember what she had been saying. Her teeth sunk into her lower lip as he cupped her buttocks with his palms and lifted her with every thrust. The tension was building, becoming unbearable. . . .

Her spine arched as she convulsed. She cried out as wave after wave of pleasure struck her.

Ku'aihelani . . .

"Lani, look at the porpoises!" Cassie leaned over the rail and pointed. "They're following the ship. Do you remember the first time you took me swimming with the porpoises at Hanlua Bay?"

Lani chuckled. "How could I forget? You almost drowned. You wanted to follow them forever."

Cassie smiled as she watched the sleek gray bodies cleave through the water. "It was wonderful . . . so much love and joy. I felt like one of them."

"Unfortunately, you don't swim well enough to become a porpoise, so you'll have to live on shore. At least you have Kapu." A smile lingered on Lani's lips as she shook her head. "Though I've often wondered if the reason you insisted on swimming with Kapu was that you wanted him to join you and the porpoises in some underwater playground."

"Don't be silly. I wouldn't be so childish. I know nature has rules that can't be broken."

"One part of you does, perhaps, but another believes that you'll find a Ku'aihelani where porpoises and horses frolic together and all is right with the world."

"Do you see that baby? Isn't he wonderful?"

Laughing, Cassie glanced at her. "And I don't think that's so bad a dream."

"No, it's beautiful." She paused. "But you must be wary of what you dream."

Cassie's smile faded as she realized Lani was no longer talking about porpoises. It was bound to come. Lani had kept her silence for the last four weeks, but Cassie had been aware she was uneasy.

How strange those weeks had been. Persephone. She had scoffed at Jared's comparison, but sometimes she had felt as if she were balanced between sunlight and darkness. During the day she and Jared almost ignored each other. They seldom spoke, merely nodded in passing like strangers. Even at the supper table they never conversed directly. Only when she entered his cabin at night did the pose of indifference vanish and she was drawn into the dark, carnal world ruled by Jared. She need not worry as long as she kept the two worlds separate. "My dreams are exactly what they were before I boarded this ship."

"And all goes well with you?" Lani asked. "He pleases you?"

Heat scorched her cheeks as she remembered Jared the night before, his head between her thighs and his tongue darting, plunging. She swallowed. "He pleases me."

"And I know you please him. When you aren't looking, he stares at you as if he wants to devour you."

Cassie's glance shifted back to the porpoises. "Isn't that what we wanted? To make him want to keep me close once we reach England?"

"Yes, that's what we wanted." The note of uneasiness was still in Lani's voice. "But I still think it would have been better if I'd been the one to couple with him. I don't like—"

"What?"

"I should have known you'd dive into carnal pleasure the way you do everything else. You're too intense." She made a face. "It's like the porpoises—I'm afraid you may drown."

Cassie reached out and covered Lani's hand on the rail. "I won't drown."

"Not while I'm here to rescue you." Lani sighed. "But I'm afraid it's too late for me to take your place. At this point I doubt if he'd accept Venus as your replacement in his bed." She smiled with an effort. "I feel in the mood to play a game of cards. Shall we?"

Cassie shook her head. "I want to watch the porpoises for a while and then go down and check on Kapu."

Lani nodded. "I thought as much. I suppose I'll have to find Bradford to substitute." She turned and strolled away. "He's usually willing to accommodate me if he's not too deep in his cups."

Cassie turned back to the porpoises. Bradford was not only willing but eager to do anything Lani wished, she had noted. He was almost painfully anxious to please and accepted Lani's sharp jabs and cool words with equanimity. Yet Cassie had an idea Lani enjoyed Bradford's wry wit. During the past weeks the two had established a guarded relationship that was almost as unusual as the one Cassie and Jared shared—No, what was she thinking? There was no comparison. Blazing heat, instead of coolness. Civilized banter, instead of tense, explosive ejaculations.

Someone was watching her.

She glanced over her shoulder. Jared was standing on the bridge a few yards away. She inhaled sharply as she saw his expression. Though fully dressed and impeccably groomed, this was the sinuous, naked savage who waited for her in his cabin, not the elegant daylight stranger. Lord of the Underworld, not the Duke of Morland.

When you're not watching, he stares at you as if he wants to devour you.

She could feel her body ripen, ready, as she gazed helplessly up at him. It was not supposed to be like this. She had thought she could keep the lines drawn, but they were merging, melting. Sunlight and darkness . . . one.

Something flared in his face, and he took a half step toward her.

No! Panic seared through her. The lines must be forced apart and kept apart.

She turned her back on him and stared blindly out at the porpoises.

She heard his low exclamation. She tensed, expecting him to come to her in spite of the rejection.

He did not.

A few minutes later she glanced over her shoulder.

He was gone.

But it was not over. Her rejection had been too blatant, and she would pay for it later.

But not now. Now the barriers were still in place. He had not been allowed to come out of that secret darkness to dominate the daylight.

Cassie stopped in the doorway in surprise. Not even the dim glow of a candle lit the cabin.

"Come in," Jared said.

"I can't see you," she said as she took a hesitant step toward him.

"I know, but I can see you. Shut the door."

Now that her eyes were becoming accustomed to the darkness, she could discern him on the bunk across the cabin—a paler silhouette against the deeper shadows. She shut the door, and an immediate uneasiness rippled through her. Now she could see nothing at all. "Light the candle," she said.

"Afterward." She could hear the rustle of movement across the cabin. "I don't want you to see my face at the moment."

"Why not?"

He was there before her, untying her sarong. He threw it aside. "It might frighten you."

She took an involuntary step back but collided with the door. Smooth, cool wood pressed against her naked back and buttocks. The darkness sharpened every sense: the sound of his breathing, the scent of him, the warmth of his body only inches from her own. He was looming over her, and she was suddenly acutely aware of the power of his body and the fragility of her own. "I've never been afraid of you."

"You've proved that by coming here tonight. I was wondering if you would."

She had not even considered not coming to him. She had been drawn as inevitably, blindly, as if answering a siren call. It was night . . . and he was waiting. "Tonight is no different from any other."

He took her hand and pulled her toward the bed. "Wrong. You're an intelligent woman, and you realize that one response requires another."

"I suppose you're saying you're angry with me."

He pushed her down on the bed. "Extremely."

"There's no reason."

"I can be an unreasonable man. Turn over."

"What?"

"You appear confused. You were eager to turn your back on me this afternoon. Why not now?"

"Because I don't know why—" She stopped and rolled over on her stomach. "Satisfied?"

"No, but I will be." He sat down beside her and began to stroke her. He started at her shoulders and moved slowly down her spine. Her stomach muscles clenched; his callused palm was a sensual abrasion against the softness of her own flesh. The darkness made him a stranger, and yet his touch had the same familiar mesmerism. He asked in a low voice, "Why did you turn your back on me?"

Her heart was beating so hard and fast she could barely breathe. "You know why."

"Perhaps. You think I broke those damnable rules you set." His hand moved down to her buttocks, stroking, squeezing. "But don't ever do it again. Do you understand?"

She didn't answer.

He muttered a curse and his hands were suddenly beneath her, lifting her to her hands and knees.

"What are you doing?" she asked, startled.

"You seem to have taken a dislike to facing me." He moved behind her on the bed. "I thought you'd prefer accepting me this way."

He held her hips steady as he positioned himself. Then carefully, slowly, he slid into her.

She gasped as the tightness resisted and then gave way. His hands were on her buttocks again, squeezing, petting. The position was incredible; her breasts hung heavy, ripe, and she was so full of him, she couldn't move.

He bent over her, pushing, letting her feel all of him. "Do you know how I felt when you turned your back on me?" he whispered. "It was as if you'd slapped me and then pushed me away."

It was what she had meant to do, she thought in despair. To push him back where he belonged.

"I wanted to come down from the bridge and bend you over the rail." He started to move, punctuating each word with a deep thrust. "I wanted to lift up the skirt of your gown and come into you like this . . . and this . . . and this . . ."

Her mouth was open as she tried to breathe. Her arms were so weak they could barely hold her as waves of pleasure struck her with every touch, every stroke.

Wildness. Fever. Possession without surcease and without mercy. She didn't want mercy. She wanted *him*.

But, suddenly, she didn't have him. He was gone. No, he was there in the darkness, plucking at her breasts, arousing her to fever pitch but not giving her the fullness she needed.

"Jared . . ." She started to turn over but he stopped her.

"No, stay where you are." He was in her again, moving, caressing her stomach, folding her around him. "I want it like this."

Arousal and withdrawal and then arousal again. Madness. It went on until she thought she could bear no more. When he finally allowed them both the explosion they craved, she was sobbing with frustration and need.

The climax was without parallel.

She collapsed onto the bed, exhausted, nerveless, and totally helpless. She could not have lifted a hand if she'd tried.

He lay beside her, his breathing as labored as her own. "Don't do it again."

She felt a frisson of annoyance through the haze of pleasure enveloping her. "Was this supposed to be punishment? I thought you'd learned you couldn't succeed in chastising me in this manner. I enjoyed it very much."

He stiffened.

"And I think when I regain my strength, we will do it again."

"The hell we will." He was silent and then suddenly began to chuckle. "I can't believe you. You're not like any woman I've ever met." He pulled her into his arms. "Thank God."

He wasn't angry any longer. She relaxed against him. "Don't the other women you bed like this way? I found it very interesting."

He kissed her temple. "But, then, you like everything I do to you. You're delightfully pagan . . . Kanoa."

He had not called her by that name since the first night. She felt a pagan when she was with him. This wild coming together in the erotic dimness of the underworld was becoming a sensual ritual she found irresistible. "But I don't believe I like to be taken in anger. It will be better next time."

"Will it, indeed? You'll have to wait awhile for me to recover. I'm not sure it wasn't myself I was punishing." He added dryly, "Someday I'm going to find a way to avoid being the victim in our encounters."

"It's very simple. Don't become angry without reason. I only turned my back on you. Why should it matter?"

"It mattered. It hur—It bothered me." He stroked her hair. "I found my response as peculiar as you do. I must be growing weary of this damnable arrangement."

She felt a pang at his words. "I don't have to come to you."

"Yes, you do." His arms tightened around her. "Every damn night." He paused. "But that's not enough. I want you to move your things to my cabin."

She went still. "No." She pushed him away and sat up. "I told you that—"

"I know what you told me. I don't care. I want you here when I want you." He pulled her back down beside him. "I want to reach out and touch you. I want to be able to have you when—" He kissed her roughly. "God, I wanted you this afternoon."

"Let me go," she whispered.

"You don't want to go."

No, she didn't. She wanted to stay and be one with him. But if she didn't leave now, she might give in to him, and that must not happen.

You won't betray him if you get up and walk away.

Lani's words. True words. Darkness and sunlight. Already bits and pieces of their lives were becoming revealed to each other. A casual comment, a question, every word brought them closer. She must not cross the line from passion into intimacy, or she would be lost.

She pushed him away again, sat up, and swung her legs to the floor.

For an instant she thought he would try to hold her, but he did not. She stood up, searching for her sarong in the darkness.

"Someday you'll stay." His quiet voice followed her. "Every time we come together, you yield a little more."

She found her sarong and hurried to the door, trying to shut out his words and his certainty, which frightened her more than any boast would have done.

"I can wait."

"I love your hair. Sometimes in the middle of the night long after you've left me, I think I feel it brush me." He spread her long hair over his shoulders and pulled her down on top of him. He was silent a long time, and then his voice came out of the darkness. "It's not going to matter, you know."

"What?" she asked. The beating of his heart sounded like golden thunder beneath her ear, she thought dreamily.

"This. I can't let it matter." His hands stroked her hair. "Delilah . . ."

She was jarred from the euphoria. Papa. He was talking about Papa. Jared never mentioned her father, and neither did she. He was always there in the background, but as time passed, he seemed to fade in and out of her memory like a phantom. Everything was blurred by the fever of her coming together with Jared. "I'm not Delilah."

"So you said." His hands moved down her back. "Then why can't I let you go? I thought I'd grow tired . . ."

That had been her hope also. After that explosive night two weeks ago she had tried to convince herself the hold Jared had on her senses was lessening, but she knew it wasn't so. Lani had said passion seldom lasted, but she could not get enough. Perhaps there was something wrong with her. She had only to catch a glimpse of him on deck, and she began to tremble. She couldn't wait until she walked through his door, and she knew it was the same for him. He took her each time as if he were starved for her.

His words were muffled in her hair. "I don't want lies between us. I just want you to know. I can't let it matter."

But it already mattered or he would not say this to her. Despite his denial, she had reached him. Lani had been right: he was not completely hardened. It bothered him to know that the daughter of his enemy was bringing him pleasure. If she continued to please him, he might soften even more. She should feel happy, even triumphant. That she was neither frightened her. She would have to face that fear soon, but not now. There was time, and she instinctively sought to lose herself once more in the erotic realm that had become her haven.

"We'll talk about it later." She raised her head and looked down at him. "That's not what I want from you now."

He smiled sardonically. "What a demanding wench you've become. No, conversation isn't what we want from each other." He rolled her over and moved on top of her. "I beg pardon, Delilah."

She closed her eyes to hide the hurt she should not have felt. She had only thought of remaining close to him; never had she considered it her duty to play the temptress.

He was inside her, his lips tugging at her breast.

She gasped, her nails digging into his shoulders as the rhythm started.

"So tight . . . mine. Christ, so much mine." His eyes were closed, sensuality heavy on his face. She had seen that expression innumerable times in the past weeks. But the soft breath of a word that came from his lips she had heard only twice before.

"Delilah . . ."

Nine

"Bradford says we should be arriving in England within a few days," Lani said.

"So soon?" Startled, Cassie turned away from the rail. "I thought the journey would be much longer."

"It's been a very long voyage." Lani raised her brows. "Though it's understandable the time would get away from you. You've been very . . . distracted."

Lani's words were without emphasis, but Cassie felt heat rush to her cheeks. "It's not—I haven't—It's not true."

What was she thinking? she thought, shocked. He had always been the enemy, and that she had considered him as anything else only showed how dangerous a foe he was.

Lani smiled gently. "I wouldn't mention it, but he's a powerful man, and you have a great zest for living. Could he be leading you into dangerous waters?"

"He's not leading me anywhere."

Was that entirely true? Lately, when she was with

him, she had begun to forget everything but what he wanted her to remember. Touch, scent, the beautiful rhythms of pleasure. A memory rushed back to her of that recent night when she had shied away from thinking of duty, pushed it into the background.

Betrayal.

Sickness churned through her. She didn't want it to be true. She wouldn't let it be true.

"Cassie?" Lani's soft voice that would never reprove her.

But she blamed herself. She had forgotten her purpose and remembered only the pleasure. She had thought herself strong enough to use Jared but had been caught in the web of seduction he wove.

But that didn't mean she had to remain in the web.

"I have to go." Her voice sounded shaky and distracted even to herself. She turned away from the rail and moved quickly down the deck. She had to escape and regain her composure before she faced Lani again. "I can't stay. . . ."

The sunlight was on her face, brilliant, hiding nothing. Not like the secret darkness of the cabin where he waited every night. A shudder went through her as she realized that, guilt or no, she still wanted to go to him. How many nights would it have taken for him to make her forget her purpose entirely? No, she couldn't believe it would ever have reached that point.

It hadn't happened. It wasn't too late. She was strong enough to put this madness behind her. She would just have to recognize that her strength was not absolute and act accordingly.

She was assailed by the image of Jared bending over her, wicked, sensuous, smiling as he moved slowly, rhythmically. Her breasts were swelling, her muscles tensing, readying even at the mere thought.

He would not want to let her go. She would have to be blind not to realize that Jared, too, was caught in the sensual web he'd woven around her.

Dear God, it was going to be difficult.

A troubled frown wrinkled Lani's brow as she watched Cassie walk away. She had known it would take only a word to bring Cassie back to the path they both must walk. She had done what was necessary, but she took no pleasure from it.

"What did you say to her?" She turned to see Bradford strolling toward her. "She seemed upset. I can't believe you were actually quarreling."

"Cassie and I never quarrel."

"Because she believes your wisdom is second only to that of the angels. She saves her strength to battle with the rest of the world." His speculative gaze returned to Cassie's retreating figure. "Jared?"

She pretended to misunderstand him. "As far as I know, she didn't quarrel with Jared, either."

"But she will." He turned to look at her. "Won't she?"

She gazed at him without expression.

"Because you've decided it's time to wake her up and break the spell."

"Spell?"

"Jared has the facility for making most women's heads whirl if he puts his mind to it. He's almost as good with women as he is with horses." He smiled. "And I'd wager he's been exerting himself to the utmost. He appears to be pretty dizzy himself this time."

"I don't know what you mean."

"I may be a drunkard but I'm not blind. They've

both been like sleepwalkers since you tossed him our enchanting Cassandra."

She stiffened. "You think I sent Cassie to him to use?"

"Didn't you?"

"No." She added with biting anger, "And you're wrong. You must also be blind if you think I'd force Cassie to do my will."

"I'm relieved." He leaned against the railing. "I didn't want to believe you'd go that far to save Deville." He made a rueful face. "Though I'd probably accept it."

"My actions are not yours to accept or refute. Your opinion is nothing to me."

"Oh, I think it is. It annoys you, but you do find me both charming and witty."

"Indeed? And modest, too, no doubt."

He shook his head, ignoring the irony. "You're too good a judge of character to make that mistake, but you're definitely drawn to me."

"I'm not drawn to you. I find you amusing on occasion, but that is all." She added, "It must be drink that's befuddling your senses."

He flinched. "Cruel."

"Truth."

"Cruel," he repeated. "And you're never cruel to anyone else. Don't you find that curious?"

She hadn't thought about it, she realized. The response had been pure instinct. "It annoys me."

"Why? I'd judge you to be the most tolerant of mortals. You even managed to live with that Kidman harridan."

"It just does." She added with sarcasm, "And Clara cannot help the poison in her soul, but you ingest poison into your body every day."

"But that poison serves to make me a less potent foe. Surely that should earn your approval." He raised his brows. "I fear your reasoning is grievously at fault. No, my reading of the situation is the right one. You're definitely drawn to me."

She gave an inelegant snort.

"You see? I'd be willing to wager that you'd never make that crude sound in the presence of your Deville. His ideal mate is a cultured gentlewoman, and he molded you in the way he wanted you to go."

"I molded myself."

"To fit his vision."

"The vision of all foreigners. You all want the same thing."

"And what is that?"

"A gracious lady at the dinner table and a pagan in bed."

"I admit it's the perfect combination. But if you gave Deville his ideal, why didn't he marry you?"

"I never asked it."

"It's usually the gentleman who asks."

"I don't want to discuss this any longer."

"Because it hurts?"

It did hurt. She had thought she had come to accept the blow to her pride, but it was suddenly there before her. "I don't need marriage. It's you foreigners who require vows."

"Yes, we do." He paused and then said with great formality, "Will you do me the honor of marrying me, Lani?"

She stared at him in shock. He could not have said what she thought she'd heard.

"I'm considered a good match. I'm not as rich as Jared, but I can keep you in fine style. I'm not completely beyond the pale as far as society is concerned."

"What are you saying?" she whispered.

"Oh, one more thing." He looked directly into her eyes and his low voice rang with sincerity. "I will love and honor you all the days of your life."

She felt as if she had been struck by lightning. Stunned . . . and unutterably touched. She did not want to feel this moved. She pulled her gaze away and looked out at the sea. "Or until you overhear one of your friends talking about the terrible mistake you made wedding a Polynesian savage. Much better just to make a whore of her."

"No, that would not end my affection for you." His voice was very gentle. "Just the life of the man who said those words."

"I can imagine your fighting over a case of French brandy, never a woman."

"Another blow. You see, you are trying to be cruel to me. I take that as definitely encouraging."

She whirled on him. "Then you're a fool. I have no affection for you. I love Charles Deville."

"Why?"

"Because he's kind and gentle and—"

"I'm kind. I can be gentle." He paused. "And I need you as much as he does. More. That should tip the scales in my favor."

"That's nonsense."

He shook his head. "I believe you're a woman who was born to give. You require someone to lavish care upon." He self-mockingly tapped his chest. "Look to me, fair damsel. I'm a bottomless well of need."

She was shaken. She had not dreamed he had studied her enough to perceive that about her character. "I'm sure you have a bottomless thirst, but that can be accommodated by a—"

"I'll quit drinking."

"What?"

"It's getting in the way and giving you an excuse to push me aside." He waved a hand. "It's gone."

She gazed at him skeptically.

"I control my habits, they don't control me. It's gone," he repeated. "Though I may be making a mistake. My drinking made you feel safe and appealed to your nurturing qualities."

"Safe?"

"You need not take a drunkard seriously," he said simply. "But now you'll be forced to consider my suit."

"I won't consider it. I love Charles."

"You've just grown accustomed to the idea of loving him." He frowned. "No, perhaps you do love him. You have a warm heart, and it's big enough to hold more than one love. I may have problems with that. But he's not worthy of you. I feel no guilt in taking you away from him."

"Particularly since you believe he killed your brother," she said scornfully.

"I detested my brother. John was a bully and a fool. He made my life miserable from the moment I was born until I escaped from Morland into the pleasant depravities of London. The only person he treated with any degree of affection was Jared. He adored him." He wrinkled his nose. "Pity. If he'd been as cruel to his son as he was to the rest of the world, Jared wouldn't be so obsessed with the thought of revenge."

"Evidently your brother cared enough to try to rescue his cousin from the guillotine."

"It was an adventure. I never said he wasn't a brave bastard."

"So you're willing to spare Charles because you hated your brother."

He nodded. "I've no driving lust for vengeance, and I do have a driving passion for you. I've never felt like this before. It's . . . extraordinary."

"Because I'm Polynesian."

"Because you're the most beautiful, strong, clever woman I've ever met." He reached out as if to touch her and then stopped. "You were meant for me, Lani. You were meant to live in my love and under my protection. You were meant to banish all the emptiness in my life. Jared doesn't believe in destiny, but I do. I have to believe in it. It's my only hope."

His words were halting, and so intense, they were almost painful to hear. She wanted to comfort him, hold him, stroke those tousled gray-flecked curls. She could not do it. She swallowed. "You have no hope." She smiled with an effort. "And you will soon forget this passion you have for me when you see all those fair-skinned Englishwomen again."

"Dammit, I will not forget—" He stopped and drew a deep breath. "You require proof. I can understand after the way Deville treated you."

"Charles treated me very well."

"So you've convinced yourself." His smile lit his rough features with warmth and sweetness. "But not the way I'll treat you. I've never had a treasure of my own. I'll know how to burnish it and keep it safe."

She felt again that rush of tenderness and pushed it firmly away. "I'm not a copper pot hanging in the kitchen," she said tartly. "I need no burnishing. Particularly not from you."

"Most particularly from me." His gaze raked her face. "But I think I'd better go away and leave the burnishing for later. I've given you enough to think about."

He turned and strolled away.

More than enough, she thought dazedly. Of course, she would not consider anything he said. She loved Charles, and Bradford was as unsteady as a weather vane. The next time she saw him, he would probably be deep in his cups and have forgotten his declaration.

Yet she had glimpsed a surprising depth and strength in Bradford today. He had shown her a side to his character she had never seen before.

And had not wanted to see.

The realization came with a sudden impact too strong to be denied. Bradford was right: she had used his inebriation as a reason to distance herself. From the first moment of their meeting she had known there was strength and intelligence beneath that careless manner. It had angered her, and then it had made her—

Cautious. She substituted that word for the one that came immediately to mind. Only cautious.

And she would remain cautious. She had told Cassie they must return to the real world, and she must not be distracted from her purpose.

She had an uneasy premonition that this Bradford she had just become aware of might be a force with which to be reckoned.

Where the devil was she?

Jared shifted restlessly before swinging his legs to the floor and standing up. Cassie would come soon. It meant nothing that she was late, he told himself.

But she had never been late before.

He moved toward the window and looked out at

the sea. Smooth and serene tonight. No reason for her to be with Kapu.

Perhaps she was ill.

He felt a leap of alarm. Had she appeared unwell at the supper table tonight? No, just quiet and remote as she usually was when they encountered each other outside his cabin. When she walked through that door, there was nothing remote about her. She was all fire and beauty. God, she came *alive*.

He felt a heavy aching in his loins. How had he come to this? It had never been like this with other women. She was like a sickness, a fever in his blood.

Why was he just standing there, waiting? He should throw on some clothes and go to her cabin as he had threatened. He half turned and then stopped.

Shame. She had averted her eyes when she had asked him if he would insist on coming to her. She had been too proud to plead with him, but he had known she had desperately wished not to be shown vulnerable to Lani. She had been like an uncertain little girl, and he had softened.

As he was softening toward her now, he realized in exasperation. No matter how angry and frustrated he was with her, he could not bring her shame.

But, dammit, where was she? He *needed* her.

He was striding toward her down the deck.

Cassie didn't turn away from the sunlit sea but watched Jared approach from the corner of her eye, bracing herself. He looked completely His Grace, the Duke of Morland, today, his expression impassive, his manner imperturbable. Perhaps it would not be as bad as she had feared.

"Good morning." His tone was silky. "I trust you slept well?"

"Well enough."

"You lie." She suddenly became aware of the controlled ferocity beneath the smooth facade. "You're pale and pinched, and I'd wager you didn't sleep a wink all night. I can't tell you how much that pleases me."

"How very inconsiderate."

"I don't feel considerate. I'm angry and impatient, and I'd like nothing better than to throw you to a passing shark. Look at me."

She kept her gaze on the sea.

"Look at me!"

She reluctantly obeyed. Faint dark circles were smudged beneath his ice-blue eyes, and the skin was stretched taut over his cheekbones. Sleeplessness may have diminished her, but it had sharpened him. He seemed to glitter like a drawn sword in the sunlight. Impossible, she thought wearily. The restless night she'd spent dreading this encounter was making her imagine things.

"Were you ill?"

"No."

"I didn't think so." He drew a deep breath and his hand reached out to grasp the rail. "Then why didn't you come to me?"

"It was time for it to end." She looked away from him. "We'll soon be in England."

"Very soon. Tomorrow."

"Really? I thought it would be a few—" She broke off as he grasped her shoulders and jerked her around to face him. "Let me go!"

"End?" he said through his teeth. "You had no plans for it to end with the voyage. Should I remind you? You were going to stay close and use me for your own purpose."

"The situation has changed. I've decided it's best I no longer couple with you."

"Best for whom? Not for me and, by God, not for you, either. You want what we have as much as I do."

"It's true that I find coupling with you enjoyable," she said haltingly. Then she met his gaze directly and deliberately used his own words. "But I can't let it matter to me."

His grasp tightened on her shoulders. "You find it more than enjoyable, dammit."

"As Lihua said, you're very good at pleasure making. I've had no experience with other men, but I believe she's right." She swallowed. "But we both know that's not important."

"If it's not important, why shouldn't it go on?"

"Because I find it distracting. It's time I walked away."

"And what if I won't let you?"

"I've learned enough about you to know you will not force me. Brutality offends you."

"Who knows?" He smiled without mirth. "I might learn to like it."

She shook her head. "Not you. Even when you were most angry with me, you did me no harm."

"So you're going to give up your plan of turning me from my chosen path?"

"Of course not. But that doesn't mean I have to remain in your bed. It's clear I cannot sway you in that manner. You told me so yourself." She paused and then said in a rush, "But I'm not sure I entirely believe you. I think you'll find it much harder to kill my father now."

"Don't count on it."

She had to count on it. She had to believe she had accomplished something and those last weeks of madness were not pure self-indulgence. "And though I'm your hostage, I doubt if you'll throw me into a dungeon once we reach Morland. As long as I'm free, I have a chance to save my father."

"And use me to do it?"

"I've never lied to you about my intentions."

His lips twisted. "No, you haven't. Use me and walk away. Isn't that the way of it?"

"Yes." She wished he would leave. Every minute he stayed, the pain grew more and more. "That's the way of it."

"But you're not walking, you're running like a scared rabbit."

"If you choose to think so."

"I know so." His gaze blazed down at her. "And I'm not going to let you do it. You'll be back in my bed within a week."

She shook her head.

"You will." His voice deepened with intensity. "You *will*."

His determination was beginning to shake the little composure she still retained. "How are you going to make me? I suppose you could threaten to take Lani to your bed again."

"Dammit, you know I don't want Lani. This is between the two of us. You'll come to me because that's what you want to do, what you have to do. You need what we have together." He smiled grimly. "And I'll be waiting for you. My chamber at Morland is much larger than the cabin, but you won't notice the difference. It will be the same for us."

The same heat, the same urgency, the same wild mating. She shivered at the memory. No, she could never go to him again. It was too dangerous. "Let me go."

After a moment, his hands suddenly loosened and dropped to his sides. "Not for long. I told you once I'd never let you walk away from me."

She stepped back and drew a shaky breath. This painful scene was almost over. He had not given up, but he had accepted rejection for the present. "Watch me."

She strode down the deck toward her cabin, her spine straight, her head held high. She could feel his gaze on her and was tempted to glance over her shoulder. She knew what she would see: anger, frustration, and that unshakable confidence and determination. The confrontation had been difficult enough; she didn't want to carry that vision away to haunt her.

She had done it. The bond was broken. She had banished any possibility of betrayal.

She had only to keep to her resolve, and everything would be fine.

"I must say I much prefer this method of deboarding, Jared," Bradford said as he watched Cassie carefully lead Kapu down the gangplank to the dock. "My nerves would have been horrendously strained if she had to swim ashore."

"I'm glad you approve." Jared smiled sardonically. "I'm sure we would all have hated to cause you any discomfort." He turned away from the rail. "Are you ready?"

"More than ready. I'm weary of this mariner's life. When you return your hostage to her homeland, you'll have to do it without me. I wish to stay on dry land for the foreseeable future." He followed Jared toward the gangplank. "You do intend to return her to her island, don't you?"

"I haven't thought about it. Certainly not when she might still prove of value."

"In what capacity?" Bradford murmured.

Jared had been waiting for the attack; it was long past due. "Say it."

"I beg your pardon?"

"I've been wondering when you'd get around to voicing a protest."

"I never waste my time. Once the seduction was a fait accompli, it would have done no good to try to intervene. You would have merely told me to jump overboard."

"It was *not* a seduction. She came to me."

"And you didn't try to convince her to stay?" He shook his head. "Of course you did. You used every wile and allure you could muster to keep her. A blind man could have seen it."

"Why not?" He smiled recklessly. "She said she wanted to use me. I was merely being accommodating." His smile faded. "You've made your protest. Let it alone. Don't interfere, Bradford."

"I'm afraid it may become necessary." He nodded at Lani, who was starting down the gangplank followed by several seamen carrying boxes and portmanteaus. "A new ingredient has been thrown into the mix. If you had not been caught up in your own concerns, you would have realized it."

"What do—" Jared's eyes widened. "You've bedded her?"

"No, but it's my most earnest hope to do so." He met Jared's gaze. "However, I may have to wait until the lady consents to wed me."

Jared inhaled sharply. "Bradford . . . no."

"Yes." He held up his hand as Jared opened his lips

to speak. "And it's you who will not interfere. I will not have it."

Jared had rarely heard that steely firmness in his tone. "You're a fool. She's Deville's mistress."

Bradford made a face. "That is an obstacle. Your thirst for vengeance is another." He nodded at Cassie on the dock. "And your lust for Lani's little friend is still another. It didn't get in the way when the girl was willing, but that's changed now. I won't have you making my task more difficult by keeping Lani on edge all the time. I want her free to think only of me."

"She doesn't think of anyone but Deville." He paused. "For God's sake, she was even planning on bedding me to help him."

"I thought as much. Lani's very determined, and she would see nothing wrong with using copulation to help a loved one. It was fortunate for me that it didn't happen." He smiled pleasantly. "And will never happen now that you know I'll beat you senseless if you make the mistake of taking her up on her invitation."

"Goddammit, I have no intention—"

"I know," he interrupted. "But it never hurts to clarify matters. At any rate, I wish you to facilitate this business of capturing Deville as quickly as possible. It's getting in my way."

Jared followed him. "My apologies. I'll try to take care of the matter before you're seriously inconvenienced. You might remember I've been wanting it done for more than a decade. I'm sending a message to Guillaume in Paris before we leave the dock. Will that be soon enough for you?"

"It will have to do." Bradford started down the gangplank. "What quarters are you giving the ladies once we reach Morland?"

"You needn't worry. I'm not going to throw them

into the dungeon. I'll make sure they're guarded carefully, but I don't think they'll be eager to escape until they're sure Deville has reached France."

"And how will they know that?"

His smile was twisted. "Why, through me, of course. Cassie has made no bones about the fact that I'm to be used. She will do her best to spy out any information. I suppose it's useless to tell you that you should also be on your guard?"

Bradford nodded. "Completely. I can't promise to be on your side this time, Jared."

"Then I'd best keep my own counsel." He hadn't felt so alone since the first night he'd come to Bradford's town house. Well, so be it. He straightened his shoulders and smiled recklessly. "But don't you act the spy, Bradford. I'd find that kind of betrayal unforgivable. I'm afraid I'd become very angry and exact a high penalty." He glanced at Cassie on the dock. "A very high penalty."

"I'm not worried. I believe you'll find making war on women distasteful."

Jared didn't answer as he watched Cassie smile and speak to Lani. But her expression became shuttered as he approached.

He smothered the irritation her response brought. "Welcome to England, ladies," he said lightly. "I hope you find it pleasant."

"We do not," Cassie said. "It's a cold and barren place." Her gaze went to the trees bordering the path up the hill. "And the trees are bare."

"It's autumn and the leaves have already fallen. I regret that we can't provide you with flowering shrubs such as those in the paradise you left behind."

"It doesn't matter. We'll be here only a short time."

"One never knows," Jared said.

She met his gaze. "I know."

Lani interjected quickly. "How far is this port from Morland?"

"A few miles. They keep horses for me here at the stables at the inn. We should be at Morland by afternoon." He added, "I'll allow you the freedom of the grounds, but naturally you'll be watched."

"Naturally," Cassie said. "You need not worry about us leaving until there's a reason to do so. Then we will go and you won't be able to prevent it."

"I'd be curious to see how you accomplish—"

"Come along, Cassie." Lani moved toward the inn Jared had indicated. "I'm growing chill here by the water. I want to be on our way."

Cassie turned at once and followed her down the dock.

Jared stood watching them go, frustration and irritation coursing through him. She would go anywhere, do anything, Lani asked, but he received only defiance.

"Feeling a tad at a loss?" Bradford asked. "I didn't think it would happen already."

"I'm *not* at a loss."

Jared stalked down the dock toward the inn.

Ten

"Very splendid," Lani said in an undertone to Cassie as they watched Jared move down the long line of servants gathered in the courtyard to greet him. "It seems the English may know more of ceremony than we do." She wrinkled her nose. "Though they could use a bit of color. What a somber collection. Do you suppose we could persuade them to trade those stiff, dark uniforms for a few decent sarongs?"

"I doubt it." Cassie chuckled as Bradford helped her down from Kapu. Bless Lani, for an instant she had actually felt a little nervous at this display of power and prestige. Cassie could barely remember the palaces and châteaus of France, but she was sure they could not have been as imposing as Morland. Still, Lani was right: this castle might be very grand, but their island was much more beautiful. Jared might be king here, but they were used to a royalty with its own set of customs. "Are you going to try?"

"Dear God, please don't," Bradford groaned, his glance going to an elderly gray-haired woman whose body resembled a plump partridge. "Mrs. Blakely dandled me on her knee when I was barely out of the nursery. I don't think I could become accustomed to her without her starched skirts and high collars."

"That's very selfish of you," Cassie said, smiling. "Think of her. How can her body breathe swathed in all that material? It's almost as bad as the gowns Clara chose for me."

"Impossible," Jared said as he approached them.

Cassie's smile faded and she instinctively braced herself. It was the first word he'd spoken to her since they'd left the dock. "Then you must approve of Lani's plan."

He frowned. "What plan?"

"Why, Lani thinks that sarongs would be much more appropriate garb for your servants."

"Not bloody likely," he said distinctly. "No sarongs. Not here. Do you understand?"

"Lani was joking."

"But are you?"

She turned away and changed the subject. "Where's the stable? I have to get Kapu settled."

He would not be deterred. "Were you joking, Cassie?"

"Perhaps. Your England is so cold, it's no wonder everyone bundles up." Her glance fell on a long, low outbuilding across the courtyard. "Is that the stable?" When Jared nodded, she started toward it, brushing aside the young boy who rushed forward to take Kapu's reins. "Don't bother going with me. I don't need your help."

"How kind of you to dismiss me," Jared said. "Will you go with her, Bradford? I'll escort Lani to her quarters."

"Delighted," Bradford replied. "I'm very proud of

the horses in that stable, as I had a hand in choosing a good many of them. I think even Cassie will have to admit their excellence."

"Not if they don't wear sarongs," Jared said sarcastically.

Bradford chuckled as he moved after Cassie. "Good God, what a picture that brings to mind." He opened the door of the stable and stepped aside for Cassie and Kapu to pass. "I'm afraid we've irritated dear Jared. I've noticed a certain lack of humor in him since you appeared in our lives." He closed the stable door behind them and gazed at Cassie expectantly. "Well?"

"It's so . . . clean." An understatement: the stable was bright and well scrubbed; even the brass latches on the stalls gleamed as if just polished. The main stable area was enormous; spacious stalls accommodated at least thirty horses. Through an arched opening in the west wall she glimpsed a carriage room that was even larger than the stable.

"Jared believes that cleanliness keeps animals healthy. He's very particular." Bradford stopped before an empty stall. "Will this do? No horse on either side of him. Your Kapu isn't used to company."

"It will be fine." She led Kapu into the stall and began unsaddling him. The familiar duty was soothing, as comforting as the smell of horse and straw that surrounded her. Her sense of strangeness and tension began gradually to ebb away. "It's like a palace compared to his stable at the cottage. Thank you, Bradford."

"My pleasure." He leaned against the stall gate, watching her. "Exceptional animal. How fast is he?"

"I don't know. I've never timed him." She smiled

over her shoulder. "We don't have horse races in Hawaii."

"Will you let me time him?"

She frowned. "Why?"

"Because I've an insatiable curiosity where horses are concerned. I have to know everything about them." He smiled coaxingly. "Please?"

She softened as she looked at him. Bradford had never been anything but kind to her, and it was a small thing to ask. "If you like."

"Tomorrow morning. Eleven?"

She nodded. "But it makes no difference how fast he is."

"It does to me." His smile was luminous. "Speed is part of the glory. Not all of it, however. There's nothing more beautiful in the world than a fine horse running like the wind."

She had a sudden memory of Kapu streaking down the beach, mane blowing, muscles bunching, gathering, gleaming with every powerful stride. "No, there isn't," she said softly.

They exchanged a glance of complete understanding.

Bradford nodded and straightened away from the gate of the stall. "I'll leave you to get him settled. I'll go see if Lani is comfortable and then meet you in the front hall of the castle in an hour. Will that be enough time?"

She shook her head. "I'll find my own way. Kapu may need me to stay with him." She began to wipe the stallion down.

"Well, promise you won't stay the night. There's nothing here that can harm him."

"If he settles well."

"Please make the effort. Jared's stable boys aren't

accustomed to ladies occupying the horses' stalls. It will disconcert them."

She grimaced and didn't answer.

"I didn't think that would be a convincing argument." Bradford started to turn away.

"Wait!"

He glanced at her inquiringly.

"Which horse is Morgana?"

He smiled. "Ah, the Queen? I should have known Jared would have told you about her." He motioned for her to follow him. "Come see her. She's at the end of the stable."

Cassie gave Kapu a pat and left the stall. "He didn't really tell me anything about her." She had stopped him, afraid she would be drawn further into the net by confidences. She felt no such threat with Bradford and was curious to see the mare Jared had said was finer than Kapu. "Why do you call her the Queen?"

"You'll see." Bradford stepped aside and gestured to the horse in the end stall. "Her Majesty."

Cassie inhaled sharply and took a step closer. She was a truly beautiful bay, much smaller than Kapu, but every line of her body sang with beauty, strength, and power. She could indeed see why Bradford called her the Queen; she had never seen a horse with such a regal air. "Lovely," she murmured. She reached out a hand to touch the mare's muzzle, but Morgana shied away. "Good," she told her softly. "You have spirit and you're particular. I should have let you get to know me first."

"At least she didn't take your hand off at the wrist, as your stallion would have done," Bradford said.

"But she's not docile." Dear heaven, she was beautiful. "Will she let anyone but Jared ride her?"

"I've ridden her on occasion. When Her Majesty

permits. She definitely has a mind of her own." He drew closer and held out his hand and, when Morgana didn't flinch, began to stroke her muzzle. "It's like sailing on a smooth sea. I imagine the ride on your Kapu is a world of difference."

"Yes." Riding Kapu was like harnessing a storm— exciting, a little unstable, but exhilarating power in every stride. "Very different. How long has Jared had her?"

"Four years. He got her as a foal from Sheikh Galen Ben Hassan of Sedikhan."

"Sedikhan?" She frowned, trying to place it. "I've never heard of it."

"Not many people have. It's a barbarous desert land very far from here." He smiled. "The sheikh also has his barbaric moments, but Jared and he hit it off. He has a magnificent stable, and horsemen always have common ground."

"And he bought her from this sheikh?"

"No, the sheikh wouldn't sell. Jared won him in a wager."

"What kind of wager?"

For the first time Bradford looked a trifle discomforted. "Just a wager," he said vaguely.

"What kind of—"

"No," he said with firmness. "Forget it. I should not have mentioned it. Such details are not for your ears."

She was tempted to pursue the matter, but it was evident he would not be moved. "I'm surprised he wanted a filly so badly."

"Look at her."

"As a foal she wouldn't have looked like this. There's nothing more awkward and disproportionate."

"Jared has infallible instincts where horses are concerned. Besides, he saw the dam. He knew Morgana would be a queen." He glanced at her sideways. "And fast. She's the fastest horse in England. There's not a man in the ton who wouldn't give his soul to own her."

"Jared told me he races her."

"Of course, Jared is a very competitive man. He enjoys winning."

She already knew that about him. "But does Morgana?"

He nodded. "Oh, yes, racing is bred in the horses of Sedikhan. It offends her royal dignity to be put in the same class as lesser beings, but she loves leaving them in the dust."

It was an amusing picture, and a smile tugged at Cassie's lips as she visualized the proud disdain of the filly. "I like her." She chuckled. "Not that she cares."

"She will care. Let her get to know you. She has a great heart."

But Cassie might not be here long enough for the magnificent filly to get to know her, she thought with a pang. A month or two and she might be in France or, if all went well, on her way back to Hawaii. Not that she regretted it, she assured herself quickly. She wanted nothing more than to be gone from here and return to her old life. It was just that the filly was extraordinary. . . .

But not as wonderful as Kapu. Kapu was her own, her heart. She had no need for another horse when she had the stallion. When this was over, she would take him back to Hawaii and she would find him a mare worthy of him and start her horse farm. She wouldn't be—

A mare worthy of him.

She stared at Morgana, stunned. Where would she find a mare worthier of Kapu than Morgana? Perfection and perfection. Royal rogue and haughty majesty.

"What is it?" Bradford was staring at her. "What's wrong?"

"Nothing." It was a lie. Something was very wrong. Now that she had seen Morgana, she would never be satisfied with another mare with which to breed Kapu. Well, she would have to be satisfied with a lesser consort. She knew she could not have Morgana. But, dear God, how she *wanted* her for Kapu.

"Don't compare the two," Bradford said. "They're both splendid in their own way."

He thought she was having doubts about Kapu's superiority and trying to be kind. "There's nothing to compare." She smiled with an effort and turned away from the mare. "I have to get back to Kapu."

"I suppose we aren't going to see you at dinner?"

"No, even if I return to the castle, I'll eat in my quarters from now on."

"I thought that particular social pretense was at an end." He paused. "Jared won't like it, you know."

"Then he doesn't have to feed me."

"I realize you eat and sleep horses, but I believe you'd find hay and grain a poor repast."

She reached Kapu's stall and resumed wiping him.

Bradford sighed as he moved toward the stable door. "I suppose this means Lani won't join us either."

"Lani makes her own decisions. You'll have to ask her."

"Oh, be assured, I will."

Cassie finished wiping Kapu down and threw aside the toweling. He wasn't as nervous as she had feared. Perhaps because he was so glad to get back on land.

She stepped closer and laid her head against Kapu's mane. "It's a fine, lovely stall, but don't get too used to it," she whispered. "We don't belong here. We've still got to find our own place."

She heard a soft neigh from down the corridor. Morgana? It could be any of a dozen horses, but she instinctively knew it was the mare.

Kapu went still and his ears pricked forward.

"She's beautiful, boy. But she doesn't belong to us either. It's just as well she's too far away for you to see her."

But she felt an aching sense of loss as she remembered those beautiful lines, the proud lift of the mare's head. What a pair they would have made together.

The distant crunch of footsteps . . .

Cassie drowsily lifted her head from the straw. She had been just about to fall asleep when the sound had disturbed her. It was probably nothing. A young stable boy had come to check on the horses shortly before dark, but after she had sent him to his bed, there had been no one.

A soft jingle of bells.

It was coming from the carriage room.

A door slammed!

She sat bolt upright, her heart pounding wildly. It didn't have to be anything ominous. She knew nothing about castles, yet it didn't seem likely that anyone would be wandering about the stables in the middle of the night.

There's not a man in the ton who wouldn't give his soul to have Morgana.

Horse thieves.

It was certainly a possibility. If Morgana was considered such a jewel, then there would always be men who would pay to obtain the treasure.

She found herself rising to her feet even before she made a conscious decision. She would never let them have that beautiful filly. The mare belonged to Jared, and here she was treated like the queen she was.

Kapu neighed softly as she left the stall.

"Shh," she whispered. Her hand was shaking as she lit the lantern and took it down from the post. She had no weapon, but the heavy lantern might be used as a bludgeon. "I'll be right back."

Why was she whispering? If the intruders heard her, they might think they were discovered and flee. She moved toward the cavernous opening leading to the carriage house.

Maybe they were already gone. After all, a door had slammed. Perhaps they had taken whatever booty they had wanted and left.

Let them be gone, she prayed as she crossed the threshold of the carriage house.

The light from her lantern caused the dozens of coaches and phaetons to cast eerie shadows on the wall—giant monsters ready to pounce on her own shadow as she slowly walked down the long aisle.

A sharp metallic squeak.

She skidded to a halt. Where had it come from? Her throat was dry with fear as she called, "I know you're here. Where are—"

The door of the carriage on her left flew open!

She caught only a fleeting glimpse of a slim, boyish figure as it launched itself at her.

The breath left her body as she hit the floor.

Her assailant was immediately astraddle her.

She fought darkness and struck out.

He grunted in pain as she connected with his eye.

She rolled over, taking him with her. Now he was beneath her, and she reached for the lantern that had dropped from her hand. She lifted the lantern. If she could knock him out and then run to the castle for help . . .

"Blast it, wait! I give up."

Cassie froze in place. The voice had been furious, disgusted, and undoubtedly feminine. Slowly, she lowered the lantern and looked down at her attacker.

Green eyes glared up at her from a face as angelic as the ones in the pictures in Lani's Bible. Short pale-gold curls rioted around the girl's thin face. She looked a mere child—certainly no more than fifteen or sixteen. "Let me up!"

"Why should I? So you can attack me again?"

"I didn't attack you. I just jumped on you. If I'd attacked you, I wouldn't have let you get the best of me."

"You knocked the breath out of me."

"But I didn't try to hit you with a blasted lantern. Let me up."

"When you tell me what you're doing here. Are you one of the servants' children?"

She said defiantly, "It's none of your business."

"Then we'll stay here all night."

"You'll get bored or Jared will come for you."

Jared. If the girl was one of the servants' children, she would not be so familiar.

"Perhaps he's missing you already," the girl said. "Let me up and go to him."

"He knows where I am." She added, "And what is His Grace to you?"

"More than he'll ever be to a scraggly tart who pleases him only in bed." Her scathing glance traveled over Cassie's worn riding habit. "Where did he get you? London?" She shook her head. "His lady birds from London are much more comely. He must have gone directly from Tahiti to the dock and picked you up. I overheard one of Jared's friends say a man becomes desperate after long weeks at sea."

Unexpectedly Cassie found her anger lessening. The girl was helpless, facing an unknown threat, and still had the courage to spit defiance. In similar circumstances she hoped she would have done the same.

"What are you doing here in the middle of the night?" she asked.

The girl set her jaw and was silent.

"Who are you?"

The girl didn't speak.

"Very well. I'll go ask Jared."

A sly expression crossed the girl's face. "Good idea. Go ahead."

And when she came back, the girl would be gone. Again she had a notion of vague familiarity. "After I find a rope to tie you up."

"No!" The girl hesitated and then said grudgingly, "My name is Josette."

"And your surname?"

"Get off me. You're crushing my stomach. You must weigh as much as Morgana."

"You know Morgana?"

"Of course I do." Her eyes narrowed suspiciously. "What were you doing creeping about in the stable in the middle of the night? Did someone pay you to bed Jared and then try to steal Morgana?"

"I'm not a horse thief. In fact, I thought the same about you. That's why I decided to search the carriage house."

Josette snorted. "You came after a horse thief with

only a lantern? What were you going to do? Set him on fire? Not likely."

"Believe what you like. I'm not the intruder here. I have permission to stay with my horse." It wasn't precisely true. She had actually given herself permission. Oh, well, close enough. "And I'll wager no one gave you leave to be here tonight."

Josette frowned. "What's wrong with your horse? Is he sick?"

"He just feels a little strange. It's his first night here."

"And his last," Josette said fiercely. "Jared will toss you out of his bed and your horse out of his stable before you can blink."

"No, he won't. I don't occupy his bed." She grimaced. "And, I assure you, he would never let Kapu leave if he had his way."

"Kapu?"

"My stallion. I brought him from Hawaii."

"Where is that?"

"An island." When the girl still looked confused, she added, "Near Tahiti."

"Jared brought you from Tahiti?"

"No, I brought myself. And from Hawaii."

"And the other woman at the castle, too?"

It appeared the girl knew a good deal about what was going on at the castle. "How did you know about Lani?"

"Is that her name?" Josette shrugged. "Someone told me about the women who came to the castle." She said with deliberate cruelty, "She must be the pretty one."

"No," Cassie corrected. "She's more than pretty, she's beautiful."

"Then she's the one in Jared's bed," Josette said flatly. "He always chooses the best."

"The choice is not always the man's."

"Of course it is. Are you going to get off me?"

"Yes." She swung off the girl and rose to her feet. "You're no threat, and I can't waste any more time on you. I have to get back to Kapu. Do what you have to do in here and be gone. I need to get some sleep."

Josette looked at her in astonishment. "You're going to let me go?"

"I can't sit on top of you all night." She moved toward the arched opening leading to the stalls. "You were truly concerned about Morgana, so you're not a horse thief. I don't care if you steal every coach in this room, as long as you leave the horses alone."

"I'm not a thief!" She jumped to her feet and followed Cassie. "And that's a stupid remark. How could I steal a coach without a horse to pull it?"

Cassie found herself smiling. "True. Then you might not steal the coaches either."

"I don't have to steal. Jared would give me any coach I wished."

"Would he? Then you're very fortunate. Good night." She moved down the corridor.

"I think I'll come with you."

Cassie looked back to see Josette swaggering after her. The girl wasn't as small as she had first thought, but she was undoubtedly a youngster. No wonder she had thought her a boy. Her slim hips were lost in those rough wool trousers, and the blue shirt hid any hint of breasts.

Josette stopped, glaring at her. "Stop staring at me." She lifted her chin. "It's these trousers, isn't it? Well, I like them. I can't help it if you disapprove. I'll wear what I like."

Cassie's eyes widened, and then she started to laugh. She had said almost those same words to Jared. "I don't disapprove. A woman should always wear what she wishes. I assure you, on occasion I wear apparel that's much more shocking."

Josette was a trifle deflated. "Oh."

Cassie turned and resumed walking.

"What kind of apparel?" Josette was beside her.

Cassie shook her head.

Josette was silent a moment, then asked, "Is it interesting being a whore?"

"I'm not a whore."

"But you're not shocked at the question, either," Josette said shrewdly. "Why did Jared bring—Why did you come to Morland?"

"Because I chose to do so."

"That's no answer."

"I've not been getting many answers myself."

Josette scowled. "All right. Jared is my guardian."

Cassie looked at her in astonishment.

"You didn't know he was anybody's guardian." It was a statement. "That's no surprise. Jared doesn't like to let it be known."

"Why not?"

She shrugged. "There are reasons. Anyway, I attend Lady Carradine's School for Young Ladies except when Jared or Bradford is here. Carradine Hall's only a short distance away, and this afternoon when I heard they had returned, I decided to come home."

"Jared sent you a message?"

"No." She added quickly, "But he would have. Probably tomorrow or the next day. He truly cares about me. I just decided to come on my own a little sooner."

Cassie looked back at the carriage room.

Josette rushed on. "Oh, I didn't want to disturb anyone in the middle of the night. I was going to sleep in the coach tonight and see Jared in the morning."

"I see." She felt a surge of pity. She thought she was beginning to understand. The child clearly adored Jared, and he couldn't be bothered about her. "How did you get here from your school?"

"I walked."

"And how far is it?"

"Not far."

"Two miles?"

"Eight," Josette admitted. "What difference does it make? I wanted to do it."

The answer made perfect sense to Cassie. "Who told you that Jared had come home?"

"I have friends here," Josette evaded.

And the child would not betray the servant who had sent her word. Cassie was beginning to respect as well as admire the girl.

"But Jared would have come for me anyway. We're like brother and sister."

"I'm sure he would have," she said gently. "Go back to the coach and go to sleep. Do you need a blanket?"

Josette looked at her uncertainly. "You won't go running to tell him I'm here?"

Cassie shook her head.

A radiant smile lit the girl's face. "Good—Jared's temper is always better after a good night's sleep." A bit of bravado returned. "Not that it would have mattered."

"Good night." Cassie started down the aisle again. "I'll wake you before I go to the castle in the morning."

"Thank you." She fell into step with Cassie again. "I'll just go along with you. I'm not really tired."

"After walking eight miles?"

"If you don't want me, just say so," Josette flared. "I've no desire for your company. I only wanted to see your horse."

In spite of the challenging words Cassie realized she had hurt her. "Then stop quarreling and come see him. He's in the stall just ahead."

Josette strode toward the stall Cassie had indicated. "If Jared likes him, he must be fairly decent. Though you may have—Great God in heaven."

Cassie smiled with satisfaction.

Josette stood gazing at Kapu with an admiration near reverence. "Magnificent . . ."

"Yes." Then, as Josette stepped closer to Kapu, "No, don't do—"

Kapu was standing still, allowing Josette to stroke him.

"Don't worry, horses like me. Not as much as they do Jared, but they know I won't hurt them." She glanced over her shoulder. "What's his name?"

"Kapu."

"What a silly name. I'll think of one of my own."

"His name is *not* silly. It means 'taboo,' 'forbidden.' " Though it seemed the idiot horse was embracing the whole world these days, she thought crossly.

"Oh, I understand." She stroked Kapu's nose. "You wanted to keep him yours."

"I named him that because he's dangerous to ride, and it seemed a fair—" She met Josette's knowing gaze. "How did you know?"

"If I had a horse like Kapu, I'd want him to be mine alone." Her expression was wistful as she added, "It's important to have something of your own."

Cassie glanced around the stable. "You surely have a horse here. There are so many."

"But none that I've won, none that—" She broke off. "You don't understand. Nobody does."

She had an idea she knew exactly what Josette meant. "None that you've had to coax and tend and fight the world to keep."

Josette nodded. "It's not that Jared's not generous. He even lets me ride Morgana. It's just that—" She turned back to Kapu and her tone became gruff. "You're right, Jared won't discard you as long as he thinks he has a chance of getting this beauty." She grimaced. "I shouldn't have said that, should I? Lady Carradine would say it's the height of rudeness."

Cassie laughed. "So would Lani, but not for the same reason. She claims if truth causes pain, then silence is better."

Josette didn't look at her. "Did I cause you pain?"

"No, I told you, neither Lani nor I occupy his bed. Your Jared cannot discard what he doesn't possess."

Josette heaved a sigh of relief. "Good, I really didn't mean to hurt you that time. It just slipped out." She changed the subject. "How fast is Kapu?"

"I have no idea. Bradford is going to clock him tomorrow morning."

"Can I be there?" Josette's face was alight with eagerness.

She smiled indulgently. "If you like. I don't see why it's so important. I don't intend to race him."

"Of course you will. Everyone races here. It's very exciting. What hour?"

"Eleven."

"I'll be here." Her expression clouded. "Maybe. If Jared isn't too displeased with me and sends me packing."

"Would that be so bad?"

"Yes." She added haltingly, "They hate me there."

She could not imagine anyone hating this urchin. In spite of her prickly nature and swaggering bravado there was something very appealing about Josette. "I'm sure you're wrong."

"What do you know? They *hate* me." She shrugged with a pretense of carelessness. "Not that I care."

"Why would they dislike you?"

"Because they're stupid and jealous." She added, "They say I'm a foreigner and the enemy."

Cassie looked at her in bewilderment. "Foreigner?"

"I'm Josette Brasnier, the Comtesse de Talaisar." She rolled the title off her tongue with flamboyant grandeur. "And a French comtesse is far better than any of their puny English titles."

Foreigner. Brasnier. French. The words whirled wildly in Cassie's mind. She had heard that name only once before, but it was one she would never forget.

"What's wrong?" Josette asked, stiffening.

The words were difficult to form, "Who was . . . the Compte de Talaisar to you?"

Josette frowned. "My father, of course."

The child. Cassie had been so stunned at the murderous implication against her father, she had forgotten completely about the child Jared's father had rescued from the soldiers. This must be the only survivor of the family Jared claimed her father had betrayed. "Danjuet."

"You've heard of my home?"

"Yes." The story Jared had told her was suddenly coming alive in the form of this young girl. She didn't want that past to come alive; she wanted to push it away from her.

"Did Jared tell—"

"I think it's time you went back to the carriage room," she interrupted harshly as she opened the door of the stall. "You may not want to sleep, but I do."

"What did I do?" Josette asked, bewildered. "What did I say to—" She broke off and then lifted her head proudly. "It's because I'm French, isn't it? You hate me because of that beast Napoléon. You're like all the others."

"No."

"You lie. It's because I'm not English. Why else would you change so quickly? I can feel you going away from me."

It would be easier to let Josette think that it was her French birth that offended Cassie—but she couldn't do it. She herself had been balanced too long between two worlds. "It's not because you're French. My father was French, and if anyone's a foreigner in this land, it's I." She didn't look at her. "Ask Jared."

"I'm asking you."

"And I'm not answering you. Ask Jared." She lay down on the straw, drew her blanket over her, and turned her back. "And after you do, I doubt you'll care what I think."

She could feel Josette's gaze on her back. She felt as if she had struck a puppy. Ridiculous. Josette was much more like a young tigress. When Jared told her that Cassie was the daughter of the man responsible for her parents' death, she would probably launch a lethal attack.

She heard Josette's soft exclamation and then retreating footsteps.

Go to sleep. Nothing had changed just because she had met one of the people who had shared that terrible experience at Danjuet. It wasn't as if Josette would ever have been a friend to her, anyway. She must make no friends here at Morland. She must keep everyone at a distance.

Yet Josette had not allowed her to distance herself; she had plummeted into Cassie's life and forced a place for herself. Almost from the first moment Cassie had felt as comfortable with Josette as if she had known her all her life.

Well, the incident was over. The girl meant nothing to her. This strange bond of familiarity between the two of them could not hold firm when tested by the information Jared would give the young comptesse.

She heard the slam of the coach door in the carriage room. Josette was settling for the night.

Cassie shivered and drew the covers around her shoulders. The early-morning chill was beginning to creep into the stable.

She should have made Josette take one of Kapu's blankets. . . .

It was barely dawn when Cassie left the stable. She was only halfway across the courtyard when Jared opened the front door and stood watching her come toward him. He was without a coat, his shirtsleeves rolled up and his dark hair tousled. His appearance at this hour could not be a coincidence. He had been waiting for her.

Dear God, she did not want to face him now. She felt grimy and sleepy, and she was still suffering that odd sense of loss.

"I hope Kapu had a better night than I." Jared's gaze raked her face. "Or you."

"I slept." It was true that after much tossing and turning she had finally managed to snatch a few hours' sleep.

"I didn't." He smiled mockingly. "I sat in my chair in the library and waited for you to abandon your vigil."

"I told you I wasn't going to come to you."

"You malign me." He opened the door and stepped aside to let her pass. "I had no lustful motives . . . this time. I merely stayed to see that you found your way to your quarters. Morland has three wings and many chambers. It would have been very distressing to the servants to have to search for you if you became lost."

"I would have just waited on the doorstep until the household woke. Besides, I never became lost on the island. I doubt if I would here."

"But the island is your home, your territory." He smiled. "This is mine."

She didn't need him to remind her. Now that she was away from the familiar sights and scents of the stable, she was beginning to feel very much alone and far from home. "Will you stop boasting and show me where I'm to sleep?"

"I wasn't boasting, I was merely pointing out the similarities between—" His smile faded as he studied her. "I'm not going to lie to you. There are very few similarities between your island and England. You're going to hate it here." He paused. "Unless you let me help you."

"A bargain, I suppose?"

His lips tightened. "No, goddammit, what's between us is a thing apart. I brought you here and that makes me responsible for you. I don't want you hurt."

"I won't be hurt." She turned and started for the stairs. "Did you put me in a chamber close to Lani?"

"No, I put you in the chamber next door to me." He moved past her and up the stairs. "So close I may be able to hear you breathe. I think I'll enjoy lying in my bed and listening for every little sound." He looked at her over his shoulder, and his voice deepened to silken sensuality. "It will be almost like being beside you."

A wave of heat surged through her as she met his gaze. Blast it, this was exactly what he wanted her to feel. She gave him a deliberately derisive glance. "These walls appear too thick to hear anything but a cannon shot."

His lips twitched. "True. Too bad you noticed."

"And I want to be next door to Lani."

He preceded her down a long hallway. "Guests have no choice in their quarters here at Morland. Placing you near Lani might prove inconvenient later."

He meant when she changed her mind and came to his bed. "I can't foresee any possible inconvenience."

He stopped before a door. "I can." He threw open the door. "I can foresee an endless variety. So you'll remain here." He nodded at the brocade bellpull on the wall across the room. "Ring if you need anything. I'd say a bath is in order." He turned away. "I'll send you breakfast at ten. You were going to meet Bradford at eleven, I believe."

"He told you?"

"Of course, he knew I'd want to be there."

"I don't want you there."

"I didn't think you would. But I'll be there all the same."

"Then I won't let Kapu—"

"Yes, you will," he interrupted. "You promised Bradford and you won't break your word." He strolled to a door only a few yards away. "I'll see you at eleven."

Cassie watched the door close behind him before she shut the door of her chamber. He was always so maddeningly confident of his knowledge of her. She should deliberately stay away from the stables to confound him. No, that would be childish. Bradford would be disappointed, and she would not let Jared's actions force her into doing anything she would not ordinarily do. These weeks at Morland would be difficult enough without allowing him to confuse her in that fashion.

Her glance traveled indifferently around the chamber. She supposed it was considered very grand, with its canopied bed draped in burgundy velvet and the heavy, rich oak furniture and high ceilings, but she found little to admire. Houses were only a place to shelter when she wasn't in the stable or outdoors. The cottage had been just as adequate as this castle for that purpose.

But Jared was right—after the night in the stable she did need a bath and a meal. She moved quickly toward the bellpull across the room.

Eleven

Bradford was standing by Kapu's stall when Cassie arrived at eleven. Jared was not with him.

Bradford gave her a smile. "We'll have to wait a bit for Jared."

"I agreed to let you, not Jared, time Kapu." She entered the stall and gave Kapu a greeting pat before turning to the saddle in the corner. "If he's not here when I've finished saddling Kapu, we go on without him." She threw the saddle onto Kapu's back. "Or we don't do it at all."

He grimaced. "I believe I detect a hint of displeasure toward Jared. Has he particularly annoyed you recently?"

"It's rude not to be punctual."

"Jared is always punctual. Something unexpected came up this morning." He paused. "As I understand you might know. Josette tells me you encountered each other last night."

"Did she?" She fastened the girth.

"You upset her."

She didn't answer.

"But she liked you." He grinned. "But, then, I knew she would."

"Why? We have little in common."

"Because she's a comtesse? That doesn't matter. She uses the title only when she wants to protect herself. Tell me, when you met her didn't you feel—"

"I felt bruised. She jumped on top of me."

"You know that's not what I meant. Did she remind you of anyone?"

"Very well, she seemed familiar. I don't know why."

"Look in the mirror. She could be your twin."

She frowned. "What do you mean? We're nothing alike."

"Not on the outside. But you definitely should have felt a bond. I didn't know you at sixteen, but I'll wager that most of your responses were exactly like Josette's. She's constantly in trouble, defiant, eager, impulsive." He chuckled. "And if she were transported to your island, she would be wearing a sarong instead of those trousers that so horrify Lady Carradine."

It was true. Now that he had held up the mirror, she could see herself in Josette. No wonder she had felt comfortable with the girl so quickly. "Will Jared punish her for running away from that school?"

"I doubt it. He won't let her off easily, but Josette usually manages to persuade Jared to do as she wishes. She even persuaded him to name his ship after her."

The *Josephine*. Cassie had not made the association. "Then why does he make her go to that school? She doesn't like it."

He shrugged. "It's the finest in the county. Josette would hate the restrictions of any school."

Cassie shuddered as she remembered the threats to

send her to a convent. She would have been as miserable as Josette if Clara had prevailed. "He should let her stay here. If she causes him trouble, it's because she's unhappy."

"It's not possible. We try to have her for long visits, but she would be ruined if she stayed at Morland."

"Ruined?

He hesitated and then shrugged. "I was searching for a discreet explanation, but that's not necessary with you. The Lady Carradines of our set don't entirely approve of the goings-on at Morland."

"What goings-on?"

"Oh, racing, gambling, drinking, and . . ." He made a vague gesture. "Other things."

Those other things probably included carnal debauchery with the women from London, with whom Josette appeared very familiar. "As long as Josette doesn't do those things, why should it matter?"

"Ah, so speaks the clear-eyed young sage. Poor Cassie, you've come to a land in many ways more savage than your own. It should not matter, but, believe me, it does."

"She's right to ignore such foolishness."

"Unfortunately, she doesn't ignore it, she strikes back. She needs constant supervision, and Jared and I are continually traveling."

"Then you should forget about hounding my father and stay home."

He lifted his brows. "It seems Josette has a new champion."

"I'm not her champion. She's nothing to me." She opened the stall door and led Kapu out. "And I'll be less than nothing to her when she finishes talking to Jared."

"Possibly. One can never be sure which way

Josette's going to jump. She's as unpredictable as you are."

She wished he'd quit comparing them. "It doesn't matter to me which way she jumps."

"You mean you won't let yourself care. Josette would respond in the same way."

He had done it again. She said through her teeth, "I'm not waiting any longer for Jared. Where is this race course?"

Bradford gestured to the rear entrance to the stable. "Out those doors and beyond the meadow. It's a half mile north. Go outside. I'll have Joe saddle my horse and I'll be with you in a minute."

She would have to lead Kapu past Morgana's stall, she realized with a mixture of anticipation and reluctance. Well, she was certain to see them together sometime; Jared must ride the mare frequently. He might even choose to do it today.

"Something wrong?" Bradford asked.

"No." She started down the aisle. "I'll wait for you outside."

Morgana ignored Kapu.

The mare took one glance at the stallion and then discreetly turned her head.

Kapu was equally oblivious. He trotted past the stall as if it were empty.

Cassie smiled ruefully. She might believe that they were perfect mates, but the horses were clearly not impressed with each other. It was an entirely natural response. Stallions were seldom interested in mares out of season. She had been foolish to expect anything else.

Jared arrived at the race course, riding Morgana, as Kapu was finishing his third run.

Cassie didn't look at him as she reined in beside Bradford, breathless, exhilarated, cheeks stinging from the cold wind. "That's enough. Kapu doesn't like all this starting and stopping. He's been on that ship for weeks, and I need to let him go. Where is there terrain safe enough to let him loose?"

"How fast?" Jared asked Bradford.

"Better than Morgana's best time on the first run. Less on the second, the third about the same."

"Christ." He turned to Cassie, his eyes glittering with excitement. "One more run."

"No." Cassie kept her gaze on Bradford. "I've done what you asked, Bradford. We're both tired of this nonsense. Now, where can I let him go?"

"I want to see it myself," Jared said.

"Then you should have been here."

"Dammit, I couldn't be here. I had to—" He stopped as he saw the stubborn set of her jaw. "I'll show you a safe path." He turned Morgana. "Come along."

"You can just tell me."

"The devil I will. If you won't let me time him, I'll at least see him in motion. There's a five-mile path along the cliff that's free of brush and potholes."

"Can I ride on the beach?"

"Too many rocks.

Craggy rocks, gray skies, biting wind, and glowering castles. Being in this unfriendly England was like being on another planet. "Are you coming, Bradford?"

He shook his head. "I think I'll see if I can find Lani. I'm surprised she didn't come with you."

Cassie smiled. "She discovered the library. She said she had never seen so many books. She may not come out for the rest of the time we're here."

"Good God, that may mean I'll have to stuff more learning into this noggin. What a coil." He lifted a hand in farewell and the next moment was galloping back toward the stable.

"Ready?" Jared asked. He didn't wait for an answer but kicked Morgana into a gallop and raced across the meadow in the direction of the cliff.

Cassie trailed behind, deliberately holding Kapu back, watching Jared. He and the mare were incredibly beautiful together. She had seen Jared on horseback only that one brief, explosive moment on the beach, and that didn't really count. Lean, tight grace and centaur strength merged with the high-spirited beauty of the mare. He effortlessly controlled Morgana yet used no force.

He reined in, glancing over his shoulder.

She nudged Kapu into a faster pace in response to the silent demand. Demand and response. In the hot darkness of the cabin she had become accustomed to meeting every need even before he voiced them, just as he had met her own. But now everything was different; she must break the habit. She deliberately slowed Kapu again as she drew near Jared.

He smiled crookedly. "Lower your guard, for God's sake. Every minute doesn't have to be a battle. I've no devious purpose at the moment. I just want to watch Kapu run. Is that so terrible?"

She could hardly object when she had lingered behind to see Jared and Morgana together. "No." She paused. "But it's your fault I'm on guard. You always make remarks . . . and threats."

"Very well, I'll curb my tongue."

The surrender was unexpected, therefore suspicious. "And your intentions?"

"Temporarily."

"Why?"

"I had a long time to think last night. It's not fair play to pursue you on unfamiliar ground. It annoys me exceedingly, but I believe I'm forced to give you time to grow familiar with Morland before I pounce."

It did annoy him. She could sense the barely leashed frustration beneath the mocking tone. She responded slowly, "Bradford said you were a just man."

"On occasion. I know it's a disappointment to realize I'm not completely lost to virtue."

He was right. She didn't want him to be honorable or just; he was robbing her of weapons to fight him. "You didn't seem overly virtuous this morning."

"I'm being patient, not foolish. I have every intention of seducing you to my way of thinking. I just promise not to snatch . . . for a while."

"Thank you."

He ignored the irony of her tone. "But I'll require something from you in return." He held up his hand when she opened her lips to object. "The opportunity to seduce. I won't touch you against your will, but you'll come to supper every night, and you must give me some portion of the day to persuade you to come back to my bed."

"I don't have to give you anything."

"Christ, you're stubborn. Can't you see I'm trying to make this easier for you?"

She looked away from him.

"Would you prefer threats? I can make it very uncomfortable for you at Morland. The master of the castle is also the master of the stable." His gaze went meaningly to Kapu. "What if I forbade you access to the stallion?"

Her gaze flew to him in alarm. "You wouldn't do that."

"Why not? Don't you think I'd do anything to—" He broke off, then said wearily, "No, I wouldn't do that to you. I'd find another way."

Yet he had discarded the one weapon that would have forced her to his will. He had known she would have yielded almost anything for Kapu. "There's no other way," she whispered.

"I'm wagering there may be one." He met her gaze. "Fair play, Cassie. You don't like to be bound by it any more than I do, but you can't turn your back. I'm giving a great deal, including Kapu, and asking very little."

If she did as he asked, it would be a way to be close to him without returning to that sensual underworld. She might be able to learn something that would help Papa. She felt a scalding rush of emotion at the thought. Betrayal. Betrayal of Jared.

Dear God, she should not be ashamed to think of her father at this moment. Why else was she here? "It's not going to change anything. Papa . . ."

He knew at once what she was trying to say. He smiled mirthlessly. "I didn't think it would. I'm not trying to seduce your soul, only your body. You claim the two are separate, don't you?"

"Yes." Yet in those last days on the ship she had begun to have doubts and had broken the bond. What he was offering now was time spent in a sunlit world. Surely it was the coupling that had been dangerous, the pleasure intoxicating. It was the blending of the darkness and the sunlight that she had feared. "I suppose we could . . . ride together."

"Not a splendid concession. It's difficult to seduce a woman on a horse." He pretended to think about it. "Though not impossible. And what shall we do if the weather is inclement? Never mind, I'll think of something."

It had seemed a small concession, but she was suddenly beset by doubts. "Perhaps I shouldn't. . . ."

"Come on," he interrupted. "There's a cliff just ahead. Don't let Kapu veer off the path, or you'll find yourself falling a hundred feet onto some very sharp rocks."

"Kapu isn't stupid enough to fall off a cliff. I'll just show him the edge and he'll avoid the danger."

"Ah, how I envy those splendid instincts. But sometimes the thrill of dancing on the edge is worth the danger." He changed the subject. "You met Josette last night. What did you think of her?"

"It doesn't matter what I think." She paused. "Did you tell her why I'm here?"

"Yes. I could hardly keep silent when you told her to ask me. I didn't mention our intimacy on the ship, but I told her all about you and Lani . . . and your father."

"What did she . . . never mind. I don't want to know."

He answered her anyway. "She was shocked, of course. She was little more than a babe when I brought her to Morland and has only a vague recollection of her parents."

She veered away from the thought of the doomed Compte and his wife. "She said she was a comptesse."

He nodded. "Thanks to the terror, there was no one else to inherit. However, the revolutionary government confiscated the estate, so she has only the title."

If Papa was to blame for her parents' deaths, then he was also to blame for Josette's loss of her birthright.

If? The thought had come out of nowhere, and yet she knew it must have been lying dormant. It was the first time she had ever questioned his innocence, and she must not do it again. All she had to sustain her was her trust. "I'm sure you'll make certain she wants for nothing."

"We try." He grimaced. "But Josette's needs are for more than food and shelter. It was easier when she was a little girl running about Morland, caring only about the horses and her boat."

"Boat?"

He glanced at the vast gray ocean. "In case you didn't notice, we live by the sea. Josette has had a small sailboat since she was old enough to handle it. When she's not on a horse's back, she's sailing."

"She seems to spend more time penned up in this Lady Carradine's school than doing either."

His lips tightened. "It was necessary."

"Because you didn't wish to modify your lewd actions to make a home for her."

"Who told . . ." He shook his head. "Bradford."

"You should not have made her your ward if you wished to fornicate with all those women."

"I suppose I should have left her alone in France," he said sarcastically.

"I didn't say that. You told me once that every action has a response. Perhaps in some instances action also requires adaptation."

"Bradford and I didn't know anything about raising a young girl. We did the best we could."

"By letting her run wild and witness your debauchery."

"She did not witness—" He stopped, thought back, and modified the statement. "Much. And it did no harm when she was a child. She was happy. It was only later that I realized—Dammit, I was only a boy. I didn't know anything about being a guardian."

"You're not a boy now, and your conduct in Hawaii and shipboard was carnal in the extreme. I see no sign that you've changed your ways."

He scowled. "I'm not a monk. Nothing I did away from her could have affected Josette." His eyes suddenly narrowed. "Why are you so passionately concerned about my behavior? You ran wild yourself as a child, and in your philosophy coupling is of no importance. Isn't that right?"

"That's right." She wasn't certain why the idea of him in bed with those other women had so upset her. She had been irritated when Josette had casually mentioned them the night before, and Bradford's confirmation had added salt to the wound. She pounced on the first reasonable answer that occurred to her. "But Bradford says that such unfettered conduct is condemned here. Condemnation can hurt, and to cause pain to another is never good."

"I don't believe that Josette's pain is your entire reason for attacking me." He smiled. "But I won't pursue the matter, since I'm not sure you're aware of it yourself." He reined in and gestured to the path. "Here we are, you can let Kapu go now. Stop at the forest. The ground becomes rough there."

Hiding her relief, she carefully nudged Kapu past Morgana. "Aren't you coming?"

He shook his head. "I want to watch him run. Even if I can't time him, I'll be able to judge his speed."

"I don't see why it's important. You saw him run the first night I met you."

He smiled. "But I wasn't able to concentrate on the stallion. I was definitely distracted."

She could feel heat rise to her cheeks as the memory of that night came back to her. It had been no mere distraction for her. He had walked out of that thatch of trees into her life, changing it forever.

She bent over the stallion's neck and loosened the reins. "Go, Kapu!"

It was the only invitation he needed. He streaked like an arrow down the path. Cassie clung to him, gripping with thighs and calves.

Wind whipped her cheeks and snatched away her breath.

Kapu's stride lengthened until he scarcely touched the ground.

Sea, sky, and earth became a blur.

"That's right," she murmured. "Run!"

He ran! She could hear his labored breathing as the pace increased and then increased again.

Dear Lord, she had missed this almost as much as Kapu had.

She felt as if she were floating, anchored to the earth only by the thunder of the stallion's hooves.

They reached the edge of the forest too soon for either of them. She reluctantly reined him in and turned back toward the castle.

Jared met her when she was halfway back to the stable, his eyes blazing with excitement. "My God, he's wonderful."

"Yes," she said simply. Contentment flowed through her as if he had praised her child. She was too filled with sheer joy to feel antagonism or wariness for anyone in the world. "It was a good run. He feels better now."

"And so do you."

She nodded. "Maybe this England isn't completely bad. The wind is sharp, but battling it causes a certain exhilaration." She patted Kapu's neck. "We enjoyed it, didn't we, boy?" She glanced at Jared. "Well, did you judge his speed?"

He blinked. "No!"

"Why not?"

"I was watching him and, dammit, I forgot all about it."

She burst out laughing. She had never known Jared not to be in control, and now he looked like a cross little boy.

Her lips were still twitching when she said, "I assure you, he was very fast indeed."

"I know." His tone was distinctly surly. "And I don't like to be laughed at."

Her eyes were dancing as she accused, "You were dazzled."

His gaze was fixed bemusedly on her face. "Completely." He glanced away from her. "I still am."

Her smile vanished. Warmth and humor and amusement were all there in his expression. In a way, such emotions were more dangerous than lust. She hurriedly glanced down at Morgana. "She's a magnificent mare."

"As I told you."

"But not as fine as Kapu."

"And what makes the stallion better?"

"Because he's mine," she said simply.

He laughed. "Why doesn't that statement surprise me?"

"Aren't you the same? Don't you think that Morgana is finer because she belongs to you?"

"I suppose I'm a bit biased, but I try to control it. For instance, I'm ready to admit that Kapu may be faster."

She grunted in disgust. "I don't see why you're all

so excited about how fast they are. Bradford could talk about nothing but the races you have here."

"I admit I'm also guilty. I'd love to see Morgana and Kapu race."

"I won't allow it," she said quickly. "I don't want them ever pitted against each other."

"Why not?"

"Because I like Morgana."

"And?"

"Can't you see? They don't like each other. They're only ignoring each other now, but I won't have them enemies."

"They're not ignoring each other."

"Of course they are."

"Oh, they're not being obvious about it, but I've noticed a few sidelong glances."

She frowned. "You're wrong."

"Watch them. Perhaps I'm more accustomed to such subtleties than you are." His glance shifted away from her to the fence bordering the meadow. "There's Josette. She's waiting for you."

Cassie stiffened as her gaze followed his to the small figure sitting on the top rail of the fence. "There's no reason for her to want to speak to me. She's probably waiting for you."

His lips twisted. "I assure you that after our talk this morning she won't want to see me for a while. Besides, she came up with a rather unique suggestion regarding you. She probably wants to discuss it."

The girl probably wanted to see her drawn and quartered, Cassie thought gloomily.

"At any rate, I'll leave you alone and let her have her chance." He nudged Morgana into a gallop and headed for the stable. He nodded at Josette as he passed, and she gave him a wary glance. Then her attention shifted to Cassie.

"You've been a long time. I've been waiting for hours." Her gaze went to Kapu. "How fast is he?"

"You didn't wait for me to find out how fast Kapu could run." Cassie rode the stallion up to the fence and braced herself. "Did you?"

"Well, not primarily, but I'm always interested." Josette soberly met her gaze. "You think I'm going to blame you for what your father did."

"For what Jared says my father did," she corrected.

"He's usually right about most things."

"He's not about—"

Josette waved her hand to silence her. "I'm not here to argue. The quarrel's between Jared and him, not us. I'd never blame anyone for being born to the wrong father or the wrong country. I've suffered too much myself for my birth."

Cassie felt a rush of relief. She had not realized until this moment how much she had dreaded Josette's condemnation. "Thank you. You're being very generous."

"Not as generous as you think." Josette's eyes were suddenly twinkling. "There's a price to pay. When can I ride Kapu?"

Cassie shook her head. The girl was impossible. "He'd kill you."

"Maybe not. I told you, I'm good with horses." She jumped down from the fence and moved forward to open the gate. "Come on. I'll help you put him up."

Cassie felt bewildered. She had feared this encounter since she had discovered the girl's identity, and Josette was being almost casual about it.

Josette's gaze narrowed on her face. "It's not so strange," she said as if she had read her thoughts. "I was very young when my parents were killed. Jared and Bradford are the only family I remember. Did you know that after his father was killed, Jared brought me to England himself?"

"No."

"He was holding me when they murdered his father. His wrists were bound, but he managed to slip into the underbrush and hide in the forest for three days. Then he made his way to the ship his father had arranged to meet them. He wasn't able to get the ropes off, and his wrists were still tied and bloody when he reached the coast."

I hate to be bound.

No wonder. He must have felt terribly helpless and frustrated, bound, bereaved, with a small child to tend. The experience would have scarred anyone.

"So you wouldn't find me understanding if you or your father did something to hurt Jared." Josette closed the gate behind Cassie. "But you're very interesting. I can't stand those ninnies at school. I believe I'll enjoy your stay here at Morland. You can tell me all about that odd place where you lived, and we'll ride and have great fun."

"Indeed? Jared regards me as a hostage, you know."

Josette made a face. "A very peculiar hostage, who's permitted to ride freely over the estate. I don't see that as a problem." She opened the stable door. "Now, what about this Lani? Is she really your father's mistress?"

Cassie stiffened. "Yes."

Josette didn't seem to notice the change in her demeanor. "Many of Jared's friends have mistresses, but they don't usually let me meet them. Once at one of

Jared's house parties I saw one of his lady birds slip into his room."

"Lady birds?"

"Light of loves, cyprians." When Cassie still looked at her blankly, she said baldly, "Whores."

Heat stung Cassie's cheeks. "Lani is not a whore. Don't you dare compare her to one. She's as respectable as—"

"I didn't know," Josette interrupted. "My apologies. Here in England mistresses are not considered—" She broke off and gave a deep sigh. "I always say the wrong thing. I meant no offense."

The girl was so clearly penitent that Cassie's anger ebbed away. "She's my friend."

"Will I like her?"

"Maybe." Cassie thought back to those first days after Lani had come to the cottage. Cassie had been rebellious and full of jealousy and resentment, and it had taken time for Lani to win her over. Josette was not as young as Cassie had been then but was just as independent and proud. "Perhaps not at once, but then you'll love her."

"Oh, she's like Jared." Josette nodded in understanding. "Sometimes I want to throttle him. He's always so right about everything." She smiled. "But then he does something absolutely splendid, and you forget all the rest."

Clearly the girl adored Jared even when she wanted to do him injury, Cassie thought. What had he done to deserve such affection? "Jared's not at all like Lani," she said dryly as she dismounted.

Morgana was already in her stall, and as Cassie led Kapu past her, she watched closely for the sidelong glances Jared had mentioned.

Blast it!

How had he noticed something almost imperceptible? She could fully sympathize with Josette's annoyance over Jared's disgusting habit of being right.

"You're frowning. Are you still angry with me?" Josette asked anxiously.

She smiled. "No, I'm not angry."

"Then after we get Kapu comfortable, will you introduce me to your Lani?"

Cassie nodded. "Very well. We'll go to the library when we finish."

As soon as Cassie and Josette left the stable and started across the courtyard, they spied the handsome carriage pulled up before the front entrance of the castle.

"Oh, no!" Josette's eyes widened in alarm. "She's here!"

"Who is here?" Cassie asked.

"Lady Carradine." Josette grabbed Cassie by the arm and pulled her away. "I didn't think she'd be here this soon. She could at least let me have a few days before she pounced."

"What difference does it make? You said Jared had promised to let you stay."

"It's not that simple. I had to convince him it wouldn't hurt my reputation to come back. I thought everything would be fine, but she didn't give me time enough to—Listen, this is the way it is." She spoke quickly. "You're my second cousin, Cassandra Deville. Your father left France to go to Tahiti years ago, and he became a farmer. He grew . . ." She searched wildly. "Rum."

"Rum's a drink made of sugar cane."

"Well, then he grew sugar cane. They grow sugar cane in Tahiti, don't they?"

"I don't know, I'm from Hawaii."

"I keep forgetting. Jared was going to Tahiti. Well, it won't matter. Who ever heard of Hawaii, anyway? Well, maybe that Captain Cook, but—"

"I don't know what on earth you're talking about."

"I need a chaperon, or Jared won't let me stay."

Cassie looked at her dazedly. "I'm supposed to be a chaperon as well as a hostage?"

"Well, you're not really old enough to be a chaperon, but I thought your Lani would do. Of course, she can't be your father's mistress, she has to be his widow." She half pushed Cassie up the stairs. "But she's old enough to be considered past her prime."

Cassie remembered her last glimpse of Lani in the library—youthful, vibrant, gloriously beautiful. "It won't work," she said flatly.

"We can try." She stopped outside the library door and gazed pleadingly at Cassie. "Please try. I don't want to go back with her."

Cassie hesitated. The entire scheme was mad, but Josette's desperation was hard to resist. As long as she was forced to be here anyway, it would be cruel to deny Josette her freedom. "Jared agreed to this?"

"He thought the plan had possibilities. He had to have a reason for your presence here." She drew a deep breath. "You don't owe me anything, but I'm asking you for a favor. Don't make me go away." She turned the knob and flung open the door. "Lady Carradine, I didn't expect you."

The woman to whom Jared was talking turned at Josette's words. Lady Carradine was small of stature and exquisitely fair, and the cool perfection of her features reminded Cassie of a lady on a cameo. "I didn't expect to have to run after you. I have better things to do with my time, Josette." Her glance disapprovingly ran over the young girl. "And you're wearing those terrible trousers again. I told you they weren't acceptable." Her attention shifted to Cassie. "Who is this?"

"Lady Carradine, may I present my cousin, Cassandra Deville?" Josette's grasp tightened on Cassie's arm as if she were afraid Cassie would flee. "My *older* cousin."

"Evidently not old enough to know decorum." The woman's gaze went over Cassie's worn habit. "A divided skirt? Good heavens, such conduct must be a family trait. That garment is little better than those hideous trousers."

Cassie felt a flare of anger. "It's served me well. I don't see—"

"Clothes are hardly important, Carolyn," Jared said quickly as he stepped between them. "I do appreciate your coming to make sure this urchin of mine is safe, but you can see all is well."

"I see nothing of the sort," Carolyn Carradine said. She took a step closer to Jared and placed her hand on his arm, smiling sweetly up at him. "Jared, be guided by me in this. We must be very careful of Josette. Let me take her back to Carradine Hall, where no breath of scandal will touch her."

"No scandal will touch her here."

She shook her head and her smile became arch. "We've discussed this before. You've been too much a rake for anyone to believe you've reformed. Not while you're still unmarried."

"But I have a chaperon." Josette turned to Jared. "Did you tell her about Madam Deville?"

"Since you weren't here, I had that privilege," he said dryly.

"A widow." Josette added for good measure. "And old. Almost thirty."

Lady Carradine, whom Cassie judged to be over thirty, was not pleased. Her lips tightened. "I'd like to meet Madam Deville."

"She's ill and not able to receive visitors," Jared said. "She's a fragile creature, and the journey was too much for her."

"Then she should not have the custody of two young girls."

"She'll be better in a day or two," Cassie said. The words tumbled from her lips unbidden. She had not meant to involve herself any more than she was forced. "Lani has a strong constitution."

"Lani?" Carolyn Carradine's tone became speculative. "What a strange name."

"Not as lovely as 'Carolyn,' certainly," Jared said with a warm smile. "You can meet Madam Deville at a later time."

"I'd like to meet her now. Isn't it—" She met Jared's gaze and accurately read the inflexibility of his expression. She surrendered at once and gave him another brilliant smile. "Of course, if she's not well, I'll not disturb her. But I feel it necessary to make sure dear Josette is in safe hands. I'm giving a small ball in six weeks' time. If Madam Deville's as resilient as you say, I should be able to meet her then. You'll make sure she's there?"

"Who would dare miss one of your soirees?" Jared lifted her gloved hand to his lips. "Of course we'll be there."

She lingeringly removed her hand and patted his cheek. "Splendid." She turned and moved brusquely toward the door. "And I want to hear no more of these trousers. You must exercise some control over your ward, Jared."

Jared gave Josette a barbed glance. "You're probably right. I've noticed she's been somewhat out of control lately." He followed Carolyn to the door. "Let me escort you to your carriage."

Josette gave an explosive sigh as the door closed behind them. She plopped down onto a chair. "Thank heaven that's over."

"I'm not sure it's over. It sounded like a postponement to me."

"Well, at least it was a good beginning." She threw one leg over the arm of the chair and began to swing it. "I was afraid it would go much worse."

"She seems quite . . . determined. I'm surprised she gave up so easily."

"She didn't want to cross Jared when she saw he wouldn't bend. She wants to be a duchess." She raised her brows when she saw Cassie's expression. "Why are you surprised? Half the women in England want to marry Jared."

She shouldn't be shocked. She had thought of Jared in connection with mistresses but not marriage. She tried to make her tone casual. "Have they known each other for a long time?"

"Over seven years. She was married to a friend of Jared's, Lord Marcus Carradine. When his horse threw him and he was killed, she was left with nothing but a few pounds and Carradine Hall. She turned it into a school for young ladies."

Cassie tried to be fair. "Very commendable."

"Ambitious," Josette corrected. "She's insinuated her way into the most powerful houses in England through their daughters. She's now looked upon as the standard setter for decorum in the county. She'd like nothing better than to extend her influence to Prinny's court through Jared."

"Prinny?" Cassie asked.

"The king's son, of course."

"I see." She remembered the seductive smile Jared had bestowed on Carolyn Carradine. "And how does Jared feel?"

"Well, he won't tolerate my insulting her. I don't know if it's because he wants to encourage respect and keep the peace, or if he likes her." She started to swing her other booted foot. "Is your Lani as comely as Joseph said?"

"She's truly lovely."

"Then I'm glad she wasn't here. The gargoyle doesn't like beautiful women around Jared, and it would have caused endless trouble." She grinned. "It's just as well you're looking so plain and frumpy today. She paid little attention to you."

"Very fortunate," she said with irony.

"Oh, I didn't mean—I told you my tongue runs away from me."

"At full speed," Jared said dryly from the doorway. "What indiscretion have you committed now?"

"Is she gone?" Josette asked.

"Yes." He shut the door and came toward them. "And none too soon. I felt as if I were going to trip any second on one of those lies you concocted."

"You're much too clever to do that." Josette grinned. "You did very well."

He bowed mockingly. "Thank you. But it would have been more clever of you to change before running in here. You know she hates those trousers."

Cassie frowned. "You're not going to forbid her to wear them?"

Josette chuckled. "Why would he do that? Jared gave me my first pair of trousers when I was four years old."

"Fashion is all very well, but riding sidesaddle is a death trap if a horse falls," Jared said. "That divided skirt you wear is safer, but there's still too much material. You'll wear trousers, too, while you're here."

She did not question the intense pleasure she received at his small defiance of Josette's "gargoyle." "Then you deceived Lady Carradine."

He smiled crookedly. "On any number of issues. There's usually a price to pay for deceit. I hope it doesn't prove too high."

"Well, I think everything is proceeding splendidly," Josette said. "And the only price would be for Lady Carradine to expel me from school, and that's no price at all."

His smile disappeared. "It's a very great price, and one I won't have you pay. Carolyn can have you ostracized from the ton with two sentences. I won't have her say those words."

Josette made a disgusted snort. "You care little for your own reputation. It's not fair to make me—"

"Hush." His hand gently covered her lips. "A woman is different, the consequences are heavier." He smiled warmly as he coaxed. "Trust me in this. Have I ever done anything that wasn't for your good?"

"No." She kissed his palm and pushed it aside before saying gruffly, "But I still don't think it's fair. I should make the decisions as to what is important to me."

"When you're older." He leaned down and brushed her forehead with his lips. "I'm not the best guide for a young girl, but I'm all you have. You don't want me torn with guilt, do you?"

Cassie felt an aching loneliness as she watched them. She had never seen Jared this tender before. The strong affection between the two was bright, warm, and clearly of long standing. For some strange reason it hurt her to look at them together. She quickly turned to leave. "I have to see Lani. She's not truly ill, is she?"

"No. I had Bradford whisk her away when I saw Carolyn's carriage. I thought it best."

Josette smiled slyly. "Because the gargoyle is too vain to tolerate comely women?"

Jared's lips tightened. "How many times do I have to tell you not to refer to her by that term?"

"Sorry," she said. "But she is vain."

"A trifle," Jared allowed. "At any rate, I thought it best not to complicate matters." He glanced at Cassie. "And there was no reason to distress Lani."

"How kind."

He frowned. "Dammit, I'm trying to do what's best for everyone."

"Then I'm sure you were right to whisk Lani away. She's lovely enough to make anyone jealous." She moved toward the door. "While, as Josette pointed out, I'm too plain and frumpy to present any threat at all."

"Plain?" he said thickly. "My God, plain!"

She glanced over her shoulder and inhaled sharply as she saw his expression. She quickly tore her gaze away and encountered Josette's speculative stare. The girl was too shrewd not to realize the implication in that single expletive. "I have to see Lani," she repeated in a muffled voice as she jerked open the door.

"May I go?" Josette asked. "You promised to introduce me."

"Not now." She needed to get away from both of them. "Later." She slammed the door behind them and fled down the corridor.

"Cassie." Jared was beside her. "What the devil is wrong?"

She didn't look at him. "What could be wrong? Other than that I seem to be getting deeper and deeper into a web of lies."

"You could have told Carolyn the truth."

"I didn't want to hurt Josette."

"Neither do I. And I also didn't want you hurt. Your presence here could be looked upon as improper. It seemed to be the way to serve both purposes."

"Proper?" She looked at him in disbelief. "Propriety is the least of my concerns. You know why I'm here. What do I care what any of your friends think of me?"

"I care," he said harshly. "And I hate it. I don't know why I care, but I do. Do you think I like being as strict and mincing as some pruny old dowager?"

She looked at him, shaken. "I won't let that—" Then the full impact of his words hit home, and she suddenly started to laugh.

He scowled. "I don't see anything amusing."

"I was just picturing you mincing into a ballroom." She shook her head. "I really don't think you're capable of 'mincing,' Jared."

"Lord, I hope not." He smiled grudgingly. "Perhaps a poor choice of words." He moved to take advantage of her softening. "Helping Josette will do you no harm. Will you continue the charade?"

She thought about it. "If it doesn't prove too difficult." She frowned. "This ball you promised to attend is—"

"More than a month away," he finished. "Who knows what will happen in a month? If you're still here, we'll just have to think of some reason to avoid it."

If she was still here.

The phrase gave her a feeling of desolation. Foolishness. If she was not here, she would either be on her way to France to Papa, or they would both be on a ship bound for Hawaii. Either journey should bring her only satisfaction.

She nodded. "Very well, if Lani agrees."

"I don't believe there will be any difficulty with Lani." He hesitated. "Why do you look like that? What's wrong?"

Intimacy. Laughter. Involvement. All the things she had avoided on the ship. All of this was very wrong, and she suddenly felt helpless to keep the bombardment at bay. "Nothing," she muttered.

She turned and hastened away from him.

Cassie took Josette to the library to meet Lani before they went riding the next day.

"The gargoyle mustn't ever see you," Josette said as soon as she caught sight of Lani. She emphatically shook her head. "Not even a glimpse from a mile away."

"Gargoyle?" Lani asked.

"Lady Carradine."

"Oh, yes, Cassie has told me about her," she said. "Surely to refer to her as 'gargoyle' is a little cruel?"

"Actually, it's cruel to gargoyles." Josette paused and then said awkwardly, "Cassie said you'd agreed to help me. I . . . thank you."

Lani chuckled. "Why should I not help you when all it means is not running to this unpleasant person and telling her you had lied? It's true that I prefer to be honest, but this is no sin."

"We're going riding," Cassie said. "Will you come with us, Lani?"

Lani shook her head. "I'll stay here by the fire. It's too cold for me."

"It's only fall," Josette said. "It's not cold at all. The snows won't come for another two months."

"Snow?" Lani shuddered. "I've read about this snow, and I think it's best viewed from a window. Though Cassie remembers it with pleasure."

"It doesn't snow on your island?" Josette asked. "How odd."

"Not odd at all. It's snow that's against nature." Lani smiled. "Someday you must come and see how beautiful it is in our land."

"Maybe," Josette replied. "But Cassie says they don't have wonderful horses as we do here."

"A serious fault, I agree," Lani ceded solemnly. "Much greater than your abundance of snow."

"Are you laughing at me?"

"Yes."

"I don't like people who laugh—" Josette stopped and then said grudgingly, "But I owe you gratitude for helping me with the gargoyle. You may laugh at me, if you like."

"Only with kindness," Lani said gently. "Laughter is a balm for the soul. It would be an arid world without it."

"Those silly girls at school laugh at me, and they don't mean it kindly." She raised her chin. "But I pay no attention to them."

"Only with kindness," Lani repeated, meeting her gaze. "I promise."

Josette stared at her for a long moment. "You mean it?"

"Lani always means what she says," Cassie said.

A sudden mischievous smile lit Josette's face. "Then I guess I'll not put cockroaches in her soup as I do those ninnies." She waved her hand airily. "It's too much trouble catching them, anyway."

"Much too much trouble," Lani said. "But you have imagination. Cockroaches in the soup are far more disgusting than the frog Cassie put in my bed when I first came to the cottage."

Cassie laughed. "I was younger than Josette."

Lani exchanged a smiling glance with her. "But we had our own gargoyle."

"Did you?" Josette asked, curious. "Who?"

Lani waved a hand. "Cassie will tell you about her. Run along and have your ride."

Cassie moved toward the door but Josette hesitated. "I'd like . . . You're not like those other—" She stopped and then said in a rush, "Come with us."

Lani was touched. The girl was clearly so accustomed to battling that to accept an adult readily was nearly impossible for her. Should she go? No, she would be in the way of the two girls getting to know each other. Cassie was going to find it very difficult here, and if she made a friend of Josette, it could only be for the best. "Another time," Lani said. "But you're welcome to come to me here whenever you wish."

Josette nodded jerkily and strode toward the door.

Lani moved toward the window and watched them as they crossed the courtyard. They were both talking animatedly, Josette gesturing, Cassie nodding. Lani felt a wave of loneliness. She had a sudden urge to open the window and call out to them to wait, that she had changed her mind. Books were always friends, but she needed human companionship in this grim fortress.

She did not call.

She turned away from the window and picked up the book she had laid down when Cassie and Josette had come in to the library. They would be better off without her, and she needed time to herself to call up memories of Charles and home. That she found those memories slipping away frightened her. In this cold, chilly land it was difficult even to think of Charles and their life together. If France was like this England, no wonder Charles had been so happy after his flight.

Yet he had still clung to his foreign ways and traditions and had never been able to embrace fully the island ways. Why? She understood his reluctance even less now than she had before.

Why was she brooding about things she had accepted years ago? Think of the good times. Charles's sweetness to her, his need of her.

"May I come in?"

She turned to see Bradford standing in the doorway, smiling at her. That almost boyish smile was always so surprising in his lined, craggy face.

She should send him away. She had been about to refresh her memories of—

"Please?" he coaxed. "I'm lonely."

It was a lonely day in a lonely land. She should not condemn herself for seeking to ease that loneliness for them both.

"Come in." She settled herself in her chair before the fire and opened her book. "But don't expect to be entertained. This book is much too interesting for me to put down."

"Cassie!" Josette's shout echoed off the hall rafters.

"I'm in the library with Lani," Cassie called.

"Well, both of you come and meet Rose."

"Rose?" Cassie exchanged glances with Lani.

Lani shrugged and stood. "Coming."

The thin woman standing beside Josette was nearing forty, with a lovely fair complexion and a pleasant expression. She beamed as Cassie and Lani approached. "Ah, lovely. What a pleasure you'll be to dress." She bustled toward the staircase. "Now, come along to Josette's room. I must get your measurements."

Neither Lani nor Cassie moved.

Rose turned to Josette. "They don't trust me. Tell them how splendid I'll make them." She proceeded up the steps.

"Rose?" Cassie asked Josette.

"Rose Winthrop. She's the finest seamstress in Cornwall. She made me my first pair of trousers." She made a face. "She was disapproving, but Jared convinced her."

"She's going to make me a pair of trousers?" Cassie asked.

"And a few gowns."

"I don't need any gowns."

"Jared thinks you do, and after seeing you last night at dinner, I agree."

"I'll take the trousers, but I—"

"It will do no harm to accept a few gowns," Lani interrupted. "I'm growing weary of seeing you in those garments Clara chose for you."

"And what if someone sees you when they drop in

to visit Jared?" Josette asked. "They would never believe Jared would permit a kinswoman to receive guests in those hideous garments. They're terribly out of fashion, and he's far too knowledgeable about females' wardrobe."

Cassie had no doubt on that score. "Then I'll hide in the stable."

Lani smiled and shook her head. "Don't be foolish."

She was being silly, Cassie realized. A few gowns would make no difference, and arguing would only lend Jared's action importance. "Very well, if you'll have a gown made, too."

"Of course," Lani said as she started up the stairs. "Several. I intend to make use of the man in every way possible."

That should be her attitude also, Cassie thought. Yet every time she made use of him, she found herself more deeply entrenched in his life.

"You'll see, it will be no trouble," Josette told her. "You won't have to make any decisions. Jared has already told her what he wants." Josette took Cassie's hand and pulled her up the steps. "And you'll like Rose. She's very quick, and she'll be careful not to stick you with pins."

"That's encouraging," Cassie said. "It would be most uncomfortable trying to ride Kapu with pinholes in my bottom."

Two pairs of trousers and shirts and jackets arrived for Cassie the next week. The gowns arrived three weeks later.

Four of the lovely garments were in delicate pastel shades. The fifth gown was a brilliant scarlet silk.

Josette shook her head. "You can't wear this. It's

far too . . . too bold. What could Jared have been thinking?"

She knew exactly what Jared had been thinking.

A reminder of those nights in the cabin. A silent assertion that he had not forgotten his intention to have her back in his bed. She stared blindly at the gown while memories rushed back to her.

"Cassie?" Josette was looking at her, puzzled.

Cassie tore her gaze from the gown. "I seldom have any idea what Jared is thinking." She quickly crammed the gown into the rear of her armoire and out of sight. "But you're right, it's far too bold."

"You look very peaceful. Where's Cassie?" Bradford asked as he strolled into the library, carrying a silver tray burdened with cups and teapot.

"Where is she always?" Lani looked up from her book with a smile. "Out riding with Josette."

He set the tray down on the table before her and settled himself in the chair opposite her. "Good. Then I'll have you to myself."

He poured her tea, then added the milk and dollop of sugar she preferred. He always remembered. From the first day he had come to the library to seek her out several weeks ago, he had subtly insinuated himself into her life. Sometimes he stayed for only an hour, other days he curled up by the fire with a book and stayed until it was time to dress for supper. At first having him constantly around had made her uneasy, but she had gradually become accustomed to his presence.

He poured his own tea and took a sip. "Do you know, I'm beginning to like this. I never dreamed I'd say that about such an innocuous brew."

She smiled. "But not as much as your brandy?"

"It's not the stimulant I'd choose." He leaned back in his chair. "But if you're hinting I regret no longer drinking, it's not true. I've been amply compensated." He studied her. "You're looking quite beautiful today. I like you in yellow."

"Do you?" She paused, then said deliberately, "So does Charles."

He stared down into the amber depths of the tea in his cup. "Not as much as I do." He abruptly changed the subject. "Do you resent Josette?"

She looked at him, shocked. "I like Josette very much."

"Everyone likes Josette. That's not what I asked. Do you resent her?"

"Why should I resent her?"

"Cassie seems to spend more time with her than she does with you."

"I'm not a jealous child," she said curtly. "It's perfectly natural for Cassie and Josette to be in each other's company. They're both mad about horses, they're close to the same age, they have similar natures. Of course I don't resent her."

He made a face. "Then you're more tolerant than Jared. I believe he's less than pleased they spend most of the day together." He paused. "And I think you're feeling a little lonely yourself."

"Perhaps." It would have been mean-spirited to envy Cassie her time with Josette, but she was willing to admit to loneliness. "She was never one to stay inside when she could be out and about, but I saw more of her on our island. Or it could be that I was busier there than I am here." She added hastily, "But you must not mention it to her. When we're together, it's just as it always was, and being with Josette is good for Cassie. I was always mother as well as friend to her. Now, in a smaller way, she must take the same role with Josette."

He said dryly, "I haven't noticed her acting particularly maternal. Yesterday she was demonstrating to Josette how to stand upright on a horse's back."

Lani chuckled. "I've seen her do that at a full gallop. It frightened me at first, but she never falls. I gradually became resigned to it."

"Jared didn't show signs of resignation. He pulled her down from the horse, shook her, and told her he never wanted to see her repeat that little trick."

"What did she do?"

"She said she'd ride her horse in any fashion she pleased. Then she stomped away from him."

"She'll do it again," Lani said.

He nodded. "Without doubt." He went back to the original subject. "If you don't want me to bring Cassie to a sense of her responsibility to you, what—"

"She has no responsibility to bear me company."

"Don't interrupt. You said that you were less lonely because you were busier on your island. It appears the remedy is to set you to work."

She raised her brows. "In what manner?"

"Will you take the task of overseeing the castle?"

"Jared already has a housekeeper."

"Mrs. Blakely is a competent soul, but every household needs a mistress."

She frowned. "What makes you think that I could rule this vast place? I've never had a home of my own. Clara even acted as housekeeper at the cottage."

"With you going behind her and smoothing the way, I'd wager."

She did not deny it. "A cottage is not a castle."

"My dear lady, will you stop dithering? We both know you could rule England if you chose."

She smiled. "From what you've told me of your king, it would be no challenge to do better than you Englishmen."

"Then you'll do it?"

"Rule England?"

He grinned. "Later, perhaps."

She thought about it. The offer was very tempting. She was not accustomed to idleness, and it was fraying her nerves. "What would Jared say?"

"Jared doesn't care a whit about how Morland is run if all goes smoothly. Well?"

She nodded slowly. "You'll speak to the servants?"

"I've already done it. You'll find them both obedient and cooperative."

"You knew I'd do it?"

"I know *you*," he said softly. "It's been my pleasure to study you for some time now."

She met his gaze, then glanced hurriedly away. "It was kind of you to take the trouble to consider my needs."

"I'll always consider your needs and fulfill them," he said. "I'm not like Deville. There won't ever be a time when you won't come first with me." He rose to his feet before she could answer. "Now, come along and we'll talk to Mrs. Blakely." He strode toward the door. "You know, I'm going to miss not knowing you're tucked in this library every hour of the day. Now I'll have to seek you out in all kinds of uncomfortable places."

As usual he had struck, then neatly sidestepped any rebuff from her. He would say something that disturbed or touched her, then skip away before she could formulate an answer. She should confront him, be stern with him, perhaps even forbid him to come to her. Not that it would do any good. She had learned that beneath that indolent exterior Bradford could be completely immovable.

Or was she surrendering too easily? she wondered with sudden uneasiness. She couldn't deny she now looked forward to Bradford's company. No day was complete without seeing that rough, craggy face. Silent or verbose, he made her feel . . . treasured.

He stepped aside and held the door for her. "Just promise me that you won't spend too much time in the scullery. I willingly embraced all those books you love so much, but I've no liking for cookery."

Now that she would not spend so much time with Bradford, surely there was no harm in postponing a total rejection. She smiled serenely as she passed him. "No cookery. I'd not endanger our stomachs. Actually, I planned on setting you to the task of plucking the chickens."

"It's young Joe Barry watching the stable tonight." Cassie let the heavy velvet curtain swing back to cover the deeply recessed window. "Jared could at least have sent one of the older men to stand guard on such a cold night."

Lani chuckled as she stretched out her hands to the fire. "You can tell him that at supper tonight. Somehow I don't believe he'll pay heed to your complaints as to his selection of jailers. You like this lad?"

Cassie nodded. "He's the one who sends Josette messages when she's at school." She crossed the library and dropped into a brocade chair before the fire. "And he may spy and follow me around, but he's pleasant about it. Not like that big dour Jack Ramgale, who scowls at me all the time." She leaned forward, resting her hands on her knees as she gazed into

the fire. "Josette took me down to the cove to see her sailboat this afternoon."

"And dour Jack followed you?"

"So close I thought he'd step on my heels." She made a face. "Did he think I was so stupid I'd try to sail off with him watching me?"

"Jared's servants are very loyal to him."

"But it did occur to me," she said wistfully. "We were surrounded by water. Why didn't I ever learn to sail a boat?"

"You were too interested in riding horses." She held up her hand as Cassie started to speak. "And, no, I cannot sail a boat. I've never done anything but row a canoe. We'll have to find some other way when the time comes."

When the time comes. It seemed to Cassie that the time to act would never come. "I dreamed about Papa last night."

"Ah, so this is why you're so restless today. A good dream?"

"No." It had been a blurred, disjointed nightmare. Her father had been swirling in a dark whirlpool and reaching out to her in despair. "We have to find him, Lani."

"And so you're ready to jump into the sea and swim to France to get to him." She shook her head. "He might not even be there yet. You know it's best to let Jared do our searching for us and then go to Charles. I'm in a much better position to know when messages are received now that the servants look to me for orders."

"That's true enough." How strange was their situation here at Morland: half prisoners, half guests, and since yesterday Lani was virtually commanding this vast castle. "But we must have a plan to leave when the word comes."

"We cannot leave from the port from which we arrived. It's too close, and it may take time to obtain passage. Bradford mentioned there was a small port about ten miles south of here. That's a possibility."

"I'll ask Josette about it." She was more cheerful now that there was action to be taken. Lani was right —they could not waste their scant funds in Paris. They must stay here until word came to Jared. She rose to her feet. "It's time to dress for supper."

"You go ahead. I have time to stay here awhile." She wrinkled her nose. "I don't have to wash off the smell of horse from my person."

Cassie moved toward the door. "As you say, it washes off." She paused at the door, hesitating. "Lani . . . do you dream of Papa?"

"Not often. I'm not a dreamer, but when I do, they are good dreams." She smiled. "He's doing what he believes is right, Cassie. God will be with him."

Cassie wished she could be as sure. The dream last night had frightened her. God had not been with that poor creature caught in a whirlpool.

"It was a dream, Cassie," Lani said gently. "If you have another, come to me and we will talk about it."

Run to Lani as she had done when she was a small child, and everything would be all right. The problems were bigger now, the dreams more terrifying, and she must face them by herself. Lani had her own burdens to shoulder.

She forced a smile. "I'm sure I won't have any more nightmares about Papa."

Twelve

October 1, 1806
Paris, France

"Monsieur David is in the salon, Monsieur Bonille," Gaston said as he opened the front door, then took Raoul's hat and gloves. "He's been there since before luncheon. I told him he'd have to wait a long time, but he insisted he must see you as soon as possible."

"Indeed? I'm truly flattered. Monsieur David seldom bothers with lesser mortals since Napoleon became his patron." He strolled toward the salon. "I hope you made him welcome?"

The servant nodded eagerly. "But of course, monsieur. He's a very great man, a glorious artist."

Raoul's lip curled. These peasant fools always thought those who stood beside and shared the glory with the Napoleons and the Robespierres of the world were great themselves. He could have told him that it was always the men behind the throne who were the clever ones. He threw open the delicately carved doors of the grand salon. "Ah, Jacques-Louis, how delightful to see you. If you'd let me know you were coming, naturally I'd have postponed my visit."

"I didn't know myself." David rose to his feet. "I had a visitor this morning."

Raoul lifted a brow. "Napoleon?"

David made an impatient gesture. "Would I come running to you if it was Bonaparte? No, it was someone else." He paused. "Charles Deville."

Raoul carefully controlled his expression. "How . . . surprising. How is the dear fellow?"

"Discomposed. He wants to know where Raoul Cambre is."

"And you told him?"

"No, of course not. You swore me to secrecy when you changed your name."

And sealed the vow with a thousand influential introductions and favors. "Brandy?"

David shook his head. "I must go. I've work to do. I've wasted enough light today waiting for you."

"Don't leave yet." He poured a brandy for himself. He needed it. "What do you mean 'discomposed'?"

"Disturbed, tense, frightened. He kept ranting that he had to see you, that he had to be sure. He said that he'd arrived in Paris just last night."

"And he came immediately to you. Interesting."

"He knew we were friends."

David had never been his friend, he thought contemptuously. He'd used the conceited fool as he had all the others. He smiled. "Excellent friends. What was his appearance? Does he seem to be a man of substance these days?"

"No. He was gaunt and his clothes a bit shabby." David frowned. "I felt a trifle guilty lying to another artist." He hastened to add, "Though he's not on my level, of course."

"Of course. There's no one on your level, Jacques-Louis. All Paris knows how brilliant you are."

"I don't like to lie," he said peevishly. "My life is quite comfortable now. It's very distracting having these people pop up out of your past bothering me. First there was that Jean Guillaume asking questions on behalf of the Duke of Morland, and now Deville himself."

Raoul restrained himself from pointing out that he had been responsible for a good deal of that comfort. In the chaos following Robespierre's death, he had been careful to make sure he protected all his spheres of influence. It would do no harm to remind David of their mutual past. "It's natural that some ghosts would come back to haunt us. Those were troublesome times." He sighed reminiscently. "I remember how ardent you were, with your revolutionary fervor and that wonderful vest with those buttons that had little guillotines painted on them."

David flushed. "As you say, those were different times." He rose to his feet. "Deville's your ghost, not mine. I've warned you and I'm done with it."

"But I fear he may trouble you again," Raoul said. "Disturbed men can be very embarrassing. Your glorious present may be tainted if memories are stirred. Napoleon might even think your allegiance fickle if he's forced to remember how passionately you embraced the revolution."

"Then stop Deville," David said flatly. "Talk to him. I won't be connected with this, Raoul."

"Did I say you would be?" His tone became soothing. "Of course I'll speak to him and send him on his way. I just need your help in planning a meeting. I must be discreet for both our sakes. Do you know where he can be reached?"

"He said if I discovered where you could be found, he'd be at sixteen rue Grenadier."

"Then why don't you send him a message and tell him you've located his old friend Raoul, who is eager to meet with him and welcome him back to France? I'll be at the Café Dumonde on the West Bank tomorrow night at eleven o'clock."

"Why don't you have him come here?"

"My dear Jacques-Louis." He glanced pointedly around the luxuriously appointed salon. "You said he was gaunt and shabby. It's neither kind nor wise to reveal one's affluence to those who might ask to share that wealth. I do hope you didn't boast how wealthy you were becoming under our illustrious Emperor."

He looked taken aback. "I didn't boast. You know money means nothing to me. I did tell him my fame had spread since he'd left France."

Raoul clucked reprovingly. "Then it's just as well I'm ridding us of this fellow. After you send him the message, dismiss him from your mind. I'll protect you as I've always done."

David nodded in relief. "Thank you, Raoul. You know an artist should not be troubled by these mundane matters." He strode quickly toward the door. "I'll leave it in your hands. Good day."

"Good day, my friend." As the door closed behind David, Raoul's smile vanished. He crashed his glass down on a table.

Sacré bleu, was that debacle at Danjuet always to raise its head to torment him? Letting the boy escape had been a blunder for which he'd been paying for years. All the other incriminating strings of his past life had been severed, but it had proved too dangerous to send an assassin to kill the young Duke. That wastrel Bradford Danemount had proved a surprisingly protective guardian.

Dammit, if he had managed to kill the boy, then he would not have had to send Deville to Tahiti away from his influence. He would have been able to move with less care and not have had to assume a new identity. He always preferred to work in secret, but totally new credentials had caused him a good deal of bother. Danemount was a constant thorn that must be removed.

And now that fool Deville had wandered back into his life and was threatening to disrupt it again.

"Beg pardon, monsieur, Marie would like to know if you'll be home for dinner?" Gaston inquired from the doorway.

Power, wealth, a house as palatial as Napoleon's and decorated with far more taste, servants at his beck and call, women eager to please him any way he wished. By God, he would not let Deville march back into his life and destroy all this.

"No, Gaston, I'll be out for the entire evening." He stood up and moved toward the door.

He must prepare a surprise for his old friend Deville.

"You've actually been behaving quite well, Jared," Bradford said. "I've even seen signs of knightly conduct. Extraordinary."

"I'm sure you find it so." Jared leaned on the fence, his gaze on Josette and Cassie riding toward them. "But, then, you've always underestimated my virtues."

"But never your lust. For the first week or so I thought you'd lost interest in our Cassie."

"What makes you think I haven't?"

"I opened my eyes. I admit my judgment was a bit clouded because Lani absorbs a good deal of my attention. She's a very stubborn woman."

"She's quite extraordinary. She's managed to take over the running of the household without antagonizing any of the servants."

"Who could resent Lani?" Bradford shook his head. "But we weren't discussing Lani. I was praising your restraint and celibacy."

"In order to encourage it to continue." His gaze didn't leave Cassie. Christ, she looked wonderful. Her eyes were flashing, her face alight with confidence and amusement as she chattered with Josette. Away from Clara's domination, at harsh, brooding Morland, she had bloomed like one of the tropical flowers from her island. "Don't be surprised if it doesn't."

"I'm never surprised at anything, but it would be far more peaceful for all of us." He waved a hand. "Josette and Cassie have become fast friends. Lani is moderately content. I'm making small strides in the direction I wish to go. You might shatter everything if you become . . . aggressive."

Jared's hand tightened on the fence rail. "For God's sake, I'm not going to rape her."

"But you're losing patience."

Damnation, yes, he was losing patience. It had been too long. He had only to see Cassie to begin to ready. He had thought the time they spent together would draw her closer to surrender. God knows, he was experienced with every nuance of seduction, but something always went wrong when he was with Cassie. One moment she was making him laugh, and the next she was saying something that touched him. Blast it, he didn't want to feel this bewildering gamut of emotion. He wanted to be back on the ship, where there was no thought, no conversation—only the satisfaction of their coupling.

No, that wasn't true. Lately he had been aware of a deep sense of growing contentment during those rides with Cassie, and a feeling of loss when they parted. Christ, he didn't know what he wanted.

Except Cassie back in his bed, where she belonged.

"Any recent news from Marseilles?" Bradford asked.

"Not since two days ago," he said impatiently. "I would have told you if I'd heard anything more. Deville hasn't surfaced yet."

"It's been more than a month since we arrived. There should be some sign of him soon."

"I know that." He also knew where this was leading. Bradford wanted to stress how pointless any passion for Cassie was since it would all be for naught once her father reappeared in their lives. "We'll just have to wait."

"Heavens, how patient you've become. I would have thought you'd be salivating to hear about Deville. Could you be softening?"

"No, I could not." He turned away from the fence. "I'm going to meet them at the stable. Are you coming?"

"I think not. I believe I'll wander back and see what Lani is doing. She said she might—What's this?" His gaze was on the carriage entering the gates. "We have a visitor."

Jared muttered a curse as he recognized the carriage. "Carolyn. I hoped we were rid of her."

"It seems you were mistaken." He watched Jared stride toward the courtyard. "You're going to meet her?"

He nodded curtly. "Go to the stables and tell Cassie and Josette to stay away until she leaves. I don't want any interference."

"I haven't noticed Josette seeking out her company." Bradford ambled toward the stable. "However, I'll endeavor to ensure that they're both occupied."

Carolyn and Lani were standing facing each other when Jared strode into the hall.

No, not facing, confronting, Jared thought grimly. Carolyn's attitude was bristling with antagonism, while Lani's expression was dignified but wary.

"Carolyn, what a pleasant surprise." He moved between the two women and took her hand. "I didn't expect you."

"And I didn't expect Madam Deville." She smiled with an effort. "We were just becoming acquainted."

"Then I don't have to introduce you."

"I had trouble recognizing your kinswoman." She gazed pointedly at the bright-blue silk gown Lani was wearing. "I couldn't imagine a widow putting aside her black widow's weeds and donning such a gown."

"My people don't believe in the wearing of mourning clothes," Lani said. "Mourning is in the heart. We don't need to boast to others how bereaved we are."

"Boast?" Carolyn bristled. "It's not boasting to—"

Jared quickly interrupted. "You look a trifle pale, Lani." Blast it, he wished it were true. Lani, as usual, radiated warmth and beauty, and that could only add fuel to Carolyn's venom. "You shouldn't be up from your sickbed. I'm sure Lady Carradine will excuse you."

"Madam Deville appears in excellent health," Carolyn said. "But it's difficult to tell. Unfortunately, her skin isn't fair like ours, is it?" She didn't wait for an answer but turned and walked toward the library. "By all means, leave us, Madam Deville. We will excuse you."

Seeing bright flags of color burning in Lani's cheeks Jared said to her in a low tone, "It will be better if you go."

"I won't run away. Do you think this is the first time I've faced hatred because my skin is a different color? In Mrs. Denworth's school there were many white children who were not as kind as their religion dictated." Her lips twisted. "And Clara was always ready to tell me that my race made me unworthy."

"Dammit, Clara isn't here, and I don't want you humiliated in my presence."

"Why not? I'm the mistress of your enemy."

Lani's bitterness was not in character. Carolyn's remarks must have stung more than she was willing to admit. "Go to your room." He strode toward the library. "Let me deal with Carolyn."

"This is the last time," Lani said quietly. "I won't hide myself when right is on my side."

How the devil had he come to this pass? he wondered in frustration. He wanted nothing more than to toss Carolyn out of his home like the feline bitch he knew her to be, but if he allowed himself to defend Lani, then Josette could be hurt. He had not exaggerated Carolyn's power in social circles.

Carolyn turned to face him as he closed the door. "It won't do, you know."

"I beg your pardon?"

"Having that . . . that woman here." Her lips tightened. "Even if she's your kinsman's widow, she's no fit chaperon for Josette. She should not be here."

"I disagree. She's an admirable chaperon. She's a

woman no longer in her first youth, she's well educated, industri—"

"She's not one of us," Carolyn interrupted. "I had
doubts when I heard that outlandish name. You
should have told me she was a native. That's the reason my conscience compelled me to return. As soon
as I met her, I realized my instincts were correct. She
should not be here."

As soon as she had noticed Lani's beauty, he corrected mentally. Jesus, he wished she hadn't seen her.
"I understand your concern, but I can hardly refuse
her my hospitality."

"Send her to me. I'll find respectable lodgings for
her." Carolyn smiled sweetly. "Believe me, it's for the
best. There would be too much talk if she remains
here. The ton would never understand if you accepted
this native woman into your home."

He smothered the flare of anger at her words and
smiled in return. "You're right, of course. My reputation is not of the best. It might prove a scandal . . .
unless someone of your stature intervened."

She went still. "What do you mean?"

"We're such old friends, Carolyn. I know you'll
help me."

"In what way?" she said warily.

"You have such influence that I'm certain all that
would be needed is a word or two to accomplish the
task."

"You wish me to sponsor this woman?" she asked
incredulously.

"As a personal favor to me." His voice deepening
to coaxing persuasion, he exerted every bit of charm
at his command. "I would be very, very grateful."

"I couldn't possibly do—" She met his gaze, and he
could see the scales being weighed beneath those

golden curls. "Naturally, I would never refuse you anything, but it will not be easy." She patted his cheek. "Be sure to have the woman at my ball tomorrow night. I'll introduce her there."

"Wonderful. Now that that pesky problem is solved, will you stay for luncheon?"

She shook her head. "My house is turned upside down with preparations for tomorrow night. I must get back." She paused and then added meaningfully, "I hope there will be many opportunities for us to share a meal at a later date."

Payment for favors given, Jared thought cynically, and Carolyn would be the first to collect. "Perhaps we could ride together on the afternoon after the ball?"

"I would be enchanted." She gave him another brilliant smile and swept toward the door. "Until tomorrow night. I can hardly wait."

And he wished it would never come, Jared thought grimly. He had led Cassie to believe he would find an excuse not to go to Carolyn's ball, and she would not be pleased about Lani's being forced to run a social gauntlet.

It was not until they were at the dinner table that Jared related what had transpired with Carolyn. "And I expect you all to behave with decorum," he told Josette, Bradford, and Cassie. "I've gone to a great deal of trouble, and I don't want it to be for naught."

"Lani shouldn't go," Josette said flatly. "Lady Carradine will hurt her." She beamed. "In fact, none of us should go. I think it would be a splendid idea if we all stayed home."

"We will go," Jared said emphatically. "Nothing will happen. Carolyn has promised to sponsor Lani."

Bradford raised his brows. "Now, I wonder what you did to get her to do that?"

Cassie didn't wonder. She had watched him with the gargoyle and had no doubt he had used more of the same charm and sweet words.

Jared ignored the question. "If Carolyn sponsors Lani, she can't claim she's an unfit chaperon." He glanced at Josette. "And won't have grounds to demand you return to school."

"Oh." Josette was clearly torn but finally said, "Find some other way. I don't trust her."

"There's no other way. You're the one who chose to adopt Cassie and Lani and make use of them." He mockingly inclined his head to Cassie. "I had other plans for the ladies."

Cassie's grip tightened on her wine goblet. She liked none of this. Not Jared's subtle sensuality that never failed to disturb her, and certainly not this plan to make them go to the gargoyle's cave.

"Why don't we ask Lani?" Bradford suggested. He turned to her and said quietly, "You don't have to go. If Jared says he's made arrangements, Carolyn will give you no insult, but you don't have to do anything you have no wish to do."

Lani was silent a moment. "I will go."

Cassie leaned forward and grasped Lani's arm. "I think Josette is right, I don't trust Lady Carradine." To Jared, she said fiercely, "I won't have Lani hurt, do you understand?"

He threw up his hands. "Very well, you come up with a solution to keep Josette's position with the ton secure. I'm weary of being looked on as a villain."

"I said I'd go." Lani placed her napkin by her plate and rose to her feet. "No more talk. That's the end of it." She left the dining room.

Bradford stood. "Jared, I fervently hope you're right about this. I'd really detest snapping your neck." He followed Lani from the room.

Cassie and Josette stared at Jared.

He said through his teeth, "Carolyn won't break her word. I've made sure of it."

Josette grunted derisively. Cassie glared at him.

Jared threw down his napkin and stalked out of the room.

"Is he right?" Cassie asked. "Can he control Lady Carradine?"

"She won't hurt Lani in any obvious way." Josette smiled bitterly. "She can be very clever. Never once has she made mention of my birth. She gives little lectures to the other students on the horrors that butcher Napoleon is inflicting on good, honest Englishmen and then turns her back and doesn't hear when they attack me."

"Why don't you tell Jared?"

"I don't whine." She made a face. "And she gives me nothing to grab on to. She's a coward and her cruelty is very subtle. Just once I wish she'd lose her temper and slap me. Jared would never tolerate that, and I certainly give her enough cause."

Cassie smiled. "I'm sure you do." Her smile faded. "I know nothing about your customs. Is Jared right? Is it important that you belong to this ton?"

"Not to me." Josette paused. "But it's true, those ninnies at school would dry up and die if they were so ostracized."

"Yours is a very cruel world." Cassie frowned, troubled. "I don't wish this to happen to you, but if that woman hurts Lani, I can't allow it to go unpunished."

"Really?" Josette looked intrigued. "What would you do to her?"

Cassie's expression became grim. "Something very unpleasant."

"Then don't think of me," she said magnanimously. "I'll sacrifice everything, I'll suffer any indignity. Even if I'm cast out, I'll be brave and force myself to stay here in this great barn of a place, exercising the horses. On occasion perhaps a game of chess with Jared. It will be—"

"You're enjoying this too much," Cassie said dryly. "You might be happy cast out from the ton, but Jared would be furious. We must hope it doesn't come to that." She stood up and moved toward the door. "And the easiest way to avoid that happening is to convince Lani not to go."

"Cassie, I don't want to hear any more about it. I'm not afraid of her." Lani added with great firmness, "And for the last time, I won't hide tonight."

Cassie sighed in frustration. She had been trying since the night before to persuade Lani not to go to the ball, to no avail. She had not thought this last attempt would fare any better, but she had tried. "We're here to help Papa, not go to balls. Everything is becoming too complicated."

"Do you forget Charles when you help Josette?"

"I never forget Papa."

"Neither do I. It does no harm to give to a child in need." Lani suddenly smiled and embraced her. "Now, go and get dressed. It's getting late. Bradford said we should leave by seven. What are you going to wear?"

"The white silk." She made a face. "Josette says

that, according to Lady Carradine, young, unmarried women should always wear white."

"I know you wish to help Josette, and you always look good in white." Lani turned to the armoire. "I believe I shall wear my yellow gown. I've always liked the color." She glanced over her shoulder with twinkling eyes. "And it will annoy Lady Carradine the most. It's as far from black widow's weeds as our island is from this England."

"Should you—" Cassie broke off as Lani shook her head. She should have known Lani would not change herself any sooner than she would hide. Cassie hugged her and moved toward the door. "You'll be more beautiful than any woman there."

A moment later she was standing before the armoire in her own chamber looking at the gowns Jared had provided.

The white silk was quite beautiful, the touches of lace at the round neck demure. Just the kind of gown Lady Carradine would approve for a shy young girl. Cassie took it out of the armoire.

As far from black widow's weeds as our island is from this England."

Lani's words kept repeating in her mind. This island and these people were not her own. Much as she liked Josette, she was not Lani. They had not suffered together, the years had not bonded them. She wanted only the best for Josette, but if there were sides to be taken, she could not ally herself with anyone but Lani.

She shoved the pristine-white gown back into the armoire and reached deep into the rear of the wardrobe.

"Good God." Bradford's eyes widened as she came down the stairs. "Stunning. You look magnificent."

He shook his head. "But I don't think Jared is going to like this."

"Then he shouldn't have chosen it." She glanced around the foyer. "Where is he?"

"He went on ahead to Carradine Hall to make sure everything was in order. He asked me to bring you. Lani and Josette are waiting in the carriage." He frowned. "I don't believe he meant that gown for this type of occasion."

She knew the occasion he had meant her to wear it. When she came to his bed. In spite of its simple Empire lines, it was the gown meant for a temptress. The scarlet color alone shouted bold sensuality, the deep square neckline revealed the upper curves of her breasts. "It's what I'm wearing."

"Has Lani seen you?"

"No." She had deliberately delayed dressing until she knew Lani would have no opportunity to find out in advance. "She thinks I'm wearing white. I changed my mind at the last minute."

He took the black velvet cloak she was carrying and draped it around her shoulders, carefully fastening the button at her throat. "Well, let's at least spare Jared the first shock when you walk into the ballroom."

"I can't wear a cloak all evening." Yet she did not want Lani to see the gown until they reached Carradine Hall. She might insist Cassie go back and change. She drew the cloak about her and moved toward the door. "Shall we go?"

"You've been very docile of late." His hand cradled her elbow as she moved down the steps toward the carriage. "I'd be curious to know why you chose this occasion to break the pattern."

The footman opened the door of the carriage. Bradford glanced at Lani, resplendent in her yellow silk gown and white velvet cloak, and then smiled. "Ah, that's it, you're going into battle. I always knew I had a fondness for you," he said in a low tone in Cassie's ear. "I hope a battle won't be necessary, but no one is worth fighting for more than Lani." He helped her into the carriage, then climbed in after her. "It's going to prove an interesting evening."

Lani smiled and reached for Cassie's hand. "You're late. Is all well?"

Cassie clasped her hand nervously. She didn't know whether this was a wise move or not. Jared would be angry, and she might do damage to Josette. It might all be for nothing. Perhaps Lani would not need championing at all. Oh, well, she had made mistakes before, and she would not back away now. She smiled at Lani but did not answer directly. "You look glorious tonight. Like a queen." She said with sudden intensity, "You *are* a queen, Lani."

Lani chuckled. "You must have been talking to Bradford. He claims I could rule this harsh England."

"It would certainly be a more interesting country if you did." Josette grimaced. "You can't imagine how stultifying this ball will be tonight." She settled back on the seat with a sigh. "Not at all like Jared's and Bradford's parties."

"Which you were never supposed to observe," Bradford said.

Josette giggled and told Cassie, "My nurse used to fall asleep and I'd creep down and watch from the landing until Jared caught me at it one night. He was very angry."

"He would have been angrier if he hadn't caught you at that particular moment. Such parties are not for the delectation of innocents."

"An orgy," Josette confided to Cassie with relish.

"Bacchanalian revels. Everyone seemed to be having a perfectly splendid time."

"May we talk of something else?" Bradford asked plaintively. "The subject of my wicked past is making me a trifle uncomfortable. Did you ride Morgana today?"

Josette obligingly accepted the turn of conversation and started to chatter on her favorite subject for the remainder of the journey.

Carradine House was ablaze with light. Lanterns hung from the trees bordering the long driveway that led to the stately brick manor house, revealing carriages of all sizes and description on the grass. Liveried coachmen moved briskly, tending their vehicles, or merely lolled in conversation with other servants.

"There's Jared." Bradford's gaze went to the open doorway as he got out of the carriage. "And our sweet hostess."

Cassie involuntarily tensed as the footman helped her from the carriage, and she caught sight of the two at the top of the steps. Carolyn Carradine was smiling up at Jared, glowingly lovely in pale-blue silk. Jared, in dark evening clothes, was no different from the Jared she saw every day. He always looked lean, graceful, slightly dangerous, and as wickedly handsome as a pagan god. It was no wonder that the gargoyle was staring at him as if she wished to eat him for dinner, Cassie thought with annoyance.

"Cassie?" Bradford said.

She hurriedly stepped aside so that the footman could help Lani and Josette from the carriage. Then she watched Lani approach their hostess for the evening with graceful dignity.

"Good evening, Lady Carradine." Lani smiled at

the woman. "How kind of you to invite me to your home."

Lady Carradine displayed perfect teeth returning her smile. "It's my pleasure." Her gaze ran over Lani's gown, which was revealed when she shed her white velvet cloak and handed it to a waiting footman. "And what a lovely gown. You look quite like a sunburst."

The words could have been construed as a compliment, and the woman's tone was cordial. Perhaps it was not going to be as bad as Cassie feared.

Lady Carradine turned to Josette. "Take your chaperon to meet Lady Huntley. I've told her to act in my place while I finish greeting my guests. Her daughter, Joan, was just saying how much she missed you at school."

Josette muttered something distinctly uncomplimentary beneath her breath before she shrugged off her cloak. "Missed a pincushion to accommodate her pricks, maybe." Then, as she met Jared's warning gaze, she pasted a smile on her face and took Lani's arm. "Come along. Surely Lady Huntley is not nearly as rude as her daughter."

Cassie watched Lani cross the crowded ballroom. As she passed, the men and women turned to stare at her. Well, who wouldn't look at her? She was more beautiful than any woman in the room.

"Don't be shy, my dear. Take off your cloak and run along and join them."

Cassie turned to see Carolyn Carradine aim a glowing smile at her as she placed a proprietary hand on Jared's sleeve. "We'll join you and your stepmother shortly."

"Very well." She straightened her shoulders and then rid herself of her cloak.

She heard Lady Carradine's shocked exclamation and Jared's sharply inhaled breath. After handing the cloak to the footman, she looked around to see two bright patches of color on Lady Carradine's cheeks. "That gown is totally inappropriate in a young girl. It's . . . it's—"

"A sunset?" She lifted her chin in defiance. "If Lani's gown is a sunburst, surely mine goes a step further."

"It goes a good deal further," Jared said grimly. "I'd like a word with you, Cassie."

"But Lady Carradine says I must run along and meet Lady Huntley." She shrugged. "If you wish to speak with me, I suppose you may come with me." She started across the ballroom.

Jared was walking beside her, looking straight ahead. "Why, damn you?"

"At least I didn't wear a sarong. It did occur to me."

"All you had to do was behave with a little decorum for one evening. Was that too much to ask for Josette?"

"I'll behave with decorum as long as these people treat Lani with courtesy."

"Has Carolyn indicated in any way that she won't?"

"Not yet." She glanced at him. "But we've just gotten here. I don't trust her."

"So you come to the most circumspect ball in England looking . . ."

"Like a harlot?"

"I didn't say that and I didn't mean it."

"That's why you gave me this gown. You wanted me to look like one of your lady birds. Well, here I am."

"And every man in the room is wondering if he has a chance of luring you into his bed."

She was suddenly tired of being on the defensive. She smiled tauntingly. "It's a possibility. I've been without a man for a long time, and you were an excellent tutor." She turned to him and said mockingly, "Come, Jared, introduce me to your friends. Let me choose a man to pleasure me."

He went white. He had been angry a minute ago; now he was a step beyond. "Damn you to hell."

She had never seen him more dangerous. She didn't care. She felt as she had when she and Kapu had swum through rapids, too late to stop, too exciting to turn back. She had to go on. "Why are you so angry? You would bed your Carolyn without a second thought. Perhaps you've already done it tonight. Don't I have the right to choose my own—"

"No, you do not." His voice was hoarse with searing intensity. "You no longer have any choice at all. You've just forfeited it."

"By wearing a gown you chose? By telling you a woman is not a slave? I think not. Go back to Lady Carradine. She will say anything you wish her to say." Her pace quickened as she approached Lady Huntley. "I assure you I don't mind your abandoning me. I'll make my own way with these people."

"I'm tempted to do it. Any of these women could cut you to the bone with one remark."

"Why would you care?"

"Oh, I would care." He smiled savagely. "It's a privilege I reserve for myself." He stopped before Lady Huntley, Lani, and Josette. He took Lady Huntley's hand, and his smile became totally ingratiating. "Ah, how delightful you look tonight, Amanda. That color always becomes you. May I present my kinswoman, Cassandra Deville? You've already met her gracious stepmother."

"Something's wrong." Cassie watched worriedly as Lani was taken by Lady Huntley from one group to the other, leaving Cassie and Josette to their own devices. "I don't like this."

"What is it?" Josette asked.

"I don't know." Lani was smiling, but she had the frozen expression she had worn when suffering Clara's worst abuse. "Can you find out?"

"It will take time. These people are not fond of me, either. Can't you ask her?"

Lani had committed herself to this ball to help Josette. Cassie knew Lani would not complain. "No."

Josette shrugged. "Then I'll find out." She drifted off into the crowd.

Cassie immediately felt isolated without Josette's comforting presence. She was surrounded by strangers—glittering, alien. She wanted to run away. The women's glances were shocked and disdainful, and the men did not meet her eyes at all. Her gaze searched the crowd for Bradford, but he was deep in conversation with a golden-haired young man in a corner.

And Jared was once more standing beside Lady Carradine in the foyer.

She met his gaze and recognition rippled through her. How could he dare look at her with such lust and possessiveness when he stood beside that woman? Her desolation was submerged by a flare of anger. These fine ladies would not accept her, but their men should not prove difficult. Men were seldom guided by anything but their bodies. She had no experience at the game herself, but she had spent years watching Lihua practice her mating skills. She deliberately looked away from Jared and sought out the golden-haired young man to whom Bradford was speaking. She waited until she caught his eye, then smiled.

The young Adonis broke off what he was saying to Bradford.

Good. She half lowered her lashes and ran her tongue lightly over her lower lip.

The young man was coming toward her.

She slanted a quick glance at Jared. Yes, no doubt about it, he had witnessed the little charade, and it had infuriated him. She felt a surge of fierce satisfaction. It would not hurt to goad him a little more.

She looked around the room to choose another man.

"Stop watching her, Jared," Bradford said in a low voice as he handed his nephew a glass of punch. "You're causing more stir than she is. After all, it's only a gown."

"You know better." She was a scarlet banner that every man in the room wanted to claim. And the bitch was deliberately dipping that banner in invitation. Neither she nor Lani could dance, but that did not hinder pursuit. The two women were at opposite ends of the room, but both were surrounded by men vying for attention.

Let me choose a man to pleasure me.

"That crystal goblet is going to break if you put any more pressure on it," Bradford observed. "You'll get a nasty cut."

"Then take the damn thing." He thrust it back into Bradford's hand. "I didn't want it anyway."

"It was better to have a goblet in your hand than a sword."

"I didn't have a sword."

"That didn't mean you might not acquire one." He took a sip of punch. "Tell me, whom are you going to call out? Young Fred Monteith? He appears very ardent. Or the Earl of Tempkar? No, he couldn't put up a very satisfactory fight. He must be almost seventy."

Jared shot him a sour glance. "You appear to be in fine spirits."

"Actually, I'm not at all happy at the way things are proceeding," he said. "But not because of those hounds baying at the moon. It's probably just as well they're causing a distraction. I don't like the set of Lani's mouth."

"What?"

"When she's upset, she holds her lips a little tighter and turns her head with a quick, jerky motion." He frowned. "Things aren't going well."

"I don't see any sign—"

"But, then, you can't see anything but a scarlet gown and your own lust. It might do you well to use your head instead of your nether parts for thinking." He turned to look at him. "Did you ask Cassie why she wore that gown?"

"I didn't need to ask. Defiance has a voice of its own."

"And she probably wouldn't have told you the truth anyway." He nodded at Lani. "Cassie wouldn't let her be alone even if it meant being ostracized herself."

"Very noble."

"But you don't want to believe it."

"I believe she loves Lani."

"I'm weary of arguing with you," Bradford said finally. He put his glass down on the banquet table. "I have to go to Lani. She's definitely upset."

"And you think she'll tell you why?"

"Probably not. But she'll know I'm there supporting her. Please refrain from glaring for the rest of the evening. Some of these guests think I raised you with a modicum of manners." He started toward the groups surrounding Lani and Cassie. "And you might repair the damage you've done by ingratiating yourself to our hostess again. If I'm wrong and all is going splendidly for Lani, we want it to continue."

Jared moodily glanced across the room at Carolyn Carradine. She was holding court of her own, smiling brightly, talking quickly, too quickly. She was furious. He should follow Bradford's injunction and go to her.

You would think nothing of going to bed with her.

He felt another rush of fury as he remembered Cassie's words. It was true; he had considered the necessity of bedding Carolyn to keep her well-disposed toward Lani, and it would have meant nothing to him. Why should it be otherwise? Carolyn knew the rules, but she had overestimated her influence with Jared.

Sexual desire for him lasted for only the moment and then was gone.

Until Cassie. Until that damnable little savage had come into his life and then had the temerity to tell him she would take another man with the same ease as she had taken him.

Christ.

He wanted to kill her. No, he wanted to kill every one of those libertines gathered around her like bees around honey. If he stood here much longer watching her, he wouldn't be able to keep himself from going over there and— He turned on his heel and strode across the ballroom toward Carolyn.

The evening was like a pennant shredded to pieces on a battlefield. He would have to retreat and try to save what he could. He would be charming, smooth

Carolyn's ruffled feathers, and perhaps all would be well.

If anything could go well on this damnable night.

"I have to talk to you," Josette murmured in Cassie's ear after she had insinuated herself into the crowd around Cassie. "Slip away from them and come to the punch bowl."

"I tried to do that an hour ago," Cassie answered, exasperated. When she had started this game to annoy Jared, she had not realized how irritating she would find it. "They just offer to get me what I want. How do I get away from them? I feel . . . I feel . . . smothered."

Josette chuckled. "I'll help." She raised her voice. "Faint? Oh, dear, we must get you outside for some air." She slid a solicitous arm around Cassie's waist, dug an elbow into the stomach of one of the young men who had stepped forward in concern. "Sorry." She whisked Cassie to the French doors a few yards away and out into the garden. She closed the doors with a flourish. "Done. We'll probably be safe for a few minutes." She shivered. "If we don't freeze to death first."

Cassie drew a deep breath of cold air. "I don't care. Just so I don't have to go back in there. What strange mating rituals you have here. The men do nothing but gather around and stare and say sweet words. They don't even listen. Every time I tried to speak of something of interest, they just laughed."

"Kapu?"

"The Earl of Tempkar said I should get a nice little mare so that I would come to no harm." She snorted in disgust. "They're all idiots."

"No, but they think we are," Josette said. "And

they'll be coming out here any minute. I must speak quickly."

"Lani?"

She nodded. "Lady Carradine has given Lady Huntley the task she can't do herself."

"Which is?"

"Subtle insults, little cuts that bleed but don't kill. Lady Carradine evidently prepared the way ahead of time. Outwardly she shows her support for Lani and then lets one of her minions stab her and disavows any responsibility. If Lani complains, she'll tell Jared she did everything possible, but that some people are just intractable." She added grimly, "It's much the same indirect way she finds to punish me. She chose an excellent substitute in Lady Huntley. She's almost as competent at cruelty as her daughter."

Cassie went rigid. "You're sure about this?"

"I overheard Lady Huntley telling Lani that she never dreamed savages would ever be permitted within the doors of Carradine House, but that Lady Carradine was such a Christian woman. She had even hired Negroes and those coarse brown creatures from India as servants." Josette added bitterly, "And her tone dripped honey with every word."

Cassie's hands clenched at her sides. A red tide of anger obscured her vision. How dare they hurt Lani? Couldn't these strangers see what she was? She wanted to strike out, pound them into the ground.

"What did Lani say?"

"Nothing. She only gave her a look that would have shriveled anyone who wasn't already a husk anyway." She raised a brow. "Well, what do we do?"

"You don't do anything. This isn't your concern." She whirled and moved toward the French doors. "Stay out of it."

"Of course it's my concern. All of this was done for my sake."

"Then don't let it go for nothing." She jerked open the door and entered the ballroom.

"Ah, you're feeling better," Freddy said as he approached her. "What a lovely color you have in your cheeks. A bit of air is—"

She swept by him and moved around the edge of the ballroom until she was beside Lani and Bradford. Lani took one glance at her face and said, "No, Cassie."

"Josette told me."

"A few more hours and it will be over."

"I won't stand for it."

"Stay out of this. I choose and fight my own battles."

"You're not fighting, you're enduring."

"It's not Lady Huntley. She's only a parrot. Leave it alone, Cassie."

"The devil I will." She turned on her heel, moving toward the corner where Carolyn Carradine was standing with Jared. Lani was right, she was the one responsible.

She halted before the woman. "Come outside with me."

She raised her brows. "I beg your pardon?"

"It's not my pardon you should beg. Come with me or you'll regret it."

"Good heavens, are you threatening me?"

"Not yet. Just warning you."

"What's the meaning of this?" Jared asked, frowning.

She ignored him. "Come!" She turned and strode out the front door.

Carolyn Carradine appeared a moment later, followed by Jared. "It's freezing out here. This is madness."

Cassie didn't even feel the cold. "I know what you told Lady Huntley to do."

A flicker of expression crossed the woman's delicate features. "Jared, I don't know what this is all about. I told Amanda to introduce Madam Deville to our friends while I was doing my duty as hostess."

"You told her to make a pretense of cordiality but show Lani she was not welcome here." Cassie added, "In the cruelest possible fashion."

"You can't blame me for another woman's venom."

"I do blame you. I blame you for your hypocrisy and your small soul and your cruelty." She took a step forward until she was only inches away. "They called her a savage, but you're the savage."

"Carolyn?" Jared asked slowly.

"Lies. She has no proof."

"No, I have no proof," Cassie said. "Just Josette's words and your expression when I confronted you."

Carolyn smiled. "Then I'm really too chilled to stay out here and listen to this raving." She started to turn away. "We'll discuss it later, Jared."

"No." Cassie's hand stopped her. "Not until you've made reparation. You can't hurt Lani and walk away."

Her lip curled. "And what will you do?"

"I'll be what you called her. Lani isn't a savage, but I can be one. She believes in dignity and kindness and turning the other cheek. She's tried to teach me to do that, but she never succeeded." Cassie stepped closer, glaring at her. "She never understood the warriors of Kalaniopuu, but I did."

"Kalaniopuu," Carolyn repeated. "What rambling is this?"

"Your Captain Cook tried to take the chief Kalani-opuu hostage. Do you know what they did to him?"

"Everyone knows that brave man was killed by savages."

"Then they cut the flesh off his bones and returned it to his sailors in a sack. That's what I'll do to you."

She shuddered. "You truly are a savage."

"Yes, and I would not think twice about creeping into your room and butchering you." The words flowed in a fierce, deadly stream. "Nothing would save you. I'd wait and I'd watch, and when you'd least expect it, I'd strike."

Carolyn turned pale. "Jared! Stop her."

"I'm not sure I can," Jared drawled. "She's really quite terrifying, isn't she?"

Cassie paid no attention to him. "You'll go to Lani and you'll beg her pardon. You'll tell her that you know she's a far finer woman than you'll ever be. You'll curtsy to her and—"

"Curtsy?"

"You should grovel on the floor and kiss her feet," Cassie said fiercely. "If it wouldn't embarrass Lani, I'd make you do it."

Carolyn raised her chin. "All of this is nonsense. I'm not afraid of you."

"Look at me." Cassie held her gaze. "You should be afraid. This isn't my world. I'm not guided by your rules. Every time you go to sleep at night, you'll wonder if you'll live another day."

Carolyn shivered and moistened her lips. "She's mad. Help me, Jared."

"And have her shred the flesh from my bones? I'd really rather like to keep the two together."

"Go!" Cassie shoved her toward the door. "Now! I'll be watching from the doorway."

Carolyn opened the door and glared venomously over her shoulder. "I'll never forgive you for letting her do this to me, Jared." She raised her chin. "Very well, I'll do it, but this small triumph will do you little good. I have a position here. I'm respected and feared. You are nothing." She swept across the room toward Lani. She stopped in front of her, hesitated, and then swept Lani a sketchy curtsy.

Lani gazed at her in astonishment.

Carolyn's words were muttered, but they must have been the right ones, because the guests near the two women wore expressions of bewilderment.

"Satisfied?" Jared asked in Cassie's ear.

"No, but it will have to do." She turned on her heel. "I'm leaving this place. I don't want to be here anymore."

"No more challenge?" He caught Bradford's eye across the room and motioned to him. "As I'm no longer welcome here either, I'll escort you from the premises. Wait outside while I talk to Bradford."

He joined her a moment later and placed her cloak around her shoulders. "You probably don't need this. I doubt if you're feeling the cold."

"Where's Bradford?" she asked as he helped her down the steps.

"He's coming. I'll take you back to the castle in my carriage, and he'll bring Lani and Josette." He motioned to the coachman. "I believe it's best I get you out of here as soon as possible."

She didn't argue as he helped her into his carriage and then settled onto the seat across from her. She wanted nothing more than to escape the place now that the deed was done. She drew the cloak closer about her. Jared was right: she didn't feel the cold, but she was shaking with the aftereffects of that terrible anger.

She breathed a sigh of relief when the lights of Carradine House faded in the distance.

"Would you have done it?" Jared suddenly asked.

"Butchered her? Don't be ridiculous. Even that . . . that . . . gargoyle's life has some worth. But I would have frightened her so badly that she would never have felt safe again."

"I'm not sure she will now."

"Good." Cassie leaned back and closed her eyes. The trembling was becoming worse. Perhaps if she feigned sleep, he wouldn't notice.

He didn't speak for a long time, and she thought she had succeeded in deceiving him. Then he said roughly, "Stop shaking, dammit."

"It's cold."

"Stop it!"

Her lids flew open and she said fiercely, "I can't stop it. If you don't want to see it, close your eyes. It's not as if you—"

"Shut up." He was beside her on the seat, his arms sliding beneath the cloak to draw her close. "Just shut up."

Strength and support flowed out of him, enveloping her in a warm haze. She should push him away, show him she didn't need him. Dear God, but she *did* need him. Perhaps it would be all right to accept comfort for just a little while.

She relaxed against him. "I'll be better soon. It's been . . . a difficult night."

"For all of us." His arms tightened around her. "And you tried your best to make it impossible."

She sensed he wasn't talking about Carolyn or Lani. "You weren't being fair."

He didn't answer.

It appeared he was not going to argue with her. Relief flowed through her. She'd had enough conflict and challenges tonight. She was glad he wasn't angry.

He really wasn't angry, she thought suddenly. She could sense annoyance but not anger. He had been furious earlier in the evening, and her attack on Lady Carradine should have added fuel to the fire. Why had it not done so? She had been so absorbed with Lady Carradine that she scarcely noticed Jared's response, but now that she thought back, she remembered he had not aligned himself against her. She had ruined all his plans, but he had refused to abandon her. His support was bewildering.

"Why didn't you— Lady Carradine was very angry with you."

"Yes."

"She'll find a way to punish you."

"You give her too much credit."

"Josette."

"I don't believe Josette will be returning to Lady Carradine's School for Young Ladies."

"Won't that enrage her? You said her influence could destroy Josette's position with the ton."

"I'll find a way to deal with her."

"How?"

"I'll destroy her." The words were offhand, spoken with a complete lack of expression. "She's set herself to be an example of virtue and good taste. With a few ungentlemanly words spoken at the right time, to the right people . . . It shouldn't be difficult to destroy that image."

The ruthlessness of the statement had shocked her —but it shouldn't have. That ruthlessness had driven her father from the island and sent her in pursuit. "You would do that to her?"

He suddenly chuckled. "At least I didn't say I'd butcher her and throw her flesh in a sack." He paused. "Yes, I'll do it if she hurts Josette. I may even do it if she doesn't."

"Why?"

"She lied to me and she didn't play fair."

She shouldn't have had to ask. Justice was important to him, and Lady Carradine had committed a transgression he couldn't forgive. "You believed me?"

"I saw her face." He added, "But I would have believed you anyway. I've found to my misfortune that you're honest to a fault."

She was silent a moment, and when she spoke, her words were muffled. "I'm sorry I caused you and Josette trouble. I had to do it."

"I know you did. Kanoa was in the ascendancy."

She said haltingly, "I thank you for understanding I couldn't—"

"Understand?" He pushed her back, looked into her face, and asked harshly, "Why the devil are you thanking me? Did you think I don't know that I'm to blame for what happened tonight? I trusted Carolyn, and because of my misjudgment Lani was hurt and you were distressed. You owe me no gratitude for being a fool."

"You weren't a fool. She was very clever and—"

"I made a mistake and others suffered for it." His lips twisted. "Which means reparations must be made."

"Lady Carradine already made reparations."

"Not for my blunder." His tone sharpened with frustration. "Christ, don't you know I want to believe I owe you nothing? At last, you made me angry enough to forget how vulnerable you are. If this hadn't happened, you'd have been in my bed tonight."

"No!"

"Yes!" His eyes blazed down at her. "You wanted it. You may have worn that gown for Lani, but everything you did afterward was for me. You meant to goad me until I forced you to take what you wanted."

Was it true? Her deliberate acts of provocation had not been at all like her. She had seen him with Carolyn and been filled with anger. Anger or jealousy?

"Don't worry, it won't happen now," he said. "Not until I find a way to rid myself of this damn guilt." His hands opened and closed on her shoulders. "Which better be soon."

She had wanted him and had tried to take him. She had acted blindly, and the instinctive response frightened her. How could she be sure it wouldn't happen again?

"Let me go," she whispered.

His hands tightened on her shoulders and then fell away from her. "Not for long." He moved back to his seat across from her. "I swear to you, not for long, Cassie."

She leaned back and closed her eyes again, trying to shut him out. She could sense his gaze on her face, feel his presence as if he were still touching her.

Dear God, she could not close him away. She might never be able to do it again.

Thirteen

"**A**re you awake?" Lani whispered from the doorway.

"Yes." Cassie turned over on her bed to face the door. Lani was still in her ball gown; she must have barely arrived. "I've just gotten to bed. I'll get up."

"No, we'll talk in the morning. I'll stay only a moment." Lani glided forward, set the candlestick down on the bedside table, then sat on the edge of the bed. "I just had to know how you did it."

"I threatened her with the death Kalaniopuu dealt Cook."

Lani threw back her head, and her rich laughter rang out. "And she believed you?"

"Josette said she was a coward. I was angry. You would have believed me, too."

A smile lingered on her lips. "Perhaps." She bent forward and brushed Cassie's forehead with a kiss. "You should not have done it, but it pleases me that you did. It's good to have a loving friend." She picked up the candlestick and moved toward the door. "Good night, Kanoa. Sleep well."

Jared had said Kanoa was on the ascendancy, and now Lani was calling her by her Hawaiian name. Perhaps she had been more fierce than she had thought tonight.

Lani paused at the door and glanced back at her. "Kalaniopuu, truly?"

"It seemed appropriate."

"Oh yes, extremely." Lani's lips were still twitching as she gently shut the door.

Bradford straightened away from the wall. "Did you find out what our tiger did to the bitch?"

"Only a threat." Lani smiled. "But an exceptionally intimidating one." She started down the hallway. "What are you doing here? I thought you were going to your bed."

"Not until I was sure all was well with you. I knew you'd go first to Cassie." He fell into step with her. "I'll escort you to your room."

"That's not necessary. I do know the way."

He said with sudden violence, "For God's sake, let me do *something* for you."

She looked at him in astonishment. She had never seen urbane, mocking Bradford this upset. His hands clenched and unclenched at his sides as he strode beside her down the hall.

"And don't stare at me as if there were something outrageous about my wanting to protect you. It makes me want to shake you."

"I cannot see how you can want to do both. The two seem to be at odds."

"Not when a man is as frustrated as I am. Do you know how much I envied Cassie tonight? I stood there and watched her defend you, not even knowing from what insult. You didn't let me know. You wouldn't let me help you. You never let me close enough to—"

"I didn't need defending," she interrupted. "It would have been better if Cassie had let it alone. She may have done harm to Josette."

"And the harm to Lani doesn't matter?"

"Those people could not hurt me unless I let them hurt me."

"They hurt you. I saw it in your face."

"Then you were mistaken." They had reached her door and her hand grasped the knob. "You don't know me well enough to read me."

"The hell I don't!" His hands on her shoulders, he jerked her around to face him. His eyes blazed down at her. "I know you better than anyone in this world. I know your pride and your generosity, your intelligence and your stubbornness. I know you'd go through the fires of Hades for anyone you cared about, and I want to be one of those people. I want it so badly it hurts me."

His lips crushed down on her mouth.

Sensuality and passion enveloped her, taking her breath, sending heat spiraling through her. His action was so sudden she had no time to lift barriers against it. Instinctively her mouth opened and his tongue entered her. Her breasts were swelling against the broad wall of his chest, and she felt the familiar hot, tingling yearning between her thighs.

He lifted his head and said hoarsely, "You see, this is what we could have. You need me."

Dazed, she gazed up at him. In this moment he was totally masculine, totally sensual, and she was responding as helplessly as she had when she was a young girl with her first man.

Triumph blazed in his expression.

Her arms slowly slid around his neck and her head tilted back. *Yes, come to me. Let my body sing. Let us join in the dance of—*

No!

She jerked away from him and stepped back so hurriedly she bumped against the door. She shuddered as she realized how close she had come to yielding.

"Don't do this. You need me."

She drew a shaky breath. "I don't need you." She had to drive a wedge between them. "I just need a man."

Hurt flickered across his rough features, and then he forced a smile. "Then take me. I'm at your disposal."

She shook her head. "Charles would not like it."

"You wouldn't have to tell him." His smile became self-mocking. "You see how low I've fallen. I'm even willing to share you with him. I'll take you any way I can get you. What a pitiful specimen I'm turning out to be."

His bitterness hurt her. "You're not pitiful. You're a fine man." She paused and then said in a rush, "Even if there were no Charles, can't you see it would not be good between us? You were there tonight. Your friends think me a savage. They would never accept me."

"Then they will no longer be my friends."

"I do not like your England."

"Then we'll go wherever you like."

She shook her head in despair. "You would be sorry you married me."

"Shall we see? Go get your cloak and we'll be off to Gretna Green. By morning we'll be wed." His boyish smile was eager. "Let me show you how I can love you, Lani. I'll care for your needs, I'll satisfy your body. I'll never ask you to say you love me. I won't ask anything but that you let me love."

She closed her eyes. She could imagine what it would be like to let herself be loved by Bradford. Passionate, warm, and yet with a multitude of sweet challenges. He would keep her safe and value her. She had never known a love like that. All her life she had been the one to give. What a lovely life it—

Her lids flicked open as she realized where that path was leading her. She could not believe how tempted she had been. Honor and loyalty forbade her even considering Bradford's plea. "Impossible." She suddenly found her eyes stinging with tears, and she turned her back and fumbled for the knob. "I've told you before I cannot listen to this. I love only Charles."

"No, you don't," he said fiercely. "You may care about Deville, but, by God, you care about me, too. Every day it's growing. In another month you won't even remember what it was like to do without me."

She fled inside her room and slammed the door behind her.

Her chest was constricted, and she couldn't breathe without wanting to weep. The last few minutes had been more agonizing than those hideous hours at Carradine House. Dear God, she did not want to hurt Bradford. The last thing in the world she wanted was to cause him sadness or distress.

The last thing in the world.

Dangerous thought. Threatening truth.

She staggered over to the bed and sat down. She felt battered and bruised and a hundred years old.

Every day it's growing.

If that was true, then it must stop.

And she had a dreadful feeling it was true.

Josette was standing at Kapu's stall stroking him when Cassie came to the stable the next day.

Josette turned to Cassie with a triumphant smile. "I've saddled him for you. He's beginning to like me. It's just going to take a little more time, and I'll be able to ride him." She added quickly, "If you'll let me."

She might not have even that long, Cassie thought with a pang. Soon events would be put in motion that would take her away forever. An intense wave of sadness washed over her. Of course she was sad, she thought hastily. Josette had become her friend and it was always sad to leave friends. She said impulsively, "Would you like to ride him today?"

Josette's face became luminous. "Could I? Do you think he's ready for me?"

"We could try. I'll stand at his head while you mount, in case he bolts."

"You know I'd love it. I've wanted to ride him since that first night." Some of the joy in her expression lessened. "Are you sure? You don't let anyone ride him. Not even Jared."

"Then it's time I was less selfish." She opened the door of the stall. "Lani says that to give a gift is always to receive a greater one in return." She grimaced. "It's the one island belief I find difficult to embrace when it comes to Kapu. But I'm not completely ungenerous—I do have reason to be careful. Kapu *is* dangerous. Lead him outside."

Josette grabbed the reins. "Come, boy," she crooned. "I'll be so good to you." She led him toward the door that opened to the pasture. "I thought I was going to have to settle for that gelding today."

Cassie suddenly realized Morgana's stall was empty. "Where's Morgana?"

"Jared must have taken her out. She was gone when I got here."

"We'll take the path through the forest." Jared always took the cliff road; if they went toward the forest, she wouldn't have to see him. "I'll saddle the gelding myself. Don't try to mount Kapu until I get back."

"You don't want to see Jared." Cassie nodded understandingly. "Was he very angry last night?"

"He wasn't pleased, but he was surprisingly fair."

"Jared's always fair."

"He blamed himself for misjudging Lady Carradine."

"What a stroke of luck. I was afraid he'd make us all apologize to the gargoyle."

"And he's not going to make you go back to her school."

"Really?" Her eyes lit with excitement. "I can stay here?"

"Presumably."

She dropped Kapu's reins, launched herself at Cassie, and whirled her in a giddy circle. "I knew when I saw you that good things were going to happen."

"Is that why you knocked me down?" Cassie asked dryly.

Josette waved an airy hand. "Only a minor error."

"It felt major." She paused. "Jared says he won't let you be hurt by what I did last night. I hope that's true. I couldn't let Lani—"

"Shh, I know. You warned me it might happen. I'd have done the same thing." Her expression was suddenly grave. "I can't convince Jared that none of those people are important to me. I'd die if I had to be penned up painting teacups, waiting for some gentleman to offer for me. I want *more*."

"And what do you want?" Cassie asked indulgently.

"I want hundreds of horses. I want to go on great adventures. I want to see your island. I want to go to Sedikhan and find a Kapu or Morgana of my own. I want to do everything, taste everything, smell everything. I want to—"

"Wait." Laughing, Cassie held up her hand. "I think you'd better set limits. You're not going to have time in one lifetime to do all that."

"I'll squeeze it all in." She grinned. "Look at me today. I'm going to ride Kapu!"

So young and full of life and dreams. Cassie herself had only one dream, which made life much simpler. She would miss Josette. "Yes, you are," she said gently. "Now, grab his reins again before he decides to wander off, while I get that gelding."

"Cassie!" Jared banged forcefully on her door. "Let me in!"

Cassie had been removing her gown and tensed in midmotion. She had no intention of letting him into her bedchamber. She had been scrupulously avoiding him since last night and had even gone to the lengths of missing supper. "I don't want to see you. Go to bed."

"Open the door."

"I'm not dressed."

"Then get dressed." He threw open the door.

He was without a coat, and his shirt was unbuttoned at the throat. His hair was tousled and he was smiling recklessly, his appearance vaguely reminding her of that night of the storm on board the *Josephine* when he had come to help her with Kapu. She had been relieved to see him then, but not tonight. "I didn't invite you to come into my room."

"And you're not undressed. What a disappointment."

"I told the truth. I was getting undressed. I'd just started to undo my gown."

"Then I'll have to help fasten it again." He turned her around, his fingers deft and swift on the buttons.

She stood there, bewildered. She had not expected aid in putting *on* her clothes.

"There." He gave her a pat on her bottom, snatched her cloak from the chair beside the bed, and grabbed her hand. "Now, come on."

"I don't want to—" But he was already pulling her from her room and down the corridor toward the staircase. "Where are we going?"

"To expiate a wrong." He gave her a reckless smile over his shoulder. "And clear the way."

"You're talking nonsense. I want to go back to my room."

He didn't answer.

"Tell me what's happening!"

He had thrown open the front door and was pulling her down the steps toward the courtyard. "Where are we going?"

"The stable."

She immediately panicked. "Is something wrong with Kapu?"

"No. In fact, something is going to be extremely right with Kapu and with you." He dropped her hand and threw her cloak around her. "Now, will you stop arguing and come with me?"

She hesitated, but then started across the courtyard. "I don't see why you'd have any reason to go to the stable in the middle of the night."

"It seems more fitting. There are too many people around during the day."

She was growing more and more bewildered. "Fitting?"

"Well, I thought you'd think so. Personally, I've no objection to spectators." He opened the stable doors. "But you think that horse is human."

"Not human, but he has a great soul." She walked down the corridor toward Kapu's stall. "And if we're going riding, you should have let me change."

"We're not going riding." He stopped beside Kapu's stall and patted the stallion's muzzle. "But he is. Take him out of the stall and lead him to the south meadow."

She frowned. "Why?"

He met her gaze. "Because Morgana is waiting for him there."

She went still. "What are you saying?"

"Morgana is in season."

"You want a foal by Kapu?"

He grimaced. "I want something out of this for my own."

"You'll have a great deal—Morgana, and Kapu's foal."

He shook his head. "I'll have the foal. Morgana will be yours as soon as the foal is born."

She stared at him in shock. "What!"

"Reparation," he said simply. "Isn't that what you want most in the world? The fulfillment of your dream, a mare to match Kapu?"

"Yes," she whispered. "Oh, yes."

"Then Morgana is yours."

She couldn't believe it. "You mean it?"

"I don't lie, Cassie." His lips tightened. "And I'm not trying to trick you into getting a foal by Kapu."

She had not even considered that possibility. "I know you wouldn't do that. It's just . . . I never dreamed . . ." Morgana was his prize possession, and this gift was generous beyond belief. "Are you sure?"

"Reparation," he said again. "You're not the only one who believes that sins must be atoned. I'll have to find another way to make things right with Lani, but I knew this would probably satisfy you." He stepped back and opened the stable door for her. "Take him to her."

She just stood there staring at him. Josette's words came back to her.

Sometimes he does something splendid, and you forget everything else.

He suddenly smiled at her. "I never thought I'd catch you speechless."

"I don't know— It's too—" She swallowed to ease the aching tightness of her throat and grabbed Kapu's reins. She asked gruffly, "Are you coming?"

"I wouldn't miss it." He followed her, past Morgana's empty stall. "You'll remember I do have a considerable interest in the outcome."

Morgana was at the far end of the pasture, and the bright moonlight revealed every shimmering, beautiful line of the mare. Cassie felt a surge of pure joy. Her dream, her horse. Morgana was going to be *hers*.

Kapu nudged her forcefully from behind, his ears pricking forward.

She chuckled as she realized the stallion was scenting Morgana. It seemed Kapu did not agree with her; Morgana was not Cassie's, but his mare. She took off Kapu's halter. "Open the gate."

Jared opened the gate and stepped aside.

Kapu bolted into the pasture.

Morgana froze and then bolted in the opposite direction.

"You didn't hobble her," Cassie said. It was customary to hobble the mare to make it easier for the stallion to mount her.

"I don't like ropes," Jared said. "As you may remember. Kapu will have to work for his pleasure."

It appeared Morgana was in full agreement. She raced around the pasture with Kapu at her heels for a full ten minutes, never letting him get too close. When she tired of that game, she came to a halt and started a new gamut of playful teasing, backing toward him and then, when he came near, swishing her tail disdainfully and dashing off again.

Jared chuckled and shook his head. "Poor Kapu."

It *was* comical. Kapu was totally bewildered, his dignity crushed as he helplessly chased after the mare.

Then, suddenly, everything changed.

Morgana stopped and turned to face Kapu.

"Ah, she's ready," Jared murmured.

Cassie tensed, watching as the two horses stood confronting each other. Something was passing between them, a message both mystical and primitive. A communication as old as the ages, beautiful and secret and mysterious.

All mysticism vanished with the next breath.

Kapu half reared and neighed in triumph.

Morgana turned and backed toward him.

Cassie heard Jared's muttered exclamation. Her own throat was too dry to speak. The entire night seemed compressed to contain only the two horses in the meadow.

No, Jared was here, but somehow he was part of it.

Kapu mounted Morgana. Dear heaven, how would those delicate legs support his weight?

She stood firm as he entered her.

Raw, driving power. Stallion and mare both lost in the sexual dance of life.

Heat tingled through Cassie and then became molten. She knew that primitive dance. She *wanted* it.

Jared's hand covered hers on the fence.

She shuddered but didn't look away from the two mating horses.

Kapu's teeth were sinking into Morgana's neck. She did not feel the pain, Cassie knew. At this moment you felt nothing but the drive, the emptiness being filled, the hot intruder that you had invited within your body.

Her hands were clenched so tightly on the railing that her palms felt bruised.

"Cassie?" Jared asked hoarsely.

She turned to look at him. *Kahuna.* Lust. Stallion. She closed her eyes, but the scent of him still assaulted her.

She cried out as his hands cupped her breasts; they swelled instantly in response. Her lids flew open.

His nostrils were flaring with the harshness of his breathing. "God, don't say no."

No? She could no more refuse him than Morgana could refuse in that final moment. She shook her head.

"Thank God." He picked her up and was carrying her.

"Where are you going?" she whispered.

"Not here," he muttered. "I don't think either of us would notice, but I don't want you chilled." They were in the stable. "Morgana's stall is the closest. . . ."

Soft hay beneath her, Jared above her, his hands tearing frantically at her gown. She helped him, her fingers trembling, her entire body shaking with need.

She was naked on the bed of straw. Jared parted her legs, his fingers searching.

No, this wasn't right. . . .

She pushed him away and rose to her hands and knees.

He understood at once. "Like Morgana?" He muttered. "Whatever you want. . . ."

He entered her, covered her. She expected it to be like that night in the cabin, but it wasn't. It was like nothing ever before. She was whimpering, moving backward, taking him. His hands cupped her breasts as he drove hard, harder. . . .

He was muttering wildly, his breath coming in great labored gasps. Then, suddenly, he was withdrawing, turning her onto her back.

She looked up at him dazedly. "Why . . ."

"Because you're not a mare, goddammit." He gasped as he entered her again. "You're a woman. Mine . . ." He plunged deep, again, again, again. "Mine."

Her teeth sank into her lower lip but she felt no pain. She felt nothing but him. She wanted nothing but him. Forever . . .

Climax. Different this time. Release that has no end . . .

He cried out and his back arched as he gained his own release. She saw the painful contortion slowly vanish from his face. He looked down at her and she met his gaze.

Mystery. Life. Destiny. How strange that this moment of realization had come after the act, not before as it had been with Morgana and Kapu. . . .

"Cassie . . ." A note of wonder, of bewilderment.

"No." She didn't want him to speak. She pulled him down and held him close as the last ripples of passion shuddered through him. She had given him this pleasure. A surge of joy tore through her, so intense it made the physical release pale in comparison. He was hers, as Kapu was hers, as Lani was hers.

No, more. So much more. The truth crashed down upon her, jarring her back to reality.

Dear God, how had it come to this?

She lay stunned, unable to believe she had not known before. She had not been careful enough. The Jared of daylight and darkness had merged, and she would never be able to separate them again.

"I didn't plan this." His words were muffled in her hair. "I didn't want it to happen this way. I wanted Morgana to be a gift."

"I'm certain you didn't," she said dully. She knew him so well now. She knew his humor and his impatience, his passion and sensuality, his gentleness with Josette and Bradford. She knew his strict sense of justice and his total determination. She wished with all her heart she knew less about him. "It wasn't your fault."

It was her own fault. She had done the unforgivable.

He raised his head to look down at her. "What's wrong with you?"

She shook her head without answering.

He muttered a curse, moved off her, and adjusted his clothes. "You wanted it, dammit! I did *not* rape you."

"No." She sat up and brushed the hair from her eyes.

"Then why are you acting as if I did?"

"I want to go to my room." She didn't look at him as she straightened her clothes. "Will Kapu and Morgana be all right in the pasture?"

"Yes. We'll leave them together for the night. They'll couple several times before morning."

"And you'll have your foal." She stood up and brushed bits of hay from the skirt of her gown. "Everything is working out just as you thought."

"The hell it is." He rose to his feet. "Tell me what's wrong!"

"Nothing." Her voice was halting. "I'm very grateful for your generosity in giving me Morgana. It's very kind."

"Kind? You must be ill. I've never known you to think me kind."

"You can be kind." Kind and ruthless. Gentle and erotic. Darkness and light. The tears were brimming, and she had to get away from him. "Good night . . ." She turned and fled down the corridor toward the door.

He caught her as she reached the courtyard and whirled her to face him. "Talk to me," he said through his teeth. "For God's sake, tell me what—" He broke off as he saw the tears streaming down her cheeks. "My God."

"I have to go." She started to struggle. "I have to—"

"Not until— All right, anything, just, for God's sake, stop crying." He let her go and stepped back. "But it's not the end of it. Tomorrow you're going to tell me what you're upset about."

She would never tell him.

She turned and ran across the courtyard. She could feel his baffled, frustrated gaze on her back as she tore up the stairs and into the hall. She would never commit that final betrayal.

She would never, never tell Jared she loved him.

"Cassie?" Josette was sitting on the bottom step of the staircase, dressed in night shift and robe, bare feet curled beneath her. Her eyes were wide with alarm. "You're weeping. What did he do to you?"

She wiped her wet cheeks with the back of her hands. "What are you doing here?"

"I heard you and Jared arguing in the hall. I was worried . . . I couldn't sleep." She shook her head. "You said he wasn't angry."

"He wasn't." She started up the stairs. "Go to bed."

Josette scrambled to her feet and followed her. "Then why are you crying? You never cry."

"I just am."

"Why?"

The tears wouldn't stop flowing and neither would Josette's questions. Cassie suddenly flared. "It's my concern. Leave me alone!" Then, when she saw Josette's stricken expression, she was instantly remorseful. "It's not . . . Everything is . . . it's too much."

"Is it Jared? Do you want me to talk to him?"

"No!" She tried to temper the sharpness. "Nothing is wrong. Jared didn't hurt me. He's actually been very kind. He gave me Morgana."

"You have to be jesting," Josette whispered.

She shook her head. "He's taking Kapu and Morgana's foal. So, you see, everything is fine."

"Then why are you crying?"

"Because I can't—" She stopped and then said,

"Because it's time I left Morland. I can't stay here any longer."

The words startled her as much as they did Josette, but once they were uttered, she knew no other action could result from the realization that she loved Jared. If she didn't leave him now, she wasn't sure she would ever leave him.

"No!" Josette cried, dismayed. "Why should you go? Everything is fine now. I don't have to go back to school, and Jared gave you Morgana. We could have a lovely time."

"Josette, I don't belong here. Have you forgotten my father?"

Josette was silent a moment. "I wish you could." She held up her hand as Cassie opened her lips to speak. "But I know you can't." She shook her head. "Jared won't let you go."

Cassie forced a smile. "Then I'll have to go without his knowledge, won't I?"

"Do you have any money?"

"About a hundred pounds my father left with Lani."

"Lani will go with you?" Josette answered her own question. "Of course she will." Her tone became wistful. "It's just that I've gotten so used to both of you. I'll miss you. . . ."

"We'll miss you, too."

"Truly?"

Cassie nodded her head. "Truly. But I have to go."

"It's difficult getting into French ports these days. Few ships will accept the risk." Josette frowned. "And how will you manage to arrange passage? I doubt if you could leave Morland without Jared's sanction."

"I don't know." She shook her head wearily. It was trying enough to come to terms with the knowledge that she loved Jared. She couldn't deal with anything else. "I'll think about it later. Right now I'm going to bed." She started up the stairs again. "And so should you."

"And what about papers?" Josette followed her. "I think you should stay here."

Cassie shook her head.

"Then I think I should go with you."

"What!" Cassie turned to look at her in surprise.

"Well, I could sail you across the channel in my boat. If we didn't land at a major port, you wouldn't be faced with the problem of papers immediately."

"You would do that for us?"

Josette grinned. "You need me. I've had all kinds of experience in escapes. At least twice a year since Jared sent me to Carradine Hall. Do you think it was easy getting away from the gargoyle all those times? I'm more prepared now than you'd be in a year."

"Carradine Hall isn't Morland." Cassie's first leap of hope vanished. "I couldn't let you do that for us."

She coaxed. "I'm a very good sailor. It wouldn't be that dangerous just to land you and Lani on a beach near a village and come back."

"Jared would be angry with you."

"Not for long. Besides, I'd rather face Jared's anger than worry about your safety."

It was very tempting, the answer to most of the obstacles that stood in their way. "I'll consider it."

Josette nodded briskly. "You'll see that my way is best." She turned down the wing where her chamber was located. She cast Cassie a mischievous glance over her shoulder. "And in the meantime I'll start making plans. It takes a great deal of forethought to make good an escape."

Josette's sorrow and disappointment had been submerged in anticipation and purpose. Cassie wished she could shift emotions so easily. She felt raw and desolate, and the entire world seemed dark. She wanted to run to Lani and hear her say that everything would be all right.

But she couldn't do that this time. She had crossed into territory that was forbidden to her. How could Lani understand that she loved the man who was her father's deadly enemy? How could she understand it herself? She didn't even have the comfort of knowing that Jared loved her in return. He desired her, but passion was not love. He had been consumed by hatred of her father for too many years, and it was madness to think he would ever allow himself to love her. No, his bitterness was too strong, the gulf too deep.

Dear God, the tears were falling again. She must stop this stupid weeping. There was nothing to be done but what they had set out to do. She must save Papa and then return home.

She must make a life for herself far away from Jared, a world away. . . .

Fourteen

"I don't like using Josette this way," Lani said, seated in her usual chair in the library. "It could be dangerous for her."

"Do we have a choice?" Cassie asked. She didn't like it either, but there seemed no alternative. "If she turns around and immediately goes back to England, it should lessen the risk."

Lani nodded slowly. "That's true. And the journey is only a scant twenty miles or so. My people go much vaster distances in their voyager canoes." She paused. "Have you a plan for finding Charles? Perhaps he hasn't even arrived in Paris yet. I told you of the message Jared received from his man, Guillaume, saying that he had not been seen there." She shrugged. "I suppose it's possible that Jared received another message to the contrary. He was suspiciously careless of that first message. I think he meant for me to find it."

But her father probably had not arrived, or Jared would have departed immediately for the Continent, Cassie thought. "I hope he hasn't arrived there.

When he does, he'll go directly to Jacques-Louis David for information about Raoul Cambre."

"And you think this is a dangerous move?"

She shivered. "I met Cambre only once, but I didn't like him."

"A child has no great judgment."

"But excellent instincts. I don't want Papa near him."

"And we go to this David and ask him to put us in touch with Charles when he contacts him?"

Cassie nodded. "We can find lodgings at a small pension near David's residence until he arrives."

"We are foreigners. There will be questions."

Cassie chuckled. "I may feel as if I'm a foreigner, but I was born in France, remember. I believe I'll have no trouble being accepted. We will say you're . . ." She thought about it; Lani's golden skin was both exotic and distinctive. "Egyptian. The widow of one of Napoleon's officers. He met you when he was campaigning and brought you back to Paris."

Lani said dryly, "You've been spending entirely too much time with Josette. You're getting overly proficient at falsehoods."

"Of course, it would be better if David could give us Cambre's whereabouts in case Papa finds out in some other fashion." She shrugged. "We will have to see when we arrive what is best."

Lani looked down into the fire. "And when do we leave on this journey?"

"Tonight, after everyone has gone to bed. Josette says we can slip out to the stable and through the back pasture door. It's only a mile walk to the path leading down to the shore where her boat is docked. She'll distract the guard at the stable and then join us there."

"You're leaving Kapu and Morgana here with Jared. You realize he's going to be very angry. What if he refuses to return them to you when all this is over?"

"He won't do that."

"You seem very sure."

"He keeps his promises." She wearily shook her head. "And even if he didn't, I couldn't do anything else. It's time we left Morland."

Lani was silent a moment and then nodded. "I think you're right. We've been here too long. One tends to become . . . confused."

There was an undercurrent in Lani's tone that made Cassie's eyes widen with surprise. Had she been subjected to the same temptation Cassie had known? It seemed impossible. Lani was always steady, completely loyal, never deterring from her purpose. "Lani?"

Lani looked at her and smiled. "But we will no longer be confused once we find Charles. All will be clear and the same as it was before. Won't it, Kanoa?"

It would never be the same for Cassie, but perhaps it would grow less painful. She nodded jerkily and rose to her feet. "We should each take only one valise. Pack no more than three gowns and your riding habit. Josette will take them to the stable and hide them under the hay in an empty stall. Oh, and wear a warm shawl under your cloak. Josette says it becomes very chill on the water at this time of year."

Lani made a face. "Josette appears to be completely in command of this journey."

Cassie nodded. "And she's enjoying every minute of it." She moved toward the door. "I'll see you at supper. Try to rest this afternoon. Josette's sailboat is very small, and there aren't any cabins. It won't be a comfortable journey."

Lani opened her book again. "Then you should take your own advice."

"I have to exercise Kapu. After I'm gone, he'll get little— I forgot, Josette can ride him. She did very well the other day."

"But you want to ride him anyway." Lani nodded. "Go on, good-byes are more important than rest."

Cassie closed the door and moved quickly down the hall.

This ride would not really be a good-bye to Kapu, but it would be farewell to Morland. She might have to return briefly to retrieve Kapu and Morgana, but she would never live within these walls again, never ride with Jared along the cliff path, never watch the humorous byplay between Jared and Bradford at the supper—

"Cassie!"

Jared. Her pace quickened as she heard his steps behind her.

His hand fell on her shoulder, and he spun her around to face him. "Don't run away from me, dammit."

"I'm not running away."

"The devil you aren't. You've been avoiding me all day."

"I don't have time to talk to you right now. I have to go ride Kapu."

"I'll go with you."

"No!" She moistened her lips. "Not today."

He drew an exasperated breath. "I'm trying to be patient, but this can't go on. Will I see you at supper?"

"Yes, yes, of course." One last meal together. Another good-bye.

"You promise?"

She nodded. "But I have to go now."

"Cassie . . ." His hands opened and closed on her shoulders. "I feel . . . Did I hurt you in some way?"

She kept her eyes fastened on his cravat. "No."

"I never meant to hurt you. I'd never . . . Dammit, look at me."

If she looked at him, he might realize the truth. She was so filled with love and sorrow, she felt as if they must be written on her face. She swallowed. "We'll talk about this another time."

"Tonight?"

She shook her head.

"Tomorrow? We'll settle this tomorrow?"

She would be gone tomorrow. She would be in France on her way to Paris, far away from him. "Yes, it will all be settled tomorrow."

He released her, and she fled across the courtyard toward the stable.

Josette landed the sailboat a scant two miles from a small French fishing village just before dawn the next day. "Am I not superb?" she asked triumphantly. "I told you I could do it." She grabbed one of the valises, jumped out of the boat, and waded the few feet to shore. "Now all you have to do is go to the village and ask the way to Paris."

"Is that all we have to do?" Lani chuckled as she grabbed the other valise and jumped out of the boat. "I think there are a few minor obstacles to overcome."

"Well, maybe," Josette conceded. "But I got you here."

"Yes, you did." Cassie followed Lani to shore. "And we thank you very much."

"It was nothing." Josette waved an airy hand. "For a marvelous sailor and navigator."

"And good fortune had nothing to do with it?" Lani asked.

"Absolutely not." She reached into the pocket of her jacket. "I took these francs from Jared's desk drawer. He always keeps French currency on hand for his trips abroad." She pushed the bills into Cassie's hand. "You may need them until you can find a safe way to exchange your English pounds."

"You stole them?"

"Borrowed," she corrected. "You need them more than he does." She rummaged in another pocket and brought out something that glimmered in the light. "The ruby necklace Jared gave me for my last birthday. If you need to, sell it. Otherwise send it back to me."

Cassie felt tears rise to her eyes. "Josette, I can't take—"

"Hush." She stuffed the necklace into the pocket of Cassie's cloak and delved again into her seemingly bottomless pockets. "One more thing. It was in the desk in the library, too."

She handed Lani a small dagger with a bejeweled hilt sheathed in engraved Moroccan leather. "You should have some means of protection since I'm not going with you." She held up her hand as Cassie started to speak. "I don't have time to argue." She gave Cassie a hug. "Go with God." She turned and embraced Lani. "I'll miss you."

Before they could speak, Josette was wading back toward the sailboat. She gave it a push into deeper water, then scrambled over the side. She called, "And you'll miss me. I should really go with you. You see how well everything goes when I'm in charge."

"We'll suffer through without you," Lani called. "Difficult though it may be. And Jared would be most upset if we took you along."

Josette nodded glumly. "He's not going to be pleased now." She looked at the lightening sky. "He should be reading my note soon."

"Note?" Cassie said. "You left a note?"

"Of course. I love Jared. I wouldn't worry him longer than necessary. I left a note on Kapu's stall door that told him where I'd gone and that I'd be returning by nightfall."

"You shouldn't have done that," Cassie said.

"Why not? Now that he knows I'm coming back, he'll wait until I get to Morland to question me about where you're going. That will give you time to make your way to Paris." Josette grinned. "Isn't that clever?"

She could find no fault with Josette's reasoning. "I guess it can do no harm."

Josette was busily turning the small sailboat. "You'd better change your gowns in that thatch of trees. The hems are wet and might attract attention. Be sure you think of a good story about your presence here. I really should have done it myself while we were sailing. And I think you should—" She was still giving orders when the wind took the sails and the boat skittered beyond earshot.

Josette sighed and lifted her hand in farewell before turning her full attention to the sail.

Cassie waved and kept on waving until Josette's small, valiant figure was lost in the half darkness. It had been a long journey, and Josette had borne the brunt of it. Now she must make the same journey alone. "Will she be all right?" she murmured.

"Of course she will. She'll be out of sight before it's fully light, and it's a calm sea." Lani gently took Cassie's arm. "Come along, we must obey Mademoiselle General and change our gowns."

"They're gone." Jared crushed the note in his hand. "Christ, I may strangle Josette."

Bradford took the crumpled note from him and spread it out with shaking hands. "When do we leave?"

"Send a message to have them ready the *Josephine*." He stared blindly at Kapu. "We'll leave as soon as we talk to Josette."

"If the little devil comes back," Bradford said. "She may decide to go with them."

"She'll come back. She promised. Besides, Cassie wouldn't let her endanger herself any more than necessary." But there would be danger for Cassie and Lani. Two women alone in an enemy land with no papers or friends. Panic tore through Jared as he realized they might already be facing danger while he stood here helpless. How would he even find them when he reached France?

Josette. She might know something, and, by God, he would force her to tell him.

But she could not possibly be here before nightfall, perhaps later if the winds weren't with her. So he would be forced to wait, going mad with worry.

He had to keep busy. He whirled and headed for the stable door. "I'm going to order our luggage readied and tell Mrs. Blakely to pack clothing for Cassie and Lani. They can't have taken very much on the sailboat."

As he crossed the courtyard, he was barely aware of Bradford beside him.

It was only a little after eight in the morning, but the sun was shining brightly, not a cloud in the sky.

Let there be good winds. Jesus, let them all be safe.

"You knew this was bound to come," Bradford said quietly.

"Not like this." He knew now he had deliberately kept himself from thinking about the reason Cassie was here. The time at Morland was a time apart. He had not wanted to remember Deville, because then he would have to remember Cassie would never belong to him.

But she *did* belong to him.

"They're intelligent women," Bradford said. "They'll be careful."

"Is that supposed to comfort me?" he asked savagely.

"No, it's supposed to comfort me. I really don't give a damn about your feelings at the moment."

Jared glanced at Bradford's face and for the first time realized it was both pale and drawn. Any other time he would have had a twinge of compassion, but not now. "Because you think this is my fault?"

"No, you could no more stop yourself from going after Deville than they could stop trying to save him." He smiled crookedly. "Destiny, my lad."

Destiny. Jared didn't argue with him as he had the last time. For the first time in his life he felt as if he had no control, that he was being sucked helplessly into a giant whirlpool of circumstance.

"I beg pardon, Your Grace." Mrs. Blakely met them as they came in the front door. "But a messenger came a few minutes ago and brought this." She proffered an envelope. "He said I should give it to you at once."

"Thank you, Mrs. Blakely." He took the envelope and waved her away. "I have a few tasks for you to perform. Please come to the library in a quarter of an hour."

"Certainly, Your Grace."

He broke the seal, ripped open the envelope, and scanned the letter. He felt the blood drain from his face as he finished it. Then he read it again.

"What is it?" Bradford's alarmed gaze was fastened on his face. "For God's sake, who is it from?"

"Guillaume."

Jared was standing on the dock when Josette sailed into the small harbor just after darkness had fallen.

Her expression was wary and became even more so when she saw his face illuminated by the lantern in his hand. "I had to do it. They needed me," she called. She jumped out of the sailboat and secured it before turning to face him. "So you needn't shout at me."

"I'm not going to shout at you."

"You're not?" She said uncertainly, "That's very understanding of you. I didn't think you'd—"

"Where are they?"

"France."

Jared drew a long breath. "Josette, I'm trying to be patient with you. Where in France?"

"You know I can't tell you that. They trusted me. It wouldn't be honorable."

"Would it be honorable to let them have their throats cut and be thrown into the Seine?"

Her eyes widened. "What!"

"Would it?"

"No, of course not, but they won't—" She frowned. "Are you trying to trick me?"

"I'm trying to tell you that you may have taken them to a place that will only bring them death."

"I knew there was danger, but Cassie has to find her father." She added with a touch of defiance, "Before you do."

"Charles Deville is dead."

She stared at him in shock. "You can't know that's true."

"I received a message from Guillaume, my contact in Paris, this morning." His lips curled bitterly. "It was my morning to receive unpleasant correspondence."

"It shouldn't have been unpleasant for you. You wanted him dead."

"I didn't want him murdered by Raoul Cambre. I wanted him to lead me to Cambre."

"And did he do it? How else would this Guillaume know that Cambre had killed Deville?"

"By following Cambre himself. Guillaume was watching an artist, Jacques-Louis David, who went scurrying to a Raoul Bonille after being visited by a man Guillaume suspected was Deville. Bonille met with Deville one evening at a cafe near the Seine. It was Deville's last meeting on earth."

Josette shivered. "You're sure?"

"Guillaume is sure."

"And this David had something to do with it?"

"Directly or indirectly. He did know Raoul Bonille. And Guillaume is almost certain that Bonille is Cambre." His gaze narrowed on her face. "You're very interested in David."

Josette turned to face him. "You're telling me the

truth? You're not trying to trick me into betraying Cassie and Lani?"

"Have I ever lied to you?"

"No." She moistened her lips. "But this is different. I know you've always hated Deville."

"Do you want to see Guillaume's note?"

She met his gaze, then slowly shook her head. "But I had to be certain."

"They mentioned this David?"

She nodded. "They talked about him on the boat. Cassie said that her father would go to him first. She planned on contacting him as soon as she reached Paris."

"Christ."

"You think he'll tell Cambre?"

"There's not much doubt." His lips tightened. "And Cambre doesn't want to be found. He's already killed one man to prevent it."

"But Cassie doesn't want to find anyone but her father." Then Josette nodded as she thought it through. "But one will lead to the other."

"As day follows night. Do you know where they're planning on staying?"

"They had no idea. A pension near David's residence . . ."

He turned and strode down the dock.

Josette trotted beside him. "Where are you going?"

"Where do you think I'm going? Paris. Bradford is waiting for me on the ship now."

"I want to go with you."

"You'll stay here."

"You're blaming me for their being in danger. Well, maybe I am to blame, but all this hatred seemed wrong. I didn't know this would happen—"

"I know you didn't." He wearily looked at her. "I don't blame you. Maybe Bradford is right and it's just fate." His jaw clenched. "But I won't have you running about Paris in danger, too. You'll stay here and take care of Kapu and Morgana. Cassie wouldn't thank you for leaving her horses to the stable boys, would she?"

"No, I guess not." A frown wrinkled her forehead. "But I don't like being left behind. I'll be frightened for you."

"Good—then maybe you won't act so hastily again."

"You're not being kind."

"I don't feel kind." His stride lengthened as they approached the stable. "If I wasn't more frightened than you ever dreamed of being, I'd have tanned your hide until you couldn't sit down for a month."

"You're frightened?" She gave up trying to match his stride and called after him, "I've never known you to be frightened of anything, Jared."

"Then enjoy the experience. I certainly don't." He disappeared into the stable.

"I'm sorry, mademoiselle." David gave Cassie an entirely winning smile. "I regret I've not had the opportunity of renewing my acquaintance with your father. It's not surprising, since we did not know each other well."

"But you did know Raoul Cambre very well," Lani said. "And we have reason to believe Charles will want to find Monsieur Cambre."

"Impossible." David sighed. "Alas, Raoul and I drifted apart after your father left for Tahiti. Raoul was always a solitary man."

"Then you have no idea where he is?" Cassie asked.

"Not the slightest." His gaze shifted quickly to Lani, and he changed the subject. "You're quite lovely. Did Charles ever paint you?"

"No, Charles was interested only in painting landscapes."

"A great mistake. I've done one landscape in my entire career. An artist has a duty to himself and history to mirror life. I have all the great men of France begging me to paint them."

"How fortunate for you," Lani said without expression.

"Not fortune, genius." He added quickly, "Or so I'm told. Even Napoleon praises my—"

"If my father has not contacted you yet, he will do so soon," Cassie interrupted. "You'll advise us when that happens."

"Please," Lani interjected, changing the demand to a plea. "It's very important, monsieur."

"He will not come to me," he said peevishly. "I told you he would not. I'm a very busy man. Why must you all bother—" He broke off and forced a smile. "You must understand my impatience if you reside with my friend Charles. Artists pay heed to the demands of the soul, not of the world."

"Except when Napoleon beckons you back to the world," Cassie said dryly. She rose to her feet and moved toward the door. "We'll be waiting for word from you."

Lani followed Cassie to the door. "Thank you for your time, monsieur."

"It's very valuable time," he said pointedly. "I have no desire to waste it."

Lani gave him another dazzling smile. "We'll try not to trouble you."

He grunted and had turned away before she shut the door.

"I think from now on I'll do the talking," Lani told Cassie. "You were less than courteous."

"He was lying." Cassie strode toward the hired carriage. "I know it."

"You wouldn't have to be a seer," Lani said. "He does not lie well."

"I think Papa was here."

Lani nodded as she seated herself in the carriage. "Which means that David was lying either at Charles's request . . . or that of someone else."

Cassie absently motioned for the driver to go. "You mean Raoul Cambre."

"Possibly."

Fear iced through Cassie. "Dear God, I hope not." She stuck her head out the window and called to the coachman, "Pull around the corner and stop."

"What are you doing?" Lani asked.

"David may go to Papa to warn him we're inquiring after him." She didn't want to voice the other alternative. "We'll wait here and see if he does."

"And then follow him?"

Cassie hopped out of the carriage. "I'll go to the café across the street from David's residence and watch the front door. You stay here in the carriage. When he comes out, I'll join you."

She didn't wait for an answer but moved quickly toward the corner.

"I'd forgotten what abominable taste Guillaume has in drinking establishments," Bradford said, looking around the crowded waterfront tavern. "There's so much smoke one can't even see the ceiling."

"Or the man at the next table," Jared said. "Which is the point when you don't want your presence noted." His gaze searched the room. "Where the devil is he? His note said he'd be here every evening until I contacted him."

"Then he'll be here. Guillaume may be a trifle crude, but he's very reliable."

"Crude? You call me crude?" Jared turned to see Guillaume a few feet away. The potbellied Frenchman belched with deliberate loudness. "I'm not crude —I'm merely too honest to comply with your fancy English manners."

"Where have you been?" Jared asked impatiently.

Guillaume glowered at Bradford. "Finding out information from my crude associates."

"What information?"

Guillaume waited, staring hard at Bradford.

"My abject apologies," Bradford said with a sigh.

Guillaume shrugged. "It's only what one would expect of the English."

"One also expects them to pay through the nose for information," Jared said. "What news of Cambre?"

"He had another visit from David today. According to my man, Valbain, he appeared very annoyed."

"David was his only visitor?"

Guillaume nodded. "And he stayed only a few minutes before returning to his home. Then Cambre left and visited a small pension on the rue de Lyon."

"Why?"

"He inquired after a Mademoiselle Deville."

Jared went tense. "And?"

"She was not there, so he left."

Jared's breath expelled explosively. "Thank God."

Guillaume chuckled. "But he could have retraced his steps two blocks and found her. Valbain said two ladies followed Cambre from his home to the pension. They waited until he left before dismissing their carriage and going to their chambers."

"Christ," Bradford said.

"You know these ladies?" Guillaume asked.

"We know them," Jared said. "Did Cambre return to the pension later?"

"Not before I came to meet you." He glanced resentfully at Bradford and belched again. "Of course, I stopped to have a bit of bread and cheese first. I knew you wouldn't want me to starve for want of a paltry meal."

Jared barely heard anything but the first sentence. "How long ago?"

"Two hours, perhaps."

He pushed back his chair. "Take me there."

"Now?" Guillaume shrugged. "I thought you'd want to go to Cambre. I think there's little doubt the man is your old enemy. He matches your description, and the friendship with David is—"

"Later." He had to make sure Cassie and Lani were out of danger before he moved on Cambre. During the entire journey from Morland he had been imagining Cassie hurt, even dead, and he would not take any chances.

Guillaume gave him a curious look. "After all these years of searching for him? I'd not believe— Oh, well, it's not my business." He pushed back his chair and stood up. "Come along. The pension's only a ten-minute carriage ride from here."

Cassie was a mere ten minutes away, and Guillaume had kept them waiting for *two* hours? Rage suddenly flared through Jared, and he was tempted to bang the Frenchman's head against the wall.

"He didn't know they were of any importance," Bradford said in a low voice. "Don't waste time on him, Jared."

Important? In the whole world Cassie was of the utmost importance to him, and Guillaume had left her unprotected with Cambre hovering over her like a vulture.

And she was still unprotected. His anger was submerged in panic. Bradford was right, there was no time to waste.

He picked up his hat and gloves from the table and strode after Guillaume.

"I don't want to just sit here and wait." Cassie prowled back and forth across the tiny chamber. "Let's go back to Cambre's house and talk to him."

"It's safer to have him come to us."

"Papa could be in that house."

"Do you think Cambre offered him his hospitality?" Lani shook her head. "Not if he's as evil as you believe."

"Perhaps Papa is a prisoner."

"Or perhaps he was too clever to let Cambre fool him." She paused. "Charles isn't stupid. We're not even certain that he went to Cambre's house."

"Why are you arguing with me?" Cassie's hands clenched into fists. "Anything could happen. Jared must be in Paris by now. If Cambre doesn't find Papa, Jared will."

"I'm not arguing with you. I'm trying to make you see reason."

"We should have met Cambre as he was coming

out of the pension. I should never have let you stop me."

"And what would you have done? It would have been foolish to confront him with no plan. We didn't even have a weapon. Evidently he's concerned with our presence here, or he wouldn't have set out immediately for our pension. When he returns, we'll question him in safety here and see if we can learn anything." She was sitting in the window seat and wearily leaned her head back against the sill. "Now, will you stop pacing? You're making my head ache."

"I'm sorry." She stopped in the middle of the room. "It's just—we're so close— I'm afraid for Papa."

"We can do nothing if we don't ensure our own safety."

Cassie knew she was right, but it didn't still the anxiety pounding through her. Ever since they had arrived in Paris, she had felt a constant sense of panic, as if they were living under a threatening cloud that was turning the world darker with every passing second.

She crossed the room and dropped down onto the floor before Lani. "What if we don't find Papa before Jared does?" she whispered. "I couldn't bear it, Lani."

Lani's gaze searched Cassie's face. "Oh, no."

Lani knew, Cassie realized. She wanted to deny it, to tell Lani she was concerned only about Papa. She couldn't do it. "What I feel for Jared will make no difference. If I was going to let it matter, do you think I would have come?"

"Poor Kanoa." She gently cradled Cassie's cheek in her palm. "It's a cruel path you've chosen."

"I didn't choose it. I didn't *want* it to happen." She closed her eyes. "It's not fair that I love them both.

God shouldn't have let this happen to me. What will I do if I can't keep Jared from killing Papa?"

"You will survive it."

Cassie's eyes opened and she blinked to hold back the tears. "You don't hate me?"

"For something you cannot help?" She shook her head. "How could you think I would hate you?"

"Because sometimes I hate myself." She sat back on her heels and smiled shakily. "But I'm glad you don't. I think it would break my heart."

Lani's expression was troubled. "If Cambre doesn't come to us tonight, we'll go to him in the morning."

Cassie nodded jerkily and rose to her feet. "Whatever you think best. I don't want to—"

A sharp knock sounded on the door.

Relief surged through Cassie. Cambre. At last the waiting was over and she could *do* something.

She moved quickly across the room and threw open the door.

"I'd like to throttle you," Jared said grimly.

She stared at him in astonishment. "How did—"

"You couldn't wait, could you?" He threw open the door and pushed past her into the room.

"Wait for what? For you to find him before I did?"

Bradford followed Jared and closed the door. "We understand, but your haste was ill-advised and unkind." His gaze went to Lani and he added reprovingly, "You frightened me."

To Cassie's astonishment color flushed Lani's cheeks. "I've given you no right to be concerned."

He smiled. "Ah, but I took that right long ago."

"Are you mad?" Jared's eyes blazed down at Cassie. "Why did you follow David to Cambre?"

"How did you— Cambre was being watched?"

"Guillaume's man, Valbain." He grasped her

shoulders. "You're to stay away from Cambre, do you hear me?"

"I hear you." She shook her head to clear it. "That doesn't mean I'll obey." Valbain might have told him where to find her, but how had he known she had followed the artist? "How did you know we'd gone to see David?"

"Josette."

She stared at him in disbelief. "That's not true. She wouldn't betray us."

"She would to save your life."

She shook her head. "I don't believe you. Nothing would make her—"

"She knew it didn't matter any longer." His expression changed, and his grasp on her shoulders gentled. "She knew there wasn't anything you wanted here."

"What are you talking about? My father is here."

"Not anymore." His grasp opened and closed on her shoulders. "Dammit, I'm the last person on earth who should tell you this."

She went still. "Tell me what?"

"He's dead." When she still stared at him uncomprehendingly, he said jerkily, "Your father is dead, Cassie."

Pain and horror stormed through her. Her eyes closed and she swayed. "You killed him?" she whispered.

"No!" He crushed her to him, his hand cradling the back of her head. "Cambre killed him."

The pain was too great even to feel relief. "How do you know?"

"I received a letter from Guillaume before I left Morland. Cambre met with your father over a week ago at a café near the Seine. They stayed at the café for over two hours talking. At first they seemed on cordial terms. When they left the café, Valbain followed them. It was very late, and they took a deserted street that bordered the Seine. . . ." He stopped. "You don't want to hear the rest."

"Yes, I do." She should step away from him, she thought dimly, but his arms seemed to hold the only comfort in the world. "I want to hear everything."

"They turned a corner, and Valbain lost sight of them for a few moments. When he rounded the corner, he saw Cambre rolling your father's body into the river."

She shuddered; she had passed that river a dozen times since reaching Paris. "Was he . . . found?"

"Not yet." He paused. "Guillaume says that's not unusual."

Papa lost . . . only that cold gray river for a grave. "And you didn't get to do it yourself," she said dully. "It must have been a great disappointment."

"Cassie . . ." His voice was hoarse with pain.

"You sound upset. I don't know why. This is what you wanted, isn't it?" She finally found the strength to push him away. "He's dead."

"What do you want me to say?" His expression was tormented. "God, I don't want to hurt you anymore."

"He's dead, that's what you wanted."

"Stop saying that."

"Why should I stop telling the truth?" The wild words were tumbling out, the tears running down her cheeks. "That's what this is all about. Death." Terrible word, horrible word. She said it again, "Death."

He took a step toward her.

"Don't *touch* me. How do I know Cambre even killed him? Maybe you did it."

He turned pale. "Do you want to see Guillaume's letter?"

"A letter that you could have written yourself. You said you wanted me in your bed again. If you killed my father, you knew that would never happen."

"I didn't kill him." He added harshly, "I can't deny that was my intention when I first met you. I won't even deny that I might still have killed him if I'd found him before Cambre did. I've hated him for a long time, and I don't know what I would have done." He enunciated every word with desperate distinctness. "But I did not kill him, Cassie."

She wanted to believe him, she realized with disgust. He had hated her father, and yet she still loved Jared and wanted to trust in him. It sickened her that even after Papa's death she continued to betray him.

"Go away." She ran past Bradford to where Lani sat in the window seat.

Lani's eyes were glittering with tears, and she held out her arms to Cassie. Cassie went into them, giving comfort for comfort. Lani had loved her father. Lani understood the pain.

She heard Bradford's soft voice above her. "He's telling the truth, Cassie."

But Bradford loved Jared and therefore could not be trusted either.

"We'll come back in the morning," Jared said. "I hope by then you'll have had time to realize I wouldn't lie to you." He paused. "Don't worry about your safety. Guillaume will be on guard outside the pension tonight in case Cambre returns. He's a short man, with a potbelly. If anyone of any other description approaches you, run to Guillaume."

When Cassie didn't reply, Jared muttered something beneath his breath before calling, "Come on, Bradford."

"Wait," Lani said. "Where are you going?"

Jared didn't answer immediately. "Guillaume will provide us beds in his pension."

"But you won't use them. You're going to kill Cambre," Lani said. "Not tonight. No more death tonight. We have enough to bear."

Jared remained silent.

"Do you hear me? No more horror. No more violence. Let us have this night to mourn."

"Very well," Jared finally agreed. "But I make no promises after tonight."

"If this beast killed Charles, I'll not ask you to hold your hand. Now, leave us."

"Lani, I'll stay if you need me," Bradford said.

"We don't need you," Lani said coldly. "You do not mourn."

Bradford sighed, and then Cassie heard his heavy footsteps cross the room. The door closed behind the two men.

"Lani . . . ," Cassie whispered.

"Shh . . . I know." Lani's arms tightened around her. "First we will weep for our loss, and then we will remember Charles."

"Remember?" How could she think of anyone else at this moment?

"No, that's not what I meant. We will talk of times we loved him the most." Lani kissed her forehead. "It will help us heal."

"I don't—I can't talk right now."

"Yes, you can. I'll start and you'll follow." Her tears were falling now and her voice trembled. "But not now. I cannot speak now."

It was not until several hours later that the tears

ceased and Lani's words began to flow. "Did you know I met Charles on the beach the day after my father and mother died?"

"No." Cassie had never questioned the circumstances of Lani's arrival in her life. First she had been too filled with resentment, and later it was as if Lani had always been there. "Your parents died together?"

"They were killed in the great storm when a tree branch fell on our dwelling. We were very loving together, and I was filled with sorrow, as we are now." She gazed unseeingly out of the window. "Charles had heard of their deaths, and he came to me. He didn't know me or my parents, but he could see I was mourning. He stayed with me all day and spoke gently and held my hand in comfort. Clara always said he wanted only my body, but that was not true. Later passion came to him, but that day he wanted to give kindness. He came every day for the next month and gradually I healed. I've always been grateful to him for giving me those days." She smiled reminiscently. "So I decided to give him something in return. He was shocked and filled with shame when I seduced him. He kept mumbling about my being a mere child. *He* was the child. He needed care and loving." She ended simply, "He needed me."

"Yes, he did . . . always."

"He was kind to you also," Lani prompted.

Cassie no longer needed encouragement; she suddenly realized she did want to talk about Papa. Yet there was no single incident, as Lani had related. Just bits and pieces of care and kindness, the little presents he had given her, the many times he had hidden her from Clara's wrath. "He gave me Kapu. Do you remember that night, Lani? They were going to kill him, but I would never have let it happen. I was planning on stealing him and running away. Papa tried to comfort me, but I couldn't stop crying. He was very upset when he left the cottage." She paused, thinking of his return. "But when he came back, he had Kapu. He had given the king four of his favorite paintings and paid six of Kamehameha's warriors to rope and lead Kapu up the hills and put him in the stable." It was all coming back to her now. "And there was the morning Mama died. You weren't there then, but I think you would have liked Mama. She was always gentle and sweet, and she loved Papa more than anything. Papa cried when she died, but he came to me later and held me and told me she was with the angels. I believed him because she was like an angel herself. . . ."

The reminiscences flowed in an endless stream for both of them as the hours passed. When there finally seemed no more to say, they undressed and lay down in the big four-poster bed, exhausted.

"Do you feel better?" Lani asked after a long silence.

Cassie felt weary, drained, but perhaps that was the beginning of healing. "Yes."

"You were very cruel to Jared tonight."

"I don't want to talk about Jared."

"Do you truly doubt him?"

She had to doubt him. She wanted too desperately to believe him. Now that the first tearing pain had lessened, she could remind herself that Jared didn't lie, but what if this was the exception? "There's no proof he didn't kill my father."

"There's no proof he did. Perhaps tomorrow we will know more." Lani closed her eyes, and her words were beginning to slur. "It's all very strange. . . . It's not fair to judge without . . ."

Lani was asleep.

Cassie stared into the darkness. She had thought she was exhausted enough to sleep, but she was still wide-awake.

There's no proof.

No proof Jared was not a murderer, no proof Cambre had done the deed, not even proof of her father's death. A man died and was thrown into the river like a piece of garbage, and vanished as if he had never lived. The thought brought the tears stinging again, and she willed them back. The time for weeping was past. Tears would not bring her father to life or avenge his death.

Vengeance.

The thought came out of nowhere, and yet it brought no surprise. Her father had been murdered, his life carelessly tossed away. She felt a sudden flare of rage, and for the first time, she fully understood Jared's quest for retribution. A wave of unbearable pain washed over her, mixing with the anger, as she wondered if that very quest had taken her father's life.

But there was no proof. Jared could have been telling the truth. It could have been Cambre.

But if Jared killed Cambre, she would never know.

She stiffened as she realized there was no doubt Jared would kill Raoul Cambre tomorrow. He had searched and found and would now execute. She would be forced to sit here and wait as he destroyed both Cambre and any hope she had of knowing what had occurred that night by the Seine.

She could not allow him to do it. She had to talk to Cambre first. She had to confront him, accuse him and watch his response. Perhaps then she would be certain of his guilt.

If he was guilty, such a meeting would be very dangerous.

Why was she hesitating? The risk was minimal compared to the prospect of living her life forever unsure if Jared had killed her father.

She glanced at Lani before carefully edging across the bed and from beneath the covers.

Lani did not stir.

Silently, Cassie dressed in her riding trousers, shirt, and jacket, but Lani was in such a deep sleep, she doubted if she would have heard her anyway. She started toward the window, then stopped and retraced her steps to the portmanteau.

The dagger Josette had given them.

Cassie slowly drew the dagger from the sheath. The blade gleamed cold as death in the moonlight.

Cassie stood looking at it in dread and fascination for a moment before returning it to its sheath and thrusting it into the waistband of her trousers. She moved toward the casement window overlooking the alley. Their lack of money had dictated they take this undesirable pension on the second floor overlooking the alley, where the garbage was thrown and the slop jars emptied. The location might now serve her well.

Guillaume would be watching the street entrance of the pension. No one would likely be astir in that stinking hole below.

She stepped onto the windowsill, then lowered herself to the sloping slate-tile roof overhanging the alley. Her boots scraped on the slate, and she froze, her gaze flying to the window above her.

Had the sound woke Lani?

She breathed a sigh of relief when no face appeared at the window.

Slowly, carefully, she turned on her stomach and

crawled backward down the roof, clinging with fingers and toes to the tiles. It took her nearly a quarter of an hour to reach the edge.

She paused to get her breath before looking down at the alley.

It was fully ten feet to the ground.

And the alley was not deserted as she had thought.

The ground seemed to be heaving with movement. Bright-red eyes gleaming in the darkness.

Rats.

She shuddered as she watched the dozens of rodents scurrying below her. Would they attack her as they ravaged the garbage on the ground?

Well, she could not stay here all night. She braced herself, then, clinging to the roof's edge, slowly lowered her body until she hung full length.

Fear iced through her as she heard increased commotion below.

She dropped to the ground.

Her knees buckled, and she fell.

Mud. Filth. A rat ran over her hand as she frantically tried to lever herself to her feet. They were all around her!

She ran blindly toward the end of the alley.

Scurrying tiny feet ran over her boots, glittering eyes glared at her. The dark corridor seemed miles long, the journey as far as their trip across the Channel. Her heart pounded painfully as she slid, half fell, and then righted herself.

Suddenly there were cobblestones instead of filth and mud beneath her feet. Thank God. She had reached the side street.

She stopped beneath a lamppost, her chest rising and falling with her labored breathing. Dear heaven, that alley had stunk, and now she was nearly as odorous. She had a sudden memory of her island, where everything was washed clean by wind and sea, where people did not live on top of each other. How could her father have ever stood living with this filth?

But her father was not living at all now.

She smothered the dart of pain the remembrance brought. She was wasting precious time; in a few hours it would be dawn. Cambre's residence was across the city, and she must get there before Jared stirred.

Fifteen

Dawn had not yet broken when Cassie reached
Cambre's imposing mansion. The house was
dark, and evidently no servant was stirring. Both circumstances were to her advantage . . . if she could
gain entrance.

She tried the front door. Locked.

Well, what had she expected? None of this would
be easy. When she did get inside, she would have to
find Cambre's bedchamber without being discovered
herself.

If she broke a window, she would be heard. The
garden? It was enclosed by a high stone fence, perhaps that barrier had caused someone to be careless
and leave a back door or window unlocked.

It seemed to be her night for climbing, she thought
grimly. It was just as well she and Lihua had spent so
many hours scaling coconut trees as children. But
straight, high walls were not as easily mastered as
those bent, ridged trees. It took her three tries to
reach the top of the wall.

She paused, her gaze traveling over the shadowy

bushes and graceful rectangular pool. No sound. No sign of anyone. The path leading to the back of the house was to her left, winding through a sparse thicket of trees.

As usual, it was easier descending than climbing. She jumped the last few feet and started toward the thicket.

A blur to her left.

She stopped, tensing. Perhaps it had not been a movement at all. She had caught only a glimpse of . . . of something from the corner of her eye.

"I wouldn't move if I were you. There's a pistol in your back." Something hard and round pressed into her spine.

Cambre. She had not heard that smooth, deep voice since childhood, but she would never forget it.

"I've been waiting for you, Monsieur Guillaume. I was hoping for His Grace, but he evidently prefers to send his minions." Cambre sniffed. "I wish he'd chosen an emissary less odorous."

Guillaume? Her masculine attire had evidently caused her to be mistaken, but how had he known about Guillaume?

"Light the lantern," Cambre said to someone over his shoulder. "Let's have a look at him. Though I understand he's not particularly pleasant to view."

Dear God, why had she been so careless? She should have waited after she'd scaled the wall, watched for some sign of Cambre's presence.

Because she had not expected a trap. She had thought she was the aggressor.

Light flared behind her, sending a flickering glow on the bushes in front of her.

"Well, what have we here?" Cambre murmured. He quickly searched her and withdrew the dagger.

"What an exquisite weapon, much more subtle than this crude pistol of mine." His hand touched the long queue of hair that reached to the middle of her back. "I don't remember being told Guillaume had such silky tresses. Turn around."

She didn't move.

The pistol pressed harder. "You'd be advised to obey me. I had a reason to keep Guillaume alive, but you're nothing to me."

She turned to face him.

"A woman? I thought as much. Now who could you be?" He pretended to think. "There have been only two women hindering my path of late. Mademoiselle Deville?"

She ignored his mockery and said bluntly, "I want to talk to you."

"And I want to talk to you." He sniffed again. "From a distance. I remember you as a comely little girl, and I must see if the fulfillment is as satisfying as the promise." He called to the man in the shadows, "Bring the lantern closer."

The light temporarily blinded her, but that was not what caused her to go rigid. The garden seemed to whirl around her as she stared in horror at the man carrying the lantern.

"Dear God, no," she whispered.

"You're Guillaume?" Lani demanded as she halted in front of the small man leaning against the window of the café. "Take me to the Duke of Morland."

He straightened. "I have no such instructions."

"You have instructions. I'm giving them to you."

"I don't obey women. I'm to watch the pension and keep the two of you safe."

"Then you've already failed your duty. Cassie is gone."

"Impossible. I have eyes like a hawk. No one came into that building."

"But someone came out. Take me to His Grace."

He shook his head. "You're trying to fool me."

Lani drew an exasperated breath. She wanted to shake him. "Then go see for yourself. She's gone!"

He stared at her, frowning, then slowly started across the street.

"Hurry!"

His pace quickened a trifle, and he disappeared into the pension.

Lani wished she had a spear to prick the stubborn idiot to greater speed. She had been filled with panic and foreboding ever since she woke to find Cassie gone, and she was in no mood to deal with arguments.

"Papa?" Cassie whispered.

"Do you think me a ghost?" Charles Deville smiled at Cassie as he thrust the lantern at Raoul, then stepped forward and embraced her. "Do I feel like a spirit?"

Cassie clung to him. He felt blessedly warm and strong and *alive*. "You . . . he killed you."

Cambre said, "My dear child, would I murder my old friend? We merely combined our forces to defeat a common enemy."

Cassie's head was spinning with bewilderment. "I don't understand."

Her father pushed her away. "None of this was meant for you. I had no idea you were in Paris until David came here and told us you were inquiring about me." He frowned. "You should have stayed home as I told you."

"You were here when David came?"

He smiled. "Of course. I've occupied a room here since the night of my . . . death. It's been a bit confining not being able to leave my chamber, but Raoul supplied me with canvas and paints, and I've started a lovely picture of this garden."

"But why? How?"

"The Duke of Morland was coming too close," Cambre said. "His man, Guillaume, questioned David two years ago, and Jacques-Louis sent him on a wild-goose chase to Tahiti." He clapped Deville on the shoulder. "Without my permission, of course. I was very angry with him that he'd endangered you, my friend. But I should have known you'd be too clever for him."

She'd wager any diversion from Cambre was instigated by Cambre himself, but to her amazement her father was smiling.

"With Cassie's help," he said.

"But when Guillaume came to see David again a few weeks ago, I knew he must suspect our connection," Raoul said. "And when David came to my house directly after his visit, Guillaume followed him. Since I had covered my identity well, the visit proved nothing, but we found Guillaume an obnoxiously thorough little man. On the chance that I might be a link of some kind, he set a man to watch me." His lips tightened. "I'm not a man who likes being observed. It gets in my way."

"Raoul, it's chilly out here in the garden," her father said as he urged Cassie toward the house. "And my resurrection has clearly been a shock to my daughter. Let's get her indoors."

"Certainly. How could I be so inconsiderate?" Raoul strolled beside them down the path. "Well, when Charles appeared seeking me, I looked upon it as a stroke of good fortune. Because of the nature of my occupation and the delicacy of ridding myself of this threat from Danemount, I could not trust the task to underlings. Such men come back with palms extended. Yet the Duke is a dangerous man, and I might need help. What was the solution?"

"I have no idea," Cassie answered.

"Then I shall tell you. Set a trap. Confirm the Duke's suspicion and provide myself with an ally as dedicated to destroying Danemount as I was myself. Therefore, I allowed the Duke's spy to observe your father's 'murder.' Charles swam under water until he thought it safe, then returned to the bank and made his way to my house as planned." He smiled at her father. "The waters of the Seine are colder than your warm seas, eh?"

Her father nodded. "But the clothes you provided when I reached here are much finer than any I've worn these many years."

"It was my pleasure." He turned to Cassie. "So, you see, when the Duke comes after me, he'll have another unexpected foe with which to contend. The unexpected is always the most deadly. Don't you think it was a clever plan?"

She shivered. "Very clever."

"Enough," her father said. "This talk of death and murder is upsetting her."

"Forgive me, I forget how sensitive ladies are prone to be. But I admit to being curious regarding her knowledge of your 'death.' In fact, her very presence here in Paris amazes me. You told me you had left her safely at home in Hawaii, and yet suddenly she appears asking questions of David." He smiled at Cassie. "Both your father and I were completely bewildered. I called at your flat to assure you all was well with your father, but I must have missed you."

Assurances? She wondered what else might have occurred in that pension. Cambre was everything she remembered him to be. She felt as if a cobra were gliding beside her. "I don't see why it should surprise you. I followed my father from Hawaii because I was concerned."

"But your knowledge of our little staged charade on the Seine bothers me. I'm sure there's some reasonable explanation, but only the Duke's man saw me roll Charles into the river. Now, unless you have a connection with His Grace, I can't see how you'd assume your father was dead."

"Stop questioning her, Raoul." Her father put a protective arm around her shoulders. "As you say, I'm sure she has a reasonable explanation, but she doesn't have to give it now. She needs rest and a bath."

Raoul gazed at her for a moment and then shrugged. "You're right, of course, my friend. I'll wake the servants and have them send hot water and a tub. I believe I have some female garments about somewhere to replace those extremely odorous trousers." He opened the French door and bowed to Cassie. "But I insist you join me for breakfast in an hour's time. If I have to wait any longer, I'm certain I'll perish of curiosity."

A state much to be desired, Cassie thought as she watched him light a candle from the sideboard by the door, then stroll away from them.

Her father didn't bother lighting a candle but took her arm and led her through the dark house. He was very comfortable in Cambre's fine mansion, she thought in despair, as comfortable as he was with Cambre himself.

"I told you I'd take care of this myself," he said. "You were supposed to stay home. I wish for once you'd obeyed me."

"I couldn't do that. I had to help." She burst out, "I don't understand any of this, Papa. Why were you waiting in the garden? Why did you think anyone would come?"

"Raoul set a spy on the spy. He knew the Duke would eventually come to Paris himself. When Guillaume met with the Duke and his uncle at a tavern, Cambre's man hurried back here to report to him." He had stopped and opened a door. "After Danemount's years of searching, Raoul thought he would probably wish to strike at once."

He had been right. If Lani had not prevailed on Jared to wait, he would have walked into the trap. "You would have killed him?"

"We'll talk of this later." He lit the candle on the table by the door before crossing the room and throwing back the pale-blue silk curtains. "Isn't Raoul's house beautiful? It was kind of him to give me such a fine room."

She glanced around the room. The entire chamber was decorated in ice-blue and ivory and shades of beige, the furniture finely crafted and elegant—but there was little color or warmth. "I don't like it. I don't like *him*."

He didn't seem to hear her; his gaze was fixed on the sky. "It's beginning to get light. Dawn is different here in Paris, paler, more delicate. All the colors are less vibrant here. Raoul's garden is lovely, but I miss our orchids and ginger blossoms."

"Then let's go back," she said eagerly. "Let's leave this place right now."

"I can't leave." His eyes never left the garden. "I have something to do here."

"You can't kill Jared. I won't let you." She crossed the room to stand beside him. "I know you're afraid of him, but I won't have him murdered."

"*Mon dieu*, I haven't heard such emotion in your voice since the night the king said he was going to have Kapu killed."

"Look at me." Her hand grasped his arm. "You can't do this. Can't you see Cambre is only using you? You're not like him. You're no murderer."

"But I am." His tone was sad. "I had a long time to think when I was on that American ship. All these years I tried to tell myself that I wasn't guilty because those deaths were out of my control, but it was a lie. I did kill them."

She stared at him in horror. "You couldn't have betrayed them. Jared said that his father called on you because you helped another family of aristocrats to escape."

"That was before I caught the fever. You don't know what it was like. It was . . . intoxicating. Every man had a revolutionary cockade in his hat and a story to tell. We sat in taverns and toasted the free republic and Marat and Danton. We sketched our heroes and sang the Marseilles. Then one night Raoul came along and told me how I could help the republic as a true patriot should. The Committee of Public Safety had discovered I'd helped a family of aristos to escape, but I was to be forgiven. I had only to prove my loyalty by notifying them in case I was asked to help again." He smiled sadly. "I had a wife and child; it seemed the right thing to do. Raoul was very persuasive. He promised me that any aristocrats I told him about would have a fair trial, and if they were found innocent of acting against the republic, they would only be stripped of their estates."

She stared at him incredulously. "And you believed him?"

He said simply, "I was young and I had the fever."

"But it wasn't only the Compte and his wife who were sent to the guillotine. Jared's father was murdered by Cambre's men."

"Raoul told me he had sent Jared, his father, and the Compte's baby daughter to their ship under escort. Unfortunately, they were attacked by bandits on the road and Jared's father was killed." At last he turned to look at her. "I know, I should have questioned the tale, but it was more comfortable not to. We both know I've always had a fondness for the easy way."

She felt sick. She had desperately wanted to believe Jared had been mistaken. Yet there was no surprise; somewhere deep within her she must have known this was a possibility.

"I hoped I'd never have to see you look at me like that," he said wistfully. "Don't hate me, Cassie."

Not bad, only weak and willing to blind himself to the terrible harm he was doing. "I don't hate you." She went into his arms and laid her head on his chest. No matter what he had done those many years ago, he was her father. The loving memories Lani and she had resurrected only hours before had made that clear to her. "I couldn't ever hate you."

His arms tightened around her for an instant before he released her and pushed her away. He smiled. "I do appreciate the gesture of affection, but I can't bear another minute of that terrible odor. I must see why the servants haven't arrived with that tub." He started across the room. "And when I return, we'll have to think of a good reason for your knowing about my supposed demise. We mustn't have Raoul believing you're a traitor." When he reached the door, he stopped and looked back over his shoulder. "Did you come to Paris with Danemount?"

"No, I came with Lani."

"Then would you care to tell me how you knew?"

She bit her lower lip. What could she say? Could she tell him of those nights on the *Josephine*? Could she tell him lust had become love for his enemy? "I can't let you kill him."

He studied her expression. "Ah, so that's the way of it. Fate does paint strange patterns for us poor mortals. Cambre may be more fortunate than he believes. If Danemount has an equal affection for you, he may have bait for the trap."

Panic soared through her. "He won't follow me. He doesn't know I'm here. Besides, he cares nothing for me."

"Impossible." He smiled gently. "You're a rare and lovely woman, Cassie. A man would be a fool not to love you, and Danemount isn't a fool."

"Papa, don't try to use me," she whispered. "I couldn't stand it."

"But you said you could never hate me, Cassie." He opened the door. "Ah, here's your tub and water." He stepped aside to allow the column of servants to enter. "Do hurry, dear. Raoul's an impatient man."

A thunderous knock snatched Jared from sleep.

"Let me in, Your Grace."

Guillaume, Jared identified drowsily. What the devil was he—

Guillaume had been guarding Cassie's pension! He

leaped from the bed and jerked the door open. "What is it? What hap—"

"We have a problem." Lani pushed past Guillaume and entered the room. "Where is Bradford?"

"In the next room." His gaze searched beyond her. "You're alone. Where is she?"

Guillaume said quickly, "I'm sorry to bring her here, Your Grace. I was standing across the street watching the pension, and she marched up to me and demanded to see you."

He motioned impatiently, his gaze fastened on Lani. "Is Cassie back at the pension?"

"No."

"Where is she?"

"I swear she didn't go past me." Guillaume scowled. "Who would think a lady would go jumping from windows and trekking in garbage? It's not my fault. You told me to protect her from Cambre, and that's what I did."

Jared muttered a curse and swung back to Lani. "What the devil is he mumbling about?"

"Perhaps the lady could wait outside while you dress, Your Grace," Guillaume mumbled uncomfortably.

"I've seen naked men before," Lani said curtly. "But put your clothes on, we may have little time. I have a carriage waiting outside. I don't know how long she's been gone."

"Go wake Bradford, Guillaume. Tell him to dress." Jared snatched up his shirt and thrust his arms into it. "Where did she go?"

"Where do you think she went?" Lani sat down at a small table. "I blame myself. I should have known this would happen when she had time to think."

"Cambre," Jared said. Christ, she had gone to Cambre. "He'll kill her."

"She has a dagger."

He pulled on his boots with shaking hands. "Why didn't she wait? Why didn't she let me do it? She knew I planned on killing him."

"You think she wished to murder Cambre before you had the opportunity." She shook her head. "Cassie is capable of vengeance, but not assassination." Her hands clenched on the arms of the chair. "Hurry."

"I'm moving as fast as I can." He jerked on his coat. "Then why did she go to him?"

"Guilt. She hopes to absolve herself."

"You're talking nonsense." He opened his portmanteau and pulled out his pistol. "She did nothing."

"She thinks she did." Her gaze met his across the room. "She believes she loves the man who may have killed her father."

He froze. "What?"

"And she's hoping Cambre will convince her you didn't kill Charles." She smiled grimly. "But he may murder her before she has the opportunity to question him."

"What is it, Jared?" Bradford said as he strode into the room followed by Guillaume. He was fully dressed but his hair was still tousled. "Lani?"

"Cambre. I'll tell you on the way." He started for the door. "Lani, stay here with Guillaume."

"I will not." She rose to her feet. "She's my friend and sister. I may be of help."

"And you may be a hindrance if we have to worry about your safety as well." He turned to Guillaume. "She stays here. I won't forgive you if she slips through your hands too."

She whirled on Bradford. "I wish to go."

He shook his head.

Her eyes blazed at him. "I'll not forgive you for this."

"Then so be it," he said sadly. "I won't risk losing you."

"You've never had me. If you do this, you never will. Let me go with you. You *need* me."

An expression of agony crossed his features. "Do you think I don't know what a risk I'm running? If I give in to you now, there's a chance I could slide into Deville's place in your life. I could let you take care of me and make my decisions. I could lean on your strength and bask in your affection." He drew a deep breath. "But I'm not Deville, Lani. I need to know that you're alive and well somewhere in this world even if it's not by my side."

He followed Jared from the room. Neither man spoke until they reached the hired carriage waiting outside.

"Do we have a plan?" Bradford asked. "Or is that too much to ask?"

"We're going to get her back."

"Masterly plan. How?"

God, he didn't know. He only knew she mustn't die.

"We're in enemy territory. We can't draw attention to ourselves," Bradford said. "On the other hand, it's clear Cambre doesn't want to attract any surveillance, either. Then, too, we're assuming Cassie needs rescuing, which may not be true. She's an extraordinary woman."

"How calmly you're taking all this."

"One of has to think." He opened the door of the carriage. "I'm not sure you're capable."

Jared tried to subdue his own panic and begin to reason. "We'll look the situation over, and then we'll—"

"Monsieur le Duc?"

Jared stiffened with shock as he whirled to face the man coming out of the shadows.

"How charming you look." Raoul smiled at her from the head of the table as her father seated her. "The lady who wore that gown last wasn't nearly as lovely."

"I'm not at all charming." Cassie indifferently glanced down at the sea-green gown one of the servants had brought her with the tub. "Why didn't your guest take the gown with her?"

"She displeased me. When she left, I allowed her nothing but the clothes on her back." He gestured to the silver plate overflowing with a selection of fruit. "I hope you don't mind serving yourself. I instructed the servants to go to their quarters and stay there."

"Why?" her father asked, startled.

Cambre ignored the question and continued addressing Cassie. "I was certain the gown would be useful someday. One never knows when one is going to be visited by another lady who will prove more accommodating." He smiled. "Tell me, did His Grace find you accommodating?"

"Raoul!" Her father frowned. "This is my daughter."

"A daughter can be a whore."

The bald crudity of the words caused Cassie to stiffen. Cambre was still smiling, but his eyes were cold and watchful. The cat-and-mouse game was ended. He was on the attack, and Cassie found it a relief.

"I'm not a whore." She met his gaze. "And I don't think His Grace would say I was accommodating."

"But he did tell you—"

"That my father was dead," she finished. "Yes."

"And he sent you to exact vengeance?"

"I don't go where he sends me. I came because I wished to do so."

"Perhaps you believed you were doing as you wished, but a clever man can pull the strings with such subtlety that the puppet isn't even aware of the tug."

"As you do?"

He nodded. "I'm a true master of the art." He popped a slice of orange into his mouth. "Well, were you going to stab me with that pretty dagger?"

"Possibly."

He chuckled and turned to her father. "She has courage." His smile faded. "But I think you have one more reason to dispose of our old enemy. It's clear he's dishonored this sweet *jeune fille.*"

"It's not clear to me," her father said.

"Well, why don't we ask him?" He rose to his feet. "He's waiting in the library."

Cassie's heart leaped to her throat.

Cambre's gaze was on her face. "What a revealing response," he said softly. "I think you lie. I believe His Grace must have found you overwhelmingly accommodating."

She tried desperately to wipe every hint of expression from her face. "It's a trick. He couldn't be here."

"Of course he could. I sent for him when I left you this morning."

"You didn't tell me," her father said as he slowly rose to his feet. "You should not keep secrets from me, Raoul."

"Unfortunately, you have a softness for this lovely thing, and I'm weary of waiting in moonlit gardens for the man to pounce. I thought it might be better to draw in the net and bring the matter to a close." He turned to Cassie. "I told him to come at once and unarmed, or I'd slit your throat. I wasn't sure you'd be enough lure to bring him here, but I was pleasantly surprised."

Her throat was dry. "Unarmed? He wouldn't do that. He hates you. I mean nothing to him in comparison."

"Then he's extraordinarily gallant." He moved toward the door. "I want this over. Bring her, Charles."

"I'll bring myself." She pushed back her chair and strode after him. She felt as if she were in a nightmare. Jared was a captive and it was her fault. He was going to die.

No, she couldn't let that happen.

Cambre opened the library door and stepped aside. "After you, mademoiselle. We don't want His Grace to be concerned for your welfare any longer than necessary. It would be unkind."

Jared was sitting in a chair facing the door. He went still when he saw her in the doorway. "Are you all right? He didn't hurt you?"

"You shouldn't be here," she whispered. "Why did you come?"

"I had no choice." Jared smiled. "He had something I couldn't do without."

"You're a fool. He'll kill you."

"Those aren't the tender words a man needs to comfort him in his last hours," Cambre said as he pushed her into the room. "And after sacrificing himself for your sake, too. Most ungrateful."

"I'm here," Jared said coldly. "Now, let her go." He turned to Cassie. "Bradford is waiting for you in the carriage outside. He'll take you to Lani."

"I can't leave you here."

"She's right, she can't leave you." Cambre drew a pistol from beneath his coat.

"What are you saying, Raoul?" Her father entered the library. "Cassie has nothing to do with this."

Jared's eyes widened as he recognized her father. "Deville?"

Her father ignored him. "The trap was for Danemount. No one else was to be hurt."

"Sometimes the innocent are swept away with the guilty," Raoul said as he locked the door. "But she's far from innocent. She was ready to betray you. She played the whore with your enemy."

"She never betrayed you," Jared said. "For God's sake, don't you know what she is? She traveled halfway across the world to try to save you."

"I don't need you to tell me about my daughter."

"Then tell Cambre to go to hell and send her away from here."

Her father whirled on Cambre. "We'll dispose of Danemount first and then we'll discuss Cassie. Give me the gun. I'll do it."

Raoul's gaze narrowed on his face. "How brave you're becoming. I assumed I'd have to do it myself."

"I've been running too long. I want it over, Raoul. Even if you give me a new start, he'd follow me."

"No!" Cassie moved between Jared and Cambre. "You'll have to shoot me first."

"Dammit, get out of the way, Cassie," Jared said.

"You see, Charles." Cambre smiled. "I can't give you the pistol. You don't have the courage to shoot your daughter to get to Danemount." He raised the gun and pointed it at Cassie's chest. "While I have no such compunction."

She was going to die. A bullet was going to tear through her flesh and end her life.

"Raoul, you don't want to do this." Her father started toward Cambre. "Let me have the pistol."

"Stay back." Cambre didn't shift the weapon, but his voice sharpened. "It's exactly what I want to do. As you can see, I took the precaution of arming myself with a double-barreled pistol. So much more efficient than the usual weapon when one is never sure who one's enemies may be. I'll give you one minute to get that interfering bitch from my line of fire before I pull the trigger."

Jared suddenly moved to stand beside her. He said hoarsely, "Get out of here, Cassie."

"Don't be stupid. I can't do that." She placed herself in front of him again and, facing him, put her arms around him. He muttered a curse and tried to break her hold, but she held tight with all her strength.

"How touching," Cambre said. "Quite like your Shakespeare's Romeo and Juliet, isn't it, Your Grace? I think it fitting your tableau has the same ending."

She braced herself for the bullet.

"You told me I could get Cassie away," her father said. "Keep your promise."

"Oh, very well. But it's a pity to spoil the—son of a bitch!"

Cassie turned to see her father launch himself at Cambre.

A second later they were on the floor, struggling for the pistol.

Jared thrust her aside and darted toward the two men.

A shot.

Blood spattered the Aubusson carpet.

Whose blood? Mother of God, whose blood?

"Fool!" Cambre pushed her father off him. Deville rolled limply, his hands still grasping the pistol that had killed him. Cambre tried to reach for the pistol, but Jared dived toward him, his hands locking around Cambre's throat.

"Let me—go." Cambre clawed at Jared's hands. "We can—deal. I have power. I can—"

Jared was strangling him, Cassie realized. She had never seen murder done. She supposed she should feel horror . . . something. She felt nothing but fierce satisfaction and regret that it had not been done sooner. Before that shot had taken her father's life. She moved slowly across the room toward her father's body.

"Stop . . ." Cambre gasped. Then he said nothing at all as Jared's hands tightened.

She fell to her knees beside her father. His skin was pasty and pale, his white shirt bathed in blood. "Oh, Papa, no . . ."

His eyes opened.

She inhaled sharply in disbelief. He was still alive!

"Didn't want . . . to die . . ."

"You won't die." She gathered him close. "I won't let you."

"Is Raoul—dead. Did I kill him?"

"Shh . . . yes."

"Had to—do it. Knew he—would never let—me live— Couldn't—kill—Danemount—retribution." He touched her cheek. "Lani."

"She's not here. You can see her later."

"Take care of—Lani. I—never did. Wrong. So many wrongs . . ."

"Shh, Lani loves you. I love you."

"Blessed . . . blessed . . ." His eyes closed and a long shudder went through him.

Gone.

Tears flowed down her face as she silently rocked him back and forth.

"Cassie . . ." Jared's hand was on her shoulder. "We have to leave. Someone may have heard the shot."

She gathered her father closer. "I won't leave without him. He doesn't belong here."

"I wasn't suggesting you do," he said gently. "Stay here and I'll go to the carriage and send Bradford to fetch a wagon."

"It's like losing him a second time," she whispered.

Jared's hand tightened on her shoulder and then fell away. "I'll be right back."

She watched him leave the library, then her gaze fell on the crumpled body of Raoul Cambre. His eyes were wide open and bulging from their sockets. He had not died easily.

Good.

She turned back to her father. He had not died easily either, but his expression was serene. Retribution, he had said. Had he gained absolution by that last act of sacrifice? She hoped it was true. Let him be at peace, she prayed.

Forgive him.

Let him forgive himself.

Sixteen

Jared arranged for Charles Deville to be buried the next morning in a cemetery near a small village just outside Paris. Through some machinations and Guillaume's help, he even managed to have the village priest preside at the graveside.

Cassie did not cry at the funeral. She felt frozen, barely able to think or feel.

"We can stay here in the village tonight," Jared said as he helped her into the carriage. "We don't have to go on."

She supposed he was being kind. He didn't realize that the man in the grave was no longer her father. Her father was somewhere else now. She wearily settled herself on the seat beside Lani. "I want to leave this place."

He studied her face, then nodded. "Very well. We'll leave for the coast at once." He turned away and mounted his horse.

Lani's hand covered Cassie's as the carriage lurched forward. "You're right, it's wise to go on. After you say good-bye, you must not look back in sorrow."

Cassie smiled sadly. "They won't understand the way we believe. The English think we must wear black weeds and flaunt our sorrow for months."

"Perhaps Jared is more understanding than you think."

"I don't want to know if he is."

"You wish to keep him at a distance." Lani nodded understandingly. "You think he cannot forget the past and all the bitterness. It was your father who bore the guilt, not you."

But would he ever be able to look at her without seeing her father and that scene at Danjuet? Now that she had accepted her father's guilt, it seemed incredible Jared had even wanted to touch her. "If he could forget, there would still be no life for us. I couldn't . . . It would be . . ." She was silent, then whispered, "I'm not as generous as you, Lani. I couldn't occupy his bed and not his life. I'd want *everything*. I wouldn't know how to be a duke's mistress."

"No, you wouldn't." Lani squeezed her hand. "I'll tell Jared you wish to go home."

She knew he would not accept it. She would have to stay out of his way, out of his sight. It should not be too difficult. As she had said, the English custom demanded a long period of mourning. Jared might have the reputation of ignoring tradition, but such beliefs were ingrained from childhood. "I need to leave right away."

Lani nodded. "It's best for both of us. We have no place with these people now."

Josette met them when they rode into the courtyard at Morland.

"Is everything all right? Are you angry with me? I had to tell him, Cassie. He said you were in danger, and I didn't think it would matter since—"

"I'm not angry." Cassie held up her hand to stop the flood of words that was about to pour from Josette's lips. "And I understand. But I'm very tired and would like to rest now." She started up the steps. "Is Kapu well?"

"Yes." Josette stared after her, puzzled. "Don't you want to go see him?"

"Later." She disappeared into the castle.

"Leave her alone for a time, Josette," Lani said. "She's still mourning. We buried her father yesterday." She turned to Jared. "Cassie and I spoke after the funeral. It's time we went home. Will you see to arranging passage?"

"Don't be foolish," he said roughly. "I'll take you myself."

"That's not necessary."

"It is to me."

"Then let it be done at once. She needs familiar things around her."

"It will take at least a week to put my affairs in order and ready the *Josephine* for a long voyage."

"Then start right away." She turned and followed Cassie into the house.

Jared stared after her, his hands clenching on the reins. He couldn't leave it like this. He wanted to comfort Cassie. He wanted to hold her and tell her that everything was going to be good again. He had to *do* something.

"Think again, lad," Bradford said as he dismounted. "Patience. She's not ready."

"I know that." He slid from his horse and threw

the reins to Joe. "I'm not completely mad." He started across the courtyard toward the stable.

Josette ran after him. "Where are you going?"

"For a ride."

"May I go with you?"

Jared didn't want company. He felt as tethered and on edge as Kapu when he had first been lifted aboard the *Josephine*.

"Please," Josette whispered.

He nodded curtly. None of this was Josette's fault, and he knew the pain of being closed out. Cassie had scarcely looked at him since they had left Cambre's library. "Come along."

"Do you suppose Cassie would mind if I rode Kapu? I've been exercising him since she left."

He shook his head. "She won't mind." Christ, he was even feeling envy of Josette. Cassie had never allowed him to ride the stallion, never allowed him the camaraderie she gave the girl. There had always been wariness and distrust between them. Even that last terrible confrontation with Cambre had been initiated by distrust.

"You said you were taking Cassie home," Josette said. "May I go with you?"

He shook his head. "It's too long a journey."

"I thought you'd say that." She bit her lip. "I don't want them to go. I don't want any of you to go."

"We have to go. You heard Lani." She looked so distressed that he put his arm around her. "You'll be busy here. I need you to help Mrs. Blakely and my agent oversee Morland."

"They do very well by themselves. I *really* want to go, Jared."

He shook his head.

She sighed. "I can't convince you, can I?"

He brushed the top of her head with his lips. "Not this time."

She shrugged. "Then I won't try." She opened the stable door and suddenly brightened. "At least I won't have to go back to school. I'm sure I can keep myself amused."

Jared grimaced. "I'm sure you can, too. God help us all."

The scents of the dark stable were blessedly familiar to Cassie. As usual they soothed her, eased the aching loss she had felt since she had arrived back at Morland over a week ago. Kapu nickered softly as she drew close.

"Hello, boy," Cassie whispered as she stroked Kapu's nose. "It's so good to see you. I didn't want to leave you alone this long. Have you missed me?"

"I've missed you," Jared said.

She stiffened, then turned to watch him walk out of the shadows. "What are you doing here?"

"Waiting for you." He stopped before her. "It's been eight days, but I knew you'd come here eventually. I've been waiting here every night. You might choose to avoid me, but never Kapu. You must really have been desperate to hide from me to keep away from him for an entire week."

She evaded the accusation. "Since we're going to leave tomorrow, I wanted him to know I'd be with him. You know how he hates ships."

"He'll be all right. He'll have Morgana in the cargo hold with him this time. Cassie, I—"

She quickly turned back to the stallion. "It seems such a long time since I saw him. So much has happened. . . ."

"Yes." He paused and then said deliberately, "I've killed a man and your father is dead." He took a step closer and added fiercely, "But you know I didn't kill your father, so why won't you talk to me?"

"There's nothing to say."

"There's everything to say. You would have died to save me, and now you don't think I'm worth a word?"

"I owed you a debt. You didn't have to come when Cambre sent for you."

"Of course I had to come. I could no more have stopped myself than I could have stopped breathing." He turned her to face him. "Stop looking at that stallion. I'm trying to tell you something."

"I don't want to hear it."

"You're going to hear it anyway. I'm not going to let you walk away from me this time. We've gone too far." His eyes held hers. "I know this isn't the time, but I can't help it. I came to you when Cambre sent for me because we were meant to be together and I didn't want to live without you. You stepped in front of me when Cambre was pointing that pistol for the same reason. We belong to each other, and I'm not going to let you go because of everything that's gone before. Though he may have saved my life, I'll never be able to share fond memories of your father. But you'll never hear me speak against him. It's over, we start again." He drew a deep breath. "That's all I wanted to say. I'm not going to force you. I know I have to give you time to heal. I just wanted you to—" He stopped and then the frustration exploded. "Just don't avoid me. I can't stand it, goddammit." He released her and started toward the door.

"It's not possible," she burst out. "I thought I was

like Lihua and Lani, but I'm more selfish. I can't live—"

"At Morland?" he interrupted. "Then we'll live half the year on your island."

"That's not what I mean." This was incredibly painful. She said haltingly. "I . . . cannot be your mistress."

He gazed at her incredulously. "My God, haven't you heard a word I said? I don't want a mistress, I want a wife!" He strode out of the stable and slammed the door.

She stared after him in astonishment, her head awhirl with the words he had spoken.

We were meant to be together.

I'll never let you walk away again.

Wife.

He had said everything but the word she wanted most to hear, the word that had been forbidden to them since they had first met.

She could not condemn him when she had not said it either.

She turned back to Kapu and laid her head against his. A tingling, glowing warmth was moving through her, dissolving the ice and sadness. A new start . . . Dear heaven, how she wanted to start anew with Jared. Right now, this minute.

No, not yet. In English eyes she was in mourning and therefore inviolate. She had been grateful for that belief when she had been trying to avoid Jared, but now she would have to think of a way to banish those scruples.

The *Josephine.*

She smiled as she gently stroked the stallion.

Oh yes, definitely, the *Josephine.*

. . . .

The next day Josette looked so woebegone standing alone in the courtyard as they rode through the gates that it almost broke Cassie's heart.

Blinking to keep back tears, Cassie waved to the girl. "I'm going to miss her."

Lani nodded. "But it may not be forever. Jared may let her come to us for a visit."

Cassie's gaze went to Jared riding ahead with Bradford, and joy surged through her. Lani was right, it would not be forever.

"What is it?" She turned to see Lani studying her speculatively. "You suddenly seem very cheerful."

"I'm happy to be going home."

"No, that's not all. Tell me."

Cassie smiled. "There's nothing to tell."

But there would be soon. The thought sent another ripple of pleasure through her, and she suddenly felt light as air. But first, there was something she had to do. She turned to Lani. "Did I tell you Papa said I was to take care of you?"

"No." Lani clearly found the thought startling. "You only said he had spoken of me with love. I need no one to care for me."

"You have no need but you deserve it." She smiled. "However, the task may prove too difficult for me. I think we'll have to arrange to choose someone in my stead." Her gaze went to Bradford. "I believe that's a likely lad."

"He's hardly a lad."

"He is around you."

"He drinks too much."

"Not any longer. I haven't seen him take more than a glass of wine."

"He's stubborn and contrary."

"Then you'll find him a challenge."

Lani frowned. "He made me stay in that pension when I wanted to go to you. He says he needs me and then he does not take my help. I told him I wouldn't forgive him."

"A terrible crime," Cassie said solemnly. "No wonder you haven't spoken to him since Papa's death."

Lani was silent a long time. "I am Polynesian. You saw how people behaved at that woman's ball. I will not hurt him."

Cassie knew she had reached the source; all the other excuses were barriers to protect Bradford. "You've always told me to be true to myself and that others didn't matter. Was it a lie?"

"No, it was not a lie," Lani said. "But I cannot hurt him."

"You'll hurt him if you force him to leave you."

Lani's lips quivered slightly before she firmed them. "I don't wish to speak of this."

"Then don't speak, do something. You're not a woman who can close herself away from life. Reach out to him."

"I will think about it."

Cassie said no more. She had planted a seed, but Lani would not tolerate any overt interference.

Well, perhaps a *little* interference . . .

"Cassie said you wanted to see me."

Lani turned away from watching Jared and Cassie lead the horses up the gangplank and saw Bradford beside her. His expression was eager and boyish, and she felt a melting deep within her. She wanted to smack Cassie.

"She was mistaken."

His face fell with disappointment, and she felt an impulse to gather him close and soothe the pain away.

He forced a smile. "I should have known it was too soon. You're still mourning."

"No," she said. "Charles will always be with me, but the time for mourning is past."

"But you won't have me."

She shook her head.

"Then I'll wait. I'll wait forever."

He would do it. She gazed at him helplessly. "How can I convince you this is not a good thing for you?"

"It's a wonderful thing for me. The most wonderful thing that's ever happened to me."

"We live in different worlds."

"True. Won't it be interesting?"

"No, it will be cruel and hard and—"

"You're weeping," he said in wonder.

"I'm not without sympathy for your pain."

"And your own."

She didn't answer for a moment, and when she did, the words were nearly inaudible. "And my own."

His face lit with a luminous smile. "You love me."

"I . . . have a certain affection for you."

"You love me."

"All right, I love you," she burst out. "Are you satisfied now?" She took a swift step back when he reached out to touch her. "No!"

His hand fell to his side. "I won't move quickly. Not if you don't want me to."

She desperately wanted him to touch her, but she was afraid she would flow into his arms and all would be lost. She had to remain in control of the situation, or he would destroy himself. "I can't convince you to leave me?"

"Not in the next hundred years."

"Very well." She moistened her lips. "I'll let you stay, but it will be on my terms. There will be no marriage."

He gazed at her, waiting.

"We will talk. We will take walks. We will play cards and chess."

"Whatever you want. Is that all?"

"No, we will couple."

A wide smile illuminated his face. "Anything else?"

"Babies. I like babies. Then when you leave me—"

"I like babies too."

"But you must not feel it's necessary to stay with me because I have children. My people love babies for themselves, not because of words said over them by the Church."

"I won't feel it necessary to stay with you," he promised. "Anything else?"

She shook her head. "But you must not speak of marriage."

"Oh, I won't." He smiled and held out his hand to her. "Not for a long, long time. Maybe after our third child is born."

She gazed at him in despair. What could you do with a man like Bradford?

Love him, take care of him, reach out to him.

Reach out to life.

She took his hand.

Lightning seared the night sky to the east.

Not tonight, Cassie prayed. The horses had settled down wonderfully in the cargo hold, but a storm would mean she would have to spend the night with them.

The storm was far away, though; maybe it would skirt around them.

She paused outside Jared's cabin and dropped her cloak to the deck. She took a deep breath and opened the door.

He was sitting at the desk, fully dressed, his back to her.

"You're not ready for me," she said.

He went still, the line of his spine rigid. He slowly turned in the chair to face her.

His gaze traveled from her bare feet, to her sarong-swathed hips, and then to her bare breasts. He said hoarsely, "I didn't know I was supposed to be."

She closed the door behind her. "It's all right. Things are a little different now, anyway. I even wore a cloak."

"I'm honored." His tone was guarded.

"Well, it's very chilly outside." She shook her head. "No, that's not true. It's still difficult for me not to put up barriers against you. I did it because I knew the seamen seeing me naked made you unhappy."

"I appreciate your consideration. My temper is a little frayed these days."

"Then we'll have to do something to repair it." She moved toward him across the cabin. "I have a suggestion." She stopped before him and took his hand. "You're usually very relaxed afterward." She put his hand on her breast.

A long shudder went through him. "What the devil are you doing here?"

"I don't think I could make it any plainer." Her hands went to the knot of her sarong. "But I'll try."

He snatched her hand away. "Stop it. This isn't the time. . . . Christ, what am I saying?"

"Foolishness."

He ran his fingers through his hair. "I think you're right. I should just reach out and grab . . . No, goddammit; it has to be right this time." He pulled her down to her knees on the floor in front of him. "Is it lust? Did you come here because it's the *Josephine* and it's what you became accustomed to doing? Because if it is, then you can just get out of here . . ." He muttered, "Maybe."

"There will always be lust." Her smile faded. "But that's not why I'm here." It was time. It had to be said, but she couldn't look at him when she said it. She laid her cheek on his knees. "I . . . love you. It would please me if you would marry me. I'd like to live with you all my life. I'd like you to give me children." Her throat was tight with tears and she tried to joke. "If you do, I promise I'll even let you ride Kapu."

"Then how could I resist?" She was suddenly on his lap, his face buried in her breasts. "God, I love you. I was afraid it would take months to get you to—" His words were muffled. "I didn't know what to do."

She held him fiercely close. She would never let him go again. She said shakily, "You did very well."

He lifted his head, and his blue eyes were gleaming with mischief. "I can do better." His fingers fumbled with the knot of her sarong. "Now that I know you're not just using me to quench your—"

The door of the cabin was flung open. "You've got to come quick!"

They both turned in astonishment to see Josette standing in the doorway.

"There's a storm coming. Can't you feel this deck pitching?" Josette said. "I've been trying to quiet them, but I need you." She suddenly became aware of Cassie's dishabille. "Oh, an orgy? How interesting. Well, you can do it later. Is that your sarong? You're right, it's much more shocking than my trousers. You must let me wear it sometime." She frowned as she returned to more important concerns. "Don't just sit there. I need help with the horses." She turned and vanished from the open doorway.

"I'm going to throw her overboard," Jared said through his teeth.

Cassie was still dazed. "She stowed away?"

"She must have sailed down the coast in her boat and managed to hide herself in the cargo hold before we arrived here." Jared stood up and put Cassie on her feet. "God in heaven, what am I going to do with her?"

Cassie started to laugh; she couldn't help it. Life would never go as expected for them. There would always be twists and turns, storms and sunlight. Well, what of it? Serenity would probably bore them both.

"Exactly what she told us to do. We're going to help her with the horses." She took his hand and lovingly smiled into his eyes. "And have our orgy later."

About the
Author

I RIS JOHANSEN has won every major romance writing award for her achievements in the genre since the publication of her very first novel, which earned her the Best New Category Romance Author Award from *Romantic Times*. She has won the *Affaire de Coeur* Silver Pen Award as their reader's favorite author, and most recently was honored with *Romantic Times*'s Lifetime Achievement Award.

LOOK FOR

IRIS JOHANSEN'S

NEXT NOVEL OF SUSPENSE

THE FACE
OF DECEPTION

on sale October 1998 in hardcover

Forensic sculptor Eve Duncan has a rare gift. In her hands the skulls of the long dead reveal their identities. Her work helps bring closure to parents of missing children. It helps Eve come to terms with the murder of her own daughter. And it is about to put her in mortal danger. Billionaire John Logan has an unidentified adult skull whose face he wants her to reconstruct. It seems to be a routine job—until the skull begins to reveal its shocking identity. And then it's too late for Eve to walk out. What she has seen makes her the target of some very powerful enemies. They have decided that the secret of the skull must remain in the grave—no matter who gets buried with it.

"You look beautiful," Eve told her mother. "Where are you going tonight?"

"I'm meeting Ron at Anthony's. He likes the food there." Sandra leaned forward and checked her mascara in the hall mirror, then straightened the shoulders of her dress. "Damn these shoulder pads. They keep shifting around."

"Take them out."

"We all don't have broad shoulders like you. I need them."

"Do you like the food there?"

"No, it's a little fancy for me. I'd rather go to the Cheesecake Factory."

"Then tell him."

"Next time. Maybe I should like it. Maybe it's a learning type thing." She grinned at Eve in the mirror. "You're big on learning new things."

"I like Anthony's, but I still like to pig out at McDonald's when I'm in the mood." She handed Sandra her jacket. "And I'd fight anyone who tried to tell me I shouldn't do it."

"Ron doesn't tell me—" She shrugged. "I like him. He comes from a nice family in Charlotte. I don't know if he'd understand about the way we lived before—I just don't know."

"I want to meet him."

"Next time. You'd give him that cool once-over and I'd feel like a high school kid bringing home my first date."

Eve chuckled and gave her a hug. "You're crazy. I just want to make sure he's good enough for you."

"See?" Sandra headed for the door. "Definitely first-date syndrome. I'm late. I'll see you later."

Eve went to the window and watched her mother back out of the driveway. She hadn't seen her mother this excited and happy in years.

Not since Bonnie was alive.

Well, there was no use staring wistfully out the window. She was glad her mother had a new romance, but she wouldn't trade places with her. She wouldn't know what to do with a man in her life. She wasn't good at one-night stands, and anything else required a commitment she couldn't afford.

She went out the back door and down the kitchen steps. The honeysuckle was in bloom and the heady scent surrounded her as she walked down the path to the lab. The aroma always seemed stronger at twilight and early morning. Bonnie used to love the honeysuckle and was always picking it off the fence, where the bees constantly buzzed. Eve had been at her wit's end trying to stop her before she got stung.

She smiled at the recollection. It had taken her a long time to be able to separate the good memories from the bad. At first she had tried to save herself from pain by closing out all thoughts of Bonnie. Then she had come to understand that that would be forgetting Bonnie and all the joy she had brought into her and Sandra's lives. Bonnie deserved more than—

"Ms. Duncan."

She stiffened, then whirled around.

"I'm sorry, I didn't mean to frighten you. I'm John Logan. I wonder if I could speak to you?"

John Logan. If he hadn't introduced himself she would have recognized him from the photo. How could she miss that California tan? she thought sardonically. And in that gray Armani suit and Gucci loafers, he looked as out of place in her small backyard as a peacock. "You didn't frighten me. You startled me."

"I rang the doorbell." He smiled as he walked toward her. There was not an ounce of fat on his body, and he exuded confidence and charm. She had never liked charming men; charm could hide too much. "I guess you didn't hear me."

"No." She had the sudden desire to shake his confidence. "Do you always trespass, Mr. Logan?"

The sarcasm didn't faze him. "Only when I really want to see someone. Could we go somewhere and talk?" His gaze went to the door of her lab. "That's where you work, isn't it? I'd like to see it."

"How did you know it's where I work?"

"Not from your friends at the Atlanta P.D. I understand they were very protective of your privacy." He strolled forward and stood beside the door. He smiled. "Please?"

He was obviously accustomed to instant acquiescence, and annoyance surged through her again. "No."

His smile faded a little. "I may have a proposition for you."

"I know. Why else would you be here? But I'm too busy to take on any more work. You should have phoned first."

"I wanted to see you in person." He glanced at the lab. "We should go in there and talk."

"Why?"

"It will tell me a few things about you that I need to know."

She stared at him in disbelief. "I'm not applying for a position with one of your companies, Mr. Logan. I don't have to go through a personnel check. I think it's time you left."

"Give me ten minutes."

"No, I have work to do. Good-bye, Mr. Logan."

"John."

"Good-bye, Mr. Logan."

He shook his head. "I'm staying."

She stiffened. "The hell you are."

He leaned against the wall. "Go on, get to work. I'll stay out here until you're ready to see me."

"Don't be ridiculous. I'll probably be working until after midnight."

"Then I'll see you after midnight." His manner no longer held even a hint of his previous charm. He was icy cool, tough, and totally determined.

She opened the door. "Go away."

"After you talk to me. It would be much easier for you to just let me have my way."

"I don't like things easy." She closed the door and flicked on the light. She didn't like things easy and she didn't like being coerced by men who thought they owned the world. Okay, she was overreacting. She didn't usually let anyone disturb her composure, and he hadn't done anything but invade her space.

What the hell, her space was very important to her. Let the bastard stay out there all night.

She threw open the door at eleven thirty-five.

"Come in," she said curtly. "I don't want you out there when my mother comes home. You might scare her. Ten minutes."

"Thank you," he said quietly. "I appreciate your consideration."

No sarcasm or irony in his tone, but that didn't mean it wasn't there. "It's necessity. I was hoping you'd give up before this."

"I don't give up if I need something. But I'm surprised you didn't call your friends at the police department and have them throw me out."

"You're a powerful man. You probably have contacts. I didn't want to put them on the spot."

"I never blame the messenger." His gaze traveled around the lab. "You have a lot of room here. It looks smaller from outside."

"It used to be a carriage house before it was a garage. This part of town is pretty old."

"It's not what I expected." He took in the rust and beige striped couch, the green plants on the windowsill, and then the framed photos of her mother and Bonnie on the bookshelf across the room. "It looks . . . warm."

"I hate cold, sterile labs. There's no reason why I can't have comfort as well as efficiency." She sat down at her desk. "Talk."

"What's that?" He moved toward the corner. "Two video cameras?"

"They're necessary for superimposition."

"What is— Interesting." His attention had been drawn to Mandy's skull. "This looks like something from a voodoo movie with all those little spears stuck in it."

"I'm charting it to indicate the different thicknesses of skin."

"Do you have to do that before you—"

"Talk."

He came back and sat down beside the desk. "I'd like to hire you to identify a skull for me."

She shook her head. "I'm good, but the only sure ways of identification are dental records and DNA."

"Both of those require subjects to match. I can't go that route until I'm almost certain."

"Why not?"

"It would cause difficulties."

"Is this a child?"

"It's a man."

"And you have no idea who he is?"

"I have an idea."

"But you're not going to tell me?"

He shook his head.

"Are there any photos of him?"

"Yes, but I won't show them to you. I want you to start fresh and not construct the face you think is there."

"Where were the bones found?"

"Maryland . . . I think."

"You don't know?"

"Not yet." He smiled. "They haven't actually been located yet."

Her eyes widened in surprise. "Then what are you doing here?"

"I need you on the spot. I want you with me. I'll have to move fast when the skeleton is located."

"And I'm supposed to disrupt my work and go to Maryland on the chance that you'll locate this skeleton?"

"Yes," he said calmly.

"Bull."

"Five hundred thousand dollars for two weeks' work."

"What?"

"As you've pointed out, your time is valuable. I understand you rent this house. You could buy it and still have a lot left over. All you have to do is give me two weeks."

"How do you know I rent this house?"

"There are other people who aren't as loyal as your friends at the police department." He studied her face. "You don't like having dossiers gathered on you."

"You're damn right I don't."

"I don't blame you. I wouldn't either."

"But you still did it."

He repeated the word she had used with him. "Necessity. I had to know who I was dealing with."

"Then you've wasted your efforts. Because you're not dealing with me."

"The money doesn't appeal to you?"

"Do you think I'm nuts? Of course it appeals to me. I grew up poor as dirt. But my life doesn't revolve around money. I pick and choose my jobs these days, and I don't want yours."

"Why not?"

"It doesn't interest me."

"Because it doesn't concern a child?"

"Partly."

"There are other victims besides children."

"But none as helpless." She paused. "Is your man a victim?"

"Possibly."

"Murder?"

He was silent a moment. "Probably."

"And you're sitting there asking me to go with you to a murder site? What's to stop me from calling the police and telling them that John Logan is involved in a murder?"

He smiled faintly. "Because I'd deny it. I'd tell them I was thinking of having you examine the bones of that Nazi war criminal who was found buried in Bolivia." He let a couple of moments pass. "And then I'd pull every string I have to make your friends at the Atlanta P.D. look foolish or even criminal."

"You said you wouldn't blame the messenger."

"But that was before I realized how much it would bother you. Evidently the loyalty goes two ways. One uses whatever weapon one's given."

Yes, he would do that, she realized. Even while they'd been talking he'd been watching her, weighing her every question and answer.

"But I've no desire to do that," he said. "I'm trying to be as honest as I can with you. I could have lied."

"Omission can also be a lie, and you're telling me practically nothing." She stared directly into his eyes. "I don't trust you, Mr. Logan. Do you think this is the first time someone like you has come and asked me to verify a skeleton? Last year a Mr. Damaro paid me a call. He offered me a lot of money to come to Florida and sculpt a face on a skull he just happened to have in his possession. He said a friend had sent it to him from New Guinea. It was supposed to be an anthropological find. I called the Atlanta P.D. and it turned out that Mr. Damaro was really Juan Camez, a drug runner from Miami. His brother had disappeared two years ago and it was suspected he'd been killed by a rival organization. The skull was sent to Camez as a warning."

"Touching. I suppose drug runners have family feelings too."

"I don't think that's funny. Tell that to the kids they hook on heroin."

"I'm not arguing. But I assure you that I've no connection with organized crime." He grimaced. "Well, I've used a bookie now and then."

"Is that supposed to disarm me?"

"Disarming you would obviously take a total global agreement." He stood up. "My ten minutes are up and I wouldn't want to impose. I'll let you think about the offer and call you later."

"I've already thought about it. The answer is no."

"We've only just opened negotiations. If you won't think about it, I will. There has to be something I can offer you that will make the job worth your while." He stood looking at her with narrowed eyes. "Something about me is rubbing you the wrong way. What is it?"

"Nothing. Other than the fact that you have a dead body you don't want anyone to know about."

"Anyone but you. I very much want *you* to know about it." He shook his head. "No, there's something else. Tell me what it is so I can clear it up."

"Good night, Mr. Logan."

"Well, if you can't call me John, at least drop the 'Mr.' You don't want anyone to think you're properly respectful."

"Good night, Logan."

"Good night, Eve." He stopped at the pedestal and looked at the skull. "You know, he's beginning to grow on me."

"She's a girl."

His smile faded. "Sorry. It wasn't funny. I guess we all have our own way of dealing with what we become after death."

"Yes, we do. But sometimes we have to face it before we should. Mandy wasn't over twelve years old."

"Mandy? You know who she was?"

She hadn't meant to let that slip. What the hell, it didn't matter. "No, but I usually give them names. Aren't you glad now that I turned you down? You wouldn't want an eccentric like me working on your skull."

"Oh, yes, I appreciate eccentrics. Half the men in my think tanks in San Jose are a little off center." He moved toward the door. "By the way, that computer you're using is three years old. We have a newer version that's twice as fast. I'll send you one."

"No, thank you. This one works fine."

"Never refuse a bribe if you don't have to sign on the dotted line for return favors." He opened the door. "And never leave your doors unlocked, as you did tonight. There's no telling who could have been waiting in here for you."

"I lock the lab up at night, but it would be inconvenient to keep it locked all the time. Everything in here has been insured, and I know how to protect myself."

He smiled. "I bet you do. I'll call you."

"I told you that I'm—"

She was talking to air; he'd already closed the door behind him.

She breathed a sigh of relief. Not that she had the slightest doubt she would hear from him again. She had never met a man more determined to get his own way. Even when his approach had been velvet soft, the steel had shown through. Well, she had dealt with powerhouse types before. All she had to do was stick to her guns and John Logan would eventually get discouraged and leave her alone.

She stood up and went over to the pedestal. "He can't be so smart, Mandy. He didn't even know you were a girl." Not that many people would have.

The desk phone rang.

Mom? She had been having trouble with her ignition on her car lately.

Not her mother.

"I remembered something just as I reached the car," Logan said. "I thought I'd throw it into the pot for you to consider with the original deal."

"I'm not considering the original deal."

"Five hundred thousand for you. Five hundred thousand to go to the Adams Fund for Missing and Runaway Children. I understand you contribute a portion of your fees to that fund." His voice lowered persuasively. "Do you realize how many children could be brought home to their parents with that amount of money?"

She knew better than he did. He couldn't have offered a more tempting lure. My God, Machiavelli could have taken lessons from him.

"All those children. Aren't they worth two weeks of your time?"

They were worth a decade of her time. "Not if it means doing something criminal."

"Criminal acts are often in the eyes of the beholder."

"Bullshit."

"Suppose I promise you that I had nothing to do with any foul play connected with the skull."

"Why should I believe any promise you make?"

"Check me out. I don't have a reputation for lying."

"Reputation doesn't mean anything. People lie when it means enough to them. I've worked hard to establish my career. I won't see it go down the drain."

There was silence. "I can't promise you that you won't come out of this without a few scars, but I'll try to protect you as much as I can."

"I can protest myself. All I have to do is tell you no."

"But you're tempted, aren't you?"

Christ, she was tempted.

"Seven hundred thousand to the fund."

"No."

"I'll call you tomorrow." He hung up the phone.

Damn him.

She replaced the receiver. The bastard knew how to push the right buttons. All that money channeled to find the other lost ones, the ones who might still be alive . . .

Wouldn't it be worth a risk to see even some of them brought home? Her gaze went to the pedestal. Mandy might have been a runaway. Maybe if she'd had a chance to come home she wouldn't . . .

"I shouldn't do it, Mandy," she whispered. "It could be pretty bad. People don't fork out over a million dollars for something like this if they're even slightly on the up-and-up. I have to tell him no."

But Mandy couldn't answer. None of the dead could answer.

But the living could, and Logan had counted on her listening to the call.

Damn him.

Logan leaned back in the driver's seat, his gaze on Eve Duncan's small clapboard house.

Was it enough?

Possibly. She had definitely been tempted. She had a passionate commitment to finding lost children and he had played on it as skillfully as he could.

What kind of man did that make him? he thought wearily.

A man who needed to get the job done. If she didn't succumb to his offer, he'd go higher tomorrow.

She was tougher than he'd thought she'd be. Tough and smart and perceptive. But she had an Achilles' heel.

And there was no doubt on earth that he would exploit it.

"He just drove off," Fiske said into his digital phone. "Should I follow him?"

"No, we know where he's staying. He saw Eve Duncan?"

"She was home all evening and he stayed over four hours."

Timwick cursed. "She's going to go for it."

"I could stop her," Fiske said.

"Not yet. She has friends in the police department. We don't want to make waves."

"The mother?"

"Maybe. It would certainly cause a delay at least. Let me think about it. Stay there. I'll call you back."

Scared rabbit, Fiske thought contemptuously. He could hear the nervousness in Timwick's voice. Timwick was always thinking, hesitating instead of taking the clean, simple way. You had to decide what result you needed and then just take the step that would bring that result. If he had Timwick's power and resources, there would be no limit to what he could do. Not that he wanted Timwick's job. He liked what he did. Not many people found their niche in life as he had.

He tested his head on the back of the seat, staring at the house.

It was after midnight. The mother should be returning soon. He'd already unscrewed the porch light. If Timwick called him right away, he might not have to go into the house.

If the prick could make up his mind to do the smart, simple thing and let Fiske kill her.

"You know you're going to do it, Mama," Bonnie said. "I don't understand why you're worrying so much."

Eve sat up in bed and looked at the window seat. When she came, Bonnie was always in the window seat with her jean-clad legs crossed. "I don't know any such thing."

"You won't be able to help yourself. Trust me."

"Since you're only my dream, you can't know more than what I know."

Bonnie sighed. "I'm not your dream. I'm a ghost, Mama. What do I have to do to convince you? Being a ghost shouldn't be this hard."

"You can tell me where you are."

"I don't know where he buried me. I wasn't there anymore."

"Convenient."

"Mandy doesn't know either. But she likes you."

"If she's there with you, then what's her real name?"

"Names don't matter anymore to us, Mama."

"They matter to me."

Bonnie smiled. "Because you probably need to put a name to love. It's really not necessary."

"Very profound for a seven-year-old."

"Well, for goodness' sake it's been ten years. Stop trying to trap me. Who says a ghost doesn't grow up? I couldn't stay seven forever."

"You look the same."

"Because I'm what you want to see." She leaned back against the alcove wall. "You're working too hard, Mama. I've been worrying about you. Maybe this job with Logan will be good for you."

"I'm not taking the job."

Bonnie smiled.

"I'm not," Eve repeated.

"Whatever." Bonnie was staring out the window. "You were thinking about me and the honeysuckle tonight. I like it when you feel good about me."

"You've told me that before."

"So I'm repeating it. You were hurting too much in the beginning. I couldn't get near you . . ."

"You're not near me now. You're only a dream."

"Am I?" Bonnie looked back at her, and a loving smile lit her face. "Then you won't mind if your dream stays around a little longer? Sometimes I get so lonesome for you, Mama."

Bonnie. Love. Here.

Oh, God, here.

It didn't matter that it was a dream.

"Yes, stay," she whispered huskily. "Please stay, baby."

The sun was streaming through the window when Eve opened her eyes the next morning. She glanced at the clock and immediately sat up in bed. It was almost eight-thirty and she always got up at seven. She was surprised her mother hadn't come in to check on her.

She swung her feet to the floor and headed down the hall to the shower, rested and optimistic as she usually was after dreaming of Bonnie. A psychiatrist would have a field day with those dreams, but she didn't give a damn. She had started dreaming of Bonnie three years after her death. The dreams came frequently, but there was no telling when she'd have them or what triggered them. Maybe when she had a problem and needed to work through it? At any rate, the effect was always positive. When she awoke she felt composed and capable, as she did today, confident that she could take on the world.

And John Logan.

She dressed quickly in jeans and a loose white shirt, her uniform when she was working, and ran down the stairs to the kitchen.

"Mom, I overslept. Why didn't you—"

No one was in the kitchen. No smell of bacon, no frying pans on the stove . . . The room appeared the same as it had been at midnight when she'd come in.

And Sandra hadn't been home when she'd gone to bed. She glanced out the window, and relief rushed through her. Her mother's car was parked in its usual spot in the driveway.

She'd probably gotten in late and had overslept too. It was Saturday and she didn't have to work.

Eve would have to be careful not to mention she'd been worried, she thought ruefully. Sandra had noticed Eve's tendency toward overprotection and had a perfect right to resent it.

She poured a glass of orange juice from the refrigerator, reached for the portable on the wall, and dialed Joe at the precinct.

"Diane says you haven't called her," he said. "You should be phoning her, not me."

"This afternoon, I promise." She sat down at the kitchen table. "Tell me about John Logan."

There was silence at the other end of the line. "He's contacted you?"

"Last night."

"A job?"

"Yes."

"What kind of job?"

"I don't know. He's not telling me much."

"You must be thinking about it if you're calling me. What did he use as bait?"

"The Adams Fund."

"Christ, has he got your number."

"He's smart. I want to know how smart." She took a sip of orange juice. "And how honest."

"Well, he's not in the same category as your Miami drug runner."

"That's not very comforting. Has he ever done anything criminal?"

"Not as far as I know. Not in this country."

"Isn't he a U.S. citizen?"

"Yes, but when he was first establishing his company he spent a number of years in Singapore and Tokyo trying to improve his products and studying marketing strategies."

"It seems to have worked. Were you joking when you said he probably left a few bodies by the wayside?"

"Yes. We don't know much about those years he spent abroad. The people who came in contact with him are tough as hell and they respect him. Does that tell you anything?"

"That I should be careful."

"Right. He has the reputation of being a straight shooter and he inspires loyalty in his employees. But you have to consider that all of that is on the surface."

"Can you find out anything more for me?"

"Like what?"

"Anything. What's he been doing lately that's unusual? Will you dig a little deeper for me?"

"You've got it. I'll start right away." He paused. "But it's not going to come cheap. You call Diane this afternoon and you come down to the lake house with us next weekend."

"I don't have time to—" She sighed. "I'll be there."

"And without any bones rattling around in your suitcase."

"Okay."

"And you have to have a good time."

"I always have a good time with you and Diane. But I don't know why you put up with me."

"It's called friendship. Sound familiar?"

"Yeah, thanks, Joe."

"For digging out the dirt on Logan?"

"No." For having been the only one holding back the madness that had clawed at her during all those nights of horror, and for all the years of work and companionship that had followed. She cleared her throat. "Thanks for being my friend."

"Well, as your friend, I'd advise you to go very carefully with Mr. Logan."

"It's a lot of money for the kids, Joe."

"And he knew how to manipulate you."

"He didn't manipulate me. I haven't made any decision yet." She finished her orange juice. "I've got to get to work. You'll let me know?"

"That I will."

She hung up the phone and rinsed out her glass.

Coffee?

No, she'd make a pot at the lab. On weekends Mom usually came down in the middle of the morning and had coffee with her. It was a nice break for both of them.

She took the lab key from the blue bowl on the counter, ran down the porch steps, and started for the lab.

Stop thinking about Logan. She had work to do. She had Mandy's head to finish and she had to go over that packet the LAPD had sent her last week.

Logan would call her today or come to the house. She hadn't the slightest doubt. Well, he could talk all he pleased. He wouldn't get an answer from her. She had to find out more about—

The lab door was ajar.

She froze on the path.

She knew she had locked it the previous night as she always did. The key had been in the blue bowl, where she always threw it.

Mom?

No, the doorjamb was splintered as if the lock had been jimmied. It had to have been a thief.

She slowly pushed opened the door.

Blood.

Sweet Jesus, blood everywhere . . .

Blood on the walls.

On the shelves.

On the desk.

Bookcases had been hurled to the floor and appeared to have been chopped to pieces. The couch was overturned, the glass on all the picture frames had been shattered.

And the blood . . .

IRIS JOHANSEN

LIONS BRIDE	____56990-2	$6.99/$8.99 in Canada
DARK RIDER	____29947-6	$6.99/$8.99
MIDNIGHT WARRIOR	____29946-8	$6.99/$8.99
THE BELOVED SCOUNDREL	____29945-X	$6.99/$8.99
THE TIGER PRINCE	____29968-9	$6.99/$8.99
THE MAGNIFICENT ROGUE	____29944-1	$6.99/$8.99
THE GOLDEN BARBARIAN	____29604-3	$6.99/$8.99
LAST BRIDGE HOME	____29871-2	$5.50/$7.50
THE UGLY DUCKLING	____56991-0	$6.99/$8.99
LONG AFTER MIDNIGHT	____57181-8	$6.99/$8.99
AND THEN YOU DIE...	____57998-3	$6.99/$8.99

❧ THE WIND DANCER TRILOGY ❧

THE WIND DANCER	____28855-5	$5.99/$6.99
STORM WINDS	____29032-0	$6.99/$8.99
REAP THE WIND	____29244-7	$5.99/$7.50

Ask for these books at your local bookstore or use this page to order.

Please send me the books I have checked above. I am enclosing $____ (add $2.50 to cover postage and handling). Send check or money order, no cash or C.O.D.'s, please.

Name _____

Address _____

City/State/Zip _____

Send order to: Bantam Books, Dept. FN37, 2451 S. Wolf Rd., Des Plaines, IL 60018
Allow four to six weeks for delivery.
Prices and availability subject to change without notice. FN 37 9/98